True Love Cowboy

"Tonight I want to be alone with you."

"Nice."

"You might not think that of me if you knew what I was thinking about doing to you right now."

She gave him a sexy, seductive smile. "Should I pick a safe word?"

He pressed his hand to her beautiful face and brushed his thumb across her soft cheek. "I take instruction very well. Yes. More. Don't stop." He shrugged one shoulder. "I'll do everything in my power to make sure you don't ever want to say no."

She leaned in and kissed him once. "Then, yes." She kissed him again. "More." She kissed him again, this time with her tongue sliding across his bottom lip. "Go. And don't stop."

Maybe he really had finally met his match.

TRUE
LOVE
COWBOY

A McGrath Novel

JENNIFER
RYAN

AVONBOOKS

An Imprint of HarperCollinsPublishers

Untitled excerpt copyright © 2021 by Jennifer Ryan.

First Avon Books mass market printing: September 2021

Print Edition ISBN: 978-0-06-302080-1
Digital Edition ISBN: 978-0-06-300632-4

Cover design by Nadine Badalaty
Cover photographs © 2020 Rob Lang/roblangimages.com (cowboy); ©
stock.adobe.com; © Getty Images

Avon, Avon & logo, and Avon Books & logo are registered trademarks of HarperCollins Publishers in the United States of America and other countries.

HarperCollins is a registered trademark of HarperCollins Publishers in the United States of America and other countries.

FIRST EDITION

Printed and Bound in Barcelona Spain by CPI BlackPrint

21 22 23 24 25   CPI   10 9 8 7 6 5 4 3 2 1

*For everyone out there
who fights for love and family.*

Chapter One

Trinity knocked on Mr. Crawford's door for the fourth time and still got no answer. She didn't usually walk into other people's homes, but this seemed like an emergency. What if he was too sick to make it to the door? What if he'd fallen and hit his head? She imagined any number of things keeping him from answering her knock when he knew she was coming to deliver his order. And the food she'd brought with her needed to go in the fridge before it spoiled. So she tried the knob, found it unlocked—people didn't worry about locking their doors out here—and pushed open the door.

"Mr. Crawford," she called out loud and clear, hoping he heard her and she didn't frighten him. "It's me. Trinity. I brought your order. Are you ready to go to urgent care to get that nasty cough checked out?"

She walked into the entry and noted the dirty plates and glasses on the coffee table in the living room. The TV was on, but Mr. Crawford wasn't sitting in there watching from the blanket-covered sofa.

"Mr. Crawford, I'll just put the food in the fridge for you." She hoped he'd come out soon, because her heart was racing and her mind spun a dozen bad scenarios for why he didn't answer. She went with the ordinary, most logical reason, that he was probably in the bathroom, and clung to that thought.

She loved the old ranch house. Single story with wide-plank hardwood floors throughout. The wide, tall windows off the back let in a ton of natural light. The place needed new paint and maybe some modern touches, but it felt homey.

Except for the quiet vibe that made her uneasy, because Mr. Crawford still hadn't appeared as she entered the kitchen.

A few dirty dishes sat in the sink, but the rest of the space looked clean. The garbage needed to go out. She smiled at the *Almost Homemade* containers in the trash. She needed to remind Mr. Crawford they should be recycled.

She set her heavy, insulated bag on the floor by the fridge and unzipped it. It only took her a couple minutes to stow all the food in the fridge and freezer, restocking his *Almost Homemade* favorites. He'd have plenty to eat over the next two weeks.

She retraced her steps and started down the hallway, calling out, "Mr. Crawford," one more time.

She passed an office and an empty bedroom, then turned a corner and caught her breath. She ran down the hall, dropping to her knees beside Mr. Crawford. Sprawled on the floor, he lay on his belly, head turned to the side as he wheezed in and out, struggling to get an easy breath.

She looked him over to see if anything appeared broken, but it simply looked like he'd fallen to his knees and then onto the hardwood with his hands by his shoulders. She pressed her hand to his too-warm head and leaned down to his ear. "Mr. Crawford, what's wrong?"

He moaned but didn't open his eyes. He looked like he'd lost ten pounds since she'd seen him last week.

She needed to get him to help. Now.

It would take the ambulance too long to get this far out of town. She didn't know if Mr. Crawford could wait that long for help. And air. So it was up to her to get him to her car and the hospital.

She gently rolled him onto his back. He seemed to breathe a bit easier, but then the coughing started, racking his body.

She knelt, lifted him so she could scoot her bent knees under his head and shoulders, and held him up to ease the coughing fit. His eyes fluttered, but didn't open. "Mr. Crawford, can you hear me?"

"Trini . . ." The rest of her name got lost on another round of coughs.

"Don't talk. Can you stand? I need to get you to my car."

He pressed his hand to his chest as he settled down again and shook his head.

"Okay. Try to stay calm." She wished her heart would take that order, but it thrashed in her chest as she tried to think of what to do.

She could call one of her brothers. They were only ten, maybe fifteen minutes away. Still too long to make Mr. Crawford lie here struggling to breathe.

It had to be her. It had to be right now.

She hoped all the standing and walking she did at work combined with the squats she did at the gym were enough to move Mr. Crawford. "I'm going to have to drag you out. I'll try to do it quickly and without too many bumps along the way, but I can't promise this isn't going to be difficult."

Mr. Crawford moaned and opened his mouth, trying to breathe in more air.

Decided, she hooked her hands under his arms and linked her fingers on his chest. She pulled him up and against her breasts, his head back against her shoulder, her cheek pressed to his hair. "I've got you. Let's go."

She kept her hold locked and got her feet under her. In the crouched position, she had to take small steps backward to drag him down the hall and to the entry. It took every ounce of strength she had to get him that far; she had to lay him down so she could open the door.

Trinity stood over him, sucked in a few deep breaths, reset her position to drag him again, and pulled him out of the house. As gently as she could, she maneuvered Mr. Crawford down the three wide stone porch steps. She hoped she wasn't scraping up his backside, but she couldn't worry about that now. He lost a sock on the path to the driveway. She wished she hadn't parked in front of the garage but on the circle drive by the lawn.

Silly to think about that now when she was so close to getting him to her car. It took a lot of grunting and muscling through the pain in her back and thighs to get him there, but once she did, she leaned him up against the back tire and opened the passenger door. She needed to get him inside.

She knelt next to him and rubbed her sore thigh muscles. "Mr. Crawford, I can't lift you into the car on my own. I need you to help me. Can you try to stand while I lift you, so I can get you to sit on the seat? Then I can gently lay you down back there. Okay?"

She bent each of his legs and planted his feet firmly. He lifted his arms and she hooked them over her shoulders. She put her hands in his armpits and lifted him while he did his best to put weight on his feet and stand with his back braced against the car.

"That's it. You're doing it. Almost there." Once she had him standing, she pinned him in place with her shoulder, then used her foot to help him scoot his foot over toward the open door. "Okay, now shift your weight over."

Mr. Crawford gave a huge effort and not only shifted to his other leg, but stepped sideways and kind of fell into the opening, hitting his butt on the seat. She caught his arms before he completely tumbled back and gently lowered him. Bent like a bow, he lay with his feet still on the ground. She picked up one and then the other and placed them on the doorframe. One slipped off, so she tried again. She pushed against his knees to keep his legs in place this time.

"Try to hold your legs here. I'm going to run around to the other side and pull you in."

She felt the tension and shaking in his whole body and hoped he had enough strength to get through this.

She ran to the back of the car, spotted the SUV barreling down the drive toward them, dismissed it because she had other things to worry about, and opened the other passenger door just as the vehicle came to a jarring stop and someone leaped out behind her.

The timing sucked as usual, but she flashed back to when she'd been knocked over the head, stuffed into a trunk, and kidnapped by her brother Tate's girlfriend's stalker ex, who wanted to use her to lure out Tate and Liz.

She didn't do well in the dark anymore.

She didn't like strangers running at her.

Every instinct she had kicked in, and she turned to face her attacker and put up her hands. "Stay back." The warning lacked the oomph she'd hoped for when her voice cracked.

The man kept coming. "What are you doing with my dad?"

She tried to hold on to the word *dad*, but panic short-circuited her brain. "Stay away. Don't touch me."

The man halted immediately, surprise and confusion lighting his eyes. He held his hands up. "I'm not going to hurt you. That's my dad. Is he okay?"

She kept one hand up in front of her to ward him off and pressed the other to her temple, trying to make sense of reality and nightmare as his face changed to the one she feared and back to Mr. Crawford's handsome son.

"Is my father okay?" His words found their way past the images assailing her mind and sank in. His sharp tone helped keep her rooted in reality, and she focused on his stunning blue eyes.

"He's sick. V-very sick."

Mr. Crawford needed her help. She tried to hold on to that thought alone.

The man took a tentative step forward. "Are you taking him to the hospital?"

"Y-yes." She nodded and tried to suck in a deep breath to stave off the hyperventilating that threatened to make her dizzy.

"Are *you* okay?"

"Fine," she bit out.

"Let me help you get him settled in the car." He took another step forward.

She sidestepped and moved away from the open passenger door to let him take her place.

With hardly any effort at all, he pulled Mr. Crawford across the back seat. "Hey, Dad. I'm home. Can you hear me?"

She managed to find her bearings and ran around to the other side of the car and situated Mr. Crawford's legs and feet. She had a hard time meeting the other man's eyes, but said, "Get in. I'll drive."

She closed the passenger door. So did he on his side, then they met in the front. She pulled the keys from her pocket and jammed the right one into the ignition before she remembered. "Shit. The front door is open."

The man pinned her in his gaze. "Do not leave without me."

She gave him a disgruntled frown and waited while he jumped out, rushed to close the door, then ran back. The second he was in the car, she stomped on the gas and backed out of the driveway, swung the car around in a tight turn, and raced down the road headed back into town.

The man turned in the passenger seat and studied his father. "What happened? Why is he breathing like that?"

"He called in a delivery order." She took a cleansing breath, found some calm, though her heart still wildly pounded in her chest, and let the rest of what happened tumble out of her mouth. "He sounded really bad. I offered to take him to urgent care, but when I arrived to drop off the food and take him, he didn't answer the door. I got worried, so I went in and found him lying in the hallway. He wasn't really awake, but he managed a few words when I told him I needed to drag him out to the car. He helped me a little to get him inside. Then you showed up."

He turned to stare at her. "Should you be driving in your condition?"

She breathed in and out in short pants. "I'm fine.

Why? I'm fine." She was totally talking way too fast. Her knuckles had gone white, so she eased off her hold on the steering wheel.

"You're pale as a ghost."

"It's not easy to drag a man who outweighs me by fifty or more pounds out of a house and into the car," she pointed out. True. But anxiety, a minor panic attack, and the nightmares filling her thoughts had far more to do with her current condition and state of mind.

She distracted herself by counting the reflective disk-thingies on the road.

He raked his hand over his head. "Damn. I don't know how you managed." He stared at his dad, then settled back in the passenger seat.

Because Mr. Crawford was her favorite customer, and she liked spending time with him when he placed a delivery order; she knew all about his favorite person. Little Emmy. His pride and joy.

Of course many of the pictures included Mr. Crawford's son. Jon? She was pretty sure that was his name. Mr. Crawford was so proud of the businessman, who was the first in the family to graduate college and leave their small town and make it big in California.

And if memory served, he was moving back home.

"You're Emmy's dad. I'm glad you showed up when you did. He'll be so happy you're home." Her brain started firing on all cylinders. "Mr. Crawford is head over heels for his granddaughter. He shows me pictures and tells me stories about her all the time." Talking about mundane things distracted her from the panic she couldn't control.

He glanced in the back to check on Mr. Crawford again. Nothing had changed in his terrible condition, but he didn't seem worse. "I hope whatever this is, he gets to see her again soon."

"He's going to be okay." She said it as much for him as she did for herself. She liked Mr. Crawford and looked forward to her visits with him.

"Thank you."

"For what?" She brushed her hair back from her face, then tucked her shaking hand between her knees and drove one-handed.

"Helping him. Taking care of him." He wiped his hand over his face. "I worry about him out here all alone. It's why I'm moving back. Well, part of why I'm moving back."

"He told me you want Emmy to grow up the way you did."

"I want her to know her grandfather, play on the ranch, learn to ride a horse, grow her own garden like my mother did, and spend more time in the fresh air than on her tablet."

"She'll get that here."

His words did something to her. She relaxed into the pretty picture he painted of a little girl growing up on a ranch. It reminded her of how she was raised and what she wanted for her future.

She took the next turn and sent her passenger into the side door.

Jon gripped the handle above the window and held on. "Um, you might want to slow down just a bit. Not that I don't mind the hurry, but I'd like to get there in one piece."

"Don't worry. I know these roads like the back of my hand."

He stared across at her. "You grew up out here."

"Born and raised. The McGrath place. Cedar Top Ranch, down the road the other way."

Jon turned to her. "Is Drake your brother?"

She smiled thinking about him and how far he'd come this past year, how happy he was with Adria. "He is. Along with Tate and Declan, who run the ranch for the family now."

"That makes you the little sister. Trinity McGrath."

"Yep." With three overprotective brothers. "And you're Jon, right?"

"Yeah. I graduated a year behind Drake and one ahead of Declan, I think. Drake and I hung out sometimes. You were still just a little thing back then."

She was surprised he remembered her at all. Her brothers didn't like her chasing after them so much when they hit high school.

Jon checked on Mr. Crawford again, frowning when Mr. Crawford didn't make a miraculous recovery they both wished for. "This is taking too long."

She pointed out the windshield. "City lights are just up ahead. Don't worry. I know the admitting nurse. They'll see him right away."

"Small towns. Everyone knows everyone."

"At some point, you meet everyone when you grow up here." That got her a very slight smile. "I feed most of the hospital staff on a regular basis."

"So you're a chef?"

"Yep." She sped into town and drove into the hospital emergency entrance and stopped right outside the doors behind an ambulance.

"Wow. That was fast."

A minute ago they'd been taking too long.

She shut off the engine and ran for the double doors. She found a wheelchair and pushed it out to the car.

One of the paramedics helped Jon slide Mr. Crawford out of the back seat and into the chair.

"Thanks, Pete." She recognized one of her repeat customers.

"No problem, Trinity."

"I'll help you get him inside," Pete offered.

"We've got this, but thanks." She turned to Jon, who was already headed for the doors, and ran to catch up. Inside, the emergency room was busy but not chaotic like she imagined some nights could be.

One of the doctors who frequented the shop walked out of a draped-off area. "Hey there."

She quickly glanced at the name tag hanging from his scrubs pocket. "Dr. Holt." She waved her hand toward Mr. Crawford, who was leaning heavily to one side in the wheelchair. "I found him passed out on the floor in his home. He has a fever, severe cough, and has been mostly unconscious for at least the last half hour."

Dr. Holt picked up Mr. Crawford's hand and examined it. "His fingertips are blue. He's not getting enough oxygen."

She didn't need to be told that. The sound of Mr. Crawford desperately trying to get air echoed through her and made her own chest feel tight.

Dr. Holt waved them to an open cubicle. "Let's get him up on the bed."

Jon and the doctor each took an arm and lifted Mr. Crawford to his feet. She quickly pulled the chair out of the way so they could maneuver him onto the bed.

Dr. Holt called a nurse in. "Let's get an oxygen mask on him and start a blood workup." He turned to her and Jon. "Please go to the desk and get . . ."

Jon took over. "Dennis Crawford. My father. I'm Jon."

"Nice to meet you, Jon. We'll take good care of him. Has he been ill?"

Jon actually turned to her. "I haven't spoken to him in a week. We were packing and getting ready to move here."

She turned to the doctor. "I spoke with him on the phone about two hours ago. He was congested, coughing, wheezing a bit. He couldn't catch his breath. He wanted me to deliver some soup and other food."

"Sounds like maybe he's got flu or pneumonia. We'll know more when we run some tests." With that, the doctor seemed to dismiss them by putting the stethoscope into his ears to listen to Dennis's heart and lungs, though she didn't know how he could hear anything beyond Mr. Crawford's coughing fit and labored breathing.

Anxious and worried, she couldn't stand there watching Mr. Crawford suffer and not do something. Unable to help him directly, she tugged Jon's arm to get him to come along with her to the reception desk so they could take care of the mundane while Dr. Holt took care of the emergency. "Hey, Ruth," she said to the woman at the desk. "This is Jon Crawford. We just brought in his father, Dennis."

Ruth smiled at both of them, at the same time typing on her computer. "We've got him in our system. Address on Pine Crest Road."

Jon nodded, but kept looking back to the cubicle where his dad lay with an oxygen mask over his nose and mouth.

"Any changes in his insurance?"

Jon shook his head.

"Is he taking any medications?"

"Um, I think he takes something for cholesterol and high blood pressure, but I'm not sure what."

"We'll check his records." Ruth handed over a clip-board. "Fill these out and bring them back."

Trinity led Jon into the waiting room. "Sit. I'll find us some coffee." It wasn't much, but she could at least do that.

Jon automatically sat and glanced at the papers, though he didn't seem to read the words. He looked over at his father again and just stared.

She put her hand on Jon's shoulder. "He's going to be fine."

"That's what they said about my mom. Then, she was gone." His gruff voice held a world of pain and loss that made her own heart heavy with sorrow. He didn't look at her, but continued to stare at his father.

She squeezed his shoulder, trying to give him some comfort.

He looked up at her. "I can't lose him. I just got back. It's not supposed to be like this."

"I know how it feels to realize you have no control over what's happening. Your father is in the place he needs to be to get better. You're here to look after him. That's all we can do right now. Maybe it's not as bad as we think. Maybe he just needs some medicine and time to recover from whatever is ailing him."

"He looks like he's been sick awhile. He's lost weight. His color . . ."

"He'll look much better once he gets more oxygen into him and he rests."

Jon didn't look convinced.

"Fill out those forms. I'll be right back."

He held her gaze. "Will you stay?"

She planned to even without the desperate and lonely look he gave her. "Yes. I want to be sure he's okay, too."

She tried to get him to smile. "He's one of my best customers. And he calls me sweet girl, which I love."

Jon's mouth twitched into an almost smile. "It's what he called my mom, and now he calls Emmy that, too."

"Well, now I feel a little less special," she teased.

Jon shook his head. "He only ever called them that." He met her gaze again. "And you."

"Well, I make him double-chocolate brownies with almonds."

"Not walnuts," they said in unison.

This time, Jon did smile, and a funny thing happened inside her. A strange fluttery feeling lightened her chest, and she became all too aware that she still had her hand on his strong shoulder.

She pulled it away. "Uh, it's probably going to be a long night. Coffee. On the way."

Chapter Two

Jon watched the medical team work on his dad, drawing blood, checking his blood pressure, making sure he was getting enough oxygen, and whatever else they did, while the tension built in his gut, neck, and shoulders. Most of it was for news on his dad. And then *she* walked back into the room and an unexpected sense of relief and ease hit him.

She'd come back.

She held up two sandwiches in one hand. "Strawberry or grape?"

Surprised, he went with his favorite. "Strawberry."

She slipped the bottom sandwich into his hand, sat beside him, put her sandwich on the coffee tray, and pulled a cup off for him. "Black." She held up the little carton of milk. "Want some of this? Or sugar?" She dipped her hand into her purse and pulled out several sugar packets. "I only have the real stuff. You shouldn't put chemicals into your body if you can help it."

He plucked the milk from her hand. "This is fine."

She dumped the sugar back into her purse, tore open her sandwich, and took a big bite. "Mmm." She chewed and swallowed and glanced back at him. "Sorry. Long day. I barely ate. I thought you might like something. Comfort food seemed appropriate."

"PB and J is comfort food?"

"Yes. It's nostalgic. Brings you back to a simpler time in life." She shrugged. "Besides, the cafeteria was closing, so it was this or I run over to my shop and make us something, but you asked me to stay, so here I am."

That's when it hit him.

Trinity made him feel like he mattered in a basic and simple way.

Him. A stranger to her.

He didn't want to be alone, so she sat beside him eating her sandwich, drinking her coffee, not expecting him to talk or do anything for her. She was here for him.

And his father. He got that.

But still.

He had a lot of business associates and friends back in California, but only a handful who would really miss him and show up if he called. He'd miss them, and hoped that over the next weeks and months he'd reconnect with old friends and make new ones as he settled in at the ranch with his dad.

Stephanie, his ex and Emmy's mom, would arrive tomorrow with their daughter, but she wasn't someone he could rely on for help and support without there being strings—usually tangled—attached. They weren't a good match.

"What do I owe you for dinner?" Well past seven, he was starving.

The disgruntled frown and side-eye told him she didn't expect payment and took offense to him offering.

With Steph, it was always give me more.

He didn't know what to do with Trinity's generosity.

And didn't that tell him how much he needed to spend time with other women and stop letting Steph take up so much room in his life that she made him not want to put himself out there and get burned again?

"Eat. You'll feel better." She dusted off her hands and balled up the wrapper. "If you do, I have a treat for you." She pulled two large chocolate chip cookies wrapped in plastic from her bag. "I keep a few of these with me for emergencies."

"I have a stash of Cheerios and fish crackers in my car just in case."

"Those are for Emmy, right?"

"She loves her snacks."

"A girl after my own heart." Trinity bit into the cookie, and her eyes rolled back in pure appreciation. "There is nothing better than dessert and coffee."

He couldn't remember the last time he took such pleasure in something so simple.

He took another bite of the sandwich and let the taste take him back to the joy of opening his lunch box and finding his favorite meal packed by his mom. It made him miss her, but it also made him smile.

Trinity bumped her shoulder into his. "See. You remember."

He did because of her. "Thank you."

"You're welcome." She handed over the cookie even though he hadn't finished his sandwich yet. "He's going to be okay."

He didn't know how much he needed to hear that, or understand why he believed her so easily, but the words and the certainty with which she said them had him relaxing into the chair and finishing his food.

"That cookie was amazing."

"Thank you. We make them fresh daily."

"Do you work at the grocery store or a restaurant? You said you delivered food to my dad."

"We're kinda in between a grocery store and restaurant. You can eat at the store, but mostly people come in to buy prepackaged meal kits or ready-made food that's either hot or cold to take home, or back to their office." She pulled out a to-go menu from her purse and handed it to him. "You can order online and pick up, or come in and shop."

He checked out the items list and information about the store. It was a really cool idea. "I thought you said you deliver."

"Not officially. We're a neighborhood store, so we take care of our neighbors who are unable to shop for themselves—if they're sick or housebound. Mostly for seniors."

"My dad isn't housebound."

The defensive tone made her quickly explain. "He doesn't like to drive as much anymore. Says his eyesight is going. I told him I'd take him to the optometrist, but he doesn't want to put me out." She bumped his shoulder with hers again. "Personally, I think he's stubborn. And maybe a little vain about wearing glasses. But he needs to go, so I've been working on him. I actually have an appointment set up for him in two weeks. I figure it will take me that long to get him to agree to go."

He turned to her and their knees touched. She didn't move away, so neither did he. "How long have you known my dad?"

"Not long. We opened the store about a year ago."

"And you've taken it on yourself to deliver food to him and make him eye appointments?" Jon got it. His dad probably loved her attention.

But why did she do it for someone she barely knew?

"Well, he doesn't have anyone to help him, so I do." She quickly added, "But you're here now, so you might have better luck convincing him to take better care of himself."

"I wonder if he's dragging it out just so he can see you." He'd probably do the same thing in his dad's shoes. Something about her drew him in and made him want to get closer.

Look at him now. He'd asked her to stay with no real thought as to why he needed her to do so. He could take care of this on his own. He did most everything on his own.

But it was nice having her here.

Which made him think of how he'd found her, struggling to get his father into her car, and going into an all-out panic when he showed up, acting like he was going to stop her or something.

"What happened to you at the house when I drove up?" At the time he thought she'd ask him for help, but instead she'd wanted him to stay away from her.

"Oh, sorry. I just didn't know who you were or what you were doing there. I . . . just needed to get Mr. Crawford to the hospital. That's all."

He didn't think so, but didn't push. She'd done him and his dad a huge favor. And in his mind, she might have saved his father's life. He noticed the tremble in her hand, the long scar on her temple, and ignored those, too.

Down to the dregs of his coffee, he nearly dropped the paper cup when the doctor walked in. He quickly stood, eager to hear what he had to say. Trinity ended up right beside him a moment later.

"How is my dad?"

Trinity slipped her hand in his and squeezed. He held tight to her, hoping for good news, but preparing for the worst.

"Better. It's a good thing you brought him in when you did. His oxygen level was dangerously low. He's got a bacterial infection in his lungs we're treating with antibiotics. We've moved him to a room upstairs. Third floor. We've got him on IV fluids for his dehydration. I hope to get him eating in the morning. We've given him some medicine to curb the coughing fits so he can get some much-needed rest. I expect in a couple days the antibiotics will kick in and he'll feel much better."

"You're sure?" When his mother had been sick, they'd gotten similar news. They'd thought she'd be fine, but it all went wrong.

"Well, he's very sick right now, but I don't anticipate any complications, though they do happen."

Trinity squeezed his hand. "Is Mr. Crawford resting now? Or can we go up and see him?"

"For a few minutes, but then I suggest you go home and get some rest yourselves. He should be awake and feeling better in the morning."

"How long do you think he'll need to stay in the hospital?" Jon needed to amend his plans. He should let Steph know what was going on, but right now he didn't want the hassle of calling her. She'd take it as a sign he wanted something more. He didn't.

And yet, here he stood with Trinity, holding her hand, the doctor talking to them like they were a couple or something, and it didn't bother him in the least. He didn't worry what Trinity thought about the hand-holding thing, other than she did it to offer comfort and he'd accepted that and didn't expect anything more.

Strange.

And nice.

He could get used to nice.

"I expect he'll need to be here at least two days, possibly three. We'll see how fast he responds to the antibiotics. Do you have any other questions?" Dr. Holt asked.

"No. I think I'll go see him now. Thank you for everything." Jon held out his free hand and shook with the doctor.

Trinity tugged him to come along as she followed the doctor out of the waiting area and walked to the bank of elevators. She didn't let go of his hand, so he held on to her. The connection helped him remain calm when he was really worried about his dad.

"Once you see him, you'll feel better."

"Are you always so optimistic?"

Something dark crossed her eyes but vanished just as quickly as he'd seen it. "I try to be."

He wanted to know more about what was behind her reaction at his father's place, that darkness in her eyes, and how she got the scar. Something happened to her. He wanted to know what.

And as they stepped into the elevator and rode it up in a comfortable silence, he realized he wanted to know everything about her.

He followed Trinity out of the elevator to the nurses' station where she got the room number and led him down the row of rooms to his father's. A nurse stood beside the bed, checking the machine next to him.

"Hi," Trinity whispered. "This is Dennis's son, Jon."

The nurse finished entering something in her tablet, but smiled and said, "Your father is resting comfortably now. His oxygen levels have come up considerably. I'll monitor them through the night."

"Mind if we stay for a few minutes?" Trinity touched his father's leg, offering him the same easy comfort she'd given Jon.

"Sure. Just don't stay too long. He needs to rest right now so the antibiotics can do their job." The nurse left them alone in the quiet room.

His father wore an oxygen mask, and his color looked markedly better. His breathing still seemed labored, but he didn't cough uncontrollably or wheeze.

Trinity released him and went to his father's side. Remarkably, he missed her hand in his. She leaned over and gave his father a soft peck on the forehead, and whispered, "You're going to be okay, Mr. Crawford. You get better real soon, and I will make you a double batch of all your favorite things."

He thought he saw his father's lips twitch into a slight smile.

He'd be smiling too to have a beautiful woman whispering sweet things to him while he was sick. The last time anyone had done that had been when his mom was alive and he'd gotten strep throat as a teen.

Trinity returned to his side and squeezed his arm. "I'll leave you alone with him. Take your time. I'm in no rush." She meant that.

So he waited for her to leave, even though he didn't really want her to go, and approached the bed. He laid his hand on his father's arm, then thought about how much it meant to have Trinity take his hand, so he slipped his hand beneath his father's and held it. Not since he was a small boy had he held his dad's hand, except for the occasional handshake in congratulations. The last time might have been the day Emmy was born and he'd gone out to the waiting room to tell his dad she arrived safely and absolutely perfect.

"Hey, Dad. I'm home." He didn't know that's what he was going to say until the words came out, and they felt so right. "Emmy can't wait to see you. Wait until you see how big she is now." Unexpected tears clogged his throat and blurred his vision. "I've missed you, Dad. More than I realized. I need you to get better so you can come home with me. I told you I'd help you fix the barn and clean up Mom's garden. You said you'd help me learn to be still again and not always on the run."

He pinched the bridge of his nose and fought back the tidal wave of emotions.

"I met your friend Trinity. She's . . . fantastic. She found you tonight." *And I found her.*

He needed to take a breath after that revealing thought popped into his head.

"You're going to be okay. Get some rest. I'll be here when you wake up in the morning." He held his father's hand for a few minutes, letting the quiet surround both of them. He felt connected to his dad and gripped his hand with both of his to send him strength and remind him he wasn't alone.

It took him another few minutes to finally be able to leave his father's side.

Trinity stood with her back to the wall across from the door to his father's room with her eyes closed and her hands against the wall behind her butt, elbows out.

She looked so serene.

He simply stared at her beautiful face and all that long wavy golden hair spilling down her shoulders and chest. Stunning.

Her eyes opened when she sensed him staring.

"You look like an angel."

Her smile punched him in the heart.

"Thank you."

A woman who could take a compliment. He didn't think such a creature existed, but she did.

"You look worn out. Ready for me to drive you home now?"

He hadn't been thinking. "I've kept you from having a proper meal and didn't even think to ask if you had other plans or someone waiting for you to come home." The last part sent a surge of jealousy through him.

"I enjoyed the sandwich and the company. I didn't have any plans aside from spending an hour or so with your dad after I dropped off the food to hear the latest Emmy stories."

"He tells you stories about her."

She kind of bounced off the wall, hooked her hand around his arm, and nudged him toward the elevators again. "Well, you may not know this, but we're in a kind of telephone game. You tell your dad stories and send him cute pictures and videos, then he shares them with me. No misinformation or weird relays in our thing though."

They had a thing?

Okay.

She punched the button for the elevator. "Emmy is adorable. Absolutely the most brilliant girl on the planet. I wholeheartedly agree with her assessment that ice cream is a food group. Along with chocolate," she added as they stepped into the elevator. "And wearing monochromatic outfits is the new trend. Her purple ensemble for your pizza date two weeks ago was totally on point."

He didn't know where it came from, but he laughed. "Wow. Okay. You do know a lot about us."

"Well, her. Not you. Except that your dad always

complains you work too hard and don't come home enough."

He put his hand over hers on his arm. "I think you and I should get to know each other better."

Her exuberance dimmed when she realized what he meant and that she was standing really close to him. So close that he could smell the garlic and chocolate on her from her day in the kitchen cooking, mixed with the peanut butter and jelly sandwich she ate with him.

He backtracked, thinking he'd come on too strong. "Unless there is someone waiting for you to come home."

She kind of came back to herself all at once. "Oh. No. That is, I'm not seeing anyone. I was just surprised you were interested."

"The timing and the circumstances are strange." He usually had better game than this. And timing. "But . . . I don't know. I appreciate what you did for my dad and staying with me tonight. I just got back to town. I haven't connected with anyone. Except you. I'd like to get to know you better." That might be more than he'd said to a woman, other than Steph, in a long time. He definitely needed to up his game.

The elevator dinged and let them out on the ground floor.

She slipped out ahead of him and he followed, wishing he hadn't said anything that would make her stop touching him.

He caught up to her. "Trinity, if I've said something . . . or you're just not interested—"

"It's not that." She stopped in the middle of the hospital lobby and stared at the floor.

"Great." He hoped that reassured her.

"Um, it's just been a while for me. I . . . uh . . . something bad happened . . . It's been hard to . . . trust myself lately."

Okay. He got that. "I haven't really dated in a while. And if you know anything about Emmy's mom, you know that trusting myself to know if someone is good for me or not has been hard, too."

She finally met his gaze. "I actually don't know that much about you and your ex-wife."

"She's just an ex. We never got married. Weren't even engaged." Why he wanted her to know that particular detail he didn't know, and chalked it up to full disclosure.

"Well, I've never been engaged either, but my three brothers have all gotten engaged, and two got married, over the past year, making me the perpetual bridesmaid." She rolled her eyes. "And that's a major turnoff, right? I wasn't trying to say that I want to get engaged or—"

He touched her shoulder. "Got it. But do you want to . . . spend some time together?" He heard how that sounded like a lame pickup line for sex and backtracked. "I mean hang out." What the hell was wrong with him? It was like he'd never asked a woman on a date.

She grinned at him, her eyes full of humor, then cocked her head toward the door. "We should head out."

The nonanswer confused and disappointed him. Did he blow it? Probably, because she was right; he was beyond tired.

They let the quiet, cool night surround them as they made their way to her car in the parking lot. The drive home was long. Neither of them spoke much, but listened to the softly playing country music as they relaxed next to each other and enjoyed the ride.

She pulled into the driveway, and though the lighting was dim with only the flare of her headlights beaming off the garage door, he caught the moment when it all came back to her and her eyes clouded with distress.

"You must have been really scared when you found my dad. I know I nearly freaked out when I saw you hoisting him into your car. I couldn't get down the driveway fast enough."

She took in a calming breath and let it out slowly.

He'd seen her consciously do the same thing several times during the ride to the hospital.

"I'm just glad we got him the help he needed."

"I can't stop thinking about it. What if he hadn't called in the delivery order? What if I didn't get in until late tonight or tomorrow?"

Trinity laid her hand over his on his thigh. "It all worked out."

He turned his hand and linked his fingers with hers. "Thank you for finding him, for getting him out to your car. I know you'd have gotten him there on your own no matter how hard it was for you to do alone. But most of all, thanks for staying with me and being . . . you." Because he didn't have anyone in his life who was just like her. He didn't have someone who'd take the time to sit with him and wait just so he wasn't alone.

"You're welcome." She slipped her hand free, grabbed her bag from the back, and rummaged inside until she pulled out a card. "Please call me in the morning and let me know how he's doing."

He took the card, noted it wasn't a business card, but her personal one.

"And yes, I'd like to see you again." She smiled softly with a touch of nervousness mixed in. "And maybe I'll get to meet your sweet girl Emmy someday."

"She'll want one of those double-chocolate brownies my dad likes so much."

"For her, on the house."

They stared at each other for a moment. He just took her in, then forced himself to get out of the car. "Is your place close?" He didn't like her out on the dark roads this late at night, especially when she'd had a long day.

"I live in the apartment above the shop."

Surprise punched him in the gut. "You mean in town?"

She nodded.

"Why didn't you say anything? I would have found another way home."

"Because I wanted to drive you." She gave him another shy but sexy smile, waking up all kinds of thoughts about her lying on white sheets and his hands caressing every inch of her silky skin.

He eyed her closely. "You're not an angel, you're a temptress."

She laughed. "Call me in the morning with that update on your dad."

He held up her card. "I'm calling you for a lot more than that."

She pressed her lips together, hiding a nervous grin, but her eyes were bright with interest.

He reluctantly closed the door and waved goodbye. When he walked into the dark house, he was still elated by their exchange and it made him miss her all the more.

He couldn't wait to see his father looking better tomorrow and call the beguiling woman who took him by surprise and made him want to try the whole dating, and possibly relationship, thing one more time.

Chapter Three

Jon MAY not have slept well last night, but he'd eaten a damn good spinach, bacon, and cheese breakfast quiche this morning from *Almost Homemade*. He'd found it in his father's fridge along with at least two dozen other prepared meals. He'd never tasted anything so good. No wonder his father ordered delivery from them.

After he ate, he made the long drive into town. He stepped off the hospital elevator, hoping to find his father awake, alert, and doing much better today.

The nurse at the desk stood. "Mr. Crawford?"

He stopped outside his father's door. "Yes."

"Your father should be back any minute. They took him for another chest X-ray to see if he's improving."

"How did he do last night?"

"He mostly slept comfortably, though he did have a few bouts of coughing. His fever is down. Oxygen levels are good."

He sighed out his relief. "Thank you. I'll just wait in his room if that's okay?"

The nurse nodded, then sat back in her seat to work on the paperwork in front of her.

Jon took the seat next to his father's empty bed. He wanted to call Trinity, but it was only seven in the morning and he didn't want to wake her after the long day and night she'd put in yesterday.

He'd sent Steph a text last night, telling her about his dad. Luckily, he'd sent it late enough that she hadn't responded until this morning. She and Emmy had already left for the airport. They'd arrive in a few hours.

Steph said she sympathized with the situation, but wasn't happy he wouldn't be picking them up. Instead, he'd rented her a car, so she would have something to drive until she bought a new car—her old car wouldn't have made the trip to Montana. She didn't like having to take Emmy alone through two airports and to pick up the rental car, then drive in an unfamiliar area to meet him at the apartment he'd rented for them. She had the directions, and it wasn't that complicated a trip. Given the circumstances, she could have been more understanding.

His dad needed him more this morning. And while he regretted not seeing Emmy right away and hearing all about her first plane ride, he needed to know his father was going to be okay. Jon had been away too long. He hadn't called home or visited enough over the past many years he built his business and sucked at his personal life.

He planned to change things and spend more time with his dad and Emmy, living a simpler life afforded to him by all that hard work. His businesses were making him money. He had good people he trusted running them. Aside from overseeing things, he could focus on rebuilding his family's ranch and raising his little girl.

And maybe he'd finally find a woman he wanted to hold on to and make a life with.

He thought of Trinity with her shy smile and generous heart.

Nothing like Steph, who liked to use Emmy as an excuse to get him to do what she wanted in hopes they'd get back together. He'd played that game for months when Emmy came along. But he stopped playing a long time ago.

He wasn't that gullible.

He hoped this would be a fresh start for all of them.

When he floated the idea of bringing Emmy to Montana for the summer and that he'd love to move back home and live on the ranch full-time, he never expected Steph to say, "Let's do it. Let's leave California and build a different kind of life." She had a job, family, a life in California.

But Steph had a tendency to wear out her welcome. Her coworkers didn't like that she got away with doing half as much as them. Even her family was tired of her being selfish and manipulative to get what she wanted.

She painted a pretty imaginary picture of them starting over, living and raising Emmy together. He loved her unexpected enthusiasm, and maybe he got caught up in getting back to the life he'd had as a kid on the ranch. He dreamed of horses and cows in the pastures, and Emmy chasing chickens in the yard and picking vegetables in the garden. He hoped for the best.

Steph said she wanted a new job, new people, and a chance to re-create herself. But as their plans moved forward, it became clear she really wanted them to rekindle their love affair—one that had been doomed to failure because they weren't compatible for a lot of reasons.

As much as he wanted to make the move, he'd repeatedly asked Steph if she was sure she wanted to leave her life behind and start over in a new place without her family. Because she relied on her family, and especially her dad, when life got too hard to deal with, which was often because Steph was spoiled and liked it when others did everything for her.

Despite all that, Steph pushed for them to move. Together.

He blew up that train of thought right off the tracks and made it clear they were not getting back together. She'd given him a look that said she knew better than him. He'd made it very clear he intended to stay at the ranch and she'd be in town where she'd have something to do—away from him—and work while Emmy attended school. He'd even found her a job.

He expected the next few weeks as she settled in to be fraught with a lot of anxiety. New state, new apartment, new job . . . He got it. He vowed to be patient while Steph settled in, even though he knew the best thing he could do was limit their interactions. He didn't want to give Steph false hope that they'd be doing anything more than co-parenting Emmy.

But Steph had a way of seeing things that weren't there and making something out of next to nothing.

He didn't expect the transition to be smooth, but he'd put up with Steph's drama—to a point—for Emmy's sake.

Maybe if his father was up for company today, he'd bring Emmy for a visit. She'd love it. And it might do his father good to see her.

"Jon. Son. You're here." A nurse pushed his dad, who was seated in a wheelchair, into the room.

Jon stood and helped his old man into the bed. "I got in last night. Just in time to see your friend Trinity dragging you out to her car."

He looked up at Jon, confused. "Trinity was at the house?"

"You called her, said you needed her to bring some food. She said you promised she could take you to the doctor."

His father's eyes clouded with confusion.

"You don't remember?"

His dad shook his head. "No. Not really. It seems fuzzy."

The nurse touched his dad's shoulder to get him to lie down. She helped him settle his head on the pillow, raised the top of the bed for him, pulled the covers over his lap and the oxygen tube up across his nose, then connected the oxygen sensor to his finger and walked out.

Jon wondered just how little oxygen his father had been getting and if it had left his brain altered. "Don't worry about it, Dad. The doctors and nurses will help you get better. Your color looks good." The gray pallor he'd seen in his father's face last night still haunted him. "How do you feel?"

"Better. The last few days . . . They were rough."

"You should have called me. I would have come sooner had I known you were sick." He'd have hopped on the earliest flight.

His father stared at his lap. "I knew you were busy."

Jon stuffed his hands deep into his jeans pockets, feeling the extra helping of guilt pile onto the rest he carried with him for not paying attention to his dad and making him feel unimportant. "I'm not too busy for you."

"You were packing, getting ready to move. You couldn't have gotten here any sooner."

He pulled one hand free and raked it over his head. "Damnit, Dad, I would have flown in immediately."

His dad settled into the bed and covered his mouth as

a string of coughs, less intense than they had been last night, rattled his chest.

Jon realized his anger was really fear. "I'm sorry I wasn't here. But I am now."

"Where's Emmy?" For the first time, he saw some joy in his father's eyes. Jon wished he'd been that happy to see him.

He checked his watch. "They should be landing any minute. I'm meeting them at the apartment in just a little while."

The happiness dimmed to disappointment. "Do you think Steph will like the new place?"

"Sure." He really didn't know. Steph thought she deserved the world and he should give it to her simply because he had the means. Her parents, and especially her father, had spoiled her and she expected others to do the same.

His dad gave him a look. "I thought she was excited about the move."

"She is. I think she needed a fresh start as much as I did."

His dad eyed him. "Where will you be sleeping tonight?"

"At home."

His father raised an eyebrow.

"At the ranch." He'd been honest with his dad about his troubles with Steph, but his dad still wondered if Jon would get back together with her despite all that. Not going to happen. He didn't want the illusion of a happy family, he wanted a real, honest relationship with a woman who actually made him happy.

Dad nodded. "Does Steph still hope you'll all move in together?"

Jon sank into the chair. "I made it clear from the beginning that this was the start of a new life for us, but that didn't mean we were getting back together. I got her the job, a place to live, and we'll still raise Emmy together."

"But she's still hoping for more."

"It seems that way sometimes, but then she talks about how she can be anyone she wants to be here. Like even she's tired of the life she had back in California and wants to do and be something different here. Emmy's four. After all this time, I can't believe Steph's still holding out hope for more. I just want to move on."

"Sounds like you're ready for more than just a new place and a new job."

"I didn't sell off everything. I still own a couple of the businesses that were already managed well and thriving without much help from me anymore."

"It's good to keep a steady income. Especially when you have to take care of Emmy and her mother."

He didn't owe Steph anything. What he did for her, he did because she was the mother of his child.

They had equal custody, so he didn't pay child support. Still, he wanted a decent roof over Emmy's head, so he paid for Steph's new apartment. He wanted to make things easier on Steph now that she wanted to be more responsible and go it alone without Daddy always bailing her out. Living rent free meant her income from managing the grocery store would make her financially comfortable. Unless she overspent, which she tended to do. A lot. Still, he could only set her up for success. She had to be responsible.

"I listened to what you had to say about the hours I worked, the long trips away from Emmy, and how I needed to step up and be the dad she deserves." That's why he'd initially wanted the summer in Montana.

"I know you always try to put her first, but I'm happy to see that you understand she has to be the priority all the time, not just when it's convenient for you."

"Work got in the way. Steph got overwhelmed because I wasn't around enough." He raked his hand over his head again, remembering seeing Emmy disheveled and living in a mess at Steph's place. He'd read the notes home from the teacher about her acting out. That wasn't Emmy.

"Let's hope things are better for all of you here."

The doctor walked in. "Dennis, I have your results." He glanced at Jon.

"This is my son. You can talk in front of him."

Jon stood. He didn't know why. He just needed to be on his feet to hear what the doctor had to say.

"The X-ray shows your lungs are better than when you arrived last night. Do you feel like it's easier to breathe today?"

His dad nodded. "Yes. The coughing isn't as bad either." He rubbed his hand over his ribs. "I don't know how much longer I could have endured those fits."

"The ache in your ribs will subside in a few days once those muscles get a rest. While your oxygen levels have improved, I'd like to see them remain steady before we send you home."

"And when do you think that will be?" Jon liked to plan. He wanted to make sure he got the house cleaned up and had everything his dad needed for a speedy recovery.

"Tomorrow if things progress as I hope. If not, we'll keep him an extra day or so after that." The doc pinned his dad in his gaze. "You're lucky you got to the hospi-

tal when you did. Another day and you might not have
made it. When you go home, make sure you continue
your meds for the full fourteen days."

"I will."

The doctor nodded. "Any questions for me?"

"I'm good. Thanks, Doc."

Jon waited for the doctor to leave. "I hope you
heard what he said and take that to heart. You need to
take care of yourself and let me help when you're not
feeling well." Jon had a lot of making up to do with his
dad. And Emmy. He planned to spend a lot of time with
both of them.

"About that."

Jon eyed his dad. "Do you want to tell me about the
papers I found on the dining-room table this morning?"
He hoped they were from before Jon decided to come
home.

"Are you really home? Is this really where you want
to be?"

Though his move back to Montana had gotten a
rocky start so far, excluding meeting Trinity last night,
he still felt like he'd made the right decision. Emmy
needed stability. A place where she could just be a kid
and grow up in the fresh air. She deserved his time and
attention. He could give her all of that here. "Yes. I'm
happy to be back at the ranch and looking forward to
fixing it up. Why?"

"Because although it's always been my home, I'm not
happy there anymore."

"What?" He felt blindsided. "You've lived there for
like forty years."

"The last five of them alone."

It hit Jon right in the chest with a thud that stopped his
heart. "You're lonely." No wonder his father asked him

to call all the time and couldn't get enough pictures or video chats with him and Emmy.

"I can't take care of that place all by myself anymore. It's too much. Everywhere I look, I see memories of your mother and you."

"I'm here now. I can take care of the place."

"Great. The ranch is yours."

Jon narrowed his gaze. "What are you talking about?" He couldn't wrap his mind around the fact his father practically begged him to come home and now he didn't want to stay at the ranch anymore.

This wasn't how things were supposed to go.

"Come on, Jon. Do you really want to move back in with your aging father?"

He held his hands out wide. "I don't mind."

His dad gave him a side-eye look that said he didn't believe him. "The place I picked out is for seniors, but not people who are sick and need around-the-clock care. Oh, they have a nurse and doctor on staff, but it's more for living at a place where there are things to do and people to do them with."

"Dad, you've got a lot of years ahead of you."

"And I don't want to spend them alone out at the ranch looking at the land and wasting away my remaining days."

Jon planted his hands on his hips and sighed. "You've already made up your mind."

"I have. But . . ."

Jon had already looked over the paperwork and knew why his father hadn't pulled the trigger and moved already. "It's pricey."

"I can pay for most of it on my social security and savings."

"But you'd eat up that savings in no time." Unless

he sold the ranch and lived off the proceeds at the new place. Jon didn't even have to think. "If this is what you really want, I'll make it happen." And he'd keep the ranch, because that's what he wanted for him and Emmy.

"The last thing I want to do is burden you with taking care of another person."

"Why? You took care of me. It's my turn to do it for you. Why make all that money and not do this for you after all the support you've given me over the years?"

"Well, that's different. That's not . . ."

"Money. You can say it, Dad. You need the money to make this move. If it will make you happy, if you'll be with friends, if it will make your life better, I'm happy to do it. I just wish you'd talked to me sooner."

"It wasn't all that bad when I could drive, but now I don't like to be out at night, driving along that twisty road. My eyes . . . They're not that good anymore."

"Then we'll get you glasses before you move into that place so you can see all the pretty women." Jon got it. His dad missed his wife. He deserved to find some comfort and companionship with someone. He shouldn't be alone if he didn't want to be anymore.

"Well, I don't know about . . . It's been a long time since . . ."

"Mom died," he finished for his dad. "She'd want you to be happy, too. She wouldn't expect you to sit around alone pining for her."

"I'd like some . . . company. I get bored out at the ranch. In town, I'd have more options. I could go places. Do things."

"You don't have to sell me. I said I'd get you into that place and I will."

"I checked last week. They have a one-bedroom

apartment open. I put down a deposit to hold it." His dad's eyes pleaded with him.

"How long is the hold?"

"Until tomorrow." Worry filled his eyes that he'd lose the deposit and his chance to be around others his age and have some fun and interactions instead of being alone at their remote property.

Jon shook his head. "Well, no time like the present to make a change." That didn't leave him much time to finalize everything.

"I'm sure . . . because I'm in the hospital . . . they'll hold it a day or two more." Uncertainty made his voice quaver.

"I'll go down there today and make all the arrangements." He checked his watch. "In fact, I'll head over there now. Their office should be open. By the time I finish that, I can meet Steph and Emmy at the apartment. The movers should arrive at Steph's place soon after. I told her I'd help her get settled. After that, maybe I can bring Emmy here to see you, if you're up for it."

"I can't wait to see my sweet girl."

"We'll see how you're feeling and how the day goes." If he got his father the apartment, maybe he could convince the moving guys to come out to the ranch and pick up and deliver the essentials his father would need at the new place. Everything else could wait for later when his father was up to sorting through years of accumulated stuff at the house.

An ambitious plan for one day, but Jon could probably swing it if he timed things right.

"I can see you've already got your mind working on the solutions for getting things done."

He laid his hand on his dad's arm and gave it a squeeze. "Can I bring you anything?"

"Emmy." His dad smiled up at him. "And a double-chocolate brownie wouldn't hurt."

"I'll see what I can do." Maybe he'd swing by *Almost Homemade*, see Trinity, pick up some treats for his dad and Emmy, then go over to secure his dad's new residence.

He headed for the door.

"What did you think of Trinity?" his dad called from the bed.

He turned before leaving and smiled. "I haven't stopped thinking about her." He left his father chuckling, and wheezing a bit, and headed out to find the temptress who was still calling to him this morning.

Chapter Four

TRINITY FLIPPED the sign to Open, unlocked the front door, and smiled for the handful of customers waiting to come in. Among them was a man holding a beautiful bouquet of pink roses and white snapdragons. Her heart went a little wild at just the sight of him.

Jon looked refreshed this morning, all shaved and cleaned up after his long night at the hospital. He looked damn good in black jeans and a light blue thermal. The color made his blue eyes even brighter against his dark lashes and hair. The smile he gave her made her belly flutter.

He held the flowers out to her. "Thank you for everything you did last night."

She accepted the bouquet and immediately buried her nose in the sweet scent. "They're lovely. And completely unnecessary. I was happy to help."

"You know what I like about you?"

"What?"

"You say you don't need those, and yet, you can't stop smiling or breathing them in. They are just pure pleasure to you."

"It's not often you get a surprise gift. When you do, you should enjoy it to the fullest."

"I wish those would last forever for you then."

Such a sweet statement. Of course, the flowers would fade and die, but not this memory. She'd hold on to this forever because no one, aside from her brothers on the day they opened the store, had ever given her flowers.

She ran her fingers over the soft petals. "How is your dad?"

"Better. Awake. Alert. Ready to move into a new apartment apparently."

She pressed her lips into a surprised frown. "Really?"

"At least I'm not the only one who didn't know anything about it."

She waved him to follow her into the store. She needed to put the flowers in a container and make sure her staff was handling the customers who were already shopping. "I suppose it's hard for him, living in the country, not being able to come into town as much as he'd like anymore."

"He said it plainly. He's lonely. And bored. So I have a fridge full of food thanks to you and a ranch that's all mine now."

"Uh, wow. Congratulations?"

He chuckled. "I came home to spend more time with Dad and Emmy and fix up the ranch. Dad hasn't run cattle or horses on the place since I was a teen. It'll take some time to fix up the stables and barn before I bring any animals onto the property. If the house is mine now, I guess I'll renovate. Make it mine."

"So a real fresh start."

"Absolutely. With a lot of possibilities."

She liked the way he held her gaze when he said that, and her belly tingled.

He glanced around the huge space, taking it in. "This is really something. Not a grocery store exactly, but . . .

a really great concept. The quiche I had this morning
was amazing."

She couldn't help the sense of pride that washed over
her at his praise. "I'm glad you enjoyed it. It's one of
your father's favorites."

"And so are you." The look in his eyes said she was
one of his favorites now, too, but that could just be wish-
ful thinking on her part.

"I thought I might stop at the hospital later and see
him. If you think he's up for it."

"I bet he'd love it. Who wouldn't want a beautiful
woman visiting them?"

The instantaneous blush heated her cheeks.

It intensified when Adria walked out of the kitchen
and spotted them. "Well, well, well, who's your friend,
Trinity?"

"Jon Crawford, this is my best friend and nosy partner, Adria McGrath. Adria, Jon."

"McGrath?" He looked at her.

Adria held her hand out. "And sister-in-law." She
rubbed her hand over her round belly. "I'm sleeping
with her oldest brother."

Jon laughed again.

Trinity loved the sound of it.

"Drake. We went to school together. He was a year
ahead of me. Declan a year behind me."

Adria eyed him. "So that's how you two know each
other?"

Jon shook his head. "I saw her around, but I didn't
really know her back then. We're getting to know each
other now."

Trinity got lost in the look in Jon's eyes, but found
some words for Adria. "Last night. I delivered the food
to Mr. Crawford. Jon's father."

Jon took over the storytelling. "She dragged my father out of the house and into her car. He passed out from being sick. Pneumonia. We got him to the hospital. Just in time, from what the doctor told me this morning. If not for Trinity's help last night, I don't know how I'd have gotten through it."

"Wow." Adria looked at her. "Why didn't you call and tell us you needed help at the Crawford place?"

"There wasn't time. He needed to get to the hospital, and I tried to get him there as fast as possible."

Jon stepped closer to her, though he didn't touch her. Still, she felt every bit of his presence. "I came by to give her the update on my dad, who is doing very well this morning, and thank her for the help."

Adria's gaze bounced from him to Trinity and back. "Seems like you two hit it off."

"We did." Jon smiled at Trinity, and that flutter thing happened in her belly again. "I'm hoping she can help me out again right now."

Trinity turned to him. "What do you need?"

He gave her a look that said a lot more than the words that came out of his mouth. "Double-chocolate brownies. Dad's favorite. And I'm hoping to give a few to Emmy."

"Who?" Adria asked, thinking there was some other woman maybe, judging by the side-eye she gave Jon.

"My daughter. She's four and obsessed with chocolate anything."

Trinity knew the feeling. Though she was starting to get addicted to the almost-too-good-to-be-true, dark-haired, blue-eyed man beside her. "I made several batches this morning. Let me put these in water, then I'll wrap some up for you." Trinity walked toward the back, but overheard Adria ask, "Would you like anything else?"

And Jon's reply. "Her."

She didn't know how many more of these little bursts of excitement her belly could take.

Adria joined her in the big kitchen. "Oh. My. God. He's. Hot!"

Trinity burst out laughing. "Your hormones are out of control."

Adria took the teasing with a smile. "Trinity. Seriously. He's . . . great."

"I know." And it scared her a little because it had been a long time since she'd been interested in anyone. And although she really wanted to get to know him better, he'd caught a glimpse of her crazy last night, and the last thing she wanted was for him to see the full-on version of the new reality she lived with and tried to hide from everyone.

"Please tell me you two have a date and a wedding planned."

Trinity gaped at Adria. "I just met him."

"Do not let him leave here without at least a dinner date set up."

"He literally just moved to town yesterday. He might need a minute to settle in before he starts dating anyone."

"You need to snatch him up before anyone else in town sees him and steals him."

"Seriously, dial down the hormones. You're all revved up. Maybe you should go home and"—she waved her hand back and forth in front of Adria's body—"work off some of that energy." She loved Adria, but she seriously didn't need to know how the pregnancy made her all horny for her brother. Ew! But also, good for them. Yuck for her to hear about it.

But what were best friends for?

Still. Adria and her brother. Gross.

"I'm just saying, you've been . . . off lately. Maybe this is just what you need."

Adria spent the most time with her. Trinity could hide her . . . symptoms from everyone else. But Adria caught the way she jumped when someone surprised her and how she constantly watched the customers and the door, looking for threats that weren't there. Adria knew how hard it was for her to take the trash out to the dumpster in back where she'd been abducted.

Trinity rubbed her finger along the scar on her temple.

Adria caught her hand and held it. "Maybe what you need is a sexy distraction to get you out of your head."

Adria had been that, and so much more, for Drake.

Trinity confessed a truth she couldn't ignore. "I like him. A lot."

"He seems to like you just as much. Don't let the past stop you from living your life to the fullest. Clint is dead, Trinity. He can't hurt you ever again. Unless you let him."

Meaning if she let her nightmares keep her behind locked doors and a barred heart, Clint still won.

"Don't keep Jon waiting too long."

What Trinity heard was, "Don't lose him because you're too afraid to go out." She spent most of her time in the shops or her apartment. She didn't go anywhere else unless she absolutely had to, and even then, she spent the whole time on high alert for a threat she knew wasn't really there.

Adria touched her shoulder. "I'll go make sure everything is okay out front with the staff. You put those pretty flowers in water and pack up his order. I'll let him know you'll be out soon."

Trinity stared at the flowers and wondered at the kind

gesture and how open and honest Jon had been about wanting to see her again. "I can do this."

She found a pretty vase in the office and set the flowers on the table while she packed up two containers of brownies. On Emmy's, she wrote the little girl's name vertically, then drew butterfly wings on each side and antennae over the top of the *E*.

She carried the boxes and her vase of flowers out to the front. She set the flowers next the register where she'd be able to admire them all day, then walked around the counter and met Jon in the middle of the shopping aisles where he stood looking at everything.

"This place is really great. Have you thought about expanding? I think people all over the country would love a store like this in their neighborhood. Everyone is so busy these days, they don't want to do everything themselves all the time. This is a great alternative to takeout and delivery, and probably costs less than home delivery meal kits."

She tried to contain a laugh but failed. "I know. That's why we opened two other stores. One in Billings and one in Bozeman. We're thinking of expanding further, perhaps getting some of the prepared foods into the larger grocery chains, that kind of thing. But right now, plans are stalled until Adria delivers her two little bundles of joy, and we can figure out the best location to move into next. Plus, though we're doing great business at each location, we don't want to leverage ourselves too much in case business slows down."

"I don't see that happening. In fact, I might have some ideas for you."

She held his earnest gaze. "What is it that you do exactly?"

"I buy businesses, grow them, expand them, and sell

them. At least I did before I moved back to rehab the ranch."

"We aren't for sale. Adria and I have worked too hard, too many long hours to let someone come in and take over just to make a gob of money and sell it all off for more." Didn't he think she and Adria could build the business on their own? They were doing a pretty damn good job of it so far. Of course they'd done the whole "What if someone buys us out and we're rich?" thing. But they loved working in the shop, seeing their satisfied customers, and delivering a product they were proud to make.

Jon shook his head and stuffed his hands in his pockets. "Sorry. I didn't mean to upset you."

"You didn't."

"I told myself when I moved back here that I'd take some time off, be happy with the businesses I still own, and settle into ranch life again so I can spend more time with Emmy." He looked around the store again. "I just see what an amazing thing this is that you've built and my mind automatically spins all the possibilities of what I could do with it." He sighed. "What I really need to focus on is renovating the house, rehabbing the ranch, getting my father set up at his new place, and getting Emmy ready for her new school."

She held up the brownie containers. "This should help. I cut hers into small squares. Your father's in big chunks."

He stared at the butterfly she'd made out of Emmy's name. "She's going to love this. Butterflies are her favorite."

"If you're doing her room, you could buy some wood letters at the craft store and do something just like this on the wall or her door. Put the letters up in a curve and use some paint or even string lights to make the wings. A couple of fat colorful pipe cleaners curled at the top for antennae. It would be really cute."

"Now I need to stop at the craft store. She'd love that. And we could do it together."

"She could paint each letter herself. Glitter them up. Put stickers on them. Whatever. You should take her with you to the craft store, let her decide."

"I'm going to owe you more flowers if you keep helping me out like this."

"Oh, well, it's nothing." A blush heated her cheeks.

"Emmy's been nervous about the move. She's in a new place and doesn't know anyone. I think getting her out, letting her see some of the town, doing a project like this together, will help her feel more at home."

"I'm happy I could help then." She touched his arm. "Take a picture of it for me. I'd love to see how it turns out."

"Maybe you'll come see it yourself."

She took Adria's advice and dove in the deep end of the dating pool. "Would you like to have dinner with me this coming Thursday?"

He smiled. "You beat me to it. I was going to ask you out for this Friday."

"Friday is harder to be out late, because I work the early shift on Saturday. I'm up baking and cooking at three."

"Damn." He cocked his head. "Wait. You said you made the brownies. Were you seriously up at three this morning after being at the hospital and driving me home late last night?"

She simply smiled. "I told you I wanted to drive you home. And I appreciate you coming to tell me first thing this morning that your dad is better."

"First thing? You've almost put in a full day already."

"I'll work through the lunch crowd, then catch a nap upstairs. I'm covering closing because Adria has a doctor appointment later today."

"Well, I better let you get to it. What time should I pick you up on Thursday?"

"Anytime is good. It's my day off."

"How about five? We'll have drinks, an early dinner, maybe go see a movie after that."

She was used to guys wanting to meet for drinks and not much else on a first date. Jon wanted an entire evening. "Sounds good."

"I haven't been in town in a long time. How about you pick the place?"

"Do you like rustic Italian?"

"After eating your quiche, if you like it, I know I'll like it."

"Then we'll go to Camilla's Kitchen. They have a great wine and cocktail hour from five to six."

"Perfect. I'll see you then, if not before." He hesitated for a moment before he smiled at her, then walked away.

She watched him go and got that giddy feeling again when he looked back at her and smiled before stepping out the door.

Adria stepped up beside her. "He's really dreamy."

She hadn't smiled this much in a long time. "Drinks. Dinner. A movie. Thursday."

Adria bumped shoulders with her. "I have a feeling you two are going to have something really special."

Trinity hoped she could keep her shit together and not lose it on the first real date she'd had in months, because she felt the spark of possibility and she didn't want her crazy to snuff it out before it really got a chance to burn.

Chapter Five

JON DROVE from *Almost Homemade* through town to meet Steph and Emmy at their new place. Though it was a bit more built up from when he was a kid, it was still a small town. He hoped Steph and Emmy would be happy with the slower pace.

Jon pulled into the apartment complex, where three two-story apartment buildings surrounded a grass area. He spotted Steph and Emmy running around the big lawn playing tag. He pulled into the empty spot next to Steph's rental. The back end of the Jeep Cherokee stood open, letting the cats in the two pet crates get some fresh air. He hoped the three cats made it through the flight okay.

Steph barely paid attention to them.

He really couldn't figure out if Steph loved anyone—or anything—more than she loved herself, though right now she seemed to be enjoying her time with their daughter.

He sometimes wondered if Emmy felt it. When she was younger, probably not, but she was a smart girl, even at four.

The youngest of four girls, Steph had been the spoiled baby of the family. She got whatever she wanted. Beyond beautiful, men drooled at her feet and wanted to do anything to please her. For a while. Because the shine wore off all too soon when the real Steph revealed herself.

It happened to him. He tired of the demanding princess routine right about the time Steph announced she was pregnant, they should get married, and she should stop working and stay home with their little one.

He partly blamed the sexy, willing woman and tequila for the unexpected pregnancy.

He equally blamed himself for drinking too much, thinking with his dick instead of his brain, and not using a condom.

Hit by a moment of clarity that he was going to be a father, he pictured the rest of his life being married to Steph, the girl who sounded like she had it all together but didn't. A person who couldn't function unless someone did everything for her.

If he'd only gotten out a couple weeks earlier.

But then he wouldn't have his sweet Emmy.

He stepped out of his car, checked to be sure there were no cars coming, and held his arms out wide. Emmy ran to him with a bright smile and pink cheeks. She launched herself into his chest. He wrapped her in his arms and swung her around. "Hello, sweet girl."

She hugged his neck so tight he almost couldn't breathe, but he didn't care. His heart swelled with pride and devotion. He loved her to no end. She made him smile and believe in unconditional love.

"Hi, Daddy. I missed you."

"How was the plane ride?"

"Awesome!" She leaned back and gave him a very serious look. "Mama's mad at you."

What's new?

He raised a brow as Steph joined them and gave Emmy a stern look. "I got a little upset—"

"She swore." Emmy tattled on her mom.

Steph planted her fists on her hips and stared down Emmy. "I'm talking." She set her perturbed gaze on him. "It was . . . *challenging*," she bit out, "getting her, the booster seat, our bags, and retrieving the cats. Not to mention hauling all that to our rental car on my own. The GPS thing didn't want to work at first. I got turned around leaving the airport, and I may have said a few choice words."

"But you got here." He hoped his easy tone and not making a big deal about swearing around Emmy eased her mind and settled her down.

"We did. Yes. But it would have been nice if you'd stuck to the plan and come to get us."

Steph was smart and capable when she wanted to be. It took him a while to figure out she simply didn't care to be proficient at anything when she could get by doing the bare minimum. Her beauty helped her out there. People, men especially, wanted to do things for her, hoping she'd pay them attention.

Which she did when it got her what she wanted.

Lesson learned. He wasn't blinded by her pretty face and gorgeous body anymore. That he had been made him feel like a chump sometimes.

It took him a while to figure out party Steph was fun, but regular Steph liked to get her pout on and leave life's chores to others.

If Steph had a headache, she called in sick. All the better to spend a day binge-watching a show while others did her job. She didn't care if she left work shorthanded or if something didn't get done.

If she spent too many days at the spa in a month or spent too much money shopping for clothes she didn't need, and she couldn't pay her bills, she called Daddy, gave him some sob story, and he coughed up the dough to cover her.

In the beginning, Jon had fallen into that trap himself because she'd rewarded him with a good time. Not anymore. He'd closed his wallet, except when it came to Emmy's needs.

"I needed to check on my dad at the hospital."

"Is Grandpa okay?" Emmy's eyes held too much concern for such a little girl.

He brushed his hand over her head. "Yes. He's much better this morning. I thought we'd go see him later this afternoon after the moving trucks get here."

"You're taking her later?"

Before the move, they'd agreed to a new equally shared custody arrangement. He wanted more time with Emmy and hoped it took some of the stress off Steph, because he couldn't count the number of times she called when she had Emmy to complain it was too much, she needed a break, or that Emmy wouldn't listen to her.

When Emmy started fighting him about going to stay at her mom's, he'd made her go because he told himself she needed her mother. But then she started acting out at school, the calls from Steph about how overwhelmed she was having Emmy "all the time," and the state his daughter came back to him in sent up one red flag after another.

Emmy was so good when she was with him.

How could she be so different at her mom's place?

He quickly discovered the problem wasn't his bright

daughter, but the mother who fed her crap, let her stay up to all hours, didn't keep to a schedule, and let Emmy get away with everything instead of disciplining her. When she did, Emmy argued, and Steph gave up.

He couldn't put all the blame on Steph. He'd worked a lot. He could sometimes be distracted by business when he should be focused on Emmy.

Then again, he never complained about his time with her. He tried to make it fun while giving her the stability and structure she needed.

But things were going to be different here. "The hospital isn't far. We'll only be gone an hour tops. My dad needs his rest, but he can't wait to see Emmy."

Steph gave him a sharp nod. "It'll give me a little time to unpack."

"Speaking of that, let's get the stuff out of the car and show the cats their new home." He tickled Emmy's belly, then set her on the sidewalk. "Don't move."

Jon turned to the car and pulled out the two cat crates and set them next to Emmy, who promptly squatted and poked her fingers through the grate to pet Razzle.

Steph joined him at the back of the car as he pulled out their suitcases. She held two shopping bags. "We stopped at the store for a few things to tide us over until I can do a big grocery run."

He spied several frozen dinners, chicken nuggets, pizza bites, a bag of Tater Tots, and frozen pizzas along with two bottles of wine. "Um, that's what you plan to feed Emmy?"

"What? She loves pizza and nuggets."

"I know, but she needs healthier foods than that." When he started noticing Emmy came home cranky and tired and just off, he started wondering why. He'd even asked the pediatrician what she thought and the first question she asked was, "How is her diet? Does she eat any vegetables at all?"

Emmy answered and blew his mind away. "Only at Daddy's."

He pinned Steph in his gaze. "We talked about this. The pediatrician said she needs fruits and vegetables and other healthy foods."

She set the second bag on the ground and held it open, showing him juice boxes, a bottle of his favorite bourbon, and a pack of yogurt sticks. "She loves those."

He knew she meant the yogurt, but asked anyway, just to be a smart-ass. "When did she start drinking bourbon?"

Steph laughed. She was always quick to laugh at his bad jokes. "That's for you. For when you come over. You promised we'd spend more time together as a family. The three of us."

He didn't say anything about how he didn't plan to stay for drinks. He meant to be a good example for Emmy.

Where Steph was concerned, he planned to keep his head.

Steph's expectant and hopeful eyes said she wanted them to give things another go. Not going to happen. He knew what he wanted in his next relationship. Less drama. Someone who made him think of forever. Someone who wanted to make a happy family with him and Emmy.

Someone kind, who cared about others.

Someone like Trinity.

"This is just to get us by while we settle in." She sounded sincere.

He let it go, hoping Steph followed through and bought Emmy the fruits and vegetables she needed. If she didn't, he'd have to stock up himself.

Emmy needed to see them working together, not always bickering at each other.

He put a shopping bag on top of each of the rolling bags and let Steph grab the cat crates. "Let's go check out your new place." He led the way along the path. "What did you think of the store?"

"It's fine. Not as up-to-date as the ones you own back home, but big. They have a good selection. The cashiers were moving customers along but still chatting with them. I imagine in a town like this, they know most everyone. And friendly, personalized customer service is important." Which she'd always stressed to the employees at the clothing store she used to manage.

Good. She liked the grocery store. He hoped she enjoyed the job well enough to make an effort to keep it. Although he got her in the door, it didn't mean she could slack off like she had at her last job.

They approached the apartment door. Butterflies took flight in his gut. He really wanted Steph to like the place he picked out for her and Emmy. It would make things so much easier between them. One less complaint he had to hear about.

Since he was footing the bill, he'd found them a nice place with what they needed. And because the rent wasn't as astronomical as in California, he'd been able to find a place with upgraded appliances and amenities, better than the place where Steph and Emmy used to live. They even had a bit more space and a private courtyard where Emmy could play on the fenced-in patio.

He handed Steph her set of keys. "Number one-twelve. Straight ahead." She went ahead to open the door. Emmy ran after her mom.

Jon walked into the apartment behind them.

Emmy squealed from her room down the short hall.

Steph stood in the entry, taking in the empty living room and kitchen. "It's so much nicer than the pictures you showed me." She glanced over her shoulder and gave him a genuine smile.

His concern dissipated and he breathed easy. "They put in new carpet and painted."

The apartment looked and smelled brand-new. A fresh place and start for Steph.

She swiped her hand over the stone countertop. "The kitchen is bigger than my last place." She gave him a self-deprecating grin. "Not that I'm a great cook, but it's really nice."

"I'm glad you like it." Relieved to see her happy and at ease, he smiled back at her, then set the shopping bags on the kitchen counter. He checked to be sure the re-frigerator was on and cold, then put away the groceries.

Steph came up behind him and put both hands on his back and rubbed up and down. It used to be that he wel-comed her affection. Now, he preferred keeping things simple and civil. He turned to face her, hoping she didn't take offense. In the U-shaped kitchen, she blocked him from exiting and he stared down into her earnest eyes.

"Thank you, Jon. I love the place." She waved her hand toward the sliding glass doors off the living space. "If we got a nice patio set, we could sit out back, have dinner there when the weather is nice, or just sit with a glass of wine and stare at the stars."

She painted a nice picture. And he liked this version of Steph, but he didn't plan to spend time with her and

Emmy at the apartment. He wanted to keep family time to meals out and playtime at the park.

"Sounds nice. Emmy will love it, too." He didn't want to spoil Steph's good mood, so he kept things light and didn't shoot down her suggestions.

"I can't wait for the furniture to be delivered. I'm excited to see the place come together."

Most of her stuff was nice but worn. Steph cared more about her clothes and handbags than her furniture, but maybe a new start here would change her priorities and she'd buy some new stuff and really make this place hers.

"Go check out Emmy's room," he coaxed, hoping she liked the surprise he'd set up for Emmy.

He followed Steph toward the sound of their daughter's chatter.

Steph scanned the room and the brand-new bedroom set he'd bought for Emmy, then looked at him. "How did you do this?"

Steph sold Emmy's baby set in the garage sale they held right before the move.

"I bought everything when I came to check out the apartment and asked the landlord to let the furniture guys in yesterday to deliver and set it up. I wanted Emmy to feel at home here. She's never moved before. It's a new place. New people. I wanted her to start off with everything she needs."

Steph rolled her eyes. "Of course you did. You can afford to spoil her and make me look bad." Her mouth pressed into the pout he'd come to see more and more the longer they were together.

He wanted to do something nice for his daughter. But he understood Steph's position, too, and sucked in a calming breath and tried to sooth her ruffled feathers.

"That's not what I'm doing at all. She needed the furniture, so I took care of it." Instead of asking Steph to pay her half, or buy it all herself because she should be the one supplying it in the house she shared with Emmy. He still needed to get her new furniture for his place once he settled in at the ranch.

He tried not to spoil Emmy too much, but she deserved a big girl room. He loved the white bedroom set. She'd have plenty of space in the six-drawer dresser. He'd need to make sure he set up her blue lava lamp on the nightstand before he left and make the bed with her favorite blanket and the brand-new comforter and sheet set he bought and packed in his car, too.

Steph wrapped her arms around her waist. "We could have picked everything out together. Maybe bought a few other things for the apartment." Steph was disappointed he hadn't bought all new stuff for the whole place.

He managed their relationship the best he could and tried not to give Steph false hope or the idea that she could use him to get the things she wanted.

He walked over and crouched next to Emmy and her new twin bed. "What do you think, sweet girl? Do you like your new stuff?"

Emmy jumped up and wrapped her arms around his neck. "I love it." She kissed his cheek, then held up one of the dolls that came with the dollhouse. "She looks like me."

"Kinda. It's why I picked her for you." He checked the text on his phone. "Why don't you play in here while your mom and I help unload the moving van that just arrived."

She was already engrossed in the dollhouse again.

He stood and cocked his head for Steph to go ahead

of him down the hallway. Before they walked out the entry, he slid open the pocket door next to what would be Emmy's bathroom. "You've got a stackable washer and dryer." He hoped that made up for not including her in the furniture thing and spoiling Emmy and not her.

At her last place, she had to go to a laundry room at the far end of her building and share with the other tenants. "That will be so much more convenient. It's a definite plus for this place." She gave him a small smile.

He took the win and hoped to get out of here before the tide changed again.

He headed out to the moving van to get this final chore done. It took some time and maneuvering to unload all of Steph's stuff, get her bed set up, and stack all the boxes in the right rooms, but once done, Steph looked overwhelmed but happy to have her things in her place.

"I need to follow the movers out to the ranch so they can unload my stuff." He'd also talked them into taking on the extra job of bringing some of his father's things to the new apartment since they had to come back through town anyway. It cost him extra, but his dad would be happy to have his place ready when he got out of the hospital. "I'll be back for Emmy in a couple of hours to take her to visit my dad."

"Maybe we can go out to dinner tonight," Steph suggested.

His first instinct was to say no, but instead he began like they hoped to start this next part of their lives. "A family dinner our first night here together sounds great."

Steph's eyes went wide with surprise that he'd so easily agree. "I'll be ready when you pick me up after seeing your dad."

"Sounds good."

If she was making an effort to settle into a new place and start a new job, he could meet her halfway and stick to their plan to spend time together as a family once in a while for Emmy's sake.

He found Emmy lying on her tummy on her bed. "I'm going to take my stuff out to the ranch. I'll be back in a little while for our visit with Grandpa. Okay?"

"Okay," she automatically replied without taking her eyes off the princess movie on her tablet.

He kissed her cheek and headed out with a wave goodbye to Steph as he passed the kitchen and walked out the front door. He felt good about everything right now. Steph liked the place, they managed to spend another day together without World War Three breaking out, and Emmy was happy in her new home.

As for him, he couldn't wait to settle in at the ranch, find some balance in his life, and learn to breathe again.

Chapter Six

Jon was feeling damn good about the start of his week. His father had markedly improved and was feeling better. Trinity loved her flowers and asked *him* out on a date. Steph was unexpectedly excited about putting the apartment together and decorating. He'd been so happy about that, he'd even given her two hundred bucks to buy a few extra things. Emmy liked the new place and even said she was excited about starting at the new pre-K. They all got through the family dinner they shared at a local barbecue place without any bickering. Another win.

After the movers delivered everything of his to the ranch, they helped him pack up his father's room, a few pieces from the living room, and delivered them to his dad's new apartment. By the time his dad left the hospital two days after he'd gone in, he was settled in his new place and signed up for bingo and the weekly poker game in the rec room once he was fully recovered.

When Jon had secured the apartment, the manager assured him his father would be very happy there. Jon noted that there were a lot of women in the common area. The manager gave him a knowing look and informed him the women outnumbered the men two to one and his father wouldn't want for company if he desired it.

Jon did not allow his mind to travel down that road. He'd simply gotten his father settled and gone back to the ranch to figure out what to do with his new house.

Renovations. He made a list and some calls. By the end of next week, he'd have the whole place painted, new carpet in the back bedrooms, and upgraded countertops, fixtures, and appliances in the kitchen. He needed to pick out furniture for Emmy's room at his place, along with all new furniture for the living room.

His dad told him to make the place his. They'd go through the contents soon. As for the big pieces of furniture that wouldn't fit in his dad's apartment, Jon could keep what he wanted and get rid of the rest.

Jon was sentimental about the wide plank farmhouse dining table his mother had loved. But a lot of the other furniture was old, and frankly, not his style.

If this was his chance to start over and make a new life for him and Emmy, he wanted to do it right.

So he had a contractor coming to fix up the stables. He'd start building the ranch with a couple horses. He wanted to teach Emmy how to ride. He also had a landscaping crew coming to redo the yard and get the vegetable garden area cleared out so he and Emmy could replant.

He seemed to have everything under control.

Until today. He hadn't looked forward to a date, or anything, this much in longer than he could remember. It seemed he couldn't get Trinity off his mind. Nor could he stay away from her. After he saw the bright smile on Emmy's face when he delivered the brownies, he'd stopped at *Almost Homemade* the next day to pick up a few entrées and sides she'd love to be sure Steph fed her well. But Trinity was working in their Billings store that day, so he missed her. The next day he and his father stopped by to stock his fridge at his apartment. Like him, his dad couldn't wait to see Trinity. But she'd been called to fix a problem in the kitchen at their Bozeman store and he'd missed her by five minutes.

He'd been too tied up yesterday to even attempt to see her. And he was pretty sure Adria would laugh in his face if he showed up three days in a row.

He and Trinity shared a couple of text messages, mostly him letting her know he was sorry he missed her at the store and couldn't wait to see her for their date. She'd responded right away with regrets she'd missed him, too, questions about how his father was doing, and if Emmy liked her new home and school.

All of that was nice, but he couldn't wait to be alone with her tonight.

If he even made it to their date.

Because he lived so far out of town and away from Steph's place and Emmy's school, he and Steph agreed to a new custody arrangement. He'd pick Emmy up from school on Friday afternoon and keep her for the weekend and drop her off at school on Monday. Since Steph didn't get off work until five, Emmy would stay at day care after school for a couple hours before Steph picked her up Monday through Thursday, and they'd split the cost.

But here he was on Thursday at quarter to five and Steph had called him and told him to come get his daughter. Steph was done for the week. She hung up after dropping that bomb and refused to answer her phone, making him drive to her place to see what the hell was going on.

Why hadn't she worked until five? Why wasn't Emmy still at day care?

The biggest why? Why couldn't she take care of their daughter?

He felt a trap. Or at least more of the same drama he told Steph he wouldn't put up with anymore.

Knowing this was going to take more than the five minutes he had to deal with it and still make it to his date on time, he reluctantly called Trinity.

"Hey there. I hope you're not canceling because I'm starving and deserve a cocktail after the week I've had."

Those words were like a knife to his heart. "Don't hate me. And please, for God's sake don't say you won't go out with me."

"But?" Disappointment filled Trinity's soft voice.

"I'm not saying I won't be there, I'm just going to be late. Something came up with Emmy. I'm on my way to see her right now, but I don't know how long it's going to take to sort out."

A sigh of relief boosted his confidence. "Oh. Okay. No problem. If Emmy needs you, I totally understand."

"You do?" He didn't know why he didn't expect her understanding, but it seemed so foreign to him after dealing with Steph for so long.

"Sure. She's your daughter. She needs you. That comes first."

He didn't know what to do with all that genuine understanding. "And you're not mad?"

"Not at all. Why would I be?"

He didn't know, but if he was having this conversation with Steph, it would be a whole other story. "I just really want to see you tonight and I wanted it to be perfect."

It took her a moment to respond. "I'm looking forward to seeing you, too." The shy words touched him. And gave him hope that he hadn't blown this with her. "How about I keep my dress on, you see what's what with Emmy, and let me know if we're still on for later tonight or if we need to reschedule."

Damn his luck. "You wore a dress?" He'd love to see her in a sexy outfit.

"Adria informed me it was proper date attire. Truthfully, it's been so long, I'm glad she reminded me." Her soft self-deprecating laugh lightened his heart. She was taking this really well and not making a fuss over the fact she'd taken the time to get dressed up and it might be for nothing, depending on what he found when he got to Steph's place.

"I'm sorry, Trinity. I meant to be on time, to wine and dine you, to hopefully make you laugh, and maybe if I played my cards right and you had a good time, you'd agree to a second date." And maybe he'd get a chance to kiss her. He spent a lot of time thinking about it and a lot more.

"There's still time. Take care of whatever you need to do with Emmy, then text me and let me know if we're still on for tonight, or next week sometime."

Next week?

That was too damn long to go without seeing her again.

"I'll let you know as soon as I can."

"I'll be waiting."

"I've been waiting all week to see you tonight. I really am sorry. I'll call you as soon as I know what's what." With that, they said goodbye and he pulled into the parking space outside Steph's apartment.

Emmy ran out the door just as he exited the car and

headed in her direction. Three steps away from him, she stopped short, fisted her hands at her sides, and gave him her angry face, which was still adorable to him. "I want to go home with you."

He didn't even have her room ready, but she could crash with him in his bed until he got that sorted out. Still, it was Steph's night to keep her, so he couldn't make any promises.

The door to the apartment stood open, so he walked right in and found Steph in the kitchen nursing a bottle of beer. Boxes were still stacked up in the living room. Laundry sat on the floor in a pile in front of the stacked washer and dryer. The whole place smelled like Steph burned something in the oven.

And she took one look at him and her eyes narrowed with rage. "What are you all dressed up for?"

"Daddy has a date with the brownie lady," Emmy announced.

He didn't know how she remembered that, or why he'd even told her. Probably because he was excited about seeing Trinity and he'd shared it with her.

Steph's eyebrows went up. "A date? We haven't even been in town a full week and you have a date? I know, literally, no one here." Steph loved to exaggerate. She'd met everyone at work and even told him she'd met a couple interesting customers at the grocery store. She'd even set up a playdate for Emmy with another mom at school.

He didn't owe her an explanation and knew from past bad experiences not to give out information she'd only twist and use against him. So he didn't answer her question, but asked one of his own. "Why haven't you answered your phone?"

"Because if I did, you wouldn't have come to get her."

Yep, he'd played right into her hands because if his daughter needed him he'd come running every time. "Why are you home from work early?"

Her gaze narrowed on him. "I'm not. I get off at four thirty."

"I thought you said five and that's why we set the pickup at school for five fifteen."

Her eyebrows went up. "Don't I deserve a little downtime at the end of my shift before I pick her up?"

Yes. Of course she did. But didn't she also miss her daughter after a long day?

"Why do I need to take Emmy tonight?"

Emmy took his hand. "She burned dinner and said I have to eat it. I don't want it." Emmy wrinkled her nose and shook her little head.

Exasperated by the stupid reason she'd called him here, he took Emmy's side without hearing her out. "Seriously, Steph. You can't expect her to eat burnt food."

"It's that or nothing."

"You bought plenty of food when you moved in."

"You'd think so, but she eats like crazy. And those brownies you bought are gone, too."

"Mommy ate them." Tears filled Emmy's big round eyes.

It killed him when she cried. "This is ridiculous. You work at the grocery store. There's no reason you can't grab something on your way home."

"I worked all day. I didn't think about picking anything up when I left. I was tired. I've been taking care of her all week and trying to put things away here."

At a glance, it didn't look like she'd done a damn thing since he left after the delivery guys brought everything inside. She'd been so excited to decorate, yet she hadn't done anything. Even the sink was filled with dirty dishes. He could practically make out exactly what they'd had to eat all week just by looking at them.

"Steph, we talked about this. Emmy needs a clean and organized home to live in."

She slammed her hand down on the counter. "I'm doing the best I can. It's been a long week. And you said we'd spend more time together as a family, yet you've been nowhere to be found because you've been out hunting up a new girlfriend apparently."

He wanted to refute that outright, but she had him on being out of touch since they had dinner their first night here. "I'm sorry, Steph. You're right. I did say we'd do more family things, but my dad was sick, and I had to move him. I've had a hell of a week, too."

She crossed her arms over her chest, but the anger in her eyes dimmed. "Yeah, well, you seemed to find someone who likes you. I'm pretty sure half the checkout people hate me."

"I'm sure they don't. You just started." Though Steph didn't always make a great impression. At a glance, she was beautiful. But get to know her . . . A couple of his friends outright warned him away from her. Others gave him a raised eyebrow that said clearly, "Really? Her?"

Still, he understood that she was maybe overwhelmed with the move and all the changes in her life.

"They resent that they weren't promoted to manager and I got the job." She rolled her eyes. "Well, you got it for me."

"And you'll be brilliant at it if you give it a chance," he said encouragingly.

She relaxed even more at his praise. She swept her

long straight hair behind her ears and sighed. "I forgot the groceries."

"Okay. Why don't you two go out and grab something?" It seemed the simplest answer.

Steph rolled her eyes. "Because I'm done. I just want to sit and watch TV." She downed the rest of her beer.

"Yeah, maybe driving right now isn't a good idea."

Steph's gaze narrowed. "It's one beer."

He changed the subject. "Don't forget you need to turn in the rental car on Saturday afternoon."

"What am I supposed to drive then?" Steph sold her old car in California before they moved because she'd need something more reliable here when the cold weather hit.

"You'll buy a new car this weekend."

"I guess I'm supposed to do that on my own, too."

Yes. Buying a car wasn't that hard. But he gave her the benefit of the doubt and tried to understand she felt alone and adrift here without her friends and family to lean on. "If you want me to go with you, I will, but you're buying the car." He wanted that to be clear.

"Sure. Because you don't care if your daughter is riding around in some junker." She rolled her eyes again.

He wanted to do the same. "You agreed to move here and be Miss Independent," he reminded her. "With the money you got from your other car and your new job, you can afford a decent car." Especially since he graciously paid her rent. "Now, why am I here?" Burnt dinner didn't seem like a good enough reason to throw her hands up and send Emmy home with him.

"Because she's out of control. She hates everything I say and do and throws a tantrum over the littlest thing."

"I didn't want to eat the yucky food."

He didn't blame Emmy.

"And you ate my brownies!" Emmy only ever screamed like that at her mother. And a few times to her teacher and other students at school, which prompted the notes home.

"Emmy, watch your tone," he warned, picking her up to console her.

She buried her face in his neck and he got a good whiff of her dirty, tangled hair.

Steph looked done. But she shouldn't get away with not taking proper care of Emmy.

"When's the last time she had a bath?" As far as he knew, four-year-olds didn't stink. Emmy's hair would take two shampoos to get the oil out and at least an hour to untangle. He had a feeling the only reason her clothes were clean was because everything had been washed and packed before the move.

Steph gave him a dirty look. "Seriously? I've had a shit week, and you want to pick a fight?"

He really couldn't win. And he didn't want to do this bitter back-and-forth in front of Emmy. So he gave Steph what she wanted, and hoped giving her a break and some time to herself would allow her to settle down, unpack, and get herself together.

He set Emmy on her feet. "Go to your room. Pick out five pants, shirts, sleep clothes, underwear, and socks. Grab your jacket and school backpack, too."

Steph stood at her full height, surprise in her eyes that he was going to give her what she wanted. "I thought you had a date?"

"I have a daughter who always comes first. I wish she did with you, too."

"That's not fair. You have no idea what it's been like for me this week, learning a whole new job, the school schedule, dealing with Emmy's tantrums, and stuff."

He didn't know what "stuff" she'd been doing aside

from ignoring their daughter's needs, not putting away her belongings, and leaving the apartment a mess.

"Well, for my daughter's sake, let me help you with some *stuff*." He walked past her into the kitchen, turned on the tap, opened the dishwasher, and rinsed and put the dishes in it. He ran the disposal when he was done. He noted that it took him not more than five minutes to do that chore, but he refrained from chastising Steph about it.

Steph stood there sipping a second beer with triumph in her eye because she got her way and someone else did for her what she should have done herself.

He didn't care. His daughter deserved a nice, clean home. So he wadded up all the paper wrappings Steph left all over the dining-room area when she unpacked the moving boxes. Dishes, glasses, mugs, utensils, and other miscellaneous kitchen stuff was stacked on the table instead of put in the cupboard where they belonged. He jammed the papers into one empty box, broke down the three others, then went back and forth organizing the kitchen.

Since Steph watched and didn't help one damn bit, he didn't even ask where she'd like things to go.

Next, he sorted the pile of laundry, shoved the colored clothes in the washer, added soap from the bottle next to the machine, turned it on, then headed down the hall to Emmy's room.

She'd done as she was told and stacked her clothes on the bed. He found her overnight bag in the closet and put all the clothes inside, making sure she didn't forget anything. Since they had double sets of toothbrushes and hairbrushes and such because she lived in two places, he already had a lot of what she'd need for the long weekend at his place.

With Emmy packed and the house in better condition, he scooped her up and held her at his side, then grabbed her bag. They walked down the hallway and met Steph by the door. "You've got all weekend to yourself to get this place in order before you pick her up after school on Monday."

"What about getting the car?"

"I'll pick you up on Saturday at nine."

"So early?"

"If you want my help, yes. I don't have time to wait around for you to sleep half the day away."

"Maybe we could get lunch afterward and do something together." The hopeful look in her eyes was the complete opposite of the incredulous look she gave him when he arrived.

"If we have time," he agreed, because he believed Emmy would benefit from seeing her parents together and getting along. He hoped he and Steph could pull it off. "I have plans for the afternoon."

"But you'll have Emmy."

"We're going to visit my dad."

She brushed her hand over Emmy's tangled hair. "You love seeing your grandpa. Have fun. I'll see you after school on Monday." She looked up at him, remorse in her eyes. "Thanks for coming and helping out. I just need a little time to settle in."

"Don't fall back into bad habits, Steph. You promised me and your dad you wanted to do this on your own."

"I do. It's just a lot all at once."

He nodded, understanding she couldn't change overnight. He'd have to give her some leeway to figure it all out. "I get that. But I also want you to prove you can stand on your own feet and take care of our girl."

"I can."

"You better, or we're going to have another talk about what's best for Emmy." With that warning, he stepped past her, opened the door, and walked out.

Emmy stared up at him from her car seat after he got her settled inside and stowed her bag. "Do I get to see the ranch now?"

"Later. First, I need to make a stop." If he had to cancel on Trinity, he planned to do it in person so she could see he wished he didn't have to, and so he could at the very least get a look at her in the dress she'd put on just for him.

Chapter Seven

TRINITY SAT on her sofa watching yet another episode of *The Zoo* on Animal Planet. She loved animals and missed living on the ranch. Maybe she'd head over early on Saturday so she could get in a ride before the big family dinner.

Her thoughts turned back to Jon. She hadn't heard from him in an hour. She hoped everything was okay with Emmy, but feared their date wasn't going to happen. She should probably change and find something to eat. Maybe she had a bottle of wine in the fridge.

Someone knocked on her door. She seriously hoped no one needed her in the store. This was supposed to be her day off. While most of the time her employees respected that, sometimes they really needed to ask her something or cover for someone.

She stood and walked across the small apartment in her bare feet to the door and unlocked the two dead bolts.

In her wildest dreams, she didn't expect to see Jon and Emmy standing on the small landing.

"Wow." The awe in his voice made her smile and her heart beat faster.

She waved off the employee who led Jon up to her place. He went back to work and she focused on Jon.

He stared at her, his gaze sweeping up and down her body. "You're gorgeous."

Surprise gave way to appreciation. "Thank you." She hadn't thought through the whole going-on-a-date thing until Adria asked what she planned to wear. Most days, she wore black pants and an *Almost Homemade* shirt. At her nonresponse, Adria had dragged her upstairs and rifled through her closet until she found the turquoise A-line dress with the tiny white pearls that circled the collar. Simple, yet elegant. And the color looked great on her with her blond hair and blue eyes.

Jon's eyes filled with regret. "You look amazing, and I'm sorry to say, I have to cancel."

That took her aback. "You came all the way here to tell me you can't make it?"

"Yeah. Sorry. I have Emmy. She's going to stay with me for the weekend."

Emmy gave her a shy wave, then turned her face into Jon's. "I'm hungry." Her belly grumbled. And it should. They were standing at the top of the stairs at the back of the kitchen. The smell of garlic, chicken, melted cheese, and sweet desserts filled the room.

The shop didn't close for a couple more hours.

Jon rubbed Emmy's back. "I'll make you something when we get home."

Emmy shook her head. "No. Hungry now."

Trinity went with the change in plans. "Do you still want that date?"

"Desperately, but . . ." He tilted his head at Emmy.

"Then it's a party of three. Come in." She held the door open wide and stepped back.

Jon stared at her dumbfounded and didn't move. "Are you sure about this?"

She tilted her head and studied him. "Are you turning down a home-cooked meal and me?" The uncharacteristic boldness when it came to men surprised her, but she went with it because she really liked Jon.

Eager, he didn't hesitate to walk right past her into her tiny apartment.

Emmy swiped the frizzy hair out of her eyes for the third time since they arrived. It appeared she had two ponytails on either side of her head at one time, but the rubber bands were tangled around part of her hair and the rest had fallen out of the band and been mussed up into a tangled mess. She scratched at her head and made a bad face.

"What is going on with your hair, Emmy?"

"Mama didn't do it. She pulls too hard and I said no."

Jon looked beside himself. "It's part of why I have her. Steph is . . . Steph." That didn't really explain anything, but Jon thought it somehow did by the exasperated tone he used.

"Well, I need to make dinner for us. There's a bathroom right down there. You can get her cleaned up. I have some great hair products you can use." She pointed to her long hair. "With this much hair, you need a moisturizing conditioner and a detangler. Right, Emmy?"

Emmy scratched at her oily head and gave her a confused look. "Huh?"

Trinity grinned at her.

Jon simply stared at Trinity.

"Seriously. Dinner will take at least twenty minutes."

"I actually have some clothes in the car I could change her into."

"Great." She held her hands out to Emmy, who came to her. Trinity held her close and turned to the TV. "Do you like animals? I'm watching this show about the zoo."

Emmy nodded and sat right down on the couch where Trinity put her. Trinity turned and found Jon still staring at her.

"Thank you for making this easy." The earnest words and gratitude in his eyes touched her.

"I don't see what's so hard about it. She needs a bath and her hair brushed. You can do that while I make dinner."

"I'm hungry," Emmy called out, though she was completely transfixed by the lemurs with their black-and-white-striped tails.

"Don't you feed her?" She was mostly teasing.

A dark look came into Jon's eyes. "I don't want to dump this on you. Are you sure about this?" Uncertainty warred with hope in his eyes. He wanted this date, but he didn't want to talk about why he had to pick up Emmy unexpectedly or why she was starving and disheveled.

She reached out and wrapped her fingers around his tense forearm. "I'm happy you came." He could have just texted that it wasn't a good night; they'd reschedule. Instead, he'd taken the time to speak to her in person.

He hooked his hand at her neck and drew her in slowly for a hug. He was warm and solid against her. He simply held her for a moment, like he needed to be close to ease whatever ordeal he'd been through with . . . Steph.

His ex. Emmy's mother.

Whatever happened, it was hard on him. He needed some comfort, so she gave it to him because she knew what it was like to try to deal with things on your own, and a hug from someone who cared would go a long way to making things better.

The embrace made her feel safe and a little closer to him. Like he shared something with her that he didn't often show others.

He stepped back first but kept his hand at the back of her neck, her hair laced between his fingers. "Thank you for doing this."

"I'm happy to have dinner with you and Emmy tonight."

"I am happy to be here with you." He dropped his hand and she missed the feel of it, of him touching her. "I'll be right back."

She waited for him to go before she went to her pantry to make sure she had what she needed for dinner. She could go downstairs and get some food, but she wanted to prepare something herself. "Emmy, do you like spaghetti?"

"Yep." She brushed the stray hairs out of her face again.

Trinity had a feeling she'd have to work out those knots.

Who let their child run around with their hair a mess like that and smelling like they hadn't had a bath in a week?

Steph.

No wonder Jon had to step in and take his daughter tonight.

She set aside her feelings about poor Emmy and focused on putting some good food in her belly. She took out the tomato sauce, paste, and noodles. She had some garlic cloves in the basket on the counter and fresh basil sitting in a jar of water. She grabbed a pot from the rack on the wall, filled it with water at the sink, then set it on the stove to boil.

She went over and sat next to Emmy on the couch.

"I'm going to take the bands out of your hair." At Emmy's nod, she started on the one closest to her. It wasn't easy, and though she tried to be gentle, Emmy let out a few "ows."

Jon returned with a knock on the door before he let himself in while she worked on the second band. "I've got a change of clothes."

Emmy glanced up at him and put her hand over Trinity's at her hair. "Ow, Daddy."

He frowned. "I know it hurts, but Trinity is doing the best she can not to pull on your hair."

"I've almost got it." Trinity worked fast to free the band and finger-comb out some of Emmy's tangles. She stood and headed for the bathroom. "You can use my shampoo and conditioner. When you get out and towel off, we can spray the detangler in your hair and comb it out. You'll see, it will be really pretty and smell good." She held the bottle out to Emmy to smell.

"Nice."

Jon checked out the small bathroom with a quick glance.

"It's not much, but you should be able to get her cleaned up. Dinner will be ready when you're done." She pulled a clean towel out of the cubby beside her, then left them to the shower.

Jon brushed his hand against hers as she walked out and headed for the kitchen, and it left a tingle rippling up her arm.

She salted the boiling water, pulled the spaghetti out of the box, and slid it into the pot just as Jon closed the bathroom door, but not before he gave her a look that smoldered and said thank you all at the same time.

She stood for a moment and tried to identify the emotion inside her. She hadn't expected this tonight, but she liked having them here. She liked seeing Emmy in Jon's arms and the way he looked at her. He didn't like that his little girl hadn't gotten all the love and care she deserved. And despite how much he wanted to be on their date, he'd done the only thing he could and gone to his daughter.

That said a lot about him as a man and a father.

He was a good guy.

And if the way she felt from just that simple hug was any indication, she was falling for him.

The pasta started to boil over. She grabbed a wooden spoon from the jar of utensils and stirred the noodles.

The sauce wouldn't take any time at all, but she got to work and lost herself in cooking and thoughts of her life living on the ranch with her brothers, the tragedies, traumas, and hurdles they'd all faced and overcome lately, and how she'd hidden herself away these last months after the kidnapping. She didn't want to do that anymore. She wanted a future like the ones her brothers had found with the women who had come into their lives and made it fuller and happier and just plain better. She wanted to love and be loved.

She didn't want to be scared all the time anymore.

She wanted to get to know Jon and Emmy better. Because it was nice to listen to them chatting in the bathroom about how Emmy liked Trinity's hair and wanted hers to look just like it, though Trinity's was bright blond and hers was dark. Sweet. Simple. Safe.

Jon loved his little girl. He took care of her.

Trinity could use a little of that.

She could take care of herself, but wouldn't it be nice to have a partner like her brothers had now?

They were all so happy.

And she was alone.

But not tonight.

The shower went off. She put a pan on the burner next to the cooking noodles and poured in the tomato sauce, some of the tomato paste, added chopped garlic, oregano, diced onions, and fresh basil. She turned the burner down to low and let it simmer, then walked to the bathroom door and knocked.

"Hey, need a little help in there?"

Emmy yelled, "He's pulling too hard."

Jon opened the door, though he stared back at Emmy. "I'm trying not to."

She stepped in and surveyed Emmy in her clean clothes and dripping wet tangled hair.

Jon sighed. "I thought the conditioner would help."

She pulled out her wide-tooth comb from the drawer. "You need this, plus this." She held up the bottle of detangler. "Close your eyes while I spray." She used a generous amount.

"Smells pretty."

"I'll send a bottle home with your dad." So she didn't forget, she pulled the spare bottle she kept under the sink out of the cabinet.

"Trinity, you don't have to do that."

She dropped to her knees to comb out Emmy's hair. "You're going to need it. This girl has some thick hair." She worked from the bottom up, using the comb to untangled the snarl Emmy's hair had become. Halfway through, she glanced up at Jon and caught him staring at her. "I think there's a bottle of wine in the fridge. Mind opening it and setting the table?"

He brushed his hand down her hair. "Sure."

Emmy turned to her. "Are we almost done? I'm hungry."

"Just one more section."

The last strands came loose easily. Trinity breathed a sigh of relief. She turned Emmy to face her. "Beautiful."

Emmy beamed her a smile, then pleaded, "Spaghetti."

"Let's eat."

Jon poured the spaghetti into the colander in the sink just as they walked in, then handed her one of the glasses of wine he'd poured. "This is good."

The Riesling was one of her favorites. "I'm glad you like it. It doesn't exactly go with dinner, but I thought you could use something to help you relax."

"You did that the second you invited us to stay."

Emmy interrupted the intimate moment they shared with another loud, "I'm hungry."

Trinity touched her hand to Emmy's back and nudged her toward the table. "Sit. I'll make you a plate." She waved Jon to the table, too.

He sat next to Emmy and ran his hand over her damp head. "You look beautiful, sweetheart. Does your head feel better?"

"Trinity does it soft." She took a lock of her long dark hair and brought it to her nose. "It smells good."

Jon looked up at Trinity as she dumped the spaghetti into the sauce pan and stirred the two together. "I'm definitely taking the hair stuff home with me. How much do I owe you?"

She shook her head and narrowed her eyes. "Just take it. She needs it." Trinity thought of Steph and how Emmy's hair got so bad in the first place. "Buy extra at the store and leave it at her mom's place." She caught Emmy's gaze. "You can spray it on and brush it through, right? Daddy can show you over the weekend how much to use."

Emmy nodded up and down. Her eyes went big when Trinity set the plate of food in front of her.

Jon's eyes filled with concern at the portion size. "She can't eat all that. I don't want it to go to waste."

"She's *hungry*." Trinity mimicked the desperate way Emmy kept saying it.

Jon laughed and touched Emmy's shoulder. "Do the best you can, sweetheart."

Trinity finished grating Parmesan over Emmy's noodles and held up her hand. "Hold it." She found two clean dish towels and wrapped one around Emmy's neck and tucked it into her shirt collar. The other she draped across her lap. She took the two hairbands from her wrist and used them to make a ponytail that draped down Emmy's back. "Okay, go for it."

Jon snagged Trinity's hand as she walked back to make them plates. "Thanks."

"She's all cleaned up. We don't want her getting dirty again."

Emmy didn't make a sound as she shoveled noodles into her mouth, sauce getting all over her lips. The little girl ate like she hadn't had a meal in days.

Jon watched with concern on his face and in his eyes.

She set his plate in front of him and hers at the table. She grabbed her wine from beside the stove and sat down with them. For a second, she took in the two sitting at her table, sharing a meal, and thought, *This is really nice.*

"I'm glad you guys came." She forked up some pasta but didn't get it into her mouth because she found herself lost in Jon's blue eyes and the intense way he looked at her.

"You have no idea what this means to me, or how grateful I am to have met you."

She let her hand drop down beside her plate. "I have no idea what to do with that."

"Accept it. Say yes to another date."

She said, "Thank you," for the overwhelming senti-
ment, and "Yes," to another date.

The last of the tension went out of Jon. He relaxed
into his chair and dug into the meal with as much enthusiasm as Emmy, who'd already devoured half her plate.

"Do you have a kitty?"

Trinity shook her head. "No, sweetheart, I don't."

"I have three." She held up one finger. "Puff." A
second finger went up. "Dot." And a third finger. "And
Razzle. She's orange and white."

"I love her name."

"I like kitties. Well, Razzle. She's nice. Puff and Dot
are grumpy. But I want a puppy. Mama says I can't have
one. But Dad said maybe, which means I'll probably get
one."

Trinity put her elbow on the table, her chin in her
hand, and stared at Jon. "Is that what maybe means?"

Jon's gaze bounced from her to Emmy and back. He
didn't answer, just lifted his wide shoulders and let them
fall. "We'll see."

"Peez," Emmy said, noodles hanging out of her mouth,
her eyes big and round and too sweet to not give in.

But Jon didn't commit. "I said, we'll see." He met
Trinity's gaze, and there was a definite yes in his eyes.

She smiled and thought it sweet he wanted to maybe
surprise Emmy with a pet when the time was right. It
had been a hell of a few days for Jon with his father being sick and Steph dropping the ball while taking care
of Emmy.

"I'm full." Emmy still had a big bite in her mouth, but
she chewed very slowly, all the energy going out of her.

"Finish off that bite and you can be done."

Emmy did, then leaned back in the chair, her eyes
drooping.

"She's had a long day." Trinity finished off the last few bites on her plate, then picked up Emmy's and hers and took them to the sink.

Jon followed with his plate once he'd finished. "That was really good. I can't believe you made that in such a short time."

"Pasta is easy. And I thought she'd like something simple and good. Everyone seems to like spaghetti."

"I like you more and more the longer we spend time together."

She loved how open and honest he was about how he felt. "I like you, too. You're a really good dad. She's a great little girl."

"She's everything to me." Which was his way of telling her he was a package deal.

She didn't mind. With Adria and Liz pregnant and the next generation of McGraths on the way, she'd been thinking about how nice it would be to have what her brothers found with their partners and to have a family of her own.

"I haven't been the parent I want to be. I spent a lot of time working and away from her. That's why I wanted to come back here to the ranch. She deserves the best I can give her, and I wasn't doing that back in California."

"So you changed your whole life for her." Amazing. Most men thought work was the most important thing and that's how they provided for and took care of their children. Not Jon. He understood the time he shared with Emmy counted most.

"What you saw tonight, that's just a small glimpse into how bad things were getting with Steph taking care of Emmy and me doing the weekend father thing. It wasn't working for any of us. Steph couldn't handle it mostly on her own. If I wasn't putting a fire out at work,

I was with her and Emmy every week. It got to be too much. So I made a deal with Steph. We'd move here and split the time with Emmy equally. Nothing in Steph's life is ever what she wants it to be unless someone is spoiling her rotten and doing everything for her. But she'd asked her dad one too many times to bail her out. I was on her case about taking better care of Emmy. And Steph decided she wanted to start over in a new place and prove to her dad and family she could take care of herself and Emmy if she had a less demanding job and a simpler life. So I got her a job managing the grocery store, rented her an apartment, and promised to actually co-parent Emmy and that we'd do more together as a family."

"So she wants to be independent but you take care of both of them."

"Like everything with Steph, it's complicated. I pay for Steph's apartment because that's where my kid lives and I want Emmy to have a nice place that is clean and safe and feels like home to her. Steph works, but sometimes she overspends and her family, or I, end up having to bail her out because my kid needs to eat." The resentment and anger came across loud and clear.

"I see." The picture he painted didn't shine a nice light on Steph. It couldn't be easy to have a parental partner who didn't hold up their end.

"I'm trying to uncomplicate my life." He cupped her face in his warm hands. "So thank you for being the easiest, most wonderful thing in my life right now. You helped me with my dad and now my daughter without complaint or even a sign of disappointment that our dinner out turned into dinner in."

"I really don't mind, Jon. She's—" Trinity notched her chin toward the bed in the corner of the large open room. "Asleep."

Jon's gaze shifted and he laughed under his breath. "She just made herself right at home."

Emmy had pulled the blanket at the end of the bed over her, curled up under it with her head on the sky blue chenille throw pillow, and fallen right to sleep.

Jon's hands fell away from her. "You cooked. I'll do the dishes, then take her home so she can get a good night's sleep." The frown confused her.

"What's wrong?"

"I wish I had her room set up, but I sold most of my furniture and her baby set before the move. I bought her a new set for Steph's place, but I thought there'd be something she could use at the ranch, but I guess I abused my old furniture as a kid and teen and it's junk now. Plus, she deserves something that's hers."

"I can help with that." She went to her desk and picked up her tablet. She pulled up the site she and Adria had been looking at recently for the new babies' room. For twins, Adria wanted something that would last.

She held the tablet up for Jon to see. "What do you think about this set?" All dark wood, the set included a dresser, nightstand, and crib. She scrolled down the page. "Instead of the crib, you can get a twin or full-size headboard instead."

"That's exactly what I wanted for her."

"I happen to know the store has everything in stock and delivers." She picked a pen from a jar and wrote down the store name, number, and the furniture set name for him. "Call them in the morning. You can probably have the set delivered by afternoon tomorrow."

"Name something you wish someone would do for you."

"What?" She had no idea what he meant.

"Anything. You've done so much for me, I want to do something nice for you."

"You gave me flowers. They're downstairs and still lovely. I like looking at them while I work all day."

One side of Jon's mouth drew back.

She loved that he wanted to thank her, but it really wasn't necessary. "You don't owe me anything. Most nights I'm here alone. Tonight, I had a nice dinner with you and Emmy and enjoyed the company and getting to know you better. That's enough, Jon." She truly meant it.

"When can I see you again?"

"I work most of the weekend and have a family dinner Sunday night, so probably next week."

Disappointment made him frown. "That's too long to wait, but I guess that's the way it goes."

"Dinner's a bit harder to get in since I work the later shifts. If you want to meet me for breakfast on—"

"Monday. After I drop Emmy at school."

She liked his enthusiasm. "Sounds great."

"I'll pick you up here. At eight thirty?"

"Works for me."

Jon glanced down at the papers on the desk, then touched them. "These are the plans for your expansion."

"Like I said, we're growing, but at a pace we can still maintain the quality of our product and Adria and I can manage the whole of the operation."

"I think what you've built so far is brilliant."

She appreciated the praise. They'd worked really hard and grown quickly the past couple months. Now they needed to maintain what they had, give Adria a chance to get through her pregnancy and the early stages of motherhood, then decide how aggressively they wanted to move forward with further expansion.

"Thanks. We're proud of *Almost Homemade* and the products we deliver."

Jon held up the sticky note with the furniture store information. "Thank you. Mind if I call you before our next date just so I can hear your voice?"

Her cheeks warmed with a blush she couldn't help. "I'd like that."

Jon went to get Emmy. She found a shopping bag to put Emmy's dirty clothes and her hair detangler in to take home. She met Jon by the door and handed him the bag. She rubbed her hand up and down Emmy's back as Jon held her against his chest, her little head on his shoulder. "I hope I get to see you again soon," she whispered to a very sleepy Emmy.

"Thank you for dinner." Emmy's eyes sank closed once again.

"I'll walk you out and lock up behind you."

Jon went out ahead of her and down the stairs carrying Emmy like she didn't weigh a thing. The downstairs kitchen lights were out except for the security light by the back door. Jon headed toward it.

"I'll unlock the front door for you."

"The lot was full when I got here, so I parked on the side of the building."

She never went out there anymore if she could help it. Sometimes when she did, the panic set in and she couldn't fight the nightmare.

"Trinity, are you okay?"

"Yeah. Here, let me get the door for you." She unlocked it and let Jon out, then followed him to his car, wholly aware of the darkness surrounding them, but fighting her memories of Clint sneaking up behind her and bashing her in the head before he wrestled her into the trunk of his car and kidnapped and terrorized her.

He's dead, she reminded herself, and focused on Jon. His steady presence helped calm her.

He unlocked the car, but she opened the passenger door so he could set Emmy in her booster seat and buckle her in. Jon gave the little girl a kiss on the forehead and dropped her bag of stuff on the floorboard at her feet. Trinity tried to focus on him and the sweet way he treated his little girl. He closed the door, took Trinity's hand, and led her to the back of the car. He didn't seem to feel her tremble.

"This was probably the best date I've ever had."

She chuckled. "I'm sorry you've had so many bad dates then if a simple dinner tops your list."

"It was the company that made my night." With that, he slowly leaned down, giving her time to back out if she wanted to, though she seemed immobilized by his yearning gaze and her own anticipation. He finally kissed her softly. His warm lips remained over hers, tempting her into something deeper, but she liked the buzz of electricity and lingered in the moment.

Jon leaned back just an inch and stared into her eyes. "After getting burned by my ex, I feel like I should be a hell of a lot more cautious. But the truth is I've wanted to do that since the night at the hospital when I shouldn't have been thinking about it at all. But I just couldn't help myself." His boldness matched her own when she'd invited him to stay for dinner.

So she went with it. "You should kiss me again." She didn't wait for him but met him in the middle and wrapped her arms around his neck. His tongue touched her lips and she opened to him. The slide of his tongue against hers, the very taste of him, sparked a flash of desperate need that had them locked together, bodies pressed tight to one another. She didn't think she'd ever been kissed like this. Nothing had ever felt this right and tempting and sexy and all-encompassing at once.

"Daddy?" Emmy's soft voice was the only thing that could tear them from each other.

Jon jolted back and stared into the back of the car. "Damn. That was totally worth the risk." He cupped her face in one hand and brushed his thumb against her cheek. "I'm sorry. I have to go." He rushed over to the driver's door, opened it, and ducked his head inside. "I'm right here, sweetheart. Go back to sleep while I drive us home."

He turned back to Trinity and took her in with one hot dip of his gaze down her body and back up to her face. "You look so good in that dress." The look he gave her said he'd rather see her out of it.

She smiled because her heart felt lighter than it had in a long time because of his sweet words and that sexy as hell look he gave her that said a lot about how much he wanted her. It felt so good to be wanted like that by him. "Monday. Breakfast."

"Forever from now, but I can't wait."

She waved, then walked back to the sidewalk so he could pull out. He gave her another long look before he drove away, leaving her standing in the dark in the place that frightened her most. She rushed inside and locked the door as quickly as possible.

She leaned against it, convinced her rushing heart had way more to do with the good memory he'd given her of that amazing kiss. One she'd hold on to until she saw him again.

Chapter Eight

JON KNOCKED on Steph's door for the third time. He checked his watch. Nine fifteen. He told her he'd pick her up at nine, but of course she wasn't up and ready to go. He stared down at Emmy, who looked up at him with a why-did-we-bother expression on her face.

"We should go home." She didn't really miss her mom. She said outright she wanted to live with him at the ranch. And while it made him feel good that she wanted to be with him, it also broke his heart. She should want to be with her mom, too. She should be able to count on Steph and be excited about seeing her.

Emmy tugged on his hand.

He held her in place and showed her the keys in his free hand. "I have the key. Let's go in and make sure your mom's okay." He unlocked the door and walked into the smell of Mexican food mixed with cigarette smoke.

Emmy rubbed her arm against her nose. "Yucky."

Yeah, the whole place looked gross. Steph still hadn't unpacked anything. The entire dining table was covered in dirty dishes and partially filled takeout containers. The food from at least two separate meals had dried, crusted, and congealed.

Several empty wine bottles sat on the counter. Two

wineglasses and several empty beer bottles littered the coffee table. More were out on the brand-new patio table he could see just out back.

Where the hell did that come from?

Did she use the money he gave her?

Right now, he didn't really care.

Emmy ran to the glass slider and rescued two of the three cats, who'd gotten locked out, though as far as he knew, they were supposed to be indoor cats.

Emmy sat on the floor and dragged Puff into her lap. The gray-and-white longhair cat meowed incessantly, setting off her buddy Dot, named because of the single white dot of fur on her chest in her all black coat. Razzle ran out of the back room, a streak of orange-and-white fur as she dashed straight to the empty bowls on the kitchen floor.

No food. No water.

How long had it been since Steph fed them?

Emmy yelped as Puff squirmed out of her arms, scratching her in the process. "Owie." She pressed her hand over her arm. "Bad kitty."

Jon tried to hold off the tide of frustration. "Come here. Let me see."

Emmy uncovered the small, bleeding cut.

He pulled a paper towel off the roll, doused it with water at the sink, and pressed it to the tiny injury.

Emmy stuck out her bottom lip. "Puff is mean."

"I think she's just really hungry, sweetheart."

The incessant meows from all of them and the head-bumps and body rubs made it clear they wanted him to fix the food situation immediately.

Jon cleaned the cut, then gave Emmy's arm a kiss. "All better. Let's feed the beasts."

Emmy smiled and went to the cupboard and pulled

out a can of cat food. He unscrewed the top on the dry food container and filled the big bowl. All three cats dove for the food and started to gorge. Emmy handed him the can and picked up the three other bowls from the floor. He didn't bother to clean them, just divided the wet food into three portions and doled it out. The second Emmy put them on the floor, the cats attacked them.

He filled the water bowl at the sink and set it in the middle of all three cats. They dashed from the water back to their food, unable to decide which they needed more.

Where the hell was Steph? No one could sleep through the hungry cat racket.

Emmy remained occupied with the cats, making sure Razzle didn't steal Dot's food after she wolfed down her own. Jon walked down the hall to the dark rooms beyond. Not feeling sympathetic or kind toward Steph, he flipped on the light in her room and immediately wished he'd just gone home.

Steph sat up, blinking against the harsh lights, and covered her eyes with her arm as the sheet fell to her lap, exposing her bare breasts. The guy lying spread-eagle on his stomach next to her groaned but didn't move.

"He's naked," Emmy announced.

Jon quickly covered her eyes and pushed her back down the hall. "Go to the kitchen and wait for me."

"What are you doing here?" Steph asked, her voice rough from sleep or whatever the hell she'd been smoking last night. The pungent stench in the bedroom didn't smell like cigarettes.

He took in the empty beer bottles on the nightstands, the two piles of cat shit on the floor, the blankets mostly falling off the bed, and the guy who was so hung over he simply dragged a pillow over his head to block out the light and sound.

"Nice, Steph. Real nice."

She went on the defensive. "This is my place. I can do what I want."

"Great. Get your own car. Return the rental, or you're paying the additional fees. I'm out of here." He turned to leave, but glanced back. "And don't forget to feed your fucking cats and clean their litter box before they ruin the brand-new carpet."

He headed back down the hall and confirmed his suspicions that she hadn't cleaned the disgusting cat box sitting on the floor in Emmy's bathroom. Litter coated the whole floor and the box was full, so the cats refused to use it anymore. The ammonia stench filling the small room made him wrinkle his nose and rush to get away.

He picked up Emmy and carried her out the front door, slamming it behind him.

Emmy picked up on his bad mood, stayed silent, and didn't fuss when he strapped her into her booster seat. He closed the passenger door with a gentleness he didn't really feel.

Steph ran down the walkway in her too short robe and no shoes. Her tousled hair and legs for days drew stares from the two guys walking in the parking lot to their cars. "Wait. I'm sorry I overslept. You said you'd help me with the car."

"And I showed up, but you didn't." He reined in his temper and tried to be civil. "I see you made a new friend."

She pinched her lips into a lopsided grin. "I met him at this bar. We hit it off and things got a little crazy." She shrugged one shoulder, unapologetic. "You had a date," she threw out, like his evening with Trinity was the same as her getting drunk and probably stoned and sleeping with a guy she barely knew.

"Best part of my week."

Her eyes narrowed and shock filled her gaze. "I thought you canceled because you had Emmy."

She probably wished he did and that meant she still had a chance.

He shook his head. "She had a big enough heart to include Emmy. She helped me brush out the rat's nest you let Emmy's hair get tangled into and made us a home-cooked meal."

His snide comments put Steph on the defensive. "Well, isn't she a saint. We can't all be Suzy Home-maker."

"All I want is for you to take care of yourself and our daughter. I expect you to have your act together when you're expecting me and Emmy. You should have had that guy out the door before we showed up."

Her eyes twinkled with delight. "Jealous?"

He dismissed that insane question. "Date whoever you want. But when you have Emmy or know she's coming home, you should be ready, so she doesn't walk in and see a naked stranger in your bed. You should put her first," he pleaded with her, hoping it sank in.

Her gaze softened. "I should have worked on the apartment, but I got caught up with him. He really is a nice guy."

"Great. Good for you. But you promised things were going to change." He pointed at her apartment. "You're getting drunk and smoking in the house where your daughter lives. You said you wanted to give that all up and live a better life here."

He'd given up drinking with friends and colleagues to all hours months before Emmy arrived. Steph did, too, but the older Emmy got, the harder Steph found taking care of her to be, the more she needed a glass of wine, or two, to get through the night. Most of her party crowd drifted away once Emmy arrived, and Steph stayed home more often than not. Sure, she had her nights out with the girls when he had Emmy. Fine. But this was different. This was flagrant. And maybe had something genuine behind it.

"Are you unhappy about the move?"

She raked her fingers through her hair, making her robe gape open at her chest. Steph didn't care or notice. "It's a big change. I didn't think it would be so different here." Unhappiness and uncertainty filled her weary eyes. "I talked to my dad after you left with Emmy the other night. He said he's so proud of me for stepping up."

He found some sympathy for her because she really wanted to do the right thing and make her dad proud of her. "It's only been a week, Steph. Give it some time. You'll make more friends." He notched his chin toward the apartment. "Maybe the new guy will introduce you to his friends, and you'll find a new crowd to hang with."

"He's fun, but it's not like that."

Right. Steph wanted to keep her options open and thought she still had Jon on the line and hoped to reel him back in one day.

Steph sighed. "I'll take care of the apartment, but I really would like your help buying the car."

"Fine. You've got ten minutes to get dressed and grab what you need or I'm leaving." He'd help her out for their daughter's sake, but he wasn't going to wait around for her all day.

She launched herself at him, wrapped her arms around his neck, and hugged him before leaning back. "Thank you." She kissed his cheek and dashed away, running for the apartment to change.

He shook his head and called himself ten kinds of a fool for giving in, but reminded himself that Steph needed a reliable car to cart Emmy around when she had her.

But he wanted to make a few things clear, and called out to her. "Hey, Steph."

She stopped and turned back.

"Listen, I get that we just got here and you wanted to blow off some steam, but if that place isn't cleaned up on Monday and suitable for Emmy to come home to, I'm keeping her at my place."

She planted her hands on her hips. "You can't do that." Before he assured her he would, damn their legal agreement, she sighed and said, "I'll clean it up."

"Thank you. I don't want to keep her from you. I just want her to be safe and happy in a clean home."

Steph huffed out her exasperation, but nodded, then walked back to her place.

He'd give her the ten minutes he promised and went to check on Emmy. He opened the passenger door.

"I want to go home." Emmy stared at him, boredom plain to see in her eyes.

"Mom will be back in a few minutes. We'll go buy a car, then get lunch."

"I want a chocolate shake."

"You got it." Looks like today was the day he said yes to everything.

"Are you guys fighting?"

He put his hand on her knee to reassure her. "No. I'm just upset that the house wasn't nice for you."

She gave him a soft smile that didn't reach her eyes.

At four, she'd probably forget a lot of the things he and Steph argued about and said, but he feared some things would stick in her mind and heart.

How long before she really understood him, Steph, and how they were raising her?

How long before she realized she deserved better?

How long before she blamed them for not doing right by her?

How long would he let Steph get away with this irresponsible behavior before he did something about it for Emmy's sake?

"She didn't feed the kitties." Emmy understood that was a bad thing. The tantrums she threw about staying with Steph in the months leading up to the move made it clear she didn't like the way Steph treated her either. Emmy's bad behavior had spilled over into school. The teacher asked for a meeting only he showed up to because, guess what? Steph forgot about it. The teacher pointed out that kids who acted up in school usually had problems at home. She asked if she could help provide any support.

He decided it was time to make a change for the better for all of them.

He just wished Steph wanted to be better. He'd give her the benefit of the doubt because of the stress of moving and starting a new job. But if this kept up, he'd have to seriously think about what to do next.

"If I get a puppy, I won't forget to feed him. I promise."

He had more faith in his four-year-old keeping that promise than he did in Steph right now.

Chapter Nine

Jon walked into his dad's new apartment behind Emmy, who squealed when she spotted a wrapped package on top of the new toy chest his dad bought for her visits.

"Not even a hello for your old grandpa?"

Emmy set the package down and rushed to wrap her arms around her grandpa's neck.

His dad kissed Emmy's cheek. "How is my sweet girl?"

"Daddy made me get a car. Boring."

Jon filled in his dad. "We went with Steph to buy a new car." Then he'd had to follow her to return the rental and drive her back to her apartment. It took most of the afternoon and several bribes to keep Emmy from having a complete meltdown.

"I saw a naked man," Emmy announced.

His dad's gaze snapped to his. "Excuse me?"

"Steph had company when we arrived at the apartment."

"I see." His dad set Emmy down. "Open your present."

Emmy didn't waste a second and tore into the wrapping paper. "A tea set." She held up the box for him to see. "Open it. Open it." She bounced on her toes.

Jon took the box and tore the top because of the industrial tape they used to seal it. He pulled out the plastic play set and placed the teapot, two plates, saucers, and teacups on the coffee table. "What do you say to Grandpa?"

"Thank you." She pretended to pour tea into a cup and set it in front of her stuffed bunny.

His dad turned on the cartoon channel and waved him into the kitchen and away from Emmy, who chattered with Bunny while pretending to drink tea while watching *Scooby-Doo*.

"What's going on with Steph?"

Jon tried to tamp down the frustration that always rose when he thought about her. "The usual. Apartment is a mess. She knew we were coming and was dead asleep when we got there. I had no idea she was with some random guy she picked up."

His dad raised a brow. "Is that a problem for you?"

"Only in that she should have had the guy out the door before Emmy came home."

"Are you sure?"

"Dad, seriously, there's no love between me and Steph. If we didn't have Emmy, I'd never see her again." Seeing her now only made him regret being with her in the first place. The only good thing that came out of it was Emmy. "I just wish she could get her act together. I wish things were easier between us."

"Are you concerned she won't settle in here?"

"When I told her about the ranch and how I wanted to bring Emmy here, she got all excited about a new place, a new life. Part of her wanting to come with me was because her father had laid down the law about her always going to him for help. She wants to show him she can do it on her own."

"She's old enough to take care of herself."

"One would think so." He rubbed his hand over his

stiff neck. "I'm afraid she's going to change her mind about the move."

"And if she does?"

"I'll have to go back with her." He really hoped that didn't happen.

"And you want to be here."

"I want to be here with Emmy. In my mind, the life we could have here is exactly what I want for her."

"And I'm sure after all the years you've worked so hard, you need a break, too."

He deserved it. "I loved what I did, but I won't miss the stress and long hours."

"Working a ranch is hard work," his dad reminded him.

"It's a different kind of work. I'm ready to get back to it. I never thought I'd miss early mornings on the ranch and tending the animals, but there's satisfaction in that. I've still got my hand in business. I'll get something going at the ranch. It will be enough for me, and I know Emmy will be happy there."

"And when she's with her mother?"

"I'm hoping Steph will find her footing here."

"Hope will only get you so far."

"I know that. I just really want this move to work out for all of us."

"Then I wish you luck." His dad set his iced tea on the counter. "Now, I'm going to play with my grand-daughter before we go to dinner."

Jon watched his old man sit on the floor and pretend to drink the tea Emmy poured him. The smiles on both his dad's and Emmy's faces were exactly why he'd brought her here.

He hoped he didn't have to turn around and take her back to California because Steph couldn't live on her own without her daddy's help and the safety net he provided.

Chapter Ten

THE DOORBELL rang, drawing Jon out of the numbers circling his head. He blinked his tired eyes. He'd been staring at his computer screen too long. Emmy, on the couch behind him, was still watching a Disney movie. The gardeners had finished cleaning the yard and trimming the trees and bushes. He thanked God the incessant noise finally ended. He couldn't wait to see the new plants they'd put in tomorrow.

He wasn't expecting anyone and figured the landscapers left after they finished for the day. He hoped to God it wasn't Steph after she made a big show this morning on her video chat with Emmy about how she'd cleaned and organized the apartment. He took the time to watch as she showed Emmy everything. He had to admit, she'd done as he asked. It finally looked like she and Emmy lived there. All the boxes were gone, Steph's belongings were either displayed or stored away, and everything looked clean. She'd even made a point of showing Emmy all the cats and asked about how she was and what she was doing.

All in all, they had a good call.

Progress, he hoped.

He braced himself when he opened the door, just

in case Steph wanted to make an even bigger effort by coming to see Emmy in person.

He never expected the surprise guest standing on his porch with a smile and a casserole dish.

"Hi."

"Trinity. It's so good to see you." Overwhelmed with joy, he couldn't help but smile back at her.

"I hoped you'd say that."

He tilted his head and studied her. "Why wouldn't I be happy to see you? *I* left you two voice mails and you haven't called *me* back."

"That's why I'm here. Apology peach cobbler." She held up the foil-covered dish. "And also, welcome to the neighborhood."

He couldn't believe she drove all the way out here to bring him dessert. Though she looked good enough to eat in a gauzy white shirt that dipped low enough for him to get a tempting glimpse at her cleavage, and jeans that molded to her hips and showed off her long legs.

Her lips pressed together. "Did I overstep?"

"What?" He had no idea what she meant.

She tilted her head, her long hair spilling over her shoulder and down her arm. "Showing up unannounced."

"I dropped in on you. I guess this is our thing."

She smiled and his belly did that roller coaster flying thing that amped his adrenaline. God, he was happy to see her.

"Then, are you going to invite me in?"

The shock of seeing the woman he most wanted to see finally wore off. "Yes! Come in." He'd lost his damn mind the second he'd seen her.

She stepped into the entry and came up short right in front of him because he couldn't move and just wanted her closer. "I love what you've done with the yard."

Truthfully, he'd barely glanced at it when the head of the landscaping crew waved goodbye on his way past the window where Jon had been working at the table for the last couple hours. "It's not done. They're coming back tomorrow to plant flowers."

"It'll be even prettier then."

"Nothing looks better than you."

"Will my good looks get me past the entry? Though I am wondering what is going on with all the boxes."

"The painters are coming this week, along with the carpet people, and I'm having new countertops put in the kitchen." He waved his hand out to encompass the large space. "It's a whole ordeal, but the place will look like new in a couple of weeks. I hope," he added, because it seemed like his best-laid plans got derailed more often than not.

Emmy ran up and threw her arms around Trinity's thighs. "Trinity! Come see my room." Emmy tugged on her hand.

She quickly handed off the cobbler to him and went along with Emmy.

He debated whether to shut off his computer and hide what he'd been doing, or set the cobbler down and go after them. He did the latter because he just couldn't believe she was here, and he wanted to spend every second of her stay with her, because if he remembered right, she had a family dinner tonight.

He didn't know why she didn't call him back after he left messages. He didn't much care, now that she was here. Still, he'd missed her these last couple days and that was very new for him, considering he'd been extremely busy with work on the house and being with Emmy.

He found them in Emmy's room. Trinity was lying on the double bed, staring up at the glow-in-the-dark stars he'd put on the ceiling in a swirling pattern.

"You were right. This is the softest bed ever."

He'd taken Emmy shopping at the department store to buy new sheets and blankets. If it wasn't soft as a bunny, she didn't want it, so her bed was now the softest thing he'd ever felt. She didn't like to sleep with the sheet, just the blanket he'd bought her. No comforter. She wanted two different colored soft blankies. One blue. One purple.

When the painters came on Tuesday, they'd transform Emmy's room with a new coat of pale lavender paint and trim out the windows in white. With her dark furniture and the sky blue carpet he'd ordered for her room, it would be as bright and cheerful as his little girl.

Emmy held her arms out. "Like the new furniture?"

"I do. It's perfect in here. I especially love the silver lamps."

"I picked them. Daddy helped."

"They're perfect."

One on each side of the bed on the nightstands he'd bought so Emmy could display her favorite egg nightlight, books, and assorted plastic gems and tiny toys. The furniture store even had a wood toy chest that matched the bedroom set almost perfectly. Emmy had everything she needed to feel like she was home here.

He wondered if that would become a permanent thing or not.

Steph seemed to be trying. But she was always good in short spurts.

Thoughts about Steph only made him mad, so he focused on the woman who deserved his undivided attention. And all he wanted to do was crawl up on that bed with Trinity and Emmy and hold the both of them in his arms, even if his mind conjured ten other things he'd like to do with Trinity in a bed—not in this room.

Trinity rose and sat on the edge of the mattress. "It turned out great, Jon. I'm so glad the store was able to get the furniture to you so fast."

"Me too."

"And you got the letters at the craft store."

"They spell EMMY. Daddy and I are going to paint them and put them up over my bed."

"Awesome!" Trinity touched her fingertip to Emmy's nose, making her giggle.

Jon smiled at both of them. "Once the room is painted, everything will be perfect for her."

"Daddy says we're getting horses."

Trinity looked surprised and properly excited to suit Emmy. "Really?"

"I want to teach her to ride as soon as the stables are repaired and ready."

"Did you already buy the horses?"

He shook his head. "Not yet. It's on my list. Along with three dozen other things I need to do."

She gave him a tell-me-about-it nod. "I'll have my brother Tate call you. He knows everything about horses. I bet he knows who has a couple for sale that will be good for trail riding and safe for her."

"Really? That would be fantastic and save me a lot of time."

"It's no trouble." Trinity always seemed to have a solution, never a complaint.

He liked that about her. He liked a lot of things about her.

Jon pulled his phone out of his back pocket, tapped his way to his contact list, and handed it to her. "Put his number in there. I'll call him as soon as I'm ready."

"I'll let him know to expect your call." She checked her watch. "I can't stay much longer."

"Your family dinner, right?" He wished she didn't have to go.

She seemed surprised he remembered. "Yeah. I think Declan and Skye have finally set a date for their wedding. I hope it's soon because Adria looks like she's about to pop and Liz is pregnant, too. I'm sure the happy couple wants everyone to be there, so they better hurry up."

"Wow. Your family is getting bigger by the day." He and her brother Drake were only a year apart. Drake was married with twins on the way. Declan was a year younger than him and also getting married. Jon had his little girl, but he hadn't found love.

Steph—He cut off all the bad thoughts he had about her. She wasn't the one.

But that didn't mean he wouldn't find someone to share his life with. So far, he really enjoyed spending time with Trinity. So much so, he wanted to spend a lot more time with her.

"I can't believe it. All my brothers married." Her bright smile made her even lovelier.

"You look happy for them."

"I am. They each found the one person who will have their back no matter how hard things get. They've all been tested in one way or another and come through it stronger individually and as a couple. I have no doubt they are all in it for the long haul."

Emmy leaned over Trinity's back and traced her finger

along the scar running down the side of her face at her temple. "Owie. How'd you get that?"

Jon stepped toward the bed to take his daughter's hand away. "Emmy, it's not polite to ask things like that." Though he'd wondered about the scar and how she'd gotten it.

Trinity waved him off, then turned to Emmy. "A very bad man wanted to hurt my brother and his wife. He hit me really hard and left that owie." A darkness clouded Trinity's eyes.

Emmy stared intently at Trinity. "Were you scared?"

"Yes, I was." She brushed her shaking hand along the side of Emmy's face, her eyes filled with the fear she tried to hide. She stood abruptly, said, "I have to go," then rushed past him.

He spun and went after her, catching her just before she bolted out the door. He held her arm and felt the tremble rippling through her whole body. "Hey, I'm sorry she upset you."

"It's fine. I'm fine." The words quickly tumbled out of her mouth.

He sank his fingers into her hair at the side of her head and brushed his thumb over the fading scar. "I can see and feel you're not okay."

Her gaze fell to his chest. "It comes back sometimes. I can't control it. The fear . . . it just overwhelms me."

It finally dawned on him what had nagged at the back of his mind about the way they met in the driveway when she helped his dad. "The night we met. You thought I meant to hurt you."

She pointed at her head. "It gets mixed up in there sometimes. The past. The present. Is it real or just my imagination?"

"Or a flashback," he suggested, reality hitting him

like a punch to the chest. It took a moment for the trauma she was dealing with to really settle in his mind. "What happened to you?" He really wanted to know. He wanted to understand her better.

He wanted to chase away the nightmare for good so she never felt this way again.

"Um, I can't talk about it. It . . . it makes things worse. I thought things were getting better, but then that night with your dad . . . you came out of the dark . . . I try really hard to stay grounded in the here and now. I know he can't hurt me ever again. Still . . ."

"Okay. I get it." He wished she'd confide in him and trust him enough to share. But this thing between them, although it felt so strong, it was new.

The pain looked raw in her. She needed time.

He'd give it to her.

"If you really want to know what happened, you can find the story online. Just look up my brother Tate. Most of the story is about what happened between his wife, Liz, and her stalker ex, Clint. I was just one more person he hurt."

"To get to your brother and his wife," he finished for her. She didn't feel like what happened to her mattered compared to whatever happened to them, and he didn't think that was right.

It did matter. Her fear and anxiety were as real as anything.

"Liz wasn't his wife yet, but yeah." She pulled free of his light hold. "I need to go." She said the words but didn't back away.

He tried to pull her back another way. "We're still on for breakfast tomorrow morning, right?"

"Yeah. Sure." She tried to distance herself now that she'd opened up to him. She didn't need to.

He had no intention of letting her go because of some perceived weakness she thought she had because she was still processing and dealing with what happened to her. "Trinity, whatever you're going through, whatever you're dealing with, it's not going to stop me from wanting to see you."

Her gaze fell to his chest again. "I hope not," she whispered.

He heard Emmy in her room playing tea party with her stuffed friends, so he had no reason not to pull Trinity close until her body touched his and her face was a breath away. "Nothing could stop me from doing this one more time." He kissed her softly, letting her know he was there and not going anywhere. She leaned into him, her hands sliding along his ribs and up his back. She went up on her toes, taking the kiss deeper, sliding her tongue along his, and setting him on fire.

Both his hands tangled in her mass of long blond hair. Her nails bit into his back as she held him close.

"Daddy." Emmy stood right behind them.

He and Trinity jumped apart like two teens who'd been caught making out.

With a sigh of regret, he turned to his daughter. "Yes, sweetheart?"

"I'm hungry."

"Of course you are." He glanced at Trinity, the woman he was starving for, who touched her kiss-swollen lips with two fingers and nearly had him on his knees begging, then turned back to his daughter. "I left a snack in the fridge. Go find it."

Emmy gave Trinity a big smile and said, "Kissing." She giggled.

Trinity laughed with her. "Yes, we were." She brushed her hand over Emmy's head. "Your hair looks amazing."

"Daddy did it." She ran into the kitchen to get the grapes, cheese cubes, and turkey slices he'd left for her.

Trinity smiled at him. "I love the braids."

He'd done one small one coming from each side of her head and tied them together in the back to hold the rest of her long hair out of her face. "I learned from a video on YouTube."

This time she reached out to him and put her hand on his face. "That's sweet you'd go through the trouble to learn."

"I do the best I can."

Her hand settled on his chest over his thumping heart. "I think she's a lucky girl."

He covered her hand with his. "Yeah, well, luck was on my side when I met you."

She brushed a kiss against his lips. "Yep. Sweet. I'll see you tomorrow."

"Not soon enough," he said by way of goodbye.

She was out the door far too soon, but before she walked down the path to the driveway, she turned back. "I just thought you should know, the cobbler was just a means to see if you'd kiss me again."

Damn if he didn't want to spend the rest of the day and night doing just that. "Stop by anytime. I'm happy to oblige."

Her smile was brighter than the sun as she backed away, turned, then headed for her SUV.

He reluctantly closed the door instead of going after her for what he really wanted, because he had to check on his daughter.

"What's this?" Emmy pulled up a corner of the foil on the dessert Trinity dropped off.

"Peach cobbler." Or Trinity's means to get him to kiss her again. He hoped she knew now she didn't need to do anything but show up and he'd want to kiss her over and over again.

"Do I like that?"

"I'm not sure." But he knew for damn sure he more than liked Trinity.

He grabbed a spoon from the drawer and scooped out a small bite and fed it to Emmy.

"Mmm. That's good."

"Eat your snack first, then you can have a little bit now and some after dinner if you eat all of it, too."

Emmy ran back to her plate at the counter and took it to the table. He stole his own bite of cobbler and nearly groaned with satisfaction from that tiny bite. He wished he could skip dinner and just eat that, but he needed to set a good example for Emmy.

Instead of devouring the brown sugar, cinnamon, and peach concoction, he went back to his computer and pulled up the search engine. He typed in Tate's name, added Liz and Clint to the search and hit ENTER. His eyes popped at the number of stories that filled the page. He started with the first one and couldn't believe all that Clint put Liz, Tate, Trinity, and a string of other women through. Murder, kidnapping, arson, deepfake videos, and harassment that went on for years for some of the victims.

His stomach knotted and his heart ached for her.

He thought of the scar on Trinity's temple, the ones left on her mind and heart, and he wanted to kill the asshole who terrorized her then and now.

Too bad the bastard was already dead and Jon couldn't get his hands on him.

God help anyone who tried to hurt her again.

He'd show no mercy when it came to Emmy and Trinity.

Chapter Eleven

TRINITY WONDERED how long it took Jon to look up what happened and how it would impact her current mental state. She didn't mind Emmy asking about her scar. Kids were curious creatures by nature. But she could have handled herself better. She didn't need to rush out of there that way.

Of course, Jon had been amazing, stopping her before she escaped to her car and had a full-blown panic attack.

Instead, he'd distracted her. Just his hand on her, the warm tenor of his voice as he asked about what happened and coaxed her to open up to him, they calmed her. His touch, the amazing kiss, they pulled her out of the past and right into his arms where she liked being way more than she should given the fact they barely knew each other.

Still. She appreciated his kindness and understanding. He didn't dismiss her feelings or tell her to get over it. Everyone liked to remind her Clint was dead and she didn't have anything to worry about. Intellectually, she knew that, but her brain hadn't processed that message yet. It stored away the trauma and fear, and when it got too much to hold back, it came right out, front and center, and took over her mind and body all over again.

But Jon seemed to know how to make it all go away.

Or maybe she should put into practice what her therapist told her and use distraction to change her mindset. Until now, she hadn't found anything that did that for her.

Except Jon.

She could kiss him again and again and never get tired of it.

"Please tell me that secret little smile you've got going has something to do with the new guy in your life." Her soon-to-be sister-in-law Skye bumped shoulders with her.

She couldn't help or hide the blush that only made Skye smile even wider at her. "Maybe."

"Spill it. Is he as gorgeous as Adria says?"

"Most definitely." Tall with wide shoulders and a trim frame, his body toned to perfection. Blue eyes set off by his dark hair. And the way he looked at her . . . Smokin' hot. "I could look at him all day."

Skye's eyes turned dreamy. "And he's a good guy. You'd only pick a good one."

"I think he picked me." It felt that way at the hospital when they stood in the lobby and he'd made it clear he wanted to get to know her better. "But I think I'll keep him. For now anyway." She tried to hide another smile but couldn't.

Skye touched her arm. "I'm so happy for you."

She looked at Drake leaning back against the counter, Adria in front of him, his arms wrapped around her, one big hand on her round belly. Declan was chatting with Tate, but his gaze kept drifting to Skye. And Tate stood there holding Liz's hand, their fingers linked. Everyone in the family had someone. She was here alone, but it kind of felt like she and Jon were on the right track to really start something that could last.

"I'm happy for me, too." It had been a long time since she'd really *felt* happy, not just pretended to be that way.

"I'm glad. You work so much and after what happened . . . Well, we were all worried about you."

She thought she hid her feelings so well. Adria swore she'd kept all Trinity's episodes under wraps. She didn't want anyone to know she was struggling, because then her brothers would hover and try to take over her life after she'd worked so hard to get them to see her as the strong, independent, nothing-bothers-me woman she used to feel like *all* the time.

"Why were you worried?" She knew why. Because of what Clint did to her. But she really wanted to hear Skye's take on it.

"You're the one who checks on everyone. You take care of your brothers. But after what happened, you've been . . . quiet. I think Declan said it best. Clint locked you in your head."

Like he'd trapped her in that trunk. She definitely felt that way sometimes. In the beginning, she couldn't get out of her head to save her life. It had scared her how the darkness sucked her under and wouldn't let go.

Skye rubbed her hand up and down Trinity's back. "You've excused your way out of all the other family gatherings, except for Declan's proposal and the dinner that followed. Otherwise, you always say you're too busy."

In her defense . . . "We opened two more stores."

"Adria found the time. You didn't want to, or couldn't bring yourself to take it and face us with whatever you were going through."

"I didn't want you guys to see," she confessed.

Her brothers would worry. They'd tell her what to do or order her to snap out of it. None of it would have worked. And although she'd wanted to be with them, she'd desperately wanted to be left alone.

"You should talk to Drake. He knows what it's like to live in nightmares. He might be able to help you."

"He's happy now. He's looking forward to the future with Adria and his babies. I'm okay enough not to mess that up for him by reminding him of his past."

"We all want you to be better than okay."

"I know. I'm getting there." She distracted Skye from asking more about her with another tidbit about Jon. "I have a breakfast date tomorrow morning."

Skye's bright smile returned. "Date number two. Excellent."

Feeling giddy, she admitted, "It's just a means to get him to kiss me again."

Skye nearly spewed soda all over the place. She held her fingers to her lips and swallowed while also smiling and laughing. "Well, that's a good way to do it."

"It's the first time we'll actually be alone." She couldn't wait.

"He has a little girl, right?"

Trinity nodded, her heart melting when she thought about the little one. "Emmy. She's four. And adorable."

"Sweet."

"Her mother's not." Anger flashed for Emmy and Jon. "She seems to give Jon a difficult time and doesn't seem to take very good care of Emmy."

Skye frowned. "That's sad."

"He moved back here to be a better dad and spend more time with Emmy."

Skye's eyes lit with approval. "What does he do for a living?"

"He's some kind of businessman. He owned several companies I think, then sold some before moving here. But now he wants to simplify his life. He's fixing up his family ranch." Maybe he'd like to run cattle for *Almost Homemade*. Declan and Tate had about all they could handle here, but they could partner with Jon.

Something to think about.

"Sounds like he's got his priorities straight."

He cared. And she loved that about him. "He's a great dad. Watching him with Emmy, it just makes my heart melt."

Tate overheard them. "When do we get to meet this guy?"

She met Tate's gaze across the kitchen. "Actually, I gave him your number. He wants to buy a couple horses for him and Emmy to ride. I thought you could hook him up with one of your buddies."

Tate held up his beer bottle. "No problem."

"He'll probably need your help and one of the trailers picking them up and getting them over to his ranch."

"*His* ranch?" Declan asked.

"Mr. Crawford decided to move to a senior place in town so he's not so lonely."

"So Jon is living there now, right?" Declan nudged her for more details.

"Yes. Emmy stays with him Friday to Monday. Mr. Crawford is still recovering, but Jon says he'll be chasing women and playing poker any day now."

All of her brothers smiled and saluted with their beer bottles.

She shook her head, but smiled with them.

Liz released Tate and leaned over the counter. "I heard you cooked for him and Emmy on your first date."

Adria smirked. "He walked right into the store and said he needed to see her. The man was on a mission."

Trinity tried to play it off. "Because he wanted to reschedule our date. His ex couldn't deal and asked him to pick Emmy up a day early."

Adria added, "But you invited him into your place, cleaned up the little girl, and made them dinner."

"She looked like a bedraggled rag doll. I don't know when her mother last fed her, but she devoured a plate of spaghetti like she hadn't eaten in days."

Drake's eyes narrowed. "Sounds like there's some trouble there. You sure you want to get involved in that?"

She had a fierce attachment to them already. "I like Jon. I feel for Emmy. It can't be easy for either of them to deal with the mom. Maybe his life is a bit complicated, but I'm not going to hold it against him when he's been nothing but nice and forthcoming about his situation."

"Okay then." Drake dropped it. But he'd pick it right back up if she indicated at any time that Jon wasn't treating her right.

Her brothers would be all over Jon then.

"Great. I'd at least like to get through a few more dates before you guys grill him about his intentions, or whatever."

Drake and Declan both glanced at Tate, which meant they'd leave it to him to check out Jon when they set up the horse deal.

"You knew Jon in high school," she reminded Drake.

"That was a long time ago. People change. And he wasn't interested in my baby sister."

Maybe she should have warned Jon about her brothers. Then again, he could hold his own. He'd have to if he wanted to date her because while he came with Emmy, she came with three overprotective brothers.

Tate started the questions. "When are you seeing him again?"

"Tomorrow morning. Breakfast date."

"Nice," Liz said. "He doesn't mind your wonky schedule."

"He seemed fine with an early dinner and now breakfast."

He made it clear he just wanted to see her. If the happy surprise she'd seen on his face when she showed up at his place unannounced said anything, it's that he wanted to spend a lot more time with her.

Her phone dinged with a text. She pulled it out, hoping she didn't have to go into work for some emergency, but smiled when she saw Jon's name come up.

JON: Thank you
JON: So yummy!!!!!

The picture of him and Emmy with empty plates smeared with cobbler remains made her heart melt and smile widen.

"Share," Adria called out.

If Jon was going to be a part of her life, that meant being part of her family. She flipped the phone around and showed them all the picture.

Liz touched her chest. "Oh my God, she's adorable."

Skye chimed in. "She looks like her dad. Dark hair. Those blue eyes. Wow, Trinity, he really is gorgeous."

"Hey." Declan frowned at his fiancée.

Trinity tapped her camera icon, turned her back to her entire family behind her, held the phone up so she could get everyone in the shot. "Say cheese."

They all smiled; a few of them actually complied with the order. She snapped the photo and sent it back to Jon.

TRINITY: Family time
TRINITY: The whole gang
JON: Have fun but wish you were here with us having dessert
TRINITY: Me and you and pancakes tomorrow
JON: Can't wait

Declan, Skye, and Liz carried the huge chicken divan casseroles to the table.

"Let's eat and talk about the wedding." Skye clasped her hands at her chest, excited about marrying Declan.

They were perfect for each other. And Trinity loved Skye. She'd become a part of the *Almost Homemade* family, too, when they partnered with the farm she grew up on in Wyoming where she and Declan planned to get married. Sunrise Farms was a huge collective of people who lived as a community on the property. Everyone there had been shaken when the leader of what was at the time Sunrise Fellowship murdered Skye's friend and partnered with a militia group bent on taking down the government with guns and bombs. But Skye and Declan helped the FBI take them down.

Skye reorganized the whole business. Her parents took over the new poultry and egg operation that supplied *Almost Homemade*. The other members went back to doing what they loved, working the farm and supplying the stores with fruits and vegetables.

Declan and Tate ran Cedar Top Ranch and supplied *Almost Homemade* with all the beef they needed.

They liked to keep business in the family.

And family came first.

Everyone took their seats around the long farmhouse table. While plates were filled with the yummy, cheesy casseroles, salad, and rolls, Trinity took a moment to glance around and take them all in. She loved that they made time to come together like this.

After the texts with Jon, she wished he and Emmy were here. It didn't matter if they hadn't known each other long. The connection was there. Their attraction was electric.

She really liked kissing him and hoped that turned into more.

She'd put her social life on the back burner for a long time now to get the stores up and running. She'd lived an all-work-no-fun life for too long.

And she hated that she used work as an excuse because she didn't want to admit how hard it had been to overcome the trauma after her kidnapping and find her way back to being someone who didn't shut others out for no reason but her own paranoia.

No one had really interested her until Jon.

So why not dive in, explore the heat between them, and see where things went from there?

Declan laid out the wedding plans. "So the wedding will be here. Something very similar to what Tate and Liz did for their wedding."

"I thought you were going to hold it at Sunrise Farms," Trinity interrupted.

Skye shook her head. "We'll have a small ceremony here. Family and close friends. Adria shouldn't travel right now."

"You guys don't have to change your plans because

of me." Adria rubbed her hand over her enormous belly. Twins took up a lot of space.

"We want to be surrounded by our family," Declan explained. "That includes you, sis. So Skye's parents, sister, Adria's family, and a few close friends from Sunrise will come here for the ceremony and small reception. Then, Skye and I will go on our honeymoon, and when we return, we'll have a bigger reception at Sunrise Farms."

"When is the wedding?" Trinity asked.

"We finalized all the arrangements yesterday and will hold the ceremony four weeks from this Saturday." Skye got nods from all of them.

No matter what they had planned, if anything, for that weekend, they'd all rearrange things to make it for the big day.

And Adria would love to have her sisters Roxy and Sonya, plus their husbands, here for a visit. They'd all become close.

Skye turned to her. "I'd love for you to be a bridesmaid."

Trinity expected to be asked. She'd been everyone's bridesmaid so far. "Absolutely." She'd add another dress to her collection of dresses she'd probably only ever wear once. "I assume your sister will be your maid of honor and your father will walk you down the aisle."

Skye nodded. "And Declan will have Drake and Tate stand up with him. Your parents can't wait to come home and see all of us. They're talking about getting a place in town so they'll be here for the birth of the babies and enjoy being grandparents."

"With Adria and Liz pregnant, they'll expect you and Declan to get working on the next McGrath addition soon," Trinity teased.

"That's what the honeymoon is for, right?"

Everyone stared at Declan, then looked at Skye for confirmation he wasn't joking.

She shrugged. "We want to start a family soon."

Trinity set down the beer she'd been drinking. "Wow. You guys don't waste any time." And by that, she meant all her brothers.

"When you know what you want, everything seems to fit into place." Declan had always been the practical, organized one among them. Of course he had a plan for this. Get married to the love of his life, start a family, be happy.

It seemed so easy.

Check, check, and check.

All of her brothers used the same plan.

She knew it was anything but simple. And her brothers had all been through the ringer getting to the aisle for one reason or another. So maybe it made perfect sense that once they got past all the bad, they wanted all the good.

After being kidnapped and scared for her life, she understood not wanting to waste precious time.

Maybe that's why she was so ready to wallow in the way Jon made her feel when they were together, and she was absolutely ready for more of it.

After dinner, the joking, teasing, and just having fun with her family, she helped clean up and grabbed her stuff to head back home.

Drake surprised her by taking her shoulders. "I haven't heard you laugh this much in a long time."

Declan added, "You smiled a lot more tonight."

Tate hugged her. "If this is because of Jon, we're happy you're happy again."

Trinity glanced at the other women. "What's going on?" Her brothers had never been this way with her.

Adria touched her arm. "They've been worried about you, Trinity. We all have. What happened with Clint changed you."

"You were too quiet for too long," Drake said, an understanding in his eyes.

She didn't know quite what to say except, "I'm fine."

Tate tugged a lock of her hair. "You say that all the time. Today you actually look it."

Unsure and a little embarrassed, she shook her head. "Don't worry about me. Things are good." And if that had to do with Jon, well, all the better, because she couldn't wait to see him tomorrow. It had been a while since she'd been excited about anything, so that was a good sign. For her. And for them. "I'll see you all soon. I need to get on the road."

She had the longest drive back. Drake and Adria only lived about fifteen minutes from the ranch, and Tate and Liz lived in the cabin on the property they'd renovated several months ago.

Alone in her car, the radio down low, she had plenty of time to think about what her brothers said and what it meant.

They had some idea she was still dealing with the mental fallout from the kidnapping, but somehow she'd finally managed to let that not be her mind's only focus.

As distractions went, Jon was a good one. But it was more than just him. Finally, she had hope for the future and dreams of what that could look like.

Maybe, hopefully, it included a gorgeous man and a beautiful little girl.

Chapter Twelve

SOMEHOW THURSDAY had become cursed in Jon's world.

Last week, Steph couldn't deal and made him pick up Emmy without any notice. Thank God Trinity understood and they'd still managed to have a really great evening together. That turned into cobbler and kisses on Sunday, a fantastic pancake breakfast on Monday, a fun but quick taco Tuesday at this little hole-in-the-wall Trinity knew about. She'd met him there for dinner, though she'd only had an hour off work. They'd even gone to a matinee movie yesterday.

He loved having the flexibility to meet her whenever she could carve out time. He liked it even more that she wanted to see him as much as he wanted to see her.

Which was why he'd rescheduled their Italian dinner date from last Thursday to tonight. But just when he was getting in his car to drive into town, his phone rang and Steph's number came up.

He dreaded answering, but couldn't not answer, because what if something happened to Emmy?

"Hello."

"Daddy."

Steph often called to let Emmy talk to him when

Emmy was upset or she just wanted to tell him something. But the distress in Emmy's voice sounded the alarm inside him.

"Hey, sweetheart. How's my girl?"

"I did something bad."

He didn't like the sound of that. "What did you do?" He tried to keep his voice neutral so she'd open up to him.

"I tried to make the O noodles. I got the can open. It cut my finger. It really hurts."

That worried him. "Is it a bad cut?" His stomach tied into a knot.

"Kinda." Her voice wobbled.

"Okay. I'm sure Mommy has a bandage for it."

"I can get one in the bathroom, but . . ."

His stomach dropped. "But what?"

"I put the can in the microwave." She paused.

He held his breath, knowing where this was going.

"It made lots of sparks and blew up." She softly cried.

Shit. "Did the microwave burst open or anything?" He prayed she hadn't been hit by shrapnel.

"No. But it's very messy inside and the glass cracked. Mommy is going to be really mad." She cried a little harder. "Are you m-mad?"

He expected to hear Steph bitching in the background like she always did when Emmy did something she didn't like. But he didn't hear a single complaint or snide comment. "Wait. Where is your mom?"

"I—I don't know."

That raised another alarm and awakened his usual ire when it came to Steph taking care of his daughter. "Is she home?"

Emmy hiccuped. "No. She left with the man while I was watching TV."

What the . . .

"I got hungry. Can Trinity bring some sp-spaghetti?"

Since the can of pasta rings with meatballs exploded, he got why she'd want an upgrade. She should be eating better.

"Do you have any idea where your mom is?" He jumped into his car, started it, and tore out of the driveway. He could not believe Steph would leave Emmy alone.

"Sometimes she goes to her friend's."

He wondered if the friend was the same guy he found in her bed on Saturday. "Does that person live close?"

"At one of the other doors."

So in the same complex. At least Steph was close by, not that it made leaving their four-year-old any better. He should call the cops. But that opened a whole can of worms he wasn't sure he was ready to deal with. And he hoped Steph returned soon and explained, but he couldn't think of a good excuse for her to leave their child alone.

She could have been gone two minutes or two hours for all he knew.

"I don't know which door she went to." Emmy sounded scared now.

"How many times has she left you alone this week?"

"I put myself to bed last night. I made sure to brush my teeth." She sounded very proud of herself, but he fumed. He wondered how scary it was for Emmy to be alone, in the dark, sleeping in a new place.

"Good girl. Listen, I'm on my way, but I'm going to text my friend Trinity and see if she can get to you right away so you won't be alone."

"I like her. Can she bring me something to eat? And a brownie?"

"Sure, baby. Stay on the phone with me." He didn't normally text and drive, but he was alone on the road and this was an emergency and he used the microphone to dictate his text.

JON: Trinity 911 Emmy is home alone can you please go to 1245 Harmony Lane apt 112 and stay with her I'm on my way

Jon rolled his eyes at the irony of the street name.

JON: please check cut on her finger
JON: she's hungry dinner and brownie if you can

"Daddy?"
"I'm still here, baby. I just sent a text to Trinity."
"Okay. I'm waiting."
He tried to distract her. "What are you watching on TV?"
She told him about the animal cartoon she was watching. He barely listened, instead reading the return text from Trinity.

TRINITY: Dinner brownie be there in less than ten
TRINITY: Don't worry I'll take care of her until you arrive

He breathed a huge sigh of relief. She'd be safe with Trinity.
Emmy must have gotten lost in her show.
"Hey, Emmy, how was school today?"
"Good. Teacher asked some friends to share lunch with me."

"Why?" He knew the answer, but wanted to hear it from her.

"Mommy forgot to pack lunch and my packet."

So she didn't have food or her homework. He fumed and forced himself to stop strangling the steering wheel.

Emmy sighed big and her hiccups disappeared. "Daddy, how come I can't stay with you?"

"I would like that very much, sweetheart, but your mom wants to be with you, too."

"That's not true," she whispered. "I'm always in the way."

Stupid legal system. Since he and Steph had joint custody, his lawyer told him they'd give Steph every opportunity to hold up her end. He could file for full custody, but that meant building a case against her and getting the Department of Public Health and Human Services involved. So far, nothing Steph had done until now really warranted it. His lawyer advised him that Steph not doing things the way Jon wanted wasn't enough to get DPHHS involved. Steph met Emmy's basic needs, even if she did the bare minimum.

But this. This crossed the line.

Still, he tried to console Emmy. "Mom just gets frustrated sometimes."

"*All* the time." Emmy let out another too-big-for-her sigh.

He thought about her question for the rest of the drive, about staying with him and how she must feel that he didn't do what she wanted and keep her full-time. She didn't understand that legally he couldn't just take her from her mom. And that even if she felt like Steph didn't want her, Steph would fight him to keep her. It ate away at him for every mile and minute it took to get to her.

Chapter Thirteen

TRINITY KNOCKED on the door of apartment one-twelve and held her breath, hoping Emmy opened up and was okay.

"Trinity," she called through the door.

"It's me. I have yummy stuff for you." She hoped that eased Emmy's mind about opening the door.

It flew open and Emmy launched herself into Trinity's legs and held on tight. Trinity rubbed her hand up and down Emmy's back. "There now. I'm here. You're okay."

Emmy looked up at her. "I'm hungry."

"You, my little friend, are always hungry." She tapped Emmy on the nose, hoping to tease her back into a good mood.

Emmy unhooked her arms from Trinity's legs and held the phone to her ear. "She's here." Then she handed it to her. "He wants to talk to you."

Trinity took the phone and nudged Emmy to go back inside. "I've got her."

"Thank you." The gratitude and relief in Jon's voice broke her heart. "I'm about ten minutes out myself."

"No problem. I'll feed her, put a bandage on her finger, and brush out her hair."

Emmy looked nearly as bad as she had last week when they met.

"Is she okay?"

As good as can be expected when she stayed with her mom, Trinity thought uncharitably, but it seemed correct. "She appears to be, but you'll see for yourself when you get here."

"Is the place a wreck?"

Trinity glanced at the stack of dishes in the sink, the dirty pans on the stove, the empty food containers over-flowing the garbage can. The floor needed to be mopped and the carpet vacuumed. The whole place smelled like cat piss.

"Your silence speaks volumes."

Trinity simply said, "It could be worse." If it was, she'd seriously reconsider stepping foot in the place.

She set the bag of food she'd brought on the only space available on the dining table. She put the phone on speaker, set it down, and stacked the mail that had been strewn across the table's surface. Her nose wrinkled at the dirty dishes, but she piled those up, stacking them atop the ones cluttering the counter by the already-full sink.

"Emmy, where are the forks?"

She pulled open a drawer that had two spoons and one clean fork left.

"Take a seat at the table." Trinity pulled out the hot container of pasta.

"That's not spaghetti."

"Sorry. This is the only pasta we had. It's called Alfredo. It has chicken in it."

"What's the green?"

"Spinach."

"Just try it," Jon coaxed over the phone.

Emmy pulled a noodle out, held it up, and slowly lowered it into her mouth. Once the creamy sauce hit her tongue, she smiled. "Yum."

"You eat that. I'm going to find you a bandage and your hairbrush."

"Bathroom," Emmy said around a big bite of chicken and spinach. "This is good."

"I'm glad you like it. If you eat half, you can have your brownie." She'd brought a large portion just in case once again Emmy hadn't eaten in a while.

Trinity found the bandages, hairbrush, and a band. She checked out Emmy's room across from the bathroom. Toys and stuffed animals littered the floor. Her bed wasn't made. Two cats slept side by side, nested in a wadded-up blanket on the end of her bed.

"Go away, Puff!" Emmy banged on the table.

Trinity rushed down the hall and pushed the cat who was trying to eat Emmy's dinner off the table. "Shoo."

"Do the cats have food?" Jon asked.

She looked around, spotted the empty bowls on the floor, and picked up the largest to fill with water. "No."

"Check the pantry cupboard," he called out, his voice growing more irritated with every sentence.

She found the food, filled the bowls as all three cats twined around her legs while she tried to do it, and they jockeyed for position at each bowl she filled.

Steph either didn't care or simply couldn't handle taking care of her home, pets, or daughter. Sad. But also, what the fuck? How hard was it to use the dishwasher, toss the trash, and run the vacuum once in a while?

She left the messes alone, wet a paper towel, and went to Emmy and gently wiped the cut on her finger clean, covered it with the bandage, then started working the tangles out of her hair. "So, what do you think of spinach?"

Emmy shrugged. "It tastes like the sauce."

"Who the hell are you?"

Trinity calmly ran the brush through Emmy's hair and barely spared a glance for the lanky dirty blonde, who looked anything but friendly. The deep frown and narrowed bloodshot gaze only made her look haggard, but she had the curves men loved and legs for days. "You must be Steph. Emmy's mom."

"You must be the one Jon's sleeping with," she shot back, her words slow and slurred.

"Tone it down, Steph." Jon's voice had gone cold and flat.

Steph stared at the phone on the table. "What is she doing in my house?"

"Where the hell have you been?"

"Out," she snapped. "What the hell are you feeding my kid? She hates vegetables."

Trinity lifted a shoulder and let it fall. "She likes spinach."

Emmy slurped up another long noodle, then popped a spinach-draped piece of chicken into her mouth to go with it.

Trinity started braiding Emmy's hair down the back of her head.

"Who let you in?"

Trinity raised a brow at that stupid question.

Jon took over. "Emmy called me because you left her alone. You're lucky she didn't set the house on fire when she put a can in the microwave and blew it up."

Steph rushed to Emmy, grabbed her arm, and shook it. "What did you do? I told you to eat the cereal I left out."

Trinity took a step closer to Steph. "Let her go. Now."

Jon walked in with his phone in hand, tapped it to end the call they'd been on all this time, and stared at them facing off. "Steph," he said in warning.

She released Emmy but not without some force.

Emmy frowned, her eyes glassed over, and she rubbed her sore arm.

Trinity stepped back, took the end of the braid she'd finished, pulled it tight because it had come loose when she let go, and wrapped the band around it.

Emmy sat staring at her half-empty container of food.

Trinity went to her side and touched her chin to get her to look up. "Finished?"

She nodded.

"Let's go see if the stars have come out yet while you work on that big, fat brownie."

Trinity picked up Emmy, who held her plastic-wrapped brownie against her chest.

Steph stood her ground in front of them. "You're not going anywhere with *my* daughter."

JON HAD ENOUGH. "Let them pass. You and I need to talk."

Steph spun around to confront him. "This is my night. You shouldn't even be here."

"Someone needs to be here! She's four. You can't just leave her alone in the apartment with a box of cereal." He couldn't believe she'd set the box and jug of milk on the coffee table and walked out the door. No bowl. No spoon. Did she expect Emmy to pour the milk in the box and then dump the cereal into her mouth?

And how dare she grab Emmy like she did?

How often did she lose her temper when she was drunk and do something like that, or worse?

He didn't need to hear her slurred speech to know she'd been drinking. He could smell the booze, cigarettes, and pot on her.

He didn't think he'd ever been this angry.

"She was fine. I wasn't gone that long."

"You left her alone! Whether it was two minutes or two hours doesn't matter. You should not have left her at all."

"She was watching TV. I was only a couple apartments away. She could have come to get me if she needed something."

"She's four. She didn't know where you were. How is she supposed to remember which apartment you went to? They all look alike. In a matter of minutes, she cut herself and could have burned this place down."

Steph rolled her eyes. "Don't be dramatic. She broke the microwave. Big deal."

"It's a *huge* deal!" His voice boomed through the apartment. "What if she'd turned on the stove and burned herself? What if that can had done more damage and she got caught in the blast? What if you'd taken your phone with you and she couldn't call me for help?"

"Yeah, well, I won't make that mistake again."

Shock stopped his heart for a second. "Seriously. That's what you have to say? You won't leave her a means to get help when you abandon her."

Steph's arms went rigid at her sides and she leaned in. "I did not abandon her. I went to see a friend."

"And got drunk off your ass. Mother of the Year, Steph."

The snide remark made her eyes blaze with anger. "You think your little blond friend is so great."

"She's a thousand times better than you!" He didn't often yell, but she pushed all his buttons tonight.

The hurt in Steph's eyes turned to fury. "Then get the fuck out and go be with her. Leave me and Emmy the hell alone."

"Oh, I'm leaving. And I'm taking Emmy with me."

"You can't do that. It's *my* night."

"What are you going to do about it? Call the cops? Go for it. I can't wait to hear you explain the pot smell coming off you and why you left Emmy alone in this mess."

"Fuck you. I'm doing the best I can."

"Even when you're sober you can barely take care of her properly."

"Yes, I can." Steph raked her trembling fingers through her own disheveled hair.

"Really? So Emmy didn't go to school today without her homework packet and lunch?"

She held her arms out wide. "We were running late. I overslept." Her hands fell and slapped her thighs.

"Because you were hung over?"

The suggestion made her eyes narrow with rage. "You don't know anything."

"I know I'm not leaving Emmy with you tonight."

Steph grabbed a cigarette from the pack on the table and lit up. "And what about your date with little miss perfect?" She blew a stream of smoke right in his face.

He stepped back before he gave in to the urge to do or say something he'd really regret. "She knows Emmy comes first. She'll understand."

"What a saint." Steph sneered at him. She had no

right to be jealous, but that never stopped her from acting out whenever he had someone in his life.

He tried, *again*, to push her to do the right thing. "You swore things would be different here."

"*You* can make new friends, but *I* can't?"

"You can't choose them over our daughter."

"I didn't. I wasn't gone that long." She really didn't get it. She didn't think she'd done anything wrong. "If she hadn't called you, none of this would be happening."

"So this is *her* fault and you're upset that you got caught?"

"I'm pissed that you and that bitch showed up at my house. You think you can make all the rules and I just have to go along."

"We have an agreement. If you can't hold up your end, then I will do whatever I have to do to protect my daughter and keep her safe."

Steph pointed her finger at her chest. "From me? *I'm* her mother."

"Then act like it!" He glanced past her at the wreck of a kitchen and living room. "What happened to this place?" She'd worked hard to clean and organize the apartment. It hadn't lasted long.

She rolled her eyes. "It's been a busy week. I'll clean it up this weekend."

"You better. Because Emmy's not coming back here if you don't."

Her whole body went rigid. "You can't do that."

"I will." He didn't care what the agreement they signed said. If she wanted to take him to court, she'd have to explain to a judge why he refused to comply. "Clean up your act, Steph. I'm losing patience. I've given you enough chances to get this right." He went to the entry and found Emmy's backpack and checked to make sure everything she needed for school was inside.

Steph held the chairback in a death grip. "You can't take her from me." The alcohol-fueled bravado fell flat with him.

He went to the table and rummaged through the pile of mail and found Emmy's packet. He stuffed it into the bag and turned to Steph. "Don't make me take her away from you."

With that, he walked out, closing the door behind him on a string of shouted "I hate yous" and "fuck yous."

He didn't care how she felt about him. He just wanted her to do right by Emmy.

It took him a minute to spot Trinity and Emmy across the courtyard lying on their backs on a bench with their heads at the center. Trinity's legs draped off one end, her feet planted on the ground in a pair of sexy black strappy heels. Emmy's feet hung off the other end in the new pair of purple tennis shoes he bought her.

The anger washed out of him at the sight of the two of them stargazing.

"I wish I had a baby sister," Emmy announced, startling him. "Then I'd have someone to play with."

"I have three brothers," Trinity told her.

"That's a lot of brothers." Emmy didn't sound like she wanted that many siblings.

"With all of them, I wished I could be alone sometimes."

"Your turn," Emmy prompted.

For what, Jon didn't know.

Trinity pointed up at a star. "I wish I could sing like Adele."

Emmy tipped her head back to try to look at Trinity. "I can sing. Twinkle, twinkle . . ."

Jon listened to her sing the whole song at the top of her lungs. She wasn't anywhere near as good as Adele, but Trinity clapped for her at the end like she was.

"That was amazing."

Jon leaned over the bench, his face inches from Trinity's. Surprise shone in her eyes at his abrupt appearance. "I think you are absolutely the most amazing woman I've ever met." He kissed her softly.

"What about me, Daddy?"

He stared down at his daughter. "You're fantastic, baby." He kissed her on the forehead. "Did you have enough to eat?"

"I ate the whole brownie." She held her arms out wide to show him how big a brownie she devoured.

"Trinity spoiled you."

"It was sooo good." And Emmy looked happy now that she was away from Steph.

"And you didn't save even one bite for me."

Emmy shook her head and pointed at her chest. "Trinity gave it to me."

"We need to work on your sharing." He grinned down at her despite her lack of generosity where brownies were concerned.

"Maybe she'll bring you one next time."

He really hoped he got a next time. Which meant he needed to break the bad news to Trinity, who now sat on the bench turned toward Emmy.

"It's getting late," she said. "We should get you home and ready for bed."

Wait. "What?"

"I'm sure you've got something in your fridge I can turn into dinner while you give her a bath and read her stories."

"Trinity, you don't need to do that."

"Thursday night is date night with Emmy, right?" She held out the edge of the skirt of her dress. "I wore my pretty dress to show her."

He was sure that sexy black number with the deep V neckline was just for him.

She stood and held her hand out to Emmy. "We should go."

The apartment door behind him opened. "Jon," Steph called out.

He didn't even bother to turn around before he followed the swing of Trinity's hips as she walked away. He caught up and took her hand, ready for another date night in with her.

What he wouldn't give to have her stay the night with him, too.

Chapter Fourteen

By the time he finished bathing Emmy and getting her ready for bed, his whole house smelled like spicy beef and melted cheese. Trinity took the pound of ground beef, a tomato, the jar of jalapeños, a block of cheddar, and the bag of tortilla chips he had on hand and started turning them into oven-baked nachos. It wasn't the Italian meal he still owed her, but it made his stomach rumble.

The long drive home gave him time to let his anger wane. It still simmered in the background. He needed to give some serious thought to what he was going to do about Steph and Emmy. This couldn't go on.

"Did you pick your three books?"

Emmy turned from her bookcase with four in her arms. "I can't decide which to put back."

She gave him the sad face he couldn't ignore and he caved. As usual. "Let's do four then."

She dumped the books on her bed. "I have to say good-night to Trinity." She ran from the room.

He went after her and caught up just in time to see Emmy throw her arms around Trinity's gorgeous legs.

"Good night, Trinity."

"Thank you for dinner and the brownie," he prompted her.

"Thank you." She tilted her head way back to look up at Trinity. "Will you bring me a brownie every time I see you?"

"I'll try, but sometimes it may not be possible." Trinity leaned down and rubbed her nose against Emmy's. "I had fun stargazing with you."

"Me too. Do it again next date-night-with-Emmy?"

Trinity giggled. "Sounds good. Now, off to bed with you."

"You read stories, not Daddy."

"Sweet girl, Trinity just cooked dinner. She's had a long day. I'll read to you."

Emmy held Trinity's hand. "No. Her."

"I don't mind." She opened the oven door, revealing two plates of nachos. "Why don't you take yours and eat."

He stared into her beautiful blue eyes. "I'll wait for you."

"You must be starving."

For her, yes. That dress. Those legs. Her sweet smile. All of it tempted him. She made him so damn hungry. "Let's put her to bed, then have dinner together."

Emmy smiled with her victory and ran for her room.

Jon stopped Trinity before she followed. Before he said anything, Trinity put her fingers over his lips. "Don't thank me. I'm glad you called. I wouldn't have wanted Emmy to spend another second alone while you drove all the way to town. Your ex is something else."

He rolled his eyes. "Tell me about it. She was so good with Emmy when she was a baby. I never worried about things then. But now . . ." He shook his head, trying to wrap his mind around how things had deteriorated to

Steph not caring that she left their sweet girl alone like that.

"It's none of my business, but . . ."

"What?" He really wanted to hear what she had to say.

"If you don't do something about it, it's as good as you saying what she's doing is okay."

He feared Emmy felt that way, too.

Trinity leaned in and kissed him. Best thing to happen to him all night. "You're a great father, Jon. She loves being with you. You brought her here to put her first. Do that."

He wanted to, but . . . "It's complicated. Emmy deserves time with her mother."

"Does her mother deserve time with Emmy?"

The turnabout took him aback. He hadn't really thought about it in that way. He didn't want to deny Emmy her mom. That relationship was important and essential. He loved and missed his mom and wished she was still here to give him advice and the support he could always count on. But if Steph couldn't take care of Emmy and be the kind of mom she needed, maybe she didn't deserve to see Emmy.

Trinity patted his tight chest with her palm. "No one is saying cut her off completely from Emmy. But does she need to have Emmy for days at a time?"

He sighed. "No. She doesn't." So many changes. Moving from California. His father moving. Renovating the ranch. Meeting Trinity. Now possibly taking on being a full-time single father.

He could do it all. It was just a lot all at once and in such a short time. He needed his brain to catch up.

"Looks like I'm facing another battle with Steph."

"Emmy is worth it."

"Absolutely." No doubt. But he didn't look forward

to Steph fighting him for her parental rights. She loved Emmy, and despite how hard and unfulfilling she found taking care of her, she wouldn't back down when it came to having her time with Emmy.

"It doesn't need to be a fight. If she can't tend to Emmy's basic needs and provide a safe environment for her, then you will."

He'd have to prove his case in court, and even when he did the courts tended to give parents a chance to prove themselves and often sided with the mother.

His lawyer had advised him of that when they made the original agreement and the changes prior to the move.

But after what happened tonight, he'd push the matter for Emmy's sake.

"I can't let something like this happen again. I've given her several chances before, and it goes well for a few weeks, a couple months, then the effort becomes too much. She doesn't pay attention to what or how well Emmy eats. She skips baths to get her to go to sleep because she let her stay up too late. Then Emmy is cranky and Steph is short-tempered and they end up arguing about stupid stuff. I want better for Emmy, but those things aren't reasons that a court would take Emmy from her." He raked his fingers over his head. "We keep ending up in this bad place, where I'm acting like the parent to both of them. I thought the move would be good for Steph. A fresh start. She could create a whole new life here. But she's making all the wrong choices."

"Do you believe she can make a significant change for Emmy's sake?"

No, he answered easily. "I'm so tired of doing this." He let his head fall back, then sucked in a breath and looked at Trinity again. "I'll talk to my lawyer, ask him how I move forward with getting full custody. Her in-excusable actions tonight actually help me." And if he could settle this without getting Department of Public Health and Human Services involved, all the better for Emmy.

"I don't want to push you to do something you're not ready to do. I'm just playing devil's advocate for you so maybe you see things in a new perspective."

"Oh, I'm looking at them from Emmy's point of view. She told me during her bath that she was really scared when the can in the microwave started sparking. She didn't know what to do. Luckily, I had her mom put a speed dial for me with my picture on her phone. All Emmy had to do was tap it to get me."

"You were just a phone call away. I'm sure that made her feel better."

"She shouldn't have been left alone in the first place. She's four." It still made his heart ache and the anger flare to think of her all alone and scared. What if she hadn't had the phone and Steph hadn't come home for hours?

Trinity held his arm. "Let's go read her books and set this aside for tonight."

They walked down the hall and stood in Emmy's doorway. She'd fallen asleep with the books spread out beside her and her favorite stuffed bunny under her arm.

"She had one hell of a day." Jon went to the side of the bed, kissed Emmy on the forehead, picked up the books and set them on the bookshelf, then returned to Trinity at the door.

She gave him another soft, sweet smile. "You had a hard day, too."

He locked eyes with her and closed the distance between them. "Ending my day with you . . ." He didn't have words to express how much it meant to have her here, supporting him, that the drama and chaos in his life hadn't driven her away. "I really appreciate how you make everything better."

She placed her warm hand on his cheek.

He leaned into her sweet touch and savored the feel of her skin against his.

"I'm sorry Steph put you and Emmy through that tonight. You both deserve better."

"Amazing is standing right in front of me." He slipped his hand into her hair and drew her in for a soft kiss that had her body melting against his, warming him up from the inside out. He touched his forehead to hers and stared into her smoldering eyes. "I'm really glad you're here."

She kissed him again with the same sultry slowness.

The connection between them felt like a tangible thing, growing and strengthening with each passing day and every moment shared.

Reluctantly, he ended the kiss, took her hand, and drew her down the hall to the kitchen. She'd made dinner and he couldn't wait to share it with her and a little more time alone together. He wanted to look at her beautiful face across the table, feel her presence surround him, and wallow in the peace she always brought with her.

She took her seat at the table. He pulled the two plates of nachos out of the oven. They were warm, the food a little on the dry side but still edible when he set the plates on the table. He pulled the sour cream and two beers from the fridge, grabbed a spoon, and joined Trinity at the table. He sat next to her and she immediately reached out and squeezed his thigh, then spooned sour cream onto her nachos like they did this all the time.

He cracked open her beer, then his. He held his up. She did the same.

"To you. Beautiful inside and out."

Her soft cheeks pinkened and she tapped her bottle to his. "Thank you, Jon."

He loved that she took the compliment and let the happy feeling it gave her shine in her eyes and smile.

They both sipped the cold beer and settled into the quiet kitchen and good meal.

She picked up a meaty, cheesy chip and stuffed it into her mouth, leaving a dollop of sour cream on her lip.

He brushed his thumb over it, then sucked it off, and smiled at her. "Mmm."

"Eat yours."

"I like watching you."

She gave him a sexy smile and stuffed the next chip she picked up into his mouth. He chewed and smiled at her, feeling the weight of the day disappear.

"I'm sorry another date didn't go as planned."

She locked eyes with him. "I don't know. This is pretty good."

"Only because of you." He let his gaze travel down and up her. Every part of him turned hot and desperate for her. "You wore another killer dress."

"I wanted to see you look at me just like that again."

He'd barely touched his food because all he wanted to do was soak her up.

She abandoned hers and turned to him. "It's a long drive back to town."

Disappointment hit him hard and fast.

"Maybe I should stay here tonight."

Surprise and excitement rushed through him, making his eyes go wide. "Are you sure?" He hoped he wasn't dreaming.

She leaned in until their lips were inches apart. "If you want me t—"

He cut her off with a searing kiss to let her know just how much he wanted her in his bed. "Make my night. Stay."

She stood and he followed. She wrapped her arms around his neck and pressed her body to his. In her high heels, their bodies perfectly aligned. "Sounds like you're going to make my night."

He swept his hands up her sides and around her back. She kissed him with a demand and urgency that told him she wanted this as much as he did. He backed her out of the kitchen and down the hall, still kissing her, needing to get her into his room and his bed. Now.

Just to be safe, and so they'd have no distractions, he let her loose, closed his bedroom door, and flipped the lock. In the dark, he could barely see her face, but he caught the raised eyebrow.

"Emmy sometimes wakes up in the middle of the night and sneaks into bed with me."

Trinity hooked her hand at his neck and drew him close again. "That's sweet."

Yeah, he loved it. But . . . "Tonight I want to be alone with you."

"Nice."

"You might not think that of me if you knew what I was thinking about doing to you right now."

She gave him a sexy, seductive smile. "Should I pick a safe word?"

He pressed his hand to her beautiful face and brushed

his thumb across her soft cheek. "I take instruction very well. Yes. More. Don't stop." He shrugged one shoulder. "I'll do everything in my power to make sure you don't ever want to say no."

She leaned in and kissed him once. "Then, yes." She kissed him again. "More." She kissed him again, this time with her tongue sliding across his bottom lip. "Go. And don't stop."

Maybe he really had finally met his match.

The thought drove him wild and he dove in for a searing kiss that drove them both mad with wanting.

Her fingers worked the buttons at the front of his shirt.

He slid the zipper down her back, and the sexy black dress slipped right off her and pooled at her feet. He broke the kiss and stared at her pale skin disrupted by a black lace bra and barely there strip of panties that made his mouth water. "Damn, Trinity. You're beautiful."

"You're overdressed." She slipped her hands inside his shirt at his shoulders and pushed it down his arms. Her hands went to his chest and ran over his skin as he worked his hands out of the cuffs. Those roaming hands of hers dipped to his navel and attacked his belt. He kicked off his shoes. She pushed his pants over his hips and took his hard length in one hand, rubbing it up and down over his boxers as he kissed her neck and cupped her ass in both hands and squeezed.

She reached down and slipped off one heel and then the other. He undid the bra clasp at her back and pulled the lace right off her arms and sent it flying across the room. He spun her around, pulled her back to his chest, and filled his hands with her full breasts. She slid her hands over his thighs and held tight as she rubbed her ass against his throbbing cock.

He kissed a trail across the top of her shoulder and up her neck to her ear. "I want you so damn bad." He nipped her shoulder, then smoothed his tongue over the love bite.

She moaned and slid her hand back between them and wrapped her fingers firm around his shaft. He worked her nipples to hard peaks, rolling them between his fingers as he walked her forward to the bed until her knees pressed against the mattress. He slid one hand down to her belly; the other massaged her breast. He kissed a trail down her neck and spine as he made her bend forward until she freed his aching cock and planted her hands on the bed.

He tugged at her nipple and cupped her sex in his other hand, sliding his fingers over her hot, wet center. He wanted to feel her skin against his, but to do that he needed to rid her of the sexy panties. He reluctantly left that sweet spot and drew his fingers up and over her hip to her back, trailing them up her spine, then back down again until his fingers hooked in the strings holding her thong on and he pulled it over her round ass and down her legs.

He kicked his pants off, took her by the hips, and rubbed his aching dick against her rump. She pushed back into him and it was all he could do not to pull his cock free of his boxer briefs and drive it home into her wet core.

But they had all night and he wanted to make this first time last.

If he could. Because damn, she tempted him to just take what he wanted. Hard and fast.

He leaned over her back. She immediately rubbed her ass against his dick again, making him groan. Hell, he'd beg at this point, he wanted her so damn bad. He swept her long hair to one side and whispered in her ear. "Lie down."

She turned her head to him, their bodies pressed against each other, and smiled.

He could live on that wicked grin.

She held his gaze, put one knee on the bed, pushed herself forward at the same time lying across the bedspread. The soft moonlight filtering through the window highlighted every curve of her long body. The slope of her shoulder, the dip of her waist, the swell of her ass, and those long legs.

"Perfection."

She answered with, "More."

He ripped off his socks and boxer briefs. At last he stood before her with no barriers between them. Her eyes dilated with desire and her mouth opened slightly. Temptingly.

He started at her ankle and kissed his way up to her very fine ass, then took her knee, pushed and rolled her to her back. On his hands and knees, he stared down at her lying beneath him. "I think about doing this all day long."

Her fingers slid into his hair and tightened into a fist the second he leaned down and licked his way up her soft folds to her clit with the tip of his tongue. Her soft little moan made him smile, so he did it again, glanced up at her, and licked his lips. "More?"

She pushed his head back down. He chuckled, but gave her exactly what she wanted and more, drawing her legs over his shoulders and burying his face in her sweet center. He sank his tongue deep, and she went limp on another moan. He loved her right up to the edge and kept her there with soft slides of his flat tongue and barely there brushes of his thumb against her clit.

"Jon, now." Frustration and demand filled that order, making him want to smile, but instead he gave her what she wanted, slid two fingers into her slick channel, circled her clit with his tongue, and sent her flying over the edge with her heels dug into his back.

The quake of her body against his lips and the satisfied moan echoing in his ears nearly undid him, but he held it together, distracting himself by kissing his way up her body to one peaked nipple and drawing it into his mouth. He licked the tip, then rose over her, stared down, and found her smiling up at him as her hand clamped around his hard dick. She stroked his length up and down. Her thumb found the bead of moisture and she circled the head, spreading it around and driving him crazy.

He stilled her hand with his. "I'm so damn close, I . . ."

Words eluded him when she squeezed his dick. "Condom. Now."

He'd bought a box this week and tossed it in the nightstand drawer. While he grabbed it, Trinity kissed and touched any part of him she could reach. He loved the feel of her hands and mouth on him, but it made it hard to concentrate and roll the condom on before he settled between her soft thighs and nudged the tip of his throbbing cock against her wet center.

Her hands slid down his sides to his hips and she pulled him in as he thrust deep.

"Oh God, yes," she said on a sigh.

He lost all thought and the ability to speak as their bodies moved together. She held him close, her hands sliding over his skin, their lips locked in a kiss that matched the way they made love. Steady and urgent at first, then wild and desperate until they both went up in a brilliant flash of ecstasy that pounded through him and continued to pulse even after he collapsed on top of her.

She held him with one hand on his back, the other on his head, her fingers slowly sweeping back and forth in his hair. His heart thundered against hers. He could barely catch his breath, and the only thought in his head was, *Don't let go.*

His mind didn't start with, *I think this could really be the start of something.* It went right to, *I don't want to lose her.*

Or maybe that was his heart talking.

Either way, he'd never felt this way about anyone.

He'd had hints of it since the first day they met. He knew she was special. The connection he felt to her kept getting stronger. But this. Being with her, making love to her, it opened something inside him. And she filled that empty space.

Any reservation he had, any nagging warning he should go slow, be sure, this could go wrong, disappeared, replaced with a sense that everything between them was absolutely right and perfect.

Possibly sensing something in him, she hugged him close and nuzzled her nose into his neck and kissed him softly. "Mmm. That was . . ."

She stalled a second. He held his breath.

"Amazing."

Relief eased the tightness in his chest. He wasn't the only one feeling something more now.

He had to be squishing her, so he slid his hand around her back and rolled to the side, taking her with him. She ended up tucked into his side as he landed on his back. He brushed the hair from her temple and kissed her on the head.

"I'm not sure amazing covers it." His mind was still trying to catch up to the overwhelming feelings filling him up.

She snuggled in closer.

The silence stretched until he had to ask. "What are you thinking?" Wasn't it women who always asked that? But he really wanted to know.

"I don't know how to say this, except to say . . ." She paused. He hoped from being shy about saying whatever was on her mind and not because she didn't want to tell him. "It felt different."

He rolled to face her and stared into her eyes, letting her know he really wanted to hear more. "How so?"

She placed her hand on his jaw. And though he saw the shyness in her eyes, she said, "Like it meant more." The way she said it, it almost sounded like a question.

So he immediately reassured her. "It did to me." He kissed her softly, then met her gaze again. "What we have, Trinity . . . It's good. It's what I've wanted for a while now, but just couldn't find. Until I met you."

"I've watched my brothers all fall for someone who turned out to be the right one for them." She pressed her lips together, her eyes soft and hopeful, staring back at him. "I'm hoping that's what this is."

"Me too." It felt good to know they were on the same page and feeling the same thing, even if it was new for both of them.

And all he wanted to do was hold on to this feeling and her forever.

Chapter Fifteen

Trinity walked into Jon's kitchen and found him with his back to her, phone to his ear. She slipped up behind him, wrapped her arms around his waist, and laid her cheek between his shoulders.

His hand immediately pressed to hers over his heart. "I told him I'd pay that amount nearly a year ago, but he didn't want to sell. Now his business is in real trouble and it's not worth anywhere near what I originally offered." Jon turned in her arms as he listened. "No." He shook his head and gave her a disgruntled look, though she guessed it was for the guy on the phone. "I'm not interested even if he drops the price." Jon kissed her softly, then leaned back, disgusted by whatever the guy said to him. Hopefully not because of the kiss. She'd finger-brushed her teeth when she got up half an hour ago so she could take Emmy to school on her way into work. "Yes, I could turn the business around, but it would require an infusion of cash, and I've got my eye on something else right now." He held her gaze.

She liked being the object of his affection and attention, so she slipped her hands up and over his chest, then down his belly to the thickening erection swelling behind his jeans zipper and now in her hand.

He sucked back a groan. "I'm not interested."

She raised her eyebrow.

He pointed to the phone, then closed his eyes when she gripped his length and squeezed. "Tell him he's too late. He'll have to find another buyer." Jon tapped his phone to end the call, tossed it on the counter next to them, cupped her face, and kissed her like he hadn't done it in forever, even though he woke her up this morning with a hot kiss, then made love to her, slowly, drawing out every stroke of his body in and against hers.

The long weekend had been more than amazing. Thursday night had simply been the first of several nights spent in each other's arms. She hadn't been able to spend the days with him, but each night after work, she drove out to his place and they spent as much time together as possible.

Mostly naked, because she arrived after Emmy had gone to bed.

Of course, if she got there early enough, they had dinner with Emmy, played games, read her stories, and tried to give her the kind of home life Jon wanted her to have every day.

Except today. Jon's lawyer advised him to follow the custody agreement. He'd already warned Steph she needed to get her act together or he'd fight for Emmy.

This was her last chance to get it right.

Trinity doubted she would and hated that Emmy may have to endure more neglect from her mother before Jon could get the court on his side.

Jon nuzzled his nose against her cheek and whispered in her ear, "All I want to do is take you back to bed." Instead, he gently separated them because they both heard Emmy humming her way down the hall toward the kitchen.

Trinity smiled up at him. "I can't help it. When I see you, I have to touch you."

He kissed her softly. "Don't ever stop feeling that way."

They stood close, but a respectful distance apart for Emmy's sake. Though she'd stayed overnight, they tried to be up, dressed, and presentable when Emmy woke up.

Luckily, Emmy was so tired each night when she went to bed because Jon kept her busy during the day, she didn't try to sneak into his bed.

Trinity wasn't sure what he'd say to her if she did and found Trinity already there. Maybe in time it wouldn't matter, but right now, things were new between her and Jon, even if it felt like life had always been like this.

She didn't want to remember what it felt like to be alone. She liked this feeling of connection to Jon too much to let it go.

The last few days together had brought them even closer to each other.

Still, she wanted to know more. "I don't actually know what you do for a living."

Jon chuckled under his breath. "I told you I sold most of my businesses before I moved here to rehab the ranch and raise Emmy."

She squished up one side of her mouth and gave an exasperated look. "That tells me nothing about what you do with the businesses you kept."

He laughed again. "Okay. Let's see. I used to look for small businesses that had a great service or product but not the resources or know-how to expand. I bought the business, grew it over time, then in most cases I sold it for a profit."

"Except you kept the two you own now."

"I kept them because they make great money and are

managed well. I don't really have to do anything but make the major decisions for the businesses."

"So that call, someone wanted to sell you their company."

"Yes. I made them an offer last year when the company hit the peak for what the owner could do with it, but he didn't want to sell despite the generous amount I offered him."

"How much?" It wasn't so much about the money as it was about understanding the deals he made and the . . . She really didn't know what else. The scope. And maybe the status he had in the business world.

"The company was worth about nine million. I offered him ten because I knew I could make it worth ten times that."

Okay. Millions. Wow. "So you're rich?"

He stared at her for a long moment before answering, "Yes." He took a step away. "I bought my first business with a loan, a plan, and a prayer. With lots of hard work, I made a decent profit when I sold it. So I bought another company. And I did the same thing, but instead of selling it right away, I leveraged it to buy an additional company. That one failed. Poor management. I was too busy building the other company and looking for a new one to see that the plan I'd put into place wasn't being implemented. The guy I hired to run the place thought he knew better than me and made a bad deal that tanked the reputation of the company. I had to lay off workers and close the doors because it would have cost too much to rebuild. Lesson learned."

Emmy walked into the kitchen, taking Jon's attention from the story and Trinity. "Your breakfast is on the table." Emmy set her bunny next to her plate, sat down,

and dug into the scrambled eggs and toast with strawberry jam Jon made her.

He went to the coffeepot, poured Trinity a mug, and
handed it to her. "I lost a ton of money on the deal. I
wanted to focus on the one business I was running well.
But I had a feeling about this start-up. The guys had the
idea, the ingenuity, the drive, but they needed capital
and someone who knew business to oversee the expansion from the ground up. They wanted to go with a well-
known venture capital company. I convinced them to
take a chance on me." Pride lit his eyes.

"Let me guess, you made a killing."

"It took a lot of sleepless nights, eighty-hour work
weeks, and blood, sweat, and tears, but that one far
exceeded my expectations."

"Do you still own that company?"

He nodded. "Yes. We make custom packaging and
cases for products."

"Sounds interesting."

"It can be."

She wanted to know more. "What kind of cases do
they make?"

"For instance, we work with a company that makes
high-quality earbuds. We make the case customers can
buy to hold and charge them." He shrugged.

She couldn't help but notice he kept a greater distance
than they'd shared this whole weekend between them.
He kept his answers to the information about what she
asked and didn't expand on it. She wondered why. "Do
you not want to talk about this?"

"It's fine. Why?"

"You seem standoffish all of a sudden."

"I'm fine." He didn't seem fine.

"What's the other business you kept?" She hoped her interest would show him that she cared about what he did and what mattered to him.

"It's the one I'm most proud of actually."

That made her smile. "Really? Why?"

"Because it helps the community."

"I understand why that would make you feel good. Adria and I support the cities we're in with *Almost Homemade*. You know we deliver to seniors. We also donate excess food to the local shelters and food banks near the stores. What does your business do?"

"It started as a single grocery store in an underserved community. The business was going under because of rising rents and, believe it or not, theft from the store because customers were too poor in the community to pay for their groceries. I had read an article about how people in communities like this were losing their local grocers and having to travel to larger cities to buy food, but it cost so much more, plus what they had to pay for gas or public transportation."

"So you bought the store to help the community." She loved that. It showed his big heart.

"I could have just bought it, but the man who owned it was the second-generation owner who was teaching his son to one day take over. It wasn't their fault the store was going under. They managed it well and tried to keep food costs low for their customers. So I bought the building and lowered the store's rent for a modest piece of the profits after I looked at their books, helped them negotiate better wholesale buying prices, added some security measures to cut down on theft, and basically helped turn things around for them."

"That's brilliant. And you allowed that man to keep the family business that meant so much to him."

"He was very grateful. So were the locals. So I did it again. And again. And again."

"How many store buildings do you own?"

"At last count? Twelve. I was thinking about buying the local grocery store here and expanding the chain to help out some of the more remote areas in Montana."

"Are you going to do that?"

"I'm focusing on the ranch right now. Originally, my plan was to spend summers here with Emmy and go back to California during the school year so she could be with her mom, too. But when I talked to Steph about my idea, she said she wanted a change, too. Living here would be less expensive, she could do it on her own, be more independent from her family. Anyway, I asked the owner of the grocery store to give her the open manager position. She used to manage a clothing store. I figured a grocery store wasn't much different."

"And you could keep an eye on her."

"That's exactly why I didn't buy the store. It's still on the table, but a week before the move, I had an epiphany."

"You didn't want to be her boss and that closely linked to her on a regular basis."

He smiled. "That's right, smart girl."

She waved her hand out toward the desk area he had set up in the living room during the renovations. "So what have you been working on? It looks like a bunch of grocery store stuff."

"It's similar, but something new. Just some ideas I have, but I'm not sure I'm going to do anything with them yet. I'm not sure if the owners of the business are open to my ideas."

"Well, if your track record is any indication, they'd be crazy not to partner with you."

"Why do you say that?"

"Because it doesn't seem to be about the money for you. You care about the people you work with and the service or product you deliver. What those businesses do matters more than how much you can make on them."

He eyed her. "What matters to you, Trinity?"

"I believe in delivering a quality product sourced from local producers. I believe in working in cooperation with the community for the community's benefit. That's why Adria and I partnered with our soon-to-be sister-in-law for the eggs, chicken, and produce we use. It's why we partnered with my brothers at Cedar Top Ranch for our beef. And why we buy our other ingredients from local vendors as well."

He shook his head. "That's all fantastic and why I admire the hell out of you and your business, but I'm asking what about me and what I do matters to you?"

She tilted her head and studied him. "I really don't understand what you're asking me."

"Are you interested in me because I'm a *rich* businessman?"

This time she took a step back from him. "Are you serious?" She wanted to swear, but Emmy was right there pretending to feed her bunny jelly toast. "I'm interested in you because of who you are, not what you do or how much money you have. I'm insulted that you'd even think I care about—"

He closed the distance and kissed her, cutting off her words.

She tried to push him away, because he'd made her angry, but he held her against him, ended the kiss, and pressed his forehead to hers. Remorse, deep and true, filled his eyes. "I'm sorry. It was stupid to ask such a thing when I know none of that matters."

"Why would you even think it?"

He said the one thing that made all the sense in the world. "Steph."

She remembered him saying that he paid for her apartment. She wondered what else he paid for to keep Steph happy and off his back. None of her business.

Or was it now?

She took a breath before she spoke to let the last of her anger dissipate. "I'm not her."

"I know that. I'm so damn happy you are nothing like her."

Trinity glanced at Emmy, who watched them closely now. "I need to get Emmy to school."

Jon lifted his head and looked at his daughter, then back at Trinity. "I'm sorry."

"I know you are. Forget it."

"Will you? I really don't want to mess this up, and I feel like I did because up until five minutes ago you had no idea what I did or how much I'm worth."

"I don't care. I just wanted to know more about you."

He sighed and looked completely dejected.

She took mercy on him. "I'll see you later tonight." She kissed him softly, hoping to ease his mind.

Distress and sorrow still filled his eyes when she stepped back.

Emmy hugged his legs and stared up at him. "How come I can't come back tonight?"

"It's your mother's turn," he said, brushing his hand over her hair.

"I don't want to go there. I want to stay here."

"The painters, landscapers, countertop and carpet guys will be here all week. By the time you come back on Friday, the house will be all done. Don't you want new carpet and your room painted?"

Emmy shook her head, tears gathering in her eyes. "No. I just want to stay in my room here with you and Trinity." Her bottom lip trembled.

"Please don't cry, baby. I know things with your mom are hard right now, but I spoke to her yesterday." He'd informed her that he'd spoken to his lawyer. "She cleaned the house and bought groceries, including all the things you like. She promised she won't leave you alone ever again." If she did, Jon would defy his lawyer and the custody agreement they had in place and keep Emmy, damn the consequences.

His lawyer answered Jon's early-morning email, telling him to go along with Steph so long as she proved she had done those necessary things until they filed the full custody papers and a judge ruled in his favor. So he'd made Steph send him pictures of the clean apartment and stocked fridge, giving him absolutely no reason to deny her right to see her child.

Emmy rolled her eyes and released her dad. "She promises stuff all the time." With that, Emmy walked out of the kitchen to the entry to pull on her backpack.

Trinity retrieved Bunny from the table and stopped in front of Jon as he stared after his daughter with a frown and sad eyes of his own. "She'll be okay."

"I hate making her do something she doesn't want to do."

"You're following your lawyer's advice. You'll work through the process and hold Steph accountable. If she doesn't keep her promises, there will be consequences."

"I feel terrible that Emmy doesn't want her mother. That bond should be unbreakable."

Trinity put her hand over his heart again. "All you can do is listen to Emmy. She is telling you she needs you more."

Jon walked over to Emmy and crouched in front of her. "I want you to know I'm working on changing things with your mom. The last time you stayed with her, you got scared. I don't want that to ever happen again, so I'm going to call you when you get to Mom's place tonight and check on you. We'll video chat and you'll tell me all about your day. I'll know you're all right. And you can tell me if you need anything."

Emmy nodded, some of the hurt leaving her eyes. "Okay."

"Are you okay with Trinity taking you to school? Because if you want me to do it, I will."

Emmy shook her head. "I'll go with her."

"Give me a hug, sweetheart. I am going to miss you bunches this week."

"I miss you, too." Emmy squeezed Jon around the neck, then walked to the door and out onto the porch.

Jon stood and kissed Trinity. "Do you have all your stuff?"

"Afraid I'll leave something here and it will look like I'm trying to move in?" She teased to help ease the tension and his mind.

Instead of teasing back, he asked, "Do you like the paint and carpet color I picked for the house?"

She glanced at the different colored squares he'd painted on the living room wall and the one that had a penciled X in the corner. She liked the soft gray. "I'd have gone a shade lighter with the darker hardwood floors in here. But that's just me. The new silver carpet is going to be thick and lush and will brighten those back rooms a lot. Why?"

"I want you to be comfortable here."

That made her smile, but he had to know the truth. "I'm only here for you."

Emmy called out, "Are we going yet?"

"And her," she added.

"But will you like the changes I'm making?" He seemed so earnest about it.

"You've seen my place. Your taste and mine complement each other perfectly."

That seemed to ease his mind and put a slight smile on his face. "Now that you say that, yeah, I see that now."

She chuckled under her breath, really not getting his strange mood this morning. "Good. Now will you let me go so I can take Emmy to school?"

For the first time, he seemed to realize that he'd taken her hand and linked his fingers through hers. He raised their joined hands and kissed the back of hers. "I can't wait to see you tonight."

"Me too. Don't forget it will be late."

"I know. You close. I wish you could get someone else to do that."

"Me too, but for now, it's me." She turned to go, but he tugged her back for another kiss she accepted and sank into because he seemed to need a little extra affection after their little tiff and Emmy's near meltdown about going to her mother's.

Jon still didn't release her, but walked with her out to the car so he could make sure Emmy buckled herself into the booster seat correctly and gave her one last kiss goodbye, too.

He waved to them as Trinity drove out of the driveway. She watched him in the rearview mirror, hoping they had more days like this, with him waving her off for the day and her driving their children to school.

"Can you make him let me stay with him?" Emmy stared hard at her in the rearview mirror, her eyes and voice intent on getting what she wanted.

Trinity gave her the truth. "No, sweetheart, I can't *make* him do anything. You know your dad loves you, right?"

She nodded and stared out the window, a sad frown on her face.

"He loves having you at the ranch. He'd like to have you there all the time. But he has to work that out with your mom, and it's hard to make happen right away, because she wants to spend time with you, too."

Emmy didn't look at her. "If you say so."

"Maybe it doesn't seem like it sometimes."

Emmy let out a loud and exhausted sigh.

"Emmy, if you don't feel safe when you're at your mom's, you can call your dad anytime just like you did last week. Day or night. Doesn't matter. You know that, right?"

She nodded, but didn't stop looking out the window.

Trinity hoped she hadn't stepped over some line, but she wanted Emmy to know she had a lifeline in Jon. He would always be there for her.

Too bad Emmy didn't have her own phone to call Jon if she needed him.

What if something happened and she didn't have access to her mother's phone?

She needed to talk to Jon about getting her one. Something simple she could use just in case until Jon got full custody.

It would make Emmy feel better, and probably Jon, too.

She'd feel better knowing Emmy wasn't trapped with Steph. There was a fine line between Steph being sometimes neglectful and her putting Emmy in danger. Things had turned out all right when she'd been left alone, but how did the hurtful things Steph did add up in Emmy's mind? What effect did they have on her self-esteem and sense of security?

Questions like that plagued her all the way to Emmy's school.

She was supposed to drop Emmy off in the carpool line, but instead she parked and walked Emmy to her classroom door. She crouched and looked Emmy in the eye. "You have a great day, sweetheart. I made you your favorite turkey, cheese, cucumber sandwich."

"Just the way you like it, too."

"Crunchy," they said in unison.

"I might have also snuck in the last brownie for you, too."

Emmy threw her arms around Trinity's neck. "Thank you. I love you."

Trinity hugged her close and tears gathered in her eyes. "I love you, too, sweetheart."

Emmy rushed into her classroom, leaving Trinity staring after her, her heart bursting with affection and joy and a protective streak that made her want to pick Emmy up at the end of the day and take her right back to her loving father.

She silently vowed that as she and Jon grew closer together, she wouldn't ever forget that Emmy came first for both of them.

Chapter Sixteen

JON RELEASED Emmy's hand so she could knock on the door.

His dad opened it a few seconds later with a big smile for his favorite little person. "Hey, sweet girl. I've been missing you." His dad sank to one knee and wrapped Emmy in a hug.

Jon loved seeing his little girl smile and how his dad closed his eyes, breathed her in, and held her like she was a precious gift.

She was to both of them.

Emmy leaned back. "Did you get me something?"

"Go check your toy chest."

Emmy tried to get past him, but his dad held her by the waist as she struggled to break free, giggling and laughing the whole time until his dad let her go. She raced over to the wood box, lifted the lid, and squeezed the plush gray-and-white puppy stuffed animal.

"I love him. Thank you."

Jon closed the door behind him and joined his father by the coffee table. "It's not the dog she wants, but let's hope that keeps her happy for a little while longer."

"The stables are looking good. The house is finished," his dad pointed out.

Jon got the hint. With the house done, he could take Emmy down to the local animal shelter to pick out the puppy she really wanted. Soon.

Jon spotted the boxes his dad had come by and packed up at the house. They'd finally sorted what his dad wanted to keep, what could stay, and what needed to be donated or thrown out to make room for Jon's things. "Do you need some help unpacking that stuff?"

His dad waved that off. "I'll get to it later." He lifted his chin toward Emmy. "Everything go okay this week?"

Jon nodded and tilted his head toward the kitchen so they could move away from Emmy and talk.

His dad took a jug of iced tea from the fridge and poured them each a glass while Emmy played with the puzzles she took out of the toy chest. His dad bought her something new each time they came for a visit so she'd have something to do here.

"Tell me," his dad prompted.

"The phone calls and video chats every night are helping. Emmy had a good week at school. Steph has kept the house clean, fed Emmy decent meals, and they generally got along this week."

"That's good."

"Yeah." He didn't have a whole lot of faith that Steph would do what she was supposed to without him checking on her every day.

"Well, Emmy looks good."

Jon wished he didn't have to worry about her having on clean clothes, that she'd had a recent bath, and her hair was brushed. Those things should be a given. "Yay for Steph. She made it through four days."

His dad pressed his lips tight, not liking Jon's sarcasm. "It's a start."

"Steph has had a lot of starts where Emmy is concerned."

"Take the win. Enjoy your weekend with her."

"I plan on it." Plus he'd had a great week with Trinity.

"I take it that smile has more to do with the gorgeous blonde you're seeing."

Jon couldn't help it. Just thinking about her made him happy. "I've never had anything like this."

"When it's right, it's good. Makes a man want to hold on to it."

"I can't even think about losing her. With everything going on right now, the move, the renovation, the Steph drama, Trinity has been the bright spot in all of it. She's just so easy to be around. When I'm with her . . . everything just feels right."

His dad clamped his hand on Jon's shoulder. "I'm happy for you, son. You know I like Trinity, but I especially like her for you and Emmy. She's good and kind and just what the two of you need."

"Emmy loves her. When I picked her up from school today, even though she knew we were coming to see you, she asked if Trinity was coming with us."

"You should have invited her."

"She's working. But it says so much that Emmy can't wait to see her. Emmy sees us together and she just accepts that our weekends include Trinity. They're so good together."

"Do you wish things could have been that way with Steph?"

Jon shook his head. "I always knew Steph and I were a just-for-fun kind of thing. Trinity . . . I think she's a forever kind of thing."

"Wow." His dad smiled. "I'm happy for you, son."

"I'm worried," Jon admitted.

"Why? Because of Steph?"

"What if she can't hack it here on her own and wants to go back to California? I can't make her stay. A custody battle could take years if her father backs her and pays for a lawyer to drag it out. I may have to do what's best for Emmy and go back to California and fight Steph there."

"Don't borrow trouble. She had a good week. Wait and see if she can turn that into more. Maybe she got the wake-up call she needed and is really trying to do right by Emmy and make a new life here."

"I hope so, because the thought of leaving Trinity to go back and fight with Steph leaves me cold. I'd hate to do it, but . . ."

"Trinity knows Emmy comes first. You two would work something out. Maybe your lawyer would get the courts to make Steph stay here until you settled the matter."

"I don't know. You're right. I'm worrying about what could happen instead of focusing on what's happening right now." He'd keep up the check-in calls and video chats with Emmy when Steph had her and hope that helped keep Steph accountable. He hoped the longer she lived here, the more she'd settle in and make this home.

"Forget about all this for the weekend. Enjoy the time with your girls," his dad encouraged.

He liked the sound of that. Because when he was with Emmy and Trinity, he was happier than he'd ever been.

And Emmy loved spending time with her grandpa. Tonight they'd eat pizza and take a walk to the nearby park where Emmy liked her grandpa to push her high on the swings and catch her at the bottom of the slide.

Jon hoped they didn't have to move back with Steph and leave the two people he loved behind.

Chapter Seventeen

THINGS SEEMED to finally be going Jon's way. He'd had two weeks where everything went as planned. Steph managed to work and care for Emmy on her days as scheduled. No Thursday evening phone call to come get her because Steph was done. He and Emmy had a video chat every night she was away. It seemed to ease her mind and make her more comfortable staying with her mom.

The calls kept Steph in line because she knew he was checking up on her, too.

The house renovation and redecorating was finished, and he loved how everything turned out. He'd taken Trinity's advice and gone with the lighter shade of gray for the walls. She was right. The place was brighter and felt more open and airy. The color complemented the new white quartz countertops and stainless-steel appliances in the kitchen, which Trinity loved. She used the space more than he did, and he didn't mind one bit. She was a phenomenal cook. Emmy loved helping her make meals on the weekend.

They worked together really well. Trinity and Emmy. And he and Trinity. She spent more nights with him than she did at her own place. When she wasn't with him, he missed her and couldn't wait to see her again. He'd never felt that way about anyone.

And he needed to put some serious thought into what he wanted for the future, though it seemed to be coming together the way he imagined without him even really trying.

Trinity loved being at his place. They loved being together. She was great with Emmy.

Everything seemed perfect right now.

And as much as he loved having more time to spend with Emmy, visiting his dad, and working to get the ranch ready to house some horses and the puppy Emmy hadn't stopped begging him to get her, he still found time to work on his pet project.

While Trinity kept him apprised of what she was doing at work, and how things were going with her plans to expand once Adria gave birth and was back to working full-time, he had a plan to make all their dreams a reality without them having to take out a massive loan, and travel and stay at the new locations for weeks at a time. And work sixty-plus-hour weeks to do it.

He had no idea what Trinity and Adria would say about his proposal. But he'd decided to do what he'd do with any other business owner and make the offer and let them decide.

He'd handled things badly when Trinity asked about what he did for a living. He let past experiences put him on the defensive and insulted Trinity. Money didn't seem to be a motivating factor for anything Trinity did. Not in her work, where she lived, or how she lived her life. She loved being a chef and running her business with her sister-in-law. She liked the little apartment over the shop because it was cozy and all she needed right now for herself. She didn't spend money on things just to have them.

As far as he could tell, her love for chocolate far exceeded her love of expensive shoes, handbags, jewelry, or trips.

Unlike Steph, she never asked him to pay for anything. If she brought food from the shop, she didn't hint or say outright he should pay her for it. When they took Emmy out shopping for new shoes and Trinity found a pair she wanted, she walked right up to the cashier and paid for them herself. She didn't give him a look, or even an opportunity to offer to pay for them while he paid for Emmy's.

In fact, she didn't expect anything from him, except his company and time. She never complained that she wanted to be alone with him when they had Emmy. She never suggested they get a sitter so they could go out without Emmy. She understood that time was precious for him and Emmy both, and she didn't interfere in their relationship.

And Emmy adored her because Trinity treated her like she was special. She showered Emmy with unconditional love from her great big open heart.

He'd be crazy to ever let her go. And stupid if he did something to ruin it.

Emmy might kill him if he screwed things up with her.

Which was why he hoped Trinity and Adria would be open to hearing him out about his business plan.

He couldn't remember the last time he'd been this nervous about a business meeting. He hadn't seen Trinity in two days, but he had talked to her on the phone last night and asked for this meeting to her great surprise. He didn't tell her exactly what he wanted to talk to her about, only that he had some ideas for her business and wanted to share them with her and Adria.

He walked into *Almost Homemade* right before their nine-thirty appointment, happy to see Trinity behind the counter talking to one of her employees. The store had a good number of customers shopping the shelves and hot counter.

He didn't see Adria, but figured she'd join them for the meeting shortly.

Trinity spotted him and gave him a huge smile. He walked to the corner of the counter, away from where customers were lined up to get food and check out.

"Hey, you." She eyed his dress shirt and tie. "Aren't you handsome and so serious today?"

He'd ditched his new usual tee or thermal for his old business attire up top, but he kept the black jeans because while he wanted to look professional, he was meeting his girlfriend and her partner.

"You're always beautiful and happy, and the best part of my day is seeing you."

The bright smile was his second favorite to the sexy one she gave him most nights when they seduced each other in bed.

Trinity tilted her head. "When you asked to meet with me and Adria, I didn't realize it was some kind of serious business you wanted to discuss."

The guy Trinity had been talking to when he walked in hovered nearby, sneaking glances at Trinity. If the guy had a thing for her, he was shit out of luck. Jon let him know it with a hard stare before he focused on Trinity again. "Your business is all tied up with family. While we have a personal relationship, I wanted you to know this is business. If you don't like what I have to say about my plans for *Almost Homemade*, then I'll drop it and we'll continue as we have been, no hard feelings."

Trinity raised one brow. "You have plans for my business?"

The guy lurking in the background rushed forward

and took Trinity by the shoulder, turning her to him. "I thought you said you weren't interested in selling. You've turned down every offer so far."

She'd never mentioned any offers to him. "How many offers have you received?"

Trinity shrugged one shoulder. "We get one every couple of weeks. We have since we opened the third store."

"If you're ready to sell, you should consider the offer I brought to you." The guy eyed Jon, then turned to Trinity again. "It's a good offer."

Jon wanted to jump in, but his phone rang. He spared it a glance before he readdressed Trinity about his offer, but instead told her, "Sorry, it's Emmy's school."

"Take it." She waved him off and said to the other guy, "We aren't selling the business."

Jon took a couple steps away. "Hello."

"Mr. Crawford, this is Pam at Oakhurst Elementary. I'm calling about Emmy."

"Is she okay?" His first thought was that maybe she was sick and needed to be picked up.

"Um. No, she's not. She was dropped off late this morning. In fact, she's only been here for the last twenty minutes."

She should have arrived at school over an hour ago.

Pam went on with the bad news. "It seems she and her mother had some sort of . . . disagreement this morning that resulted in a rather bad haircut. At least one of the kids in her class called her ugly. Emmy is beside herself. She won't stop crying. In fact, she's so hysterical, she's made herself vomit."

"Oh my God. I had no idea." He really didn't know what to say, but the thought of anyone calling his daughter ugly made him livid. Knowing she was that upset only made it worse. "I'm not that far away. I can be there in a few minutes."

"We'd appreciate that. She's simply inconsolable."

"I'll be right there," he assured Pam.

"You should know that we've contacted her mother as well. Because of the nature of what happened, Emmy's rather strange appearance, and how she was delivered to us, we think it best to discuss the situation with both of you present to get a better understanding of what happened."

The anger built inside him until he was holding the phone so tightly his fingers ached. "I would like to understand exactly what happened as well. Please tell Emmy I am on my way and I'm coming as fast as I can." He hung up and turned to go back to Trinity, but she was already right behind him with her purse on her shoulder.

"What happened to Emmy?"

"One of the kids in her class called her ugly."

Trinity scrunched her mouth into a disgruntled frown. "Well, that's not nice at all."

"I don't think it's all about that. Pam, the nurse, said something about her and Steph having an argument this morning before school, which is why Emmy arrived late. The school nurse called me and Steph in because they're trying to figure out what really happened." He took Trinity's hand, so grateful for her calming presence during yet another Steph mess. "They said she's hysterical, made herself ill, and is inconsolable."

Trinity squeezed his hand. "Then let's go get her." She tried to pull him toward the door.

He tugged to halt her. "I've got this. You don't want to dive into this mess."

Trinity tilted her head and her shoulders sagged. "But Emmy needs us."

Relief and deep appreciation filled him up. "She does.

But Steph is going to be there. I don't want to make a bad situation worse."

"As in, she'll see me and cause a scene."

"Yes. And I like you happy and far away from Steph's sharp tongue."

She started walking toward the door. "Then you deal with your ex, and I will take care of Emmy."

He caught up to her, took her outstretched hand, and linked his fingers with hers again. He'd given her an out and she didn't take it. He appreciated her help and support. Emmy would be happy to see her. But he'd like to keep her and Steph as far apart as possible. Then again, if he and Trinity were really building something together, they'd all have to learn to get along.

He held the car door open for her.

She climbed in and met his gaze. "I'm going to table the conversation about you trying to buy me and Adria out of our business until later, but we will talk about it." The tone didn't bode well for him, or his proposal.

Yeah, he hated to leave that hanging between them because he hadn't quite explained his plan. "It's not what you think."

He closed the door and went around to the driver's side. He didn't want her to believe he wanted to shut her out of the business she built. He drove out of the lot and headed for the school. "Really, Trinity, I just have some ideas. All I want is for you to hear me out."

"Later," she said, getting out of the car as soon as he parked in the lot. "Which way?" she asked when they met on the sidewalk.

He took her hand and led the way to the office where he supposed they'd taken Emmy. The second they walked in the door he heard a strange keening sound that broke his heart when he followed it into a room off the main lobby and found his daughter curled in a ball on the sofa, her hands over her head.

Pam crouched next to her with one hand on her back and looked up at him. "Mr. Crawford."

He couldn't speak. He went to Emmy and put his hand on her back. "Emmy, baby, I'm here. You're okay."

The eerie sound she made turned into a harsh cry.

He scooped her up and held her to his chest. "Okay, sweet girl, I'm here. You're okay," he assured her and held her tighter. "It's all right now." She clung to him with her arms wrapped around his neck and her legs around his waist. She liked to squeeze him good sometimes, but this was a desperate embrace filled with fear that he'd let her go and something bad would happen to her.

"Emmy." Trinity brushed her hand down Emmy's disheveled and considerably shorter hair. "We're both here for you, honey. Whatever happened, we'll try to help."

"I'm ugly," Emmy wailed. "She cut it off and threw it at me."

Jon raged inside, but he held Emmy and kept it contained because she'd had enough today, and the morning was barely over.

Pam met Jon's gaze. "Apparently, her mother got angry while trying to brush Emmy's hair and cut it off."

Jon couldn't really see the damage but it was apparent enough to Pam, and Trinity, judging by the frown and concern in Trinity's eyes.

Trinity tried to console Emmy again. "It's not that bad, sweetheart. We can go to the hairdresser and get it trimmed into a very pretty style."

"It's too short." Emmy buried her face in Jon's neck, but her crying had subsided as she hiccuped and tried to slow her breathing. All her long hair, which had once draped down to the middle of her back, had been cut haphazardly, as if Steph took handfuls of her hair and chopped it off, not caring that some of it was longer than other areas.

"I bet it will look really cute. Like a fairy's haircut." Trinity pulled out her phone and tapped a bunch of times, then held it up. "See. How about something like this?"

Jon loved that Trinity found several photos of models with short, chin-length dark hair that would look great on Emmy.

Emmy refused to look at first, so he tried to encourage her. "I think this one could work." He made the general statement, hoping she'd want to pick one for herself.

Finally, Emmy raised her head and glanced over his shoulder at the phone Trinity held up. "Which one?" she asked him.

"I bet my favorite is the same as yours." He wanted her to decide, because her mother obviously hadn't given her a choice this morning about lopping off her hair.

Emmy tapped one of the photos, making it larger on the phone. "That's nice."

"I think that will look really cute on you," Trinity agreed. "I'll save the picture and we'll show it to the hairdresser so she can cut your hair just like that."

"Do you think she can?" Emmy leaned back, and for the first time he got a good look at her.

He felt so sorry for Emmy. How could Steph do this to her daughter?

"Yes, it can be fixed. And I'm so sorry your mom did that to you, sweetheart." Jon hugged her close again.

"She deserved it for screaming at me." Steph stood in the doorway, her eyes narrowed on Emmy and filled with rage. "Now you've made me take time off work to

come down here because you're being a big crybaby."
Steph had never spoken to Emmy so coldly.

At least, not in his presence.

"That's enough." Jon couldn't believe Steph's behavior.

"Why don't we take this to another room?" Pam suggested. "Perhaps your friend can stay with Emmy, Mr.
Crawford."

Emmy had buried her face in his neck again and
clung to him with all her might.

He turned and whispered in her ear, "Is it okay if I
hand you off to Trinity while I talk to your mom?"

Emmy immediately turned and held her arms out to
Trinity, who took her into her arms and held her just the
way Jon had done.

"There now, my sweet girl. We'll just sit right here
and catch our breath." Trinity sat on the sofa with Emmy
on her lap and wrapped around her.

"Why are we even here? Send her back to class."
Steph blocked the doorway.

He walked right up to her. "Let's take this outside."
He didn't want Emmy to overhear their raised voices,
because right now he couldn't find the calm to speak in
a civil tone.

Steph quickly backed away.

Pam went out with her.

He went back to Trinity and Emmy and kissed both
of them on the head, then stared down at Trinity. "I'm
so glad you came with me."

"I've got her. Go deal with . . . that."

Jon touched Emmy's arm. She flinched, and that
made him even sadder. "I'm going to make sure your
mom doesn't do something like this ever again."

Emmy didn't acknowledge that at all. He didn't know

if she believed him or not. But he wouldn't let this go unanswered.

He found Steph, Pam, and a man standing outside, closer to the parking lot than the door. Good.

"Mrs. Crawford," the man implored.

And Jon set him straight. "She's not Mrs. Crawford." Emmy had his last name, so it was a good assumption for the guy to think Steph and he had once been married. "We were never married." *Thank God.*

Pam made the introductions. "Mr. Crawford, Miss Brown, this is Principal Fields. I've asked him to join us to discuss what's been happening with Emmy."

"She's fine." Steph stood defiant with her arms crossed and her head high, wearing the grocery store polo and jeans.

Jon didn't think Emmy was even close to fine, and he wanted to hear what the school had to say about it. "What exactly has been happening with Emmy at school?" He'd start there and get to Steph and what happened this morning.

Principal Fields took the lead now. "Emmy is late to school every day of the week, except Mondays." He gave Jon a direct look.

Jon easily made the connection. "In other words, she's only on time the day I drop her off."

"Well," Steph started, "if she'd cooperate in the morning, we wouldn't be late."

"You are also late picking her up more days of the week than you do on time," the principal pointed out.

"I'm a single working mother." That explained nothing.

"You get off at four thirty. You live five minutes away from here. You shouldn't ever be late." Jon dared her to contradict him with a look.

She glared at him. "Sometimes I have to work late. I am the manager."

"We've been lenient up until now." The principal's voice held a warning. He was losing patience with Steph and her callous attitude.

Jon felt the same way. "In other words, pick her up on time, Steph."

She rolled her eyes.

Pam tried for a calmer tactic. "Children do best on a schedule. That way they aren't anxious about what's going to happen. When you're late, she worries that she's been forgotten."

That hit Jon right in the chest.

Poor Emmy. He didn't want to imagine her watching all her friends get picked up and taken home on time while she sat there waiting on her mother, wondering if she'd even bother to show up.

Principal Fields continued with what he thought they needed to hear. "When children lose interest in school and act out in class, it's usually because of issues at home. They aren't getting the guidance and attention they need."

"She's acting out in class?" This was starting to sound like what had happened back in California.

Apparently, all he'd done was move the problem from one state to another.

"She argues with her classmates and teacher, she doesn't always complete her packet work, and she's even thrown a few tantrums that disrupt the class to the point her teacher has to send her to the office for a time-out." Principal Fields looked from him to Steph and back. "The question is, what is happening at home that is upsetting Emmy so much she can't concentrate in class? Perhaps it's an issue one of our school counselors can assist you in identifying and rectifying for Emmy's benefit."

Steph threw up her hands and let them drop. "She doesn't listen to me. She complains about everything. She won't do what I say."

Pam turned to him. "Is that your experience with Emmy as well, Mr. Crawford?"

He held Steph's gaze. "No. It's not. She's a good girl. Smart. Kind. Funny. We have fun together, but she does her chores and any homework she brings home on Friday, though the teacher doesn't usually assign any for the weekend."

"Yeah, you get the easy gig, playing with her all weekend. I get the hard stuff."

Pre-K homework was hard? Getting her up, dressed, fed, and to school on time was hard? Picking her up, feeding her, doing basic skills homework, bathing her, and putting her to bed on time was too much?

He could rectify that very easily.

"You and I will discuss that later. What I want to know right now is what happened specifically this morning."

Steph frowned and glared at all of them. "Of course, I'm the bad guy."

"Our daughter's hair is a mess. What happened? Why would you do that to her?"

Steph unfolded her arms and shoved her fisted hands down until her arms were rigid at her sides. "Because she deserved it."

"Our four-year-old deserved to have her hair chopped off and to be humiliated in front of her classmates? One of them called her ugly."

"Well, she was acting that way this morning." Steph raked her fingers through her hair and pulled it away from her face. She shifted from one foot to the other, clearly agitated and upset. "Her hair is too long. It's always a mess." She pinned him in her gaze. "You're always on my case about making her hair look nice."

"It's not that hard to brush it and put some of those clip things in to keep it out of her face."

"Yeah, well, that's what you think. It's like a rat's nest in the morning when she wakes up. I tried to brush it this morning, but it was all in tangles."

"Did you use the detangler spray I left you?"

Steph narrowed her eyes. "You mean the one your girlfriend gave her?"

"Yes," he said snidely. "That one."

"I'm so damn tired of hearing about how great Trinity is. It's constantly Trinity this, and Trinity that. 'Trinity doesn't pull my hair. Trinity does it softer,'" she mimicked in a snide tone.

So that's what really set Steph off.

"What the hell is she even doing here? This is between us. Emmy is *our* daughter."

Trinity wasn't the problem here; Steph's jealousy was making her act out and it needed to stop.

"Trinity cares about Emmy. She takes care of her when she's with us."

"Us? So you two are living together now. Don't think I don't know what you're doing."

He had no idea what she meant by that. "What am I doing?"

"You're trying to take her from me. You just want to be a happy family with that bitch and my daughter. I won't let you have full custody."

"I want you, her mother, to take care of her properly. That's all."

"I'm a good mother."

"You left her alone in the apartment to go party with some guy."

Pam interrupted. "If Emmy is being left alone, there are bigger issues we need to discuss. Which should include the statements Emmy has made to her teacher about her mother being mean to her."

"She's lying," Steph immediately spat out.

Jon wanted to know just what Emmy had to say to her teacher, but first he wanted to get to the bottom of what happened this morning. "We both know she's not, Steph. Look at what happened today. She's so upset, she made herself sick. You're defensive and agitated, but you won't say what happened."

"She wouldn't sit still. She kept saying I was pulling too hard and hurting her."

"You probably were. So why didn't you stop?"

"And let her video call you with less than perfect hair so you can tell me again how I'm not doing what I'm supposed to for her? I'm so tired of you picking at every little thing I do or don't do for her. All you do is threaten to take her away from me. And now she's telling me that I'm not good at stuff, that Trinity is such a good cook and does her hair without hurting her, and blah, blah, blah, blah blah."

"So this is Trinity's fault."

"She took you. Now she's trying to take my daughter." Steph had lost her mind if she thought he still belonged to her in any sort of way.

So Jon made it clear. "Trinity and I are together. She's a part of Emmy's life. She's good to her. She'd never do what you did to her this morning."

Steph tried to rein in her anger, but her frustration came through loud and clear. "There wasn't time to straighten up her haircut. We were already late. I'll fix it later tonight."

"Trinity and I are taking her to the hairdresser right

now. I hope that will repair some of the damage you did to her self-esteem and make her feel good about herself again."

Steph waved that away. "If she'd stayed still it wouldn't have turned out so bad."

Jon caught himself before he took a step toward Steph and did or said something he shouldn't and might not really regret later.

Steph glared at him. "You can't take her from school."

"I can. I am. She's too upset to stay."

Pam nodded. "I think she'll feel better coming back to school tomorrow with a new haircut and time to let what's happened settle in her mind."

"She's supposed to be with me tonight. But, of course, because I had to come down here, I'll have to work late to make up the time." She rolled her eyes in exasperation that she'd been put out.

Jon didn't give a shit that she'd had to leave work. It was her damn fault. She just didn't see it.

"Then it works out, because I'm taking Emmy home with me."

Steph fumed.

He ordered her to do the right thing. "After you go inside and apologize to her for what you did."

She gaped at him. "After the way she acted, the things she said." Steph shook her head. "No. She should apologize to me."

"So she's the only one in the wrong?"

"Yes. If she'd stayed still and shut up, none of this would have happened."

He fought to contain his rage. "You lost your temper and attacked her hair with a pair of scissors."

Steph rolled her eyes. "Her hair will grow back."

"But will she ever forget what you did to her and how

you made her feel today?" Jon wouldn't forget the devastation in Emmy's eyes or the way she'd cried like a wounded animal.

"She's four. She probably won't remember any of this." Steph shrugged it off.

"So you're going to leave it to me to fix this between you two."

"She'll get over it. What choice does she have? I'm her mother. She needs to do what I say."

He set her straight. "That's where you're wrong, Steph. She does have a choice. I've already got my lawyer working on it."

Steph rushed him and got right in his face. "I've done everything you ordered me to do. You can't take her away from me!"

Principal Fields inserted his arm between them. "Perhaps this is a discussion you can have when you've had time to calm down and you can talk amicably about what is best for Emmy."

"I'm her mother. I'm what's best for her. Not Trinity." Steph glared hard at him. "I'm calling my father and getting a lawyer to stop you."

No surprise. When things got hard for Steph, she ran to Daddy and begged him to fix things for her.

Jon wondered what her father would say when he heard what Steph had done to Emmy.

"You're going to need one because Pam and Principal Fields are required to report suspected abuse and neglect."

Steph's eyes went round when Pam nodded. "You can't do that. She's fine."

Pam gave Steph a sad but determined look. "We are mandated reporters. If we suspect abuse, a call is required."

Steph stormed off, pulling her phone out, likely to call her dad, as she crossed the parking lot.

Jon stood there, not caring if the principal and Pam stared at him, waiting for him to say or do something. He knew what was coming. He'd held off Emmy's teacher in California with promises that he'd take care of things with Steph. She'd do better.

Well, he was tired of covering for Steph. He hated that Emmy was going to have to go through this, but it had to be done if he was going to get the court to side with him instead of Emmy's mother. More than likely, they'd be lenient and give Steph more chances than she deserved to get things right. And in the process, Emmy would suffer.

He'd do his best, everything and anything he could to protect her, but if he wanted to win and keep Emmy away from Steph and her abuse in the future, he had to do it the right way.

Pam broke the tense silence. "I know this has been a difficult morning, Mr. Crawford. We appreciate you coming down to see to Emmy's needs."

"In the future, if Emmy needs one of us to come to her again, call me first."

"Of course," Pam agreed. "We don't like to insert ourselves in people's personal lives, but it is clear that Emmy needs some stability in her home life. She's falling behind in school. She's got a long way to go and starting off like this . . . arriving late, not doing assignments, acting out in class . . . Well, it will only make things harder in the future."

In other words, he needed to turn this around now before it became a hard habit to break.

"I appreciate how you've handled this and that you've provided some further insight into what is going on with Emmy on the days her mother has custody of her. If you wouldn't mind putting together the information about how many times she's been late to school and picked up late after school so I can provide that to my attorney, I'd appreciate it."

"Of course, the school records are for your information to use as you see fit." Principal Fields led them back up to the office. "They will also be provided to DPHHS."

Meaning they would make the call to the authorities now.

"We appreciate your willingness to work with us to try to make Emmy's school experience a good one."

"I'm trying. And while DPHHS will do their thing, more than likely Steph will get an attorney to make this go away. My hope is that after today she'll make more effort to have Emmy here on time and to get her after school by five. Please let me know if this pattern continues, so I can address it." He had a sudden thought. "If Emmy isn't picked up or something else comes up, can I put my girlfriend's name down as an emergency contact? She works close by and could get to Emmy much faster than me if I'm not in town."

They walked into the office lobby.

Principal Fields nodded. "Of course we can add her." He went around the desk to the computer. "I have Emmy's information here. So we'll add Trinity. What's the last name?"

"McGrath." Jon gave them her cell phone number as well as the number to her shop. Just in case.

Principal Fields typed it all in. "There we go. All finished. I've also made a note in the file that you are the primary contact, so you will be called first if any issues arise such as this, or if she becomes ill."

"Great. That eases my mind."

Pam touched his arm. "Why don't you collect Emmy? I'm sure she's worried about what we've talked about and what happens next."

"Don't worry. I'll have a talk with her." Because now strangers were going to step in and make decisions for Emmy's sake even if he didn't agree with them. Steph had tied his hands today. He couldn't stop the school from reporting. He couldn't stop DPHHS from taking Emmy from both of them if that's what they thought was best.

He didn't think it would come to that, but it was his greatest fear.

He needed to call his lawyer ASAP to get ahead of this, but right now, his daughter needed him.

He went to the little room off the main lobby and found Emmy sitting on Trinity's lap facing her. She'd released Trinity from the death grip she had on her when he left.

"You're not ugly, sweetheart," Trinity assured her.

Emmy stared down at Trinity's lap and played with the hem of her *Almost Homemade* tee. "Do you really think they can fix it?"

"Yes. In fact, I think it would be a great idea for your dad to take a before and after picture. That way you can see how great it looks when it's all done."

Jon pulled out his phone, but hesitated to hold it up when Trinity brushed her hand up Emmy's arm, pushing her sleeve up to reveal the red marks and bruises on Emmy's biceps.

"Turn and look at Daddy so he can take the picture," Trinity coaxed, but her eyes held his and were filled with concern.

He understood why when Emmy's gaze met his and he saw the red mark right under her eye. He hadn't noticed it before because she'd been crying so hard her whole face had been red.

Jon zoomed in so the marks on her were clear in the photo.

Emmy would never know this was why Trinity wanted him to take the picture. He actually took several just to be sure he documented the marks Steph put on her. She had to have grabbed Emmy's arm really hard to leave imprints of her fingers digging into his daughter's skinny little arm.

He had no idea how she'd hurt her eye, so he simply asked. "Hey, sweet girl, what happened to your eye here?" He pointed to the small but distinctive hurt. She'd probably have a little black eye tomorrow.

"Mama shook me and I banged my face on the table."

Trinity's eyes glassed over.

He had a hard time finding his voice. "I see. Does it hurt?"

"Yeah." She buried her face in Trinity's chest.

Trinity hugged her. "We'll put some ice on it later." She leaned back and gave Emmy as bright a smile as she could considering the distress she saw in her eyes. "Our appointment is in ten minutes. Let's get your stuff and head over to the salon."

Emmy glanced up at him. "Trinity said I can get my nails painted, too. And a pedi. That means my toes."

Grateful didn't begin to describe how he felt toward Trinity right now. Emmy had been so distraught when he arrived she'd nearly choked him to death, but now she smiled with excitement about getting her nails done. "Sounds like you get the full beauty treatment."

"She said it's her treat. So do I get a candy, too?"

Trinity's good heart and generosity always touched him.

"When we get home, you can have two candies out of the treat jar." Another thing Trinity had brought over. Because she liked chocolate and so did Emmy. Plus it was a way to reward Emmy for her chores, eating her veggies, and being a good girl.

"Let's get going." Trinity stood with Emmy in her arms.

Emmy stared at the floor. "Am I in trouble for being bad with Mama?"

"No. Not one bit. Your mom got angry and did something bad to you. I asked her to apologize. I hope she will because you deserve an apology. But you are not in trouble. Okay?" He brushed his hand over her head.

"Okay."

They walked out of the room.

Jon took Emmy's backpack from Pam. "Thank you."

"No problem. We'll see you tomorrow, Emmy. I can't wait to see your new haircut. I bet it's going to look really pretty."

Pam held his gaze. "Expect a visit from someone today."

Jon nodded.

Emmy managed a small smile for Pam before they walked out of the office and headed for his car.

Jon put his hand at Trinity's back and pulled her close to his side. "Thanks for coming with me."

"Absolutely. I'm looking forward to my mani-pedi, too."

Emmy reached over Trinity's shoulder and pulled her long ponytail close. "Are you going to get a haircut, too?"

"Do you think I should?"

Emmy shook her head. "It's too pretty to cut."

Trinity brushed her nose against Emmy's. "Yours is going to be way prettier. You'll see."

Chapter Eighteen

JON HELD up his phone and snapped a photo of Emmy and Trinity holding up their hands to show off their painted nails and Emmy's new do. He owed Trinity big-time for setting up the appointment right away and turning the disastrous chop job into a stylish haircut that actually suited Emmy nicely and would be easier to maintain.

"Do you love it?" He smiled to let Emmy know he sure did.

She flipped her hair back with one hand. "It's so bouncy."

The short cut did in fact bounce and swish as Emmy walked with them to the car.

Her smile delighted him, but the images of Emmy's hacked hair and the bruises on her arm and darkening under her eye still blazed in his mind and kept his anger roiling in his gut.

He expected to hear from DPHHS any minute. Nerves and anxiety made his chest tight.

They all climbed into the car and he pulled out of the parking lot and headed toward Steph's place.

Trinity glanced over. "I thought you were taking me back to the store."

"I will. I just want to do one thing first."

Emmy hummed along to the song on the radio and stared out the side window.

He used her distraction to pull onto a side street and park.

"Where are we?" Emmy met his gaze in the rearview mirror.

"I just need to make a quick stop here. Wait with Trinity. I'll be right back." He left the keys in the ignition and jumped out. He smiled and waved to Emmy to ease any concern she had about the detour.

It took him only a couple minutes to walk to the apartment from the back entrance. He knocked on Steph's door even though he didn't see her car in her assigned spot. He used his key to enter and found what he didn't want to see in the living space. Right there next to the dining table, spread all over the floor, was his daughter's long, dark hair. The pair of sharp scissors sat on the table atop a stack of unopened mail.

Because of the video calls he had with Emmy every night she stayed with Steph, the place wasn't that bad. Not spotless, but okay.

He snapped several photos of Emmy's discarded hair littering the floor to hand over to his lawyer.

Just because he was curious, and his kid lived here part-time, he opened the fridge to make sure Steph had enough food. He snapped a photo of the dismal contents. No milk or eggs or cheese. Just a bunch of condiments, an open bottle of wine, two juice boxes, some sad salad greens that didn't look edible, and half an apple that had been placed face-down on the dirty glass with no protective covering. The whole thing needed a good cleaning. And to be restocked.

He opened the pantry cupboard. A box lay on its side,

oat cereal spilled everywhere. Who knew how long it had been there? The remaining contents were probably stale and inedible now. He spotted a couple cans of chicken noodle soup, a bag of unopened rice, three bags of pasta, no spaghetti sauce in sight, and a box of strawberry Pop-Tarts. That was it.

The contents filling the garbage revealed Steph preferred the drive-through.

Seriously, Steph worked at a grocery store. How hard was it to pick up food on her way home? Even the store deli counter had better offerings than a fast-food place.

Why couldn't she take care of herself and Emmy better?

Steph's parents had done such a good job doing everything for her, she didn't know how to do anything herself. That's the only explanation that made sense.

He snapped a picture of the pantry, closed the door, made sure he didn't leave anything out of place. Not that Steph would notice.

Emmy and Trinity were probably wondering what was taking him so long. He wanted to check out the rest of the apartment, but decided against it. He'd gotten what he wanted.

He locked up behind him, then made the trek back to the car and climbed in. He handed Trinity his phone and lifted his chin toward it to get her to look at the screen.

Her eyes went wide with shock.

Seeing his daughter's hair scattered everywhere like that after hearing what happened, and trying so hard to console her earlier, hit him hard in the chest again.

"I'm glad you got this. I think it will help." Trinity handed the phone back, then glanced at Emmy. "I'll run into the shop when your dad drops me off and get you a snack for the ride home, okay?"

Emmy nodded. "Spaghetti."

"Not in the car," he quickly interjected. "But we could take some home."

Trinity reached back and patted Emmy's knee. "I'll see what we have in the shop."

"Can I pick?"

"Sure." Trinity never minded letting Emmy be involved in what they did.

"Will you be staying at the ranch tonight?" Something about Trinity seemed off and it concerned him. Maybe it had to do with all the drama with Steph and Emmy. Maybe she was worried about work.

"I've been gone most of the day. I'll probably need to close. Plus it's not a good time for us to finish the discussion we started this morning."

Shit. He forgot about his business proposal.

"Like I said earlier, it's not what you think." He pulled into the *Almost Homemade* lot and parked out front.

"It's been a long day." She slipped out of the car without another word.

Emmy unbuckled, scrambled into the front seat, and climbed out with her.

His girls walked toward the shop door hand in hand. He went after them, knowing he needed to explain, but also understanding now wasn't the time.

Emmy followed Trinity back behind the counter like she owned the place, too. Trinity picked her up and held Emmy on her hip. She grabbed a to-go container and let the little girl check out all the hot food behind the counter.

"I want the spaghetti and the cheesy thing." Emmy pointed to the chicken broccoli cheesy casserole thing that looked amazing.

"Make us a big one of that."

Trinity set Emmy down and made one large container of each of Emmy's choices, then added a salad for him, garlic toast wrapped in foil, and two big brownies to the meal she placed in the large bag.

He held up his credit card.

She stared blankly at him, shook her head, and handed the bag over.

The guy who'd interrupted his meeting with Trinity that morning came up behind her and tapped her on the shoulder. She nearly jumped out of her skin, spun around at the same time she shoved Emmy behind her, and then put her hands up to ward off an attack that never came.

The guy startled and stopped short. "Sorry. I didn't mean to scare you. I just wanted to talk to you about selling the store."

Trinity's whole body trembled. She glanced from the guy in front of her to Jon, then ran into the kitchen.

He'd seen that panicked look before and went after her, waving for Emmy to follow him. He found Trinity halfway up the stairs to her apartment, sitting with her head between her knees and completely out of breath. Her whole body shook, and sweat had broken out down her back.

He knelt on a step below her and brushed his hand over her head. "You're okay, sweetheart."

She shook her head. "No. I—I'm not. So stu-stu-pid."

"It was just a scare. That's all." He rubbed his hand up and down her back, trying to soothe her.

Emmy scooted by him and hugged Trinity. "Don't be sad."

Trinity raised her head, sucked in a deep breath to calm the ragged pants, wiped the sweat from her brow all while Emmy tried to hold her around the neck.

Trinity hooked her arm around Emmy. "I'm okay. I just couldn't catch my breath."

"When I cry too hard, Mama gives me water."

How often did that happen? Jon stood. "I'll get you a glass." He went back down into the large kitchen and pulled a paper cup from the dispenser by the sink and filled it.

Trinity stood and held hands with Emmy as they walked back down the stairs and met him. She took the cup and guzzled the water, then glanced down at Emmy. "I feel much better." Her gaze found his. "Thank you."

"Are you really okay? If there's something I can do . . ." He wished he could take away the pain and trauma that haunted her.

"I'm fine. It's . . . fine." But Trinity's eyes went wide again. "What are you doing here?"

Jon turned toward the blond guy walking up behind him.

"Didn't you see me out front at the register?"

"I . . . I guess I didn't."

The blond kept a close eye on Trinity. "Is there something going on with you and Nathan? Is he bothering you? If he is, you should fire him."

"Who is this?" Jon broke into their conversation.

Trinity quickly shook her head as if to clear it. "Sorry. Uh, this is my brother Tate. Tate, Jon and his daughter, Emmy."

Tate held his hand out. "We need to talk about the horses I found for you." But he didn't give Jon a chance to say anything about that before he turned to his sister. "You. Nathan. What's up?"

"Nothing. It's been a long day. I'm tired. I didn't see him come up behind me. I overreacted."

Emmy tapped Tate's arm. "You're Trinity's brother."

Tate bent low. "Yeah. I am. She told me how much she loves spending time with you."

Emmy beamed him a smile, then turned to Jon. "I want a brother."

Tate's eyes bounced from him to Trinity and back. "Something you want to tell me?"

"No," he and Trinity said in unison.

Tate eyed Jon for a moment and decided to drop it. "If you're having a hard time after—"

"I'm fine," she said, cutting him off. "I need to get to work. We were supposed to do inventory today."

"I took care of it."

Trinity held her arms out, then let them drop back to her thighs. "What are you even doing here?"

"When Adria found out you had to leave for a tiny-tot emergency"—he bopped Emmy on the head with his palm—"she called me in for backup at the store."

"Oh. Okay. Well, thank you."

"You're welcome." Tate turned back to Jon. "About those horses."

"I'm hungry," Emmy announced.

He knew that was coming sooner rather than later. "I'm sorry, but we'll have to discuss that another time. I need to get her home and fed. She's got a homework packet to catch up on."

Tate smiled down at Emmy. "I'm glad I got to meet you, tiny tot. I love your hair. Very sophisticated."

Emmy hid her smile and face in Jon's thigh.

Jon appreciated the way Tate engaged Emmy. Especially today of all days.

"Don't forget to take the food," Trinity reminded him.

"I really need to talk to you." He didn't want to leave things unsettled between them.

"It can wait. I need to get to work." She tried to walk

past him, but he took her trembling hand to stop her. She looked up at him, something strange and unsure in her eyes.

"You have no idea how much I appreciate having you with me today. Emmy and I needed you, and you being there made everything better. So thank you."

Trinity's eyes glassed over. "I love her."

His chest went tight. He hoped that love extended to him, too, because what he felt for her, he'd never felt for anyone else. And because it was so big and new and all-encompassing, he didn't have words to adequately express it. So he kissed her, hoping she felt everything he poured into the simple yet poignant touch.

Deep inside, he wished Trinity was Emmy's mom and that she was his forever.

He ended the sweet kiss and stared into her eyes, hoping she saw those wishes and how earnest he was about making them come true.

She put her hand on his chest and fisted his shirt in it. "I'll see you soon." She still seemed conflicted, but she wasn't backing away.

"I will explain everything."

Tate jumped in. "What's going on with you two?"

"Leave it alone," Trinity warned.

Nathan stood in the entry and interjected, "She's selling the shop."

"*Almost Homemade* is not for sale." Fed up, she gave Jon a disgruntled look, then walked back into the main part of the store.

Tate and Nathan looked to him for an answer. "This is between me and her." He picked up Emmy and followed Trinity back into the shop to pick up the food she'd packed for them, say one last goodbye, then reluctantly head home. All he wanted to do was have a conversation with Trinity, but somehow that had become complicated. And it shouldn't be. Not after all the time they'd spent together and how close they'd become.

But he needed to get home and call his lawyer and prepare for a visit from the authorities investigating whether or not Steph's neglect and abuse meant he got full custody.

Probably not. Because they always favored the mother and gave them every chance to do right by their kid. Yes, Emmy needed her mother. The psychological damage of taking her away could be deep and long-lasting. But Steph could inflict even more harm if given a chance she didn't deserve.

Trinity was helping a customer at the counter. He didn't want to hover and take her away from work any longer than he already had, so he picked up the bag of food, gave Trinity a smile, and hoped she'd call him later.

If not, he'd call her after he put Emmy to bed.

He walked out of the store and found Tate standing off to the side of the lot. They met by Jon's car as he loaded Emmy and the bag of food. He kept Emmy's door open and turned to Tate. "What's up?" He really didn't need a brotherly interrogation about his and Trinity's relationship right now.

Tate pointed his thumb over his shoulder. "What happened in there?"

"What do you mean?" He didn't give anything away.

"She got totally spooked. All the blood drained from her face and she fled."

So this was about Trinity's emotional state. He pulled his phone out and tapped the color-matching game Emmy liked to play. "Here, sweetheart, you can play this while I talk to Tate."

Emmy took the phone and he waved Tate to move to

the back of the vehicle where they could speak without Emmy overhearing them.

"Do you blame Trinity after what happened with that guy Clint? I know you and Liz had a deadly run-in with him, and so did Trinity."

Tate raked his fingers over his hair. "I was scared to death he'd kill her."

"She was, too, which is why she doesn't like anyone sneaking up behind her. It sets her off. The nightmare comes back."

Tate gripped the back of his neck. "I had no idea this was still going on. In the beginning, sure, we all saw how guarded she was and how she'd gone quiet. But I thought . . . over time . . . well, I hoped it had faded away."

"Maybe it was easier for you and Liz because you have each other. She lives alone in the place she was taken from. This is supposed to be a safe place for her. For the most part, I think she sees it that way, but I parked out back once and I could see that going out there disturbed her." He didn't want to give away all of Trinity's secrets, but Tate's deep concern allowed him to open up. "She checks the locks here and at my place at least three times. She tries to stand so that no one can come up behind her. She doesn't have nightmares most nights, but believe me, the couple times she did were not fun. She kicks and screams and wakes up in a cold sweat."

Tate stared up at the sky, taking that all in. "We knew she had some lingering anxiety and . . . overly cautious behavior. But I didn't think it was still this bad."

"She gets by most days without it really interfering in her life. I'd like to think being with me and Emmy helps her focus on good things and not the past."

"We're all happy that she has you. At the last family

dinner, we all noticed the difference in her. We hadn't seen her so relaxed and happy. She teased and engaged everyone like she used to before everything happened. It's why I was so surprised to see her kind of lose it over something that seemed as innocuous as Nathan coming up behind her."

"She told me a little about Drake. I'm sure he's got his good days and bad. Though he went through a hell of a lot more than her, it's all trauma." He glanced toward the shop, thinking about Trinity. "This thing today with Emmy was emotional. Trinity turned Emmy's distress into a day of pampering and helped her get past the bad stuff and smile again. I think that's all we can do for Trinity. Be there for her when she needs us."

"That's the thing—she doesn't lean on us."

"I think she leans on Adria the most because they work together. But she knows you're all there for her."

That seemed to ease Tate's mind and relax his tense shoulders. "Okay. But you'll let us know if things change or get worse for some reason."

"I will. Like I said, most days it doesn't intrude on her life. Others, like today, something happens and she deals with it the best she can. She's really strong. She understands it's her mind's way of dealing even if it is hard on her."

Tate shifted from one foot to the other and hit him with his next concern. "What's this about you trying to buy *Almost Homemade*?"

"I'm a businessman. I have some experience in the grocery store industry. I want to *talk* to Trinity and Adria about it. That's all." He wanted to clear things up with Trinity himself without Tate going to her and explaining for him. He wanted to make his plans for the business, and for them, clear.

"They've worked really hard to build this thing. I can't imagine they'd simply want to just sell it all."

"Their plans to expand it are impressive."

Tate tilted his head. "You believe in what they're doing."

"They are smart businesswomen. The concept is great. I'm not surprised others have made offers on the business. Getting in now, while they're still expanding, it's a smart move."

"And you're a savvy businessman."

Jon nodded, but didn't add to what he'd already told Tate, except . . . "I'm looking toward the future." With Trinity. But that was also for him and Trinity to discuss. So he changed the subject this time. "About the horses . . ."

"I can have them delivered this week if you're ready. Unless you want to check them out first."

"You're the expert. I trust you found suitable horses. But instead of just the two for me and Emmy, I want a third for Trinity, so she can ride with us."

"I can bring her horse over from Cedar Top."

"That would be great. She spends a lot of time with us, and now she'll be able to have her horse there, too."

"I'm sure Luna will be happy to spend more time with her."

"I like the name."

"Yeah, she's white with gray speckles. She looks like the moon, so that's what Trinity named her."

"Emmy will love to hear about that and see Luna."

"I'll text you with the delivery details."

"Sounds good."

"Are you planning on running cattle?" Tate studied him.

"Eventually. Right now I have my hands full with my

daughter." And the very real possibility that Steph could decide she wanted to go home to California where she had family support that would bolster her case for keeping Emmy.

"Maybe Declan and I can talk to you about that. We're looking to expand our operation to supply *Almost Homemade* as they open new stores."

That fit into his plans with Trinity perfectly. "Great idea. Let's talk soon. Right now, I need to get Emmy home."

"No problem. And hey, I like seeing the way you and Trinity are together. She deserves to be happy."

"I've never been as happy as I am with her."

That earned him a nod of approval from Tate. Not that he needed it. He intended to keep making Trinity happy.

"Get tiny tot home. I'll see you later this week." Tate waved bye and went back into the shop.

Jon went to Emmy's door to close it. She was still playing her game, but when the phone chimed with a text, she handed it to him.

He closed the game and pulled up the text.

STEPH: DPHHS came to my work!!!
STEPH: They interviewed me and are coming to my place tonight.
STEPH: My lawyer is not going to let you get away with this.

So Daddy came through and hired a lawyer for Steph. He expected it, but it still grated that her family was helping Steph continue to make Emmy miserable. And now they all had to go through this tedious process that would end with Steph doing what she had to do to keep

Emmy but ultimately wouldn't change who she was or how she acted when no one was watching.

He sighed and checked Emmy's buckle. "Ready to go, sweetheart."

"When is Trinity coming?"

"We might not see her until tomorrow." He hated that she didn't plan to drive out to stay overnight with him like she'd done so many other nights. Distance was the last thing he wanted from her.

Maybe he should have kept business out of their relationship. But when he had an idea, especially one this good, he had to go for it. And that it included Trinity, well, that just made it better.

He hoped he could get her to accept his proposal.

Chapter Nineteen

TRINITY ONCE again read the text messages Jon sent last night. They made her smile and hope for things to go back to the way they were before he had decided to talk business.

She wanted something much more personal with him.

JON: Emmy's in bed I'm alone and missing you

That was at 8:04 p.m.
At 9:22 p.m. he sent . . .

JON: I should give you a key so you can come over whenever you want

At 10:47 p.m. . . . .

JON: Why aren't you in bed with me???
JON: I miss you

She texted him back at 11:01 p.m. . . . .

TRINITY: I miss you 2 let's fix this tomorrow

JON: I want to make things even better between us
that's all
JON: If you don't like what I have to say I'll drop it
and it's just you and me and Emmy like always

At 11:04 p.m. she ended with . . .

TRINITY: I like it when it's the 3 of us
JON: I like it when you're here with me

She should have driven out to see him. They could
have cleared the air and spent the night together. She
didn't believe, at least she didn't want to, that he wanted
to buy her company and somehow cut her out of it. It
just didn't make sense. Yes, it would be a good business
deal for him. But why buy it from her and reap all the
benefits for himself? He had to know that wouldn't sit
well with her.

Which is why he wouldn't do that to her.

She wondered if it might be something like he did
with the grocery stores he helped save. Except she and
Adria already owned the buildings they opened the
shops in, so that concept wouldn't work.

She really had no idea what he wanted to propose.

She tamped down the rising hope that maybe it was
something more personal.

"How could you lie to me?" Nathan startled her out
of her thoughts.

She turned to him, her heart pounding, hands shaking,
but she kept her head and didn't let the panic overwhelm
her. "I'm sorry, but—"

"I hooked you up with Bountiful Foods. They made
you a great offer, and you turned them down. Now
you're taking an offer from your boyfriend."

She didn't understand the anger in his voice and why this seemed so personal to him.

"What I was going to say before you interrupted me was, it's none of your business what I do with *Almost Homemade*. It's *my* business. My decision. *You* work for *me*." She tilted her head and studied him. "Why are you even here? You should be at the Billings store doing your job."

"I came to talk some sense into you."

"Excuse me?" How dare her employee talk to her that way.

"Bountiful Foods is ready to pay you a fortune for your stores. You wouldn't have to work ever again. They'd expand *Almost Homemade* in a way you can't on your own. Take the deal."

"No." She didn't owe any further explanation.

"Why are you being so stubborn about this? If you want more money, I'm sure they can sweeten the deal within reason."

"You are late for work. Get back to Billings. Do your job if you want to keep it."

Nathan took a menacing step closer. "You're being unreasonable."

She held her ground even though everything in her screamed for her to run. "You've overstepped. I've given you, and them, my answer." She held his gaze when his angry eyes narrowed. "Do you want to keep your job or not?"

"You need to listen to me. I have the experience in the food industry you don't."

"That's why I hired you to run the Billings store. And you've done a great job. I've known you since culinary school. I admired your drive. I appreciate that you're passionate about the deal Bountiful offered us."

"I helped put that deal together. It's extremely generous."

She had no idea he'd worked with Bountiful Foods to put together the offer. She wondered if there was something in it for him if she took it. "As you know, Adria and I have plans to continue to expand the business. More stores. We'd love to get our products into larger grocery chains."

"Adria is about to have twins and you're wrapped up in your boyfriend and his kid. I wouldn't be surprised if you got married and had kids, too, which means you won't be able to work."

"First, that's a completely sexist and antiquated way of thinking. I can have a family and work."

The eye roll pissed her off.

"Second, my relationship with Jon is none of your business. I'm paying you to do your job. Third, while I value your input on the operation and the menu, Adria and I make the final decisions about the business."

"Maybe I should be talking to her."

"You're out of line," Adria said from directly behind him.

Nathan didn't know it, but Adria had walked into the kitchen and overheard the last part of their conversation.

His eyes went wide, he pressed his lips tight, then turned to Adria. "You've been taking more time off because of your pregnancy. You'll be home with your twins for months. You know you can't dedicate the time and attention to the business it deserves. Bountiful Foods can see your vision and make it a reality."

Adria stared hard at Nathan. "Trinity and I are on the same page, the way we always are when we come to a decision. We do not want to sell. As for me, it is the luxury of owning my own business and hiring smart, dedicated employees to oversee things in my absence that makes it possible for me to take the time I need and want for my personal life. I have a loyal partner who has my back and will keep me apprised of the business in my absence."

Trinity went to Adria and stood beside her. Them against Nathan. "We gave you the job you wanted. If your heart and loyalty are to Bountiful Foods and not *Almost Homemade*, perhaps you should go work for them."

"My job was supposed to be overseeing the opening of each new store. So far, all I've done is open Billings after you opened Bozeman. Everything else is stalled."

"Delayed, yes. Stopped, no. The other stores will open. We're just taking our time, making sure we don't stretch ourselves or our finances too thin."

"Bountiful could have ten stores open over the next year."

"Good for them. Let them open their own stores. We are doing things our way."

Nathan gave them an exasperated look. "They want the *Almost Homemade* brand and reputation."

"It's not for sale," she and Adria said in unison.

Nathan stormed out.

Adria turned to her. "What was that all about?"

"Jon." He started this.

Adria raised a brow in question. "I know I missed the meeting he asked to have with us yesterday. So tell me, what does he have to do with *Almost Homemade*?"

"I think he wants to buy it."

Confusion lit Adria's eyes. "You said he owned a company. Is it in the food industry?"

"A couple aren't, no. But he kinda helps out several independent grocery stores."

Adria leaned back against the counter. "How so?"

"He buys the struggling stores' building, then keeps the rents reasonable so the stores can stay open. He invests in the stores, helps them to expand and modernize, and takes a piece of the profits. From the way he describes it, it's more about keeping the stores open in low-income and food-scarce neighborhoods than it is about making a lot of money. Which he already has because of all the other types of businesses he owned and sold over the past ten years."

"So he's an entrepreneur."

"Apparently a very successful one. He sold most of the businesses he owned and moved here to give Emmy a more family-oriented life. He wanted to have more time for her."

"Okay. So if that is the case, why does he want to buy *Almost Homemade*, which would surely take up an exorbitant amount of his time if he plans to expand it the way we do?"

"Exactly. It makes no sense. Plus he knows we aren't looking to sell. Why would I sell him the business so he could make all the money off it and still date him?"

"Did you ask him?"

She sighed. "I didn't have time to ask him anything because of what happened with Emmy. The school called right as we were about to discuss his proposal."

"Did he say he wanted to buy us out?"

"No. Not exactly." She brushed her long hair behind her ears. "He said it wasn't what I thought, and we'd talk about it later." And it weighed on her mind.

"Okay. So if he doesn't want to buy the business, maybe he has some ideas for us, or he wants to invest."

"Maybe." That sounded more promising.

Adria touched her arm. "If he makes us an offer, we can simply say no and that's the end of it."

"I guess."

"What is really bothering you?"

"Is this why he started seeing me? So he could get the inside scoop on the business and gather information to make us the offer and I'd push it with you to make him happy?"

Adria shook her head all through that. "No. I don't believe that. I don't think you do either. You've been so happy together."

"I thought so, but then he does this out of nowhere. We talk about *Almost Homemade*, but it's more about how my day went. I suppose I've given him some idea of our financial status. I've definitely spoken about how we want to expand and what that would look like. If he wanted to know all that stuff, I guess I made it easy for him."

"You're making assumptions and creating a story that may not be true at all. The best thing to do is talk to him. See what he has to say. Call him now, get to the bottom of it so you'll have your peace of mind back."

"I wish I could, but we have a cashier out today and Sunrise Farms is due any second with our delivery."

"I can cover while you make the call."

"You're not even supposed to be here. The doctor wants you home and resting for the rest of your pregnancy."

Adria sighed and rubbed her hand over her big round belly. "I know. I promised Drake I'd pick up the paperwork and my laptop and go straight home."

"You need to take care of yourself and those babies. I can handle the stores."

"I know you can. I'm just not very good at doing nothing. If I can get the paperwork, payroll, and inventory done, then it's less for you to worry about, and you'll have more time with Jon and Emmy."

"I appreciate that. I do, but I don't want you overdo-ing it."

"Believe me, Drake won't let me." Adria glanced around the kitchen. "Did the hydroponic greens come in for the salad kits?"

"They'll deliver to all the stores early tomorrow morning. We'll switch over to exclusively using the or-ganic greens in everything we prepare, including the spinach in our cooked dishes."

"I'm so glad we partnered with the new company. Not only will the greens be locally grown, but because they're grown indoors, we'll have fresh organic lettuce all year round for less than shipping them here."

Trinity had made the connection with the hydro-ponic growers. "That's what we're about, working with and sourcing quality ingredients locally. The hydro-ponics company can set up new locations as we do to supply us. It's a win-win for both businesses."

The back door opened and the rep from Sunrise Farms walked in with his tablet in hand, ready to make delivery of their other fruits and vegetables.

Adria touched her arm. "I'll get what I need and head home. Don't let Nathan get to you. And call Jon. Let him explain what it is he wants with *Almost Home-made* and you. I've never seen you as happy as you have been since you started seeing him. I know things have been . . . complicated with his ex, but you two seem made for each other."

"That's exactly how I've felt, and I love Emmy."

"Do you love him?"

"I think I do." She loved spending time with him. When they were apart, she thought about him all the time and couldn't wait to see him again. The time they spent together at his place with Emmy . . . It really felt like they were a family.

Marriage, expanding their family, that all just seemed inevitable to her.

Steph would never be easy to deal with, but they'd make it work somehow. She and Jon would give Emmy the stability and love and home she deserved.

She didn't want to take Steph's place, but Trinity could be to Emmy everything Steph couldn't be. Maybe with her influence, Steph would step up and try harder to be the mom Emmy needed.

"I think Jon loves you, too, Trinity, for what it's worth coming from me. I see it in the way he looks at you and how he wants you with him all the time."

She regretted leaving things hanging between them and not letting him explain yesterday before he left. The panic attack had simply made it impossible for her to think reasonably.

"Would you mind telling the Sunrise delivery guy to go ahead and start loading everything they brought into the refrigerators? I'm just going to give Jon a quick call and touch base before I verify the order." She really wanted to know how the interview went with DPHHS, too. She hoped Emmy wasn't further traumatized by having a stranger question her about what happened.

"Great. No problem." Adria went to speak to the Sunrise guy.

Trinity pulled out her cell and hit the speed dial for Jon. It rang. And rang. And rang, until his voicemail picked up. She listened to his deep, rich voice tell her to leave a message, then didn't know what to say. "Hey. It's me. Um. I just wanted to talk." She really wanted to hear his voice and some reassurance that everything between them was okay.

She hung up, disappointed their talk would have to wait and wondering why, when he always answered her call, he didn't this time.

Chapter Twenty

JON LOVED his new office with the cool silver color on the walls he used throughout the house. He bought new bright white bookcases, a light-colored wood desk, black leather chairs, and a small sofa to fill out the space. To remind him of California, he'd found three large paintings of the ocean with beach dunes and sea-grass.

Every time he came in, he felt calm and ready to work.

Except today.

He sat in front of his laptop and stared at his lawyer, Elijah, on the video call.

"Beth from DPHHS took Steph's statement yesterday at the grocery store," his lawyer told him. "By the time Beth met her at the apartment, Steph must have been advised by her lawyer. The place was clean. The fridge stocked with food. Beth had no choice but to deem the place acceptable for Emmy to return to."

"What about the marks on Emmy? The butchered haircut?"

"Steph explained them away. She had never cut anyone's hair before, and Emmy wouldn't sit still. She botched the job but intended to have it fixed after school. She never got the chance to follow through because you took Emmy even though it was Steph's day to have her. Steph has every right to cut her kid's hair, even if she does a crap job. Her explanation that Emmy had a tantrum and made the process difficult to do, well . . . Beth didn't buy it, but Emmy wasn't physically hurt because of it. I know that doesn't help, but there are thresholds that have to be met.

"The bruises were an accident. When Steph pulled Emmy up from the chair, Emmy became defiant, threw a tantrum, and pulled away, making Steph hold her arm tighter to keep her upright, leaving marks on her arm. Emmy, in a fit, tugged herself free, lost her footing, and fell into the table and hit her eye."

"Bullshit. Steph was pissed and hurt her."

"Emmy's account isn't that far off from Steph's, but I agree Steph stuck close enough to what really happened and your four-year-old didn't add anything to raise a red flag."

"Emmy had a difficult time explaining what happened. If I'd been allowed to help her during the questioning . . ."

"You know they aren't going to let you do that and make it look like you coerced her to say something."

"Pam and the principal had to back up Emmy's account that her mother hurt her on purpose."

"They couldn't say that Emmy's distress wasn't caused more by her classmate calling her ugly than what her mother did to her. They didn't *see* the bruises on Emmy."

"I should have shown them." Only he and Trinity were in the room when he took the pictures of Emmy's arm and eye. Damn. He'd missed an opportunity to have witnesses.

"Emmy told Pam her mother was mean. Kids say that all the time."

"What about the photos I gave you of the apartment?"

"The ones you took when you entered the dwelling without Steph's permission." Elijah's chiding tone didn't help. "We'll hold on to them and only use the pictures if we need them. Right now, Steph looks bad, but not bad enough to lose custody. Beth's recommendation to the judge that Steph take a parenting class was accepted. Steph promised not to leave Emmy alone again, and understands if she does she could get into hot water. Beth will follow up with a home visit in two weeks."

"Do you have any idea what Steph could do in that amount of time? How much does Emmy have to endure while Steph's neglect and abuse rise to the threshold where someone finally does something about it?"

"I know it sucks, but you're doing what you need to do."

It didn't feel like he was getting anywhere. Not when he had to send Emmy back to her mother, who basically got away with what she'd done. She'd attend the parenting class, but she probably wouldn't pay attention to any of it.

"Steph's new lawyer sent over a counterclaim to our request for full custody."

Of course Daddy came through and paid for Steph's lawyer. Great. He expected a fight; it just sucked having to put Emmy through it.

Elijah went on. "She's furious and says you're trying to steal her daughter. And I quote, 'He's just being mean.' Seriously, her lawyer put that in her complaint." Elijah rolled his eyes.

Frustration got the better of him and he snarled, "Let me guess—he's buying Steph's story about what happened with Emmy."

"He's defending his client. He states this was an isolated incident that will not be repeated."

Jon grew more frustrated. "Things have escalated to this," he pointed out.

"Have you seen Steph hit or grab her hard like that before? Have you seen bruises on Emmy that can't be easily explained by normal child mishaps while playing?"

"I saw her grab her arm once before, but otherwise, no." The admission made him feel deflated. "But Emmy doesn't want to be with her anymore."

"We have to prove that it is because Steph hurts her, not because they don't get along and end up arguing with each other."

"Emmy gets sassy with her because of the way Steph treats her."

"Steph's position is clear. If you don't like the way she disciplines Emmy, she's happy to have a discussion with you about it, and come to an agreement about how you will both handle future incidents."

"What about her leaving Emmy alone?"

"It's in Beth's report. According to the document, Steph was only gone for a short time and felt Emmy was safe in the locked apartment watching TV. She said it only happened once, and like I said, she promised it won't happen again."

"Bullshit," he snapped. "Emmy said she'd done it more than once."

"You can only prove the one time because your friend found Emmy alone. Emmy's testimony would help your case, but because she is so against being with her mother, it's likely Steph's attorney would argue that you coached Emmy to say that and you've turned Emmy against Steph."

"Seriously? I've never badmouthed Steph to Emmy. Ever. I don't have to. Emmy sees her mother's bad behavior. She feels how little Steph cares about her."

His cell phone rang beside him. He sucked in a calming breath and checked caller ID, thankful to see Trinity's number and not Steph's. He couldn't deal with Steph right now. He'd probably chew her out again and make things worse.

"Do you need to take that?" Elijah asked.

"No." He hated to ignore Trinity's call, especially when their relationship seemed rocky right now. How could he blame her? Their dates got ruined because of Steph. She left work to help him with Emmy because of Steph. They constantly had to change plans or alter them because he had Emmy on days she should be with Steph.

Not that Trinity minded those things. She never complained. But it had to be wearing on her the way it was on him.

He wanted some normalcy. A routine that worked for them, and especially Emmy.

"We have a good case to go to court, but we could use more than what we've got. It's your word against Steph about the pot smoking, drinking, and neglect. If you can get pictures of that, then we'd have absolute proof she's being a bad influence. The school records help with the neglect, but the other things, like not feeding her properly, bathing her, and taking care of her the way you want her to do it . . . well, that's up to the judge to decide if he agrees with you or Steph. Beth reported that Emmy's basic needs are met when she's with her mother."

Emmy deserved better than that.

"The judge will most likely begin by instructing you to try to come to a new custody agreement, though

Steph's attorney made it clear they are not giving you full custody."

"Let me guess—she likes things the way they are."

"She wants to keep the current arrangement. She's made a good faith effort to do as you asked and have the apartment in order and food for Emmy when she has her. She's proven that on your video calls, so you can't dispute that."

No, he couldn't. But that didn't mean Emmy was safe with her mom.

"It's in your favor that despite the fact you don't have to pay child support because you have equal time with Emmy that you pay for Steph's apartment. It shows you're generous, and that even if the judge didn't give you full custody, but majority days of the week, you would be willing to forgo any child support from Steph, which could be a hardship for her, especially if you stopped her rent payments because Emmy lives with you."

"While I'd love to cut her off, I won't stop the rent payments until a judge decides the case because I don't want to look vindictive."

"Steph is already playing that card. She claims you want to keep Emmy so you and your new girlfriend— congrats by the way. I hear she's a great person and really nice and Emmy loves her, which pisses Steph off. Anyway, Steph thinks you'll get married and take Emmy and she'll be cut out of the picture, you'll poison Emmy against her, and she'll never see her daughter again."

"While things with Trinity are headed in that direction, I hope, it doesn't mean we want to cut Steph out. I just want to limit the time she has Emmy alone. At least until Emmy is older and can better care for herself and speak up when she's not being treated well and get help if she needs it."

"I've seen this a lot, Jon. All I can say is, you need to accept that this is the best Steph can do. She isn't capable of more. It's been four years and things have been steadily declining to this point. Some people are great with babies but just don't have the patience or heart to deal with toddlers and preschoolers. They don't understand that kids have a mind of their own. Steph is frustrated that raising Emmy is hard work."

"Then why won't she let me carry the bigger share of the load?"

"For better or worse, she's Emmy's mom, and she doesn't want to give up her child."

"So we fight." He'd do anything for his little girl, including going through this arduous process. And hey, it could be worse. "I am so glad I never married her."

"If you're really thinking about marrying Trinity, I'll send you a prenup."

Jon didn't want to think about how that would go down with Trinity. She was already on edge about him coming to her with a business proposal that he hadn't even explained yet. But the prenup would protect Trinity's interests, too.

"Fine. What do you suggest I do about Steph?"

"Until a judge rules on the new custody request, stick to the agreement in place, document everything, and hold Steph accountable. If we don't get full custody, I'll make our second offer. You take Emmy Monday through Friday. Steph gets Emmy nine to six Saturday and Sunday. No sleepovers, unless you agree to them. You'll alternate holidays per your original agreement."

"Even that would be better for Emmy than what we have in place now."

Elijah agreed with a nod. "I know you don't want to hear this or for anything else to happen to Emmy, but if it does, it's more ammunition for us to take to the judge. Neglect and abuse are usually a pattern of behavior. Be vigilant. Keep up your video calls with Emmy after school. Check in on her as often as you can. Don't let there be an opportunity for Steph to do any harm. Take Emmy every time Steph calls unable to care for or deal with her. Document that. It will show that shorter visitations would be beneficial to her and Emmy."

He hated that this process took so long. He just wanted Emmy here with him.

"Okay. We wait for the court date. Until then DPHHS will check in with her in two weeks. It seems so far away. And you'll be here to present the case with the attorney you're coordinating with here in Montana?"

Elijah nodded. "I've handed over all we've done here in California. I'll fly in and attend the hearing as co-counsel."

He had to pay two attorneys, but it was the safer bet to be sure nothing fell through the cracks.

Elijah knew him and Steph. It would take too long for a new attorney to get acquainted with everything they'd been through in such detail.

Steph would be at a disadvantage there.

"Don't be discouraged, Jon." Elijah always seemed confident. "If Steph continues like this, and it looks like she will, you'll get what you want."

"I just don't want things to get worse before that happens."

"We are doing all we can right now."

Jon hung up with a heavy heart. Only one person could make him feel better after that exhausting and frustrating call. He picked up his cell and tapped the screen to play the voice mail Trinity left him.

She said few words, but they packed a punch. She sounded unsure and hesitant about reaching out to him when he wanted her to know and feel like she could always count on him. He'd gone about approaching her with his business proposal all wrong. He should have been up front with her about his thoughts and ideas.

Instead, he'd kept them to himself because he wanted to have it all mapped out so she could see what he had in mind and how it would make all her long-term goals for *Almost Homemade* possible.

He called her back, eager to hear her voice and set this right, but he got her voice mail. Knowing she had a full and busy day didn't help ease his mind or the disappointment that he didn't get to talk to her. "Hey, sweetheart. Sorry I missed your call. I was on a video conference with my attorney. About Steph. And Emmy. Let's just say, it didn't go the way I wanted. You and I definitely need to talk. I'm sorry I've left you feeling like . . . I don't know what you're feeling to tell you the truth, but I know it's come between us and that's the last thing I want to happen. You're more important to me than anything, so let's clear the air and get back to being happy together. I missed you so much last night."

More than he could possibly say. Enough that it kept him up and made him think about their future and what needed to happen so they could be together all the time.

He thought moving here meant his life would be simpler. When he was with Trinity, it felt that way. Somehow, some way he was going to get everything on track. He didn't like that Emmy, Trinity, and he were all off in some way. They'd shared so many good times and days together. He wanted more of that.

He wanted more of everything with them.

Chapter Twenty-One

Trinity CHECKED the time on the voice mail Jon had left yesterday. She winced, feeling like shit for not calling him back last night. But last night had been crazy—they'd had an unexpected dinner rush, and she'd stayed to clean up. She had finally made it up to her apartment only to crash on her couch while she waited for dinner to warm in the microwave.

It was still in there in the morning when her alarm went off and she found herself fully clothed, shoes on, still sleeping on the sofa.

In a hurry to open the shop, she'd quickly showered, put on new clothes, and hauled ass downstairs to meet the morning crew to open the store. The early-morning bakers had done their jobs and were headed out when she came down.

The store was humming with activity. Adria was in the office doing paperwork. She promised she'd stay only for an hour, then go home and rest like she was supposed to do.

With the store shelves, refrigerated cabinets, and hot counter all stocked and ready for the lunch crowd, she took a seat at one of the tables by the front windows and listened to Jon's message, hoping he wasn't upset with her for not calling him back yesterday. He probably thought she was ignoring him. That's the last thing she wanted him to think. Then again, she'd been very busy yesterday, but that didn't mean she couldn't have taken the time to call and check in with him like she did most days.

She didn't like this odd state they were in and wanted to find a way to get back to where they were when everything was so good between them.

She'd never had a relationship like they shared, and she didn't want to lose it over something they hadn't even taken the time to discuss.

She could only imagine the drama, uncertainty, and strife he faced now that the Department of Public Health and Human Services had gotten involved with Emmy. Poor Jon. He wanted to do right by his daughter. And Emmy had to be feeling uncertain and confused by all of it.

She tapped the screen for her voice mail. Jon's deep voice settled her. His message was sweet, his voice filled with longing to be speaking to her instead of leaving her a message.

She really appreciated that and so much more about him.

And she hated that she hadn't even bothered to check her phone last night. She should have and called him back if only to say she'd missed him yesterday, was too tired to talk, but she'd connect with him today.

She called him now, ready to make apologies and set things right between them.

"Trinity." He didn't say hello, just her name filled with relief. "I'm sorry. For whatever it is you're thinking or feeling about the other day. Really. I'm so sorry. I just want us to get back to where we were."

All the anxiety in her heart evaporated. "Jon, I'm the

one who's sorry. I worked like a demon yesterday and didn't see your message until this morning. I passed out last night without even looking at my phone."

"I miss you. I miss *us*."

Her heart melted. "I do, too. I don't even know what it is that's come between us. You had something you wanted to say to me and I don't even know what it is, so why am I holding back?"

"You don't have to. Nothing about the business proposal is worth losing you and what we have together."

"You're not losing me. It's been a long couple days with work and the thing with Emmy and Steph and I don't know . . . I'm tired, I guess, but my wanting to be with you hasn't changed."

"Then say you'll come out to the ranch tonight so we can talk in person and put things back to the way we both want them to be."

She should stay until the shop closed, but she didn't want this thing with Jon to continue any longer. "I can probably get out of here by five." If she tried to leave any later, she'd inevitably get caught up in the dinner rush and not escape until closing.

"How about I barbecue steaks? I'll make some baked potatoes and a salad or something and we'll have dinner together and talk."

"You do the steaks and potatoes. I'll bring the salads." She could grab a few out of the refrigerator case and hold them in hers upstairs until she left tonight.

"Look at us doing things together again," Jon teased, but she sensed his relief that they'd see each other soon and work this out.

"I really can't wait to see you tonight." She wanted to reassure him. She hoped he heard how much she meant it, so much so her stomach fluttered with anticipation.

"I hope that means you'll stay. It's been too long since we've been together."

She really missed kissing him and having his arms around her. "I'll bring my overnight bag."

"Maybe you should bring some stuff to leave here." He waited a beat, then added, "Maybe you should just stay here."

Her heart pounded in her chest. "That sounds like a bigger conversation."

"All you have to say is yes."

She wanted to say it, but she held back because they still needed to get back on the same page. "It's not a no."

"Then I'll do my best to convince you to say yes tonight."

She wondered if he hoped to get her to say yes to the business deal, whatever it was, too, but didn't want to get into it right now. They'd see each other tonight, talk, and she'd know exactly what he wanted and where they stood.

"Listen, Trinity, if you need more time, I will wait however long you need to decide, but I want you to know I'm all in. I get that my life is complicated with Emmy and Steph and that's a lot for you to take on."

"Jon, I don't want you to think that because it's not the case. I mean, yes, the trouble with Steph is . . . difficult, but I love Emmy. You know I love her."

"You're everything I want for myself and her."

And that told her everything she needed to know. "How can I say no to that?" Her heart felt so full to bursting she pressed her hand to her chest.

"Don't."

"I can't."

"I know we still need to have that talk. We will. I promise. But I know everything is going to be okay now, so that makes the rest easy."

She felt the same way. "You said in your message that you spoke to your attorney."

"Beth from DPHHS interviewed me, Emmy, Steph, the people at Emmy's school."

"I had a brief conversation with her. I told her about my interactions with you and Emmy. Basically, I confirmed what you'd already told her."

"I'm sorry you had to get involved. Steph and I are at the point I hoped we'd never get to, battling for custody instead of working things out together. I knew it would come to this eventually, but when she said she wanted to move, start a new life here, I thought she was ready to make a real change." Jon sighed. "I'm worried that she'll want to go back to California. Her lawyer will probably advise her that it's best for her to show she has family support to help her."

"Does that mean you'd move back with her?"

Jon didn't say anything for a long moment. "I hope it doesn't come to that."

"But you need to put Emmy first." She understood, but it would break her heart to lose them both now. She and Jon were just getting started on what felt like something that could be a forever kind of love.

"Yes. She needs me. And I need you. I hope you know that, whatever happens."

She didn't really know what to say. Her life was here. Her family was here. Her job. Would she give it all up to be with Jon and Emmy?

Maybe.

"We have a court date coming up in two weeks, along with Beth doing another check-in with Steph. Until then, I keep a close eye on Emmy and Steph and document everything, even though I want to keep her at the ranch with me." Bitterness filled his voice and every word.

"I'm sorry, Jon."

"I've asked myself the last few days how I could ever be with her."

"It didn't last because whatever spark that brought you two together fizzled out because she wasn't right for you."

"That's for sure. Everything I ever wanted, I found in you."

"Oh Jon, I feel that way, too."

"I try not to regret my time with Steph because it gave me Emmy, but it's damn hard."

"She's the best of what you two had. Totally worth it, if you ask me." Though she wondered how long Jon and Emmy could endure Steph's bad behavior before things came to a head and ended in an all-out fight.

"I just wish Steph and I could have a nice, normal friendship, so we could parent Emmy together instead of always being at odds."

"Stop trying to get her to change and expecting her to be someone she's not. Find her strengths, work with those, and compensate for her weaknesses. Emmy will be better off for it."

"I love that you're always thinking of Emmy and what's best for her. I wish I could put you first all the time, the way you put her first."

"Jon, I understand that she needs you to make her your priority. That's how it should be. She's lucky to have a wonderful dad like you."

"Emmy and I are lucky to have you."

Her heart overflowed with . . . love. She loved him. Admitting it to herself, knowing it absolutely solidified all those dreams she couldn't wait to make a reality. With him.

She didn't want to think about him moving back to

California. Or what she'd do if faced with the decision to stay or go with them.

She hoped it didn't come to that. "I'll see you tonight."

"Not soon enough, but I'll take it."

"And Jon . . ."

"Yeah?"

"Everything is going to be all right." If they loved each other, they could work anything out. It sounded easy, but she knew it would be very hard if they were faced with a possible separation.

She hoped Steph turned things around and stayed here in Montana where she could support Emmy on her own, live a good life, and be someone new if that's what she truly wanted.

"As long as you and I stick together, I know that's true."

They said their goodbyes, and she hung up feeling a lot better and lighter for talking to him, but also worried about what came next. She couldn't wait to see him tonight. Emmy would be with her mom; they'd have dinner and time to talk, then they could reconnect in a whole other way when they were in each other's arms. They had the whole night to explore the love growing and strengthening between them.

She made a mental list of what she'd like to take with her. Something sexy, and naughty, to wear for him. The strappy black lace thong and bra set she ordered online that arrived the other day made the top of her list. She had some extra bathroom essentials she could leave at his place.

Their place?

That sounded good to her. But how long would that be if Steph wanted to move back to California?

One step at a time, the cautious part of her warned.

If she wanted to spend the night with him, and turn that into every night, she needed to get back to work so she could leave early and they could continue their conversation. But first, she went to the refrigerated cabinet, took out two salads, and brought them upstairs to her place. Later, she'd pack her bag, grab the salads, and head to his place where they'd talk about the future she hoped they had together.

Yep, that felt right. It felt perfect.

And a little scary, because with Steph involved, nothing felt certain.

Chapter Twenty-Two

JON MADE his way through the grocery store aisles, picking up the steaks, potatoes, and other groceries he needed at the house. He couldn't wait to see Trinity tonight. They needed the alone time to reconnect.

He hated dropping the bomb on her that if things went south with Steph he might have to move back to California. He didn't want to. In fact, raising Emmy on the ranch, running cattle, being with Trinity, and helping her with *Almost Homemade* sounded like a damn good life to him.

If only Steph would . . .

He let that thought go. There were too many things he hoped Steph would do.

He picked up a couple bottles of wine and a case of beer and headed for the checkout, grateful he managed to do all his shopping without running into Steph. He hoped she was holed up in the back office and he could get out of here without a confrontation.

But Steph didn't stop him before he checked out; the store owner, his buddy Henry, did.

"Jon. I was hoping I'd see you soon." Henry glanced around like he was looking for someone.

Jon had a feeling they were both avoiding the same woman. "It's good to see you. How's business?"

"We're the only store in town, so great."

"What's your take on *Almost Homemade*?"

"I like their concept. It's something I've wanted to add to the store here so shoppers can pick up quick and easy ready-made meals. We have some in the deli, but nothing like what they've done."

"Ever thought about partnering with them?" It was part of the proposal he'd put together for Trinity and Adria. No harm in laying the groundwork now. Even if Trinity didn't go along with his plan, he could connect her with Henry and they could work something out.

"Yes. In fact, it's part of why I wanted to hire a new manager here." Henry inherited the family business, but he didn't want to run the stores on a daily basis. He loved being a veterinarian, not a businessman, which was why he'd approached Jon to buy him out.

Henry's eyes filled with frustration. "Part of the directive I gave Stephanie is to connect with *Almost Homemade* and follow up on the proposal they delivered to us." He tapped Jon on the shoulder. "I'm still waiting to hear from you about buying this place." Henry held up his hand. "I know. You're still settling in. You've got plans to be a rancher. You could manage this place with your eyes closed. But I can't keep up with my day job and the stores. Which leads me to why I stopped you. Stephanie, well, it's been challenging working with her."

Great. This was the last thing he needed. "How so?"

Steph was more than qualified to do the job. She'd managed a small clothing store before the move. She knew how to schedule shifts, direct her employees, and find solutions to problems. Mostly she knew how to delegate so she did as little of the actual work as possible but still looked good because tasks got done.

Henry's eyes filled with concern. "She's late more often than not, which sets a bad example for our employees. While she does her work, she's not very conscientious about it. It's sloppy and lacks attention to detail."

Just like keeping her apartment clean.

"It's like she doesn't care."

Jon thought that about her all the time. And in relation to Emmy, it made him sad.

"I see it. The employees feel it. I'm not sure she's the right fit."

"Listen, Henry, I appreciate that you gave her the job to begin with, but I don't expect you to . . . give her special treatment. It's up to her to earn and keep the job."

And if she lost it, that might be another reason for her to move back to California, complicating his life even more, and possibly making him lose Trinity. The thought broke his heart and made it hard to breathe.

But Henry had to do what he had to do for his business.

Jon got that. "If she's not meeting your expectations and the job requirements, by all means do what you have to do to either get her in line or fire her."

It would suck. It was the last thing he needed, especially facing a potential custody battle, but he couldn't expect his friend, who did him this favor, to keep an employee who didn't do her job and made his life difficult.

"I've been reluctant to pursue the matter in any rigorous way because I didn't want to jeopardize our friendship."

"We've known each other a long time. You gave me a lot of great advice when I started in the grocery business. I asked for a favor, and you obliged me. But if it's not working out for you, I don't expect you to wring your hands and do nothing when it's affecting your business."

"Okay then. I'll start a discussion with Stephanie about my expectations going forward and consequences if they aren't met."

"I'd do the same with any employee of mine." He hoped Steph listened to Henry, took it to heart that her job was on the line, and stepped up and tried harder to keep her job. Though he hoped it wasn't one too many people scrutinizing her every move, sending her over the edge. "As for *Almost Homemade*, I'm seeing one of the partners and am very interested in their success. Maybe I can broker the deal between the two of you."

"Up to your old tricks again, Jon?"

He didn't see Steph coming and wondered how long she'd stood in the aisle next to where he and Henry stood talking.

"I see you've found your next conquest. I thought you were limiting your work in favor of being Father of the Year to *our* little girl and now you're scouting businesses again." Steph shook her head like he'd done something wrong.

"It's not your concern, Steph."

"Right. Except talking to your girlfriend is on my list of things to do. I've put off talking to *her* about the partnership with the grocery store, but it sounds like you're already stirring the pot, so I guess I better get on that before I have to do the deal with you."

"That's not what's happening."

She raised an eyebrow. "Does Trinity know just how interested you are in her business?"

"Leave it alone, Steph." His irritation turned to pure anger.

"Right. You keep her in the dark just like you did me about all your business dealings."

Henry stepped in. "Jon, this sounds like it's personal. I think I'll handle the *Almost Homemade* deal myself. Steph, you can focus on your other duties."

She glared at Jon, then turned to Henry. "I'm actually not feeling very well. I think I'll go home early and rest so I can be here bright and early tomorrow."

Henry frowned, but he couldn't do anything about Steph going home sick. Not really. Even if, like Jon, he didn't believe a word coming out of Steph's mouth.

"If you're not feeling well, I'd be happy to take Emmy tonight." He could pick her up right now and take her back to the ranch. It would derail his plans with Trinity, but she'd understand. After Emmy went to bed, he could talk to Trinity about *Almost Homemade* and Tate suggesting they work together by running cattle on his ranch.

Not that he could make any plans while he waited for the court hearing to find out if he'd get full custody. And if not, if Steph was going to do what he expected but dreaded and run home to Daddy to take care of her, creating an even bigger mess of their lives.

Steph glared at him. "No. It's my night. And I won't let you use one more thing against me to try to take my daughter from me. I'm her mother, not your precious Trinity!" She caught herself losing her shit and turned to her boss and tried to cover. "I'm sorry. I'm really feeling off today. I've been under a great deal of stress and it's causing me a lot of mental and physical upset." She pressed her hand to her stomach. "I'm going to pick up my daughter early from day care and take her home." She gave Jon a hard look, then turned and walked away.

He tried really hard to forget walking in on Steph

and that guy naked and asleep in bed, but all of a sudden he wondered if maybe she was pregnant. God, he hoped not.

Henry sighed. "Looks like I'll have to save my talk with her for tomorrow. In the meantime, I'll go over the *Almost Homemade* proposal again, refresh my memory, and get in touch with the owners myself."

He couldn't get his thoughts off Steph and whether or not she was really sick, tricking her boss into getting the afternoon off, or if she could be pregnant again. "Great. I'm sure they'd love to hear from you." He and Trinity would clear the air tonight, and he could talk to her about his discussion with Henry and moving forward with it.

He said goodbye to Henry and went to pay for his groceries. He really needed to get the cold items into his cooler for the trip home. The checkout line went quickly and so did packing up his car.

Steph remained on his mind. She really did look stressed out and ready to snap. It had to be hard on her, having everyone breathing down her neck, watching her every move. He could only imagine what her family was saying to her about DPHHS getting involved because of Steph's behavior. He'd tried to tell them, but they never quite believed him and took Steph's side by making excuses for her. Still, her father paid for her attorney.

He felt like he was fighting everyone to protect his daughter.

He needed to check in on Emmy as soon as he got home and make sure Steph was up to taking care of her tonight. While Steph would lie to his face, Emmy would spill the beans if Steph crashed in bed and left Emmy to fend for herself.

He hoped his gut feeling that this would end badly was wrong and he didn't need to rescue Emmy tonight, but when Steph was involved, things never seemed to go his way.

JON STRESSED THE whole way home and all through putting away the groceries.

One of the heads of his companies called with an emergency that required his attention and distracted him from contacting Emmy to be sure Steph picked her up on time and took her home. Was she taking care of Emmy or crashed out in bed?

If she was, he wouldn't blame her. People got sick. But she should have taken him up on his offer to take Emmy for the night.

To ease his mind, he called the second he finished his business call.

His stomach tied into a knot when she didn't answer the video call.

He tried again.

Nothing.

Dread filled his heart.

He called her and got voice mail.

It could be nothing. It could be something completely innocent.

His gut said otherwise.

He hated to put Trinity out or in this position, but he had no choice. He hit the speed dial and thanked God she picked up right away.

"Hey, sweetheart, I'm headed your way in a few minutes."

"Steph went home sick from work today. She said she was picking up Emmy early from day care and going

home. I can't reach her, or get Emmy on the video chat."
The words spilled out in a frantic tone he couldn't help.

"I'm on my way. I'll check it out."

"It could be nothing. Maybe she's giving Emmy a
bath or helping her with her homework." He didn't think
so. He felt like something was really wrong this time.

"Maybe. I'll find out. I'm in my car headed there
right now. I'll call you back as soon as I see Emmy."

"Thank you. I don't know what I'd do without you."

"I'm sure everything is fine." She tried to reassure
him, but he knew she was just as worried as he was right
now. "I'll be there in a few minutes and call you back
with good news."

Steph and good news didn't go together.

And waiting for news nearly killed him.

Chapter Twenty-Three

TRINITY PARKED the car in a visitor's spot, got out of the SUV, and noticed Emmy playing alone on the grass. Her heart sank. How could Steph leave her daughter outside alone, unsupervised? Especially after DPHHS warned her about neglecting Emmy.

She was about to call out to Emmy, but Steph's door opened and a man stepped out and yelled, "Get back in here!"

Emmy ran for the door, trying to dodge the guy, who went out of his way to swat her on the butt. The force of the slap sent her to her hands and knees. Emmy looked over her shoulder, crying. The guy snickered as he left the apartment, slamming the door behind him and walking four doors down and into what she presumed was his place.

Bastard.

Furious to see someone treat Emmy so harshly, Trinity rang the bell. No one answered. She pounded on the door with her fist. "Emmy, sweetheart, it's Trinity. Open the door."

The door eased open and Emmy stared up at her with watery eyes and red marks on her bare knees where she'd skinned them on the rug. She flung herself into

Trinity's thighs and wrapped her arms around her waist and held on for dear life.

Trinity rubbed her hand up and down Emmy's back. "Hey, sweetheart. I'm here. It's okay."

"I want Daddy."

"Okay." Trinity had no trouble making that happen. But first, she needed to find Steph.

The apartment smelled like cigarettes, cat pee, and something she hadn't smelled since walking through the senior parking lot after every football game. If she didn't leave soon, she'd get a contact high. Emmy, too.

"Let's tell your mom we're leaving."

"She's asleep. She won't wake up now for a long time."

"Yeah? How often do you play outside alone?"

"All the time. She won't let me in the house when *he's* here."

Protect her from one thing while endangering her at the same time. Apparently Steph hadn't learned her lesson.

Trinity fumed, but brushed a reassuring hand over Emmy's head. "Let's go in."

Emmy let her loose. Trinity followed her into the living space. Steph lay passed out on the couch. She looked like she'd fallen asleep sitting upright and toppled over. Her feet were on the floor, but the rest of her was bent sideways.

On the coffee table sat a huge bong and an open tea tin with a plastic baggy sticking out filled with pot. Bottles of beer stood on the table all lined up like soldiers. Three across and three deep. If they were all from today, it had been one hell of a party for two.

The gray-and-white cat sat on the floor licking something off a discarded paper plate. One of the cats had peed on the pile of mail sitting on the dining room table—right next to Emmy's breakfast dishes. The leftover milk in the bowl had congealed and left a sour scent in the air barely discernible with all the other pungent odors clogging Trinity's nose.

The floors were dirty and stained. The kitchen sink overflowed with dishes. The counters were covered in spilled food and crumbs.

Steph probably figured she had time to clean up before DPHHS came back.

"Okay, Emmy, please go get your backpack. Make sure it has everything you need for school. Do you have enough clothes at your dad's?"

She nodded.

"Great. Hurry up."

Emmy scrunched her mouth. "Are you going to wake her up?"

"In a minute." First she wanted to document what she'd found for Jon's case against Steph. "I need to tell her we're leaving." She'd love to just take Emmy and see how Steph reacted when she discovered she was alone in the house and had no idea where Emmy was, but that would be wrong.

But boy did she want to stick it to Steph for once.

"Don't wake her up. She gets really mad." Worry filled Emmy's big blue eyes.

Trinity didn't care what Steph thought or felt. "Please go get your things and meet me by the door." She waited for Emmy to run to her room, then she took out her phone and texted Jon.

TRINITY: Bringing Emmy home with me
TRINITY: This should explain most of it

Then she started taking pictures of the apartment and Steph passed out. In all, she sent Jon eight photos of the gross apartment and Steph's sick day playdate.

Her phone rang immediately.

She swiped the screen to accept Jon's call, but didn't say anything because Steph sat up, rubbed her bloodshot eyes, raked her hair out of her face, and asked, "What are *you* doing here?"

"I'm taking Emmy to Jon's. You're in no shape to keep her tonight."

"You can't do that," she slurred.

"Or I could just call the cops and let them deal with you, but I hate to put Emmy through that. Or Jon."

Steph laughed under her breath, in a way that held more vengeance than humor. "You think he wants you. You're so stupid. He's using you. All he wants is your business. That's what he does. He comes in and takes over everything."

Trinity felt that like a punch to the gut. She didn't want to believe it. Steph was lashing out. But it rang a little true. And she'd make Jon answer for it when she saw him.

"Like I said, I'm taking Emmy to Jon's."

"No, you're not." Steph smacked her tongue on the roof of her mouth, trying to work up some saliva. It only made her look drunker and more out of it. "You may have taken Jon"—she slurred out the words—"but you're not taking Emmy away from me, too."

"You're drunk. You're stoned. You left her playing alone outside while you were passed out on the couch. Whoever that guy was partying with you, he hit Emmy on the way out the door just for fun. There's no fucking way I'm leaving her with you."

Steph's gaze went to Trinity's phone and a burst of energy made her stand up. "What did you tell him? Is he listening to this?"

Emmy stood in the entry with her backpack on. "I'm ready."

Trinity turned to walk out with Emmy and call the cops because, yeah, it would suck for Emmy and Jon, but Steph and that asshole who hit Emmy should pay for what they'd done. But she was getting Emmy out first.

She held her hand out to Emmy, but she never reached her. Something cracked against the back of her head. Stars burst in her eyes. In slow motion she saw Emmy's eyes go wide, her mouth open, and a piercing scream echoed through Trinity's ears before her knees hit the floor and she fell face-first into the disgusting carpet.

Something whacked her head again, and then something even bigger and heavier stomped on her back and slammed into her ribs and side over and over, relentlessly.

Someone screamed again and again. She heard crying. And in the chaos she heard Emmy yell, "Mommy, no. You're killing her!"

Trinity fought the pain and rolled over and blocked another blow from Steph's foot with her arms, but her head spun and flashes went off in her eyes, making it hard to see and focus.

"Daddy!" Emmy yelled.

Steph grabbed Emmy's arm and spanked her butt. "Shut up! Go to your room." She spanked her again and shoved her toward the hallway with another hard blow to the back.

Emmy fell, got hit again, scrambled on her hands and knees, then rose to her feet and ran.

Trinity tried to get up, but could barely make it to her hands and knees.

"You are ruining everything!" Steph spat out and hooked her arm under Trinity's and hauled her up, dragging her toward the entry. Steph was surprisingly strong. Maybe it was all adrenaline. That seemed to be the only thing keeping Trinity from passing out.

"You're not taking my daughter." She shoved Trinity into the entry closet. Off-balance, Trinity didn't turn fast enough to escape and the door slammed shut, leaving her in the dark.

"She's mine!"

Trinity went from one nightmare to another, her mind taking her back to being locked in the trunk with no escape when she'd been kidnapped. She clawed at the door and tried to turn the handle, but the door wouldn't budge.

"Let me out! You can't leave me in here! Please!"

"You can't take her!" Steph screamed over Trinity begging at the top of her lungs, "Let me out!"

Her nails bit into her palms, and her fists ached from pounding on the door. She clawed and kicked at the wood and banged on the handle. She screamed and screamed and screamed until nothing came out of her dry throat. She could feel the tears gathered in her eyes and streaming down her cheeks, but she couldn't see anything.

And then the only thing she felt was her heart pounding so hard she thought it might burst out of her chest, and she couldn't get any air no matter how hard she tried to suck it in. She was suffocating in the dark where there was no escape.

And then the blackness swallowed her whole, and she fell into the nothingness.

Chapter Twenty-Four

Aᴛ ꜰɪʀꜱᴛ, Jon was relieved to finally receive a text from Trinity, until he saw what it said. Then the pictures started popping up and he grew livid. He didn't think he could be any angrier until he called her and heard Steph's drunk-ass voice.

He didn't know why Trinity didn't say anything to him. She had to have her hands full with Steph and getting Emmy out the door with her.

But his heart nearly stopped when he heard a thunk and Emmy screamed, "Mommy, no. You're killing her!"

He didn't think. He ran for his car, pulling his keys out of his pocket the second he cleared the door and hit the path to the driveway. He was behind the wheel and peeling out of the driveway before he really registered he was on his way.

Emmy screamed, "Daddy!"

His heart shattered. She needed him and he wasn't there.

The screams echoed in his ears along with the thuds and the slam of a door.

Nothing prepared him to hear Trinity's wailing voice plead with Steph to let her out.

Everything seemed to happen at once and all on top of each other as the miles passed by in a blur. His mind had trouble following him trying to keep the car on the road, listening to what was happening to Trinity and his daughter, and him having to make the devastating decision to put the call on hold so he could conference in 911. Somehow he managed to hold it together when the dispatcher answered.

"Nine-one-one. What is your emergency?"

"My ex is trying to kill my girlfriend."

"What is the address of the emergency?"

He rattled off Steph's address. "Hurry. Please. My four-year-old is in the house, too. I have an open line to them." He tapped his screen to put all three of them on the line together like he did with so many of his business calls these days.

Trinity screamed one last time, "Let me out!" Then everything went silent.

"We have an officer two minutes out."

That wasn't fast enough.

Why couldn't he hear Trinity anymore?

He was too late.

"Where are you, you little brat?" Steph yelled in the background far away from the phone. "Come out of there right now, Emmy!"

Emmy didn't answer. At least he couldn't hear her say anything.

"Sir, who is in the house?"

"Emmy is my daughter. Steph is her mother. Trinity is my girlfriend. Please, you have to help them. Emmy said her mother was killing Trinity and now I can't hear her at all."

"The officers just arrived. Do you know if Steph owns a gun?"

"I don't think so." He didn't know. And he should since his daughter lived in the house.

"I said come out of there, Emmy!" More distant pounding.

"I think Emmy might have locked herself in the bathroom. I told her to do that if she ever felt unsafe." Why did he have to tell his four-year-old something like that?

Thank God he did.

Something crashed closer to the phone.

"Police! Get down on the floor!"

For a second Jon breathed a sigh of relief. Help was there.

"Down on the floor!"

"I didn't do anything," Steph slurred, her voice disgruntled and defiant. "This is my house. She tried to take my kid!"

Jon relayed what really happened. "Steph went home from work sick and said she was picking up my daughter early. I tried to call them to be sure everything was okay. She didn't answer, so I sent my girlfriend over to check on Emmy. When Trinity arrived, Steph was passed out on the couch, drunk and stoned based on what the pictures she sent me show. She texted me that she was bringing Emmy home with her. I called when I received the pictures and heard Steph tell Trinity she wasn't taking Emmy. Then Emmy screamed that her mom was killing Trinity. So tell me, is Trinity alive or dead!" His voice shook and he prayed as hard as he could that she was alive.

Oh God, please.

"The officers have one in custody. Your daughter is locked in the bathroom. Alone, she says. Once officers have her out, they'll search the apartment. We have an ambulance standing by outside."

Those ominous words squeezed his heart. "Trinity's cell phone is somewhere in the apartment. If the officer can find it, I can talk Emmy out of the bathroom."

"Just leave her in there to rot," Steph yelled to the officers in the house.

"I told you to keep your mouth shut," the officer ordered.

The dispatcher came back on the line. "One of the officers is searching for the phone now."

Jon tried to listen to every little sound. The officers' voices in the background talking to Emmy, though he couldn't really make out the words. Steph grumbling incoherently. The shuffle of footsteps. The creak of . . . a door maybe.

"Found her. She's bleeding and unconscious. I feel a pulse. Ma'am. Ma'am. Wake up. Are you all right? There you go."

Jon thanked God for the officer's patient and kind voice and how he relayed everything to the dispatcher, even as Jon overheard it on Trinity's phone at the same time.

And then all hell broke loose again.

"Let me go! You can't keep me in here!" Trinity shouted. Something fell and scraped on the floor.

"Damnit. Where are you going?" More scuffling, then nothing.

"What's happening?" Jon asked the dispatcher.

"Not sure. Hold while I get the information."

Every second felt like an eternity that ticked by with the pounding of his heart. He was still five minutes away from the apartment complex despite driving like a maniac and breaking every speed law and running three very yellow lights and one that was definitely red as he raced to help his girls.

"Sir, it appears Trinity was found locked in a closet. When she came to, she was disoriented and frightened by the officer. She ran from the apartment and the officer had to chase her down. She's apparently experiencing some kind of panic attack."

"She was kidnapped and held inside a trunk months ago. She's having a fucking flashback."

"I'll relay that to the officers and paramedics assisting her right now."

Jon finally pulled into the apartment complex and parked behind one of the cruisers with its lights flashing. "I'm here." He didn't know if the dispatcher heard him or not, and he jumped out of his car and ran toward the path that led to Steph's place, but stopped short when he spotted the ambulance with the back doors open wide, an officer holding Trinity's arms as she thrashed on a stretcher, and a paramedic filling a needle.

An officer came out of nowhere. "Are you the man who called this in?"

"Yes." He took a step toward the ambulance so he could help Trinity, but the officer took his arm and held him still. "Is it your daughter locked in the bathroom in the apartment?"

He stopped trying to pull free of the officer and turned to him. "Yes."

"We need your help. She's very distraught. We're trying to talk her out without having to break down the door and traumatize her more."

He knew he needed to help Emmy, but he also needed to get to Trinity and help her.

"Sir, Trinity's in good hands. They'll take care of her. We need to take care of your little girl."

Jon let the officer pull him toward the apartment and away from Trinity.

It felt like he was being ripped in two. Everything inside him wanted to be in two places at once.

He barely noticed the neighbors milling around outside their apartments watching the scene unfold. He tried to take in the apartment as the police officer led the way to the hall. One of the dining room chairs was lying on its side in the entry by the wide-open closet door. Steph must have used it to lock Trinity inside. He stared at the red smears on the stark white panel and smudged all over the handle.

The officer turned back because Jon had stopped in his tracks, transfixed by what he saw but his mind couldn't comprehend. "She tried to claw her way out." The officer filled in the information he didn't want to believe.

"You can't take her from me, you bastard!" Steph tried to shove her way past the officer standing next to her in the living room, but he held her arm in a firm grip.

"Sit down, or I'll make you."

Jon stared at Steph, not seeing the woman he'd fallen for once, but someone he truly didn't recognize. "Not only can I take her. I will. You handed her right over to me. You tried to kill Trinity. You're going to jail. For good, I hope."

"She deserved it. She tried to take my kid."

Jon noticed the broken beer bottle with blood on it on the floor. Trinity's blood.

"I won't let you near either one of them ever again." He walked down the hall behind the officer. A third officer knelt at the door with one of those universal keys that opened indoor privacy locks.

"The apartment manager brought one of these over. I didn't want to open it until you were here. I think she'd feel safer seeing you."

Jon nodded, waited the two seconds it took the officer to open the door, then he filled the doorway so Emmy saw only him, though she'd scooted herself into the niche between the cabinet and toilet with her knees up to her chest and her face buried in them.

"Emmy, sweet girl, it's Daddy. You're okay, now, sweetheart. I'm here." He slowly crouched in front of her, his nose wrinkling from the overwhelming stench, and his shoes crunched the cat litter dusting the floor. He put his hand on her head. "Baby, come out of there now."

Her little wet face rose and her devastated eyes met his. "She killed Trinity." Her bottom lip trembled, and she burst into tears and launched herself into his chest and cried her little heart out.

Jon's heart broke into a billion pieces. He'd never forgive Steph for doing this to their daughter. "No, sweetheart. Trinity is alive, sweet girl. I just saw her. She's hurt, but she's going to be okay." God, he hoped he wasn't telling a lie right now. He had no idea how badly Trinity had been hurt or how, other than being bashed over the head with that broken beer bottle.

"Mommy hit her, then she kicked and kicked and kicked. She wouldn't stop." Emmy sobbed.

"Sir, let's get her to the ambulance so the paramedics can look her over."

He held tight to Emmy, covering her head as he walked her out of the apartment and past Steph. He didn't want her to see her mom. It would only make her more hysterical.

One of the officers caught up to them with one of Emmy's soft blankets from her bed. He draped it over Emmy, and Jon wrapped her up good as he walked to the ambulance, anxious to see Trinity, only to find the ambulance empty. "Where is Trinity?"

"They already took her to the hospital. She's got a major head trauma, possibly some broken ribs. Her hands were in pretty bad shape, too," the officer informed him.

His heart sank. He should be with her. He needed to see her. She needed to know he was there and he'd take care of her.

"Please take a seat," the paramedic instructed. "We'll take you both to the hospital and have a pediatrician check Emmy out."

Jon sat on the gurney. The paramedic had raised one end up into a sitting position. He leaned back and held Emmy tight.

The officer closed the back door, blocking out the flashing lights and commotion outside.

Emmy seemed to calm and burrow into his chest, though there was nowhere for her to go.

"Do you think I can get her vitals?" The paramedic waited patiently.

Jon rubbed Emmy's back, soothing her as the crying subsided and she rested against him, hiccuping from the bout of tears. "Hey, baby, we're just going to get a look at you to be sure you're okay." Jon gently eased the blanket off her back, but Emmy winced and tried to move away from where he brushed his hand against her. "Does something hurt?"

Emmy nodded.

"Can I see?"

Emmy reached back and pulled her shirt up a bit. He helped ease it up a little farther. The paramedic winced and turned to a cabinet, pulled out a pack, cracked it, then gently laid it on the bruises on Emmy's lower back and disappearing into her little leggings.

Jon met the paramedic's questioning gaze. "I heard Trinity say that she'd seen a man at Steph's place and he hit Emmy."

The paramedic nodded, then looked at the guy sitting up in the driver's seat. He immediately exited the vehicle, presumably to tell the officer waiting outside.

"Mommy hit me, too," Emmy whispered. "Lots. She was very mad."

"That won't ever happen again," he vowed. He didn't care what he had to do. Steph would never lay a hand on Emmy again. She'd be lucky if she got to see their daughter again.

He held the ice pack to Emmy's back while the paramedic listened to her heart and took her blood pressure. Exhausted, Emmy fell asleep in his arms. He took that as a good sign that she felt safe enough to let go.

The driver climbed back behind the wheel. "The cops found the guy. They've arrested him along with the woman."

Jon sighed with relief, but it was short-lived. The second they drove out of the apartment complex, he took out his phone and made the call he dreaded.

"Jon. You ready to talk horses?" Tate sounded pleased to hear from him.

Jon hoped Trinity's brothers didn't kill him over this. "You need to get to the hospital. Trinity was just taken into the emergency room. I don't know everything, but she's got a head wound, possibly broken ribs, damage to her hands, and she suffered a very bad flashback after being locked in a closet after she was clocked with a beer bottle and beaten by my ex." He waited for the cussing, accusations, and death threats.

"Anyone else hurt?" Tate's voice was calm and controlled.

Jon choked up. "Em-Emmy. Though she's f-far better than Tr-Trinity."

"Okay. Hold on. We'll meet you there." Which meant Tate would call the rest of Trinity's family. They'd take care of her.

He nuzzled Emmy closer. He'd take care of her, but he wished he could be with Trinity right now, too.

Chapter Twenty-Five

TRINITY COULDN'T put one thought together with the next to figure out what was happening. All she knew was overwhelming fear and a sense that she needed to get away. With her heart pounding and her lungs seized, she felt like she was suffocating.

She couldn't move her hands. They were strapped down. Why? She didn't know.

The people dressed in blues and whites around her kept assuring her she was okay, but she felt anything but.

She needed to find someone but she didn't know who. Tate? Liz? Emmy? Images came and went, and she couldn't make out now or then or reality versus nightmare.

Someone poked another needle in her arm.

"What are you doing?"

"It's just a mild sedative to help you calm down. Breathe, Trinity."

She wished she could, but something seemed very urgent and necessary. "Where is Jon? I need to . . . tell . . . him . . . about Emmy. Did they . . . find . . . Clint? Where . . . is . . . Tate?" She couldn't get all the words out without gasping for every breath.

"We'll find out. But first we need to take care of you." The man with the white mask and plastic face shield had earnest brown eyes that made her believe he'd help.

"You have to . . . find them."

"We will," he assured her. "Let's get a chest X-ray. Is CT ready for her?"

"Yes," someone answered. "We're ready to move her."

Trinity's head spun as the lights and ceiling tiles moved overhead, making her have to close her eyes to stop the queasy feeling in her stomach from getting worse.

"Trinity!" Jon's deep and urgent voice made her turn her head.

"Jon." Just his name hurt her throat to say. She didn't know why she couldn't make her voice louder than a whisper.

The masked man appeared over her again. "You need to stop talking so your throat can heal."

Jon hovered over her, his face and eyes filled with anguish. He leaned down and kissed her forehead. "I'm so sorry, Trinity."

She tried to raise her hand, but the restraint held it down, though she spotted the bloody bandages covering her fingers. "What happened?"

Jon turned to look at the masked man, who spoke to him. "She's having trouble thinking clearly. The paramedic said something about a flashback from a previous event."

"Did they get Clint?" she asked Jon, desperate to be sure he hadn't hurt Tate and Liz.

Jon brushed his hand over her forehead. "Clint is

dead. That was months ago, sweetheart. Steph did this. You were trying to help Emmy."

She tried to get up, but the masked man . . . No, a doctor. And Jon. They gently held her down. "She hit Emmy." She tried to see past them. "Where is she? You have to help her."

"Emmy is safe. She's right over there."

The doctor put his hand on Jon's chest and pushed him back. "We need to get her to CT."

Jon elbowed his way back to her side and pressed his forehead to hers. "Let the doctor help you. I need to stay with Emmy, but I'll come see you again as soon as they bring you back." He kissed her head again. "Your family is on the way," he assured her, then disappeared, making her turn to find him, but they were moving her again and the dizziness and lights made her close her eyes.

"We need to do some imaging," the doctor said from beside her. "Then we'll get you back to your family. But now you know your little girl is okay."

Her heart calmed. Emmy. She was safe. Jon had her.

And oh, it sounded and felt good to think of Emmy as her little girl.

She'd like that. She'd try her very best to be a good mom to her.

Bits and pieces came back to her about what happened, how Steph attacked her. Unprovoked. Her deadly intent clear.

Trinity was done playing nice. She vowed Steph would pay for what she did, for hitting Emmy, and for trying to kill her.

Chapter Twenty-Six

JON HATED leaving Trinity's side. Seeing the blood drenching her hair, the thick pad on the back of her head, the bandages around her hands because she'd literally tried to claw her way out of the closet, and her wide eyes filled with desperation as she struggled to understand what was happening. They'd restrained her to keep her from hurting herself more. It was all too much to bear. But she needed him to hold on, take care of Emmy, and be there for her when they brought her back.

If he was going to do that, he needed help.

And it arrived just in time. He glanced up when the hospital-room door opened. His father stared at him, then Emmy, and back in the dim room they'd moved them to because the noise in the ER agitated Emmy and they wanted to keep her calm.

"Dad." He'd never been so relieved to see his father.

"How is she?"

Emmy lay curled up on her side in the golden glow from the single light at the head of the bed. She twitched and made odd noises in her sleep, but she didn't wake up. The pediatrician who examined her warned him about nightmares and Emmy being afraid and feeling unsafe for a while.

He'd managed to change her into a tiny hospital gown and held two ice packs on the bruises on her back and bottom. He couldn't believe Steph had spanked her hard enough to leave such bruises.

His father stared at his hands on Emmy. "What happened?" he whispered.

Jon kept his voice low. "I couldn't get ahold of Emmy after school. I asked Trinity to drop by and check on her. Steph didn't answer my calls because she was too busy getting drunk and stoned." He glanced at Emmy, thought of all she'd been through, and tried to breathe through it and tell his father everything he knew about what happened.

He let go of one of the ice packs and brushed his hand over her head. "The pediatrician said physically she's okay. Bruised, but no broken bones or anything. He's concerned about the emotional trauma she's suffered. We'll know more in the morning when she's awake and hopefully able to talk to us. He said it's not unusual for children her age, exposed to such violence, to stop talking for a while."

When Jon looked back at his dad, he found Tate standing next to him. "How is Trinity?"

Tate sighed. "Two cracked ribs, a skull fracture, she's got a brain bleed and swelling they're monitoring, two broken fingers, one missing fingernail, the others broken and bloody, and a very questionable mental state right now. She seems to flip between the past and present. She doesn't know if she should try to save me and Liz or Emmy."

Jon wiped the tears from his eyes. "I'm so sorry. This is my fault. I sent her there."

Tate shook his head all through that. "This is all on

Steph. She did this. To Trinity. To Emmy. That's where the blame belongs."

He wished he could believe that, but his gut was tied in knots with guilt.

Tate stepped closer, but still kept his voice to a whisper. "Do they have your ex in custody?"

He nodded. "I expect the cops to update me soon. She should be going away for a very long time after what she's done." He hoped they locked her up and threw away the key. He had a lot of other dire wishes for her, but didn't voice his anger-fueled thoughts.

"And the guy who hurt Emmy?" his dad asked, looking like he'd like some retribution there, too.

"Also in custody," Jon confirmed, wishing he could get his hands on the guy and beat the shit out of him for laying a hand on his daughter.

Tate slid his hands into his jeans pockets. "We've got the whole McGrath crew here. I've spoken to our mom and dad. They'll be here as soon as they can. But I know Trinity would want you there with her, so whenever you can get away, you're welcome to come to her room. Three-zero-two. She's mostly awake because of the concussion, but not very lucid. They'll be taking her for hourly CT scans to check the brain bleed, so if you miss her, just know she'll be back shortly. All of us will be keeping vigil either in her room or the waiting room."

Jon desperately wanted to see her now.

His dad walked to his side of the bed and put his hand on Jon's shoulder. "Go check on her. I'll sit with Emmy."

Jon glanced at his daughter, torn about staying or going.

Tate read his mind. "I'll stay here with Mr. Crawford. If Emmy wakes up, I'll come get you right away."

Jon set the ice packs on the bedside table, covered Emmy with the blanket, and stood. "It's probably enough ice for a while. The nurse will be in to check on her soon."

His dad touched his arm. "She's going to be okay."

He knew that, but the reassurance helped.

Jon checked Emmy one last time to be sure she was sleeping, then let his dad take his seat. He tapped Tate on the back in thanks and headed for Trinity.

He had no trouble finding her room. He recognized two of her sisters-in-law and her brother Declan outside her room.

They saw him coming and Declan came forward. "It's good you're here. Drake and Adria are in with her, but she keeps asking for you." Declan held his hand out. "Nice to see you again by the way even under these circumstances."

Jon didn't expect to be welcomed. He took Declan's hand and shook. "You too. Um, I don't know what to say about all this, except I'm sorry."

"Tate filled us in on what he knew, and Trinity's said enough about your ex that we understand what you've been dealing with. None of us thought it would end like this, but . . ." Declan shrugged. "How's your little girl?"

"Not great, traumatized and bruised."

"I hope she's better real soon."

"We all do," one of women said, probably Declan's fiancée, Skye.

He guessed the other one was Tate's wife, Liz, based on the baby bump. She gave him a soft smile. "She's waiting for you." She pushed the door open and held it for him.

Jon stepped in and came up short against her big brother Drake, who looked fierce and concerned all at the same time.

"Jon."

He nodded and heard the possible threat in Drake's voice, but his attention was on Trinity lying with her eyes closed in bed in the dimly lit room. The second Drake said his name, her eyes fluttered open.

"Why are you here?" She looked around the room. "Am I late for dinner?"

He stared blankly at her. "What?"

Drake went to Trinity and put his hand on her leg. "You're in the hospital. Remember? You have a concussion." Drake turned to him. "The neurologist said her brain isn't working properly right now. Her short-term memory is short-circuited."

"I'm right here." Trinity glared at her brother, then focused on him. "Where's Emmy?" The simple question came out easy enough but a split second later, her eyes glassed over and her chin trembled. "Where is she?"

Jon rushed to the other side of the bed, put his hand on her arm, and leaned in close. "She's here. She's okay. She's sleeping."

Trinity's wide eyes met his. "Something bad happened."

"I know. It's all okay now. You're going to be okay."

A tear slipped down her cheek. "Why does it hurt to breathe?"

"You've got two cracked ribs, sweetheart. Your voice is raw because you were screaming." He pressed his forehead to hers. "I know this is very confusing for you right now. You have a head injury, but you're going to be okay, too."

"We were supposed to have dinner."

He leaned back and stared down at her.

She sucked in a gasp. "You're trying to steal *Almost Homemade*."

He shook his head. "I can't steal something you own, sweetheart. It's yours. And Adria's."

Adria stood across from him next to Drake. She touched Trinity's leg to get her attention. "No one is stealing *Almost Homemade* from us. It's safe."

"But she said this is what you do." Trinity looked at him, so confused and trying to piece things together it broke his heart over and over again.

"She wanted to make you angry with me." He'd like to kill Steph for trying to turn Trinity against him with her lies.

"I took you from her."

"No, sweetheart, you didn't. Steph and I weren't together. And I only want to be with you."

"She's a terrible mother." Trinity sank down into the bed and crossed her arms, tears flowing down her cheeks now. "She hurt Emmy." She shook her head back and forth but stopped because it appeared to cause her a lot of pain. "She can't have Emmy back." She leaned her face close to his. "No! Emmy can't go back there." And then Trinity went very quiet, her face went slack, and she stared into space.

Jon looked to Drake, hoping he had some answers.

"It's the head injury mixed with the trauma. Her brain is trying to sort things out but she can't make sense of it, so her brain sort of shuts off. It should clear up as the swelling goes down."

"How long will that take?"

"They'll CT her again and see if the brain bleed is subsiding or getting worse."

"You're talking about me like I'm not here again." Trinity listened to them, but the confusion in her eyes worried him.

"I'm so sorry, Trinity. I never thought something like this would happen."

"Clint is dead now. Everything is going to be okay." She touched the scar on her temple. "I'll be fine."

Drake shook his head. "She's got sixteen stitches in the back of her head. We'll know more in the morning."

Tate burst into the room. "Emmy's awake and screaming her head off for you."

Jon gave Trinity a quick kiss and ran out of the room and down the hall to get to his little girl, but he left part of himself in the room with Trinity.

Chapter Twenty-Seven

TRINITY HAD been up most of the night. Everything ached. Her hands. Her head. Her chest. Her heart. Even her hair.

She wanted to shut off her mind, but it kept jumping around from past to present, nightmare to nightmare, and all the while her mind kept going back to Jon and Emmy.

She loved her family for staying with her all through the night, and the way Tate went back and forth between rooms to update Jon on her condition and to update her on Emmy's.

But she hated the separation, the vague answers, and her own mind not being able to hold on to a thought so that she could be sure what they told her was true and not her mind playing tricks on her.

Drake took Adria home to rest. Declan and Skye went to pick up breakfast. Tate sent Liz home so she could get some sleep, but he stayed with her.

"Once they get the results of your latest scan, they'll let us know if you can go home." Tate kept his patience with her all through the night when she asked him the same questions over and over again.

It scared her that her mind didn't work right. The

pounding headache turned to a dull throb that wouldn't quit. The flashing lights in her eyes came and went but now she had strange floaters that danced across her vision.

Tate pushed her wheelchair down the hallway. The overhead lights were far too bright for her sensitive eyes, sitting hurt her ribs, her fingers were killing her, but she wanted to see Emmy.

Tate stopped at Emmy's door, knocked, then opened it, and pushed Trinity into the brightly lit room. She winced at the light coming in from the windows. Tate handed her the sunglasses Liz luckily had in her purse and left for her to use before she went home.

Trinity waited to put them on because she wanted Emmy to see her whole face and know that she was okay.

Emmy sat on the bed, her legs crossed, holding Jon's hand as he sat in front of her in the chair, leaning in close to her.

"Why can't I see her?"

Jon smiled, though it didn't reach his sad eyes. "Turn around, Emmy. She's here."

Emmy turned, dropped her dad's hand, and scrambled off the bed and ran to her. She threw her arms around Trinity and hugged her tight.

Trinity bit back the yelp of pain moving caused her ribs and hugged the little girl back.

Emmy climbed into her lap, curled up into her, and let loose a sorrowful cry that brought tears to Trinity's eyes.

She wrapped Emmy up close, the pain in her body blanked out by the overwhelming ache in her heart. "It's okay, sweetheart. Here I am."

"I . . . I thought she killed you."

Trinity pressed her cheek to Emmy's head. "No, sweetheart. I'm just a little sore." She lied for Emmy's benefit, when in reality she could barely stand the agony. It hurt so bad, she had to close her eyes to block out the light and Jon's earnest and compassionate gaze.

His hand pressed to her face. "We're so happy to see you. Emmy wanted to go to your room, but I wasn't sure you were up for visitors yet."

"And yet I have a vague sense you've been frequently coming to check on me." She opened her eyes just a slit to confirm the agreement in his eyes.

"Emmy's grandpa was here most of the night, so I could go back and forth," Jon confirmed.

Tate went to the window and closed the blinds.

She sighed with relief and opened her eyes. "Emmy needed you."

"*You* needed me and I wasn't there." Jon stuffed his hands in his pockets, his shoulders slumped, and he looked so damn disappointed and angry with himself.

Tate tried to look out for her. "I'm going to find the doctor and see if he has your latest scan results. Getting you home where you can rest should help lower your anxiety."

"I'm fine," she automatically said.

Tate rolled his eyes and left them alone.

Jon took her hand and held it up, showing her that it trembled. He clasped it gently in both of his. "You are going to be okay. You'll need some time to adjust again. And if you'll let me, I'd like to be the one to take care of you."

"I'm okay. Sore. Foggy. But . . ."

"You can't be left alone for a while, Trinity. Not with that head injury. Drake and Declan are talking about taking you home to one of their places, but I want you to come home with us."

Emmy looked up at her. "I get to stay with Daddy. The judge said so."

Jon gave her a wary smile. "My lawyer got an emergency custody order. Emmy stays with me."

"Right where she belongs."

Emmy tugged her hair. "You have to come, too. Please."

Trinity's eyes glassed over. Both of them looked at her with imploring eyes.

"Please, Trinity," Jon begged. "Give me a chance to make this up to you."

"Make what up to me?" She didn't understand. He hadn't done anything to her.

"We'll talk about it later." Jon held his hands out to Emmy. "Come here, sweetheart. Trinity loves to hold you, but she needs to rest." Jon plucked Emmy off her lap, and she was able to breathe a little easier without her ribs screaming at her. "I don't know how you're holding it together so well."

She looked up at him, concerned that maybe she wasn't comprehending everything that was going on right now. "Are you okay?"

"I'll be better when I have you home and I know you're really going to be okay."

That sounded good to her. She really wanted to get some sleep. "Okay. Can we go soon? I'm really tired."

"Emmy should be released any time now, but I'm not sure if the doctor will let you go home yet."

"Why did Emmy have to stay here?" It finally dawned on her that Emmy stayed in the hospital last night for some reason.

Jon set Emmy on the bed and handed her his phone. "Play your game while I talk to Trinity." He came back to her and pushed her chair back toward the door, then squatted next to her. "Emmy was very scared last night," he whispered.

"I tried to get to her, but . . ." She tried to make the images in her mind clear. "I couldn't seem to reach her."

"How much do you remember?"

"It's bits and pieces. I feel like it's out of order."

Jon took her shaking hand again. "That's okay. You don't need to think about it."

"I can't explain it, but it hurts to think. It's hard for me to . . . I can't think of the word."

"Process?"

She nodded. "I feel slow. And stupid that I can't remember words and things."

"The swelling is down and the bleed in your brain has stopped and is clearing up. Those are all good signs that your head is healing. In a few days, thinking and doing things will be easier, but the doctor warned me and your family last night that it will take weeks, if not months, for all your symptoms to completely subside."

She stared at their joined hands. He held the one that had only two fingers with badly broken nails, the skin torn and raw. All of her fingertips ached. But her other hand was the worst. She'd lost one fingernail completely, half of another, and broken two fingers. They were bandaged and splinted together. "How did I hurt my hands? No one will tell me. It's one of the things that's . . . dark." That word made her whole body tremble as fear washed through her like a tidal wave.

"That's a good word to describe what happened, sweetheart." Jon glanced at Emmy, who played her game and didn't pay them any attention. As before, he kept his voice low. "I wasn't there, so I can't say exactly how it happened, but Steph somehow shoved you into the closet and locked you in by jamming a chair under the handle."

"I . . ." Her chest seized.

Jon cupped her face and made her look at him. "Breathe, Trinity."

She tried, but she felt like she was suffocating. "Something bad happened." She wrapped her arms around her aching ribs.

"You are okay. Just breathe." He took a slow breath in.

She copied him and let it out just like he did.

"There you go. Again."

She breathed in and out with him.

"Keep it slow and even," he coaxed, and she was able to calm down.

The flashing lights stopped in her eyes. She didn't feel like she was going to pass out again. "I had a panic attack."

"That wasn't so bad."

She regretted shaking her head. It really screwed up her brain. "No. In the closet."

"You had a flashback. You panicked. You ran when the police officer let you out, but he was able to catch you and put you in the ambulance."

"Where is she?" Desperation filled her words and pounding heart.

"Jail." He pressed his hand to her cheek and looked her in the eyes. "She can't hurt you or Emmy anymore. I won't let her."

Tate walked in next to them. "The doctor says your scan looks good. You can go home. He's getting your release orders ready now." Tate looked from her to Jon. "Everything okay?"

Jon stood, but didn't let go of her trembling hand. "She wanted to know some details."

"The doctor said not to overwhelm her." Tate put his hand on her shoulder.

"I simply answered her questions to help her feel less confused." Frustrated and defensive, Jon rubbed his hand over the back of his neck. "I'm trying to help her process things as they come to her."

Tate conceded. "You're right. The doctor said to help her separate the past and the present and only bring it up if she asked."

"Again. I'm right here." She understood they wanted to help her, but she didn't like that they made her feel inept.

Jon sighed with such fatigue she felt sorry for him. He'd had one hell of a night worrying about her and Emmy. "I'm sorry, sweetheart. I'm trying to do what's right here."

Tate squeezed her shoulder, but spoke to Jon. "Why don't you take Trinity back to her room and help her get dressed. Liz brought her some clothes and stuff. I'll stay here with tiny tot."

Emmy perked up on the bed. "I'm totally going to beat your score." Emmy held up the game she was playing, taunting Tate.

"No way, tiny tot. You're toast." Tate went to the bed and sat beside Emmy.

Jon stared at Emmy, relief in his eyes. Whatever he'd been through last night with her, seeing her happy and playful with Tate sure did make him feel better.

He took the handles at the back of the wheelchair and pushed Trinity out of the room and back to hers. He helped her stand because her balance was off right now and held her still so she could get her bearings, but all she wanted was to be in his arms. She stepped into him and he wrapped his arms around her and held her loosely, because of her ribs, but close.

She breathed him in.

He sighed out his relief. "I wanted to be with you last night, to hold your hand, help you through all the scans, and be here for you while the doctors checked you out and stitched and bandaged you up."

She stepped back so she could see him, but kept her hands on his arms for balance. "I'm sorry I couldn't be with you last night and help Emmy."

Jon stared down at her, surprise and puzzlement in his eyes. "Seriously? You could have died." His throat worked as he swallowed hard. "I almost lost you, and you're sorry you weren't with *me* and Emmy last night. I don't deserve that. I should have taken Emmy away from Steph a long time ago."

She hated seeing the self-loathing in his eyes. "You're close to doing just that."

"Too little, too late. She nearly killed you and Emmy is covered in bruises all down her back."

Trinity gasped. "Oh no."

"She's going to be okay," he assured her. "The point is, if I'd done what was necessary sooner, none of this would have happened."

"Steph did this. *She* was drunk and stoned and let her anger, resentment, and jealousy get the better of her."

"She should be jealous, because you're kind enough to try to understand her after what she did to you and you're the mother I want for Emmy. You're perfect."

"I'm not," she assured him. She had her flaws, but she liked that they blurred or disappeared when he looked at her.

"You are for me. That's why I love you so damn much."

She had to let loose her aching hands the second she gripped him tighter. "What?"

"You heard me. But if you're having trouble processing that, I can say it again. I love you. And while it's not the time to really talk about it, I think you know that I want a life with you. I can't lose you, Trinity. You mean everything to me." He kissed her. Long and soft, it spun out and time stopped, and she simply lost herself in him and the amazing way he made her feel.

When he ended the kiss, she felt a little dizzy and it had nothing to do with her head injury and everything to do with the buzz of electricity and love running through her.

She didn't open her eyes. She simply let herself feel and smiled with the sheer joy of it. "I love you, too."

Jon pressed his forehead to hers. "Look at me," he pleaded.

She opened her eyes and stared into his, the blue depths filled with longing. "Stay with me at my place. Let me take care of you."

"I remember thinking when I saw what was happening at Steph's place that I'd take Emmy home to be with us. In my mind . . . and my heart . . . I knew that home meant being with you."

"Then be with me."

"Then take me and Emmy home."

Jon held her for a moment. "I'm never going to let anything happen to you again."

She nuzzled his neck. "It's not your fault. And when my head is clearer and it doesn't hurt to see, we'll talk about what happens next with Steph and us."

He held her at arm's length. "Sit on the bed. Let me find your clothes, and we'll go home so you can get some actual sleep. I just hope you don't come to your senses and decide you don't want to be with me, or forget altogether that you said you love me."

She reached up with her somewhat good hand and pressed it to his jaw. "I didn't just say it. I mean it. I feel it. I am so in it."

He leaned into her palm and held her gaze. "When I was driving to get to you and I heard what was happening on the phone and Emmy screamed she was killing you . . ." Tears filled his eyes. "I really, really thought I lost you."

"Never."

The kiss they shared sealed that promise.

He made her head spin.

Or maybe that was the concussion. Either way she saw stars.

Jon gripped her waist a bit tighter and broke the kiss. "You need to sit down."

He eased her back and onto the edge of the bed, untied the bows at the back of her hospital gown, and drew it down her arms, then sucked in a surprised gasp when he saw the colorful array of bruises covering the left side of her torso.

"Holy hell, Trinity."

She glanced down at her naked chest and abdomen, but quickly looked away. She couldn't look at the marks and remember what happened. "My clothes are in that bag."

Jon reached out to touch a particularly bad spot at her ribs, but she quickly leaned back. "Don't. It hurts."

"It's got to be excruciating. How the hell did you not scream when Emmy climbed in your lap?"

"It wasn't easy, but I could see in her face how much she needed me."

He closed his eyes and sighed before looking at her

again. "The doctor thinks she should see a child psychologist to help her process what happened."

"I can't imagine how she felt watching what happened."

"I know how she felt. Desperate. Angry. Useless. Frightened beyond belief."

"Those are big feelings for adults. She's four." Feeling exposed, she wrapped her arms around her chest and middle.

Jon grabbed the bag off the end of the bed, unzipped it, and pulled out the soft lightweight black sweater Liz packed for her.

"Thank God I don't need to put on a bra."

"With those cracked ribs, no way," he agreed. He gathered the material at the neckline and slipped it over her head, then pulled the sweater over her shoulders and gently picked up each of her hands and helped her put them in the sleeves. She winced. "How bad does it hurt?"

"It's hard to describe. Everything comes in waves, radiating out from whatever body part I disturb. They held back on the pain meds because of the bleeding in my brain."

"Why would that matter?"

"In case they needed to do surgery to relieve the pressure."

Jon swore under his breath. "The cops left me a message I haven't returned yet, but I'm hoping it's to tell me Steph pleaded guilty to all the charges and I'll never have to see her again."

She took his hand. "You know you're going to have to see and talk to her."

"If I see her, I'll kill her."

"I'll bail you out and we'll run away with Emmy," she teased.

He brushed his thumb across her cheek. "I don't deserve you."

"You deserve to be loved. She never gave you that. I will."

Jon held her black leggings between his hands with his shoulders slumped. "I don't know what to say to that, Trinity. It feels like so much more than I imagined I'd have in my life. More than I feel like I deserve right now."

"Just accept it. And help me put on my pants, because I'm not leaving with my ass hanging out."

Finally, he smiled. "I'm much better at taking your clothes off, but let's see if we can do this in reverse." He slipped the pants up to her knee on one leg then the other, moving her slowly to mitigate the pain in her ribs. She stood and he pulled the leggings up and over her hips. His hands stayed at her waist as he held her close.

She held his gaze and took in the fatigue and worry in his. "We've had a hell of a night."

"I feel like I've been dragged through hell. I can't imagine how you feel."

She clamped her jaw tight, wrapped her arms around his middle, and hugged him. "Better now." Though holding her arms up like that killed her ribs, she bit back the pain and focused on Jon holding her and the feel of his strong body pressed to hers.

The doctor walked in and spotted them. "I see you're dressed and ready to go."

She eased out of Jon's embrace. "I just want to curl up in bed at home and shut off my brain."

"You're going to need to do that a lot over the next

week, but it will ease up over time. Keep screen time to an hour or less a day. You'll be light sensitive for a while, so sunglasses if you have to go outside, keep the lights down inside. Your short-term memory will be spotty. You may have trouble finding the right word or lose your thoughts before you can express them."

Jon slipped his hand around her waist and pulled her close to his side. "I've seen some of that already."

"Don't be alarmed. It should clear up as her brain heals, but it could be weeks to months before it's completely gone." The doctor focused on her. "Be very careful getting up. Dizziness and blurred vision are very common. A fall with another blow to the head could make things significantly worse."

"I see things floating in my vision. Stars in my eyes."

He nodded. "Very common. You'll probably want to shower and wash your hair. You've got stitches, so try to keep them as dry as possible, but I understand you'll want to clean the blood from your hair." He looked at Jon. "You should stand by while she showers for the first few days just to be safe."

"I will."

The doctor turned even more serious. "I understand your daughter is having some emotional issues. Trinity, do you remember our talk last night about reengaging with your therapist to help you cope with your PTSD and anxiety?"

"Vaguely. My brother Drake encouraged it this morning."

"You've been through two very traumatic experiences. Last night, you had trouble knowing the difference between the past and present. Don't be surprised if you have more episodes like that. Talking to someone, opening up about how you're feeling and working through the trauma and learning to live—"

"Doc, I've done this before. I know what I need to do now."

The doctor stared at her hand trembling at her side. "Please follow through. And if any of your symptoms worsen, contact me immediately."

"I will. And thank you."

The doctor handed her discharge papers to Jon and left them alone in the dimly lit room again.

Jon turned to her. "Have you called your psychiatrist and made an appointment?"

"Trust me, I have no doubt my brother Drake already did." She didn't want to talk about her mental state. "Let's get Emmy and go home."

Jon didn't let it go. "I'm worried about you."

She pressed her hand to her forehead. "I need some time. And sleep. Then we'll see where my head is. Right now, it's too fresh and up front and overwhelming. I want to go home!" She couldn't hide the desperation for wanting to get back to normal.

"Okay. I'll take you."

"Thank you."

"Don't thank me, Trinity. For anything. If not for me, you wouldn't be in this predicament."

She closed her eyes because she really needed to block out the light and sort of turn things down in her mind. "Jon . . ."

"You're tired. Okay. No more talk about it. Sit. I'll help you put on your shoes and I'll take you home."

"That's all I want and need right now." She opened her eyes and met his. "And you."

"You'll always have me." He helped her finish getting

dressed and packing up the few items she had with her, which included her purse thanks to one of the officers retrieving it from Steph's apartment last night and putting it in the ambulance with her.

Emmy managed a smile when the nurses, who were pushing them both out in wheelchairs, pretended to race by letting Trinity get ahead, then racing Emmy ahead to take the lead to brighten her day.

Tate, Declan, and Skye hugged her goodbye at the curb, promised they'd call and check on her first thing tomorrow, and waved as Jon drove her out of the hospital lot. Her eyes and brain couldn't take watching the scenery pass by, so she closed her eyes and settled in for the drive out to the ranch with Jon's hand on her thigh and Emmy softly humming in the back seat.

Startled awake by something, she flung her hands up to ward off an attack she couldn't really see and screamed.

Someone grabbed her by the wrists. "Stop, Trinity. It's me. It's Jon."

The fight went out of her. She wrapped her arms around her middle and sucked in a slow breath as the pain in her ribs subsided to a dull throb again, even though her heart still pounded with fear. "What's going on?"

Jon stood close, so she focused on him. "We're home."

She looked around, not recognizing anything.

"I pulled into the garage and closed the door so you wouldn't have to deal with the bright sunlight." He gently took the sunglasses from her face, making it much easier to see in the dim garage interior.

"Oh."

"Emmy's already inside. Are you okay?"

"Yeah. Sorry. I . . . I don't know what happened."

"As much as you need the darkness, it triggers too many bad memories. We'll have to figure something out." He stepped back to allow her to exit the car.

She pressed her trembling hand to her temple. "I'm sorry. I overreacted."

"After all you've been through, you're working on pure instinct. I'll try to be more aware of it and not scare you."

"It's not you."

"I know. I just want to make things as easy as possible for you right now." He followed her into the house through the door that led into a mudroom off the kitchen. "Are you hungry?"

She went to shake her head, remembered how that set off all kinds of side effects and discombobulated her, and used her words instead. "I should eat, but I'm too tired."

"I'll help you get into bed so you can sleep for a few hours."

Emmy lay on the sofa watching a cartoon on the big TV with her stuffed bunny and one of her super-soft blankets.

Trinity leaned down and kissed her on the head. "I'm going to sleep. See you in a little while."

Emmy nodded but didn't say anything.

Trinity waited until she and Jon were in their room before she voiced her concerns. "I don't like how quiet she is."

"Me either. The pediatrician said to give her some time and to coax her to talk and interact with us. I'm hoping you'll both feel better after a good night's sleep."

She dumped her purse on the floor beside the bed and kicked off her shoes. Jon pulled the covers back and she lay down and closed her eyes the second her head hit the pillow.

He brushed his fingers through her messy hair, pulling it back and away from her face. "Rest."

Her phone vibrated in her purse again. She'd been ignoring it since she woke up in the car. "It's probably one of my brothers. Will you check?"

Jon made some ruffling sounds as he dug through her purse to get her phone. "Your battery is about dead. I'll plug your charger in, but you've also got twenty-eight messages."

"Probably work stuff. Will you listen to them and call Adria with anything that needs to be handled right away?"

"Sure, sweetheart."

With his assurance that he'd handle it, she gave in to the incessant need to shut off her brain and fell into oblivion, only to wake up sometime later caught in a barrage of nightmarish images, Steph's warning ringing in her head, and a raging need to know why Jon deceived her.

Chapter Twenty-Eight

JON HAD enough to worry about with Emmy's quiet intensity and Trinity sleeping for the last sixteen hours. He truly couldn't handle anything else. If she didn't wake soon, he'd go in and try to wake her again. His last attempt an hour ago got nothing but her mumbling incoherently and pushing his hands away from her. After watching her through the night restlessly shift and move in bed and listening to her muffled screams and babbling nonsense he wished he could decipher, he just wanted to see her awake and alert, not stuck in some nightmare.

Emmy had her own nightmare during the night. It took him nearly an hour to calm her down and put her back to bed next to Trinity, which seemed to make her feel much better. He had a feeling she'd be sleeping with them for the foreseeable future.

But those weren't the only things keeping him up most of the night.

Trinity asked him to listen to her messages and relay anything urgent to Adria. The messages were dire, and when he spoke to Adria, she had no idea how to handle the situation. Added to that, she was supposed to be on bed rest and couldn't deal with the situation herself. Not without jeopardizing her health and that of her babies.

After all Trinity had been through, he couldn't let her wake up to this drama, so he offered to step in and take care of it. Adria agreed, so long as he kept her in the loop and all final decisions were made by either her or Trinity once she woke up.

So he got on the phone with the Billings store manager to assess the situation and discovered it was far worse than the original desperate messages Nathan had left Trinity.

Jon had handled a recall with one of his companies, but it had been small, voluntary, and didn't risk anybody's life.

With twelve confirmed cases of food poisoning and four people in the hospital already, this had the potential to kill someone and potentially lots of people if he didn't get the word out immediately. So he'd contacted the local news and given them all the information to warn the public.

He and Emmy sat on the sofa watching the noon news while Tate made something to eat in the kitchen.

"As we reported earlier, the FDA and *Almost Homemade* have issued an immediate recall on all prepackaged Caesar salads purchased in the last two days due to E. coli contamination of the romaine lettuce used in the salad kits." A photo of the Caesar salad with the proper *Almost Homemade* labeling appeared on the screen in a box beside the anchor with a circle around the Prepared On date. "If you purchased one of these salads, you are asked to either discard it or return the Caesar salad to *Almost Homemade* for a full refund. So far twelve people have fallen ill in the Billings and Bozeman area with four hospitalized. Anyone who has eaten one of these salads and is feeling ill should contact their doctor or seek immediate medical attention.

Next up after the break, weather." The news cut to a chicken nugget commercial with a cute kid, reminding him that he needed to pick more up for Emmy. Maybe she'd like them with some french fries for dinner. Anything to entice her to eat and talk.

"You cheated on me!" Trinity stood just inside the living room, hands on her hips, eyes narrowed against the bright light coming through the windows, and spewed that accusation at him.

Concerned she was having some sort of episode, he stood, and walked toward her. "Trinity, honey, are you okay?"

Tate came out of the kitchen, a threat in his eyes. "What's going on?"

"He . . . he cheated?" Now she didn't sound so sure about the allegation.

Jon was completely confused, but remembered the doctor's warning about her having trouble finding her words. "I'm not cheating on you, Trinity. You are the only woman I've been with since I moved to Montana. I love you. You know that. You know me. So what are you really trying to say?"

"I think she made that pretty damn clear." Tate didn't seem inclined to give him the benefit of the doubt after an accusation like that.

Trinity huffed and rubbed the back of her hand against her forehead. "You . . . you want *Almost Homemade*. You made me think . . ." She scrunched her face like she was thinking really hard. "You wanted me."

He was starting to catch on. "Yes. I want you. End of story."

Trinity scrunched her face again and shook her head, found that didn't agree with her, and put a hand on the wall to balance herself.

"Sweetheart, you need to calm down and relax. This isn't good for your head injury."

Anger flared in her eyes. "She told me." Trinity tapped her temple several times with her finger. "I hear her. I'm stupid. You used me."

He got it now. "Steph told you that all I want is your business. I come in and I take over."

She pointed her finger at him. "Yes. You used me."

"Do you really believe that after everything we've been through?"

Tears gathered in her eyes, and it killed him to see them and the confusion making her so distressed and distrustful. "Something is wrong. We were supposed to talk and we didn't and she said . . ."

"I know, sweetheart. We were supposed to talk about the business ideas I had for you and Adria, but then Nathan thought I wanted to buy the company, and we had to go to Emmy's school. Remember?"

She nodded.

Jon continued filling in the blanks for her. "And we never talked about it. You were upset that you thought I wanted to buy the company and expand it without you."

"Yes." Understanding filled her eyes.

"But that's not true. And it doesn't matter now. I threw the proposal away, because all I want is you, your love, and our life here together. Remember? We talked about that in the hospital."

She still looked upset and unsure.

"Sweetheart, I swear to you, all I'm trying to do is what you asked and help Adria with *Almost Homemade* until you're feeling better."

She went still. Her eyes locked on him. "Wait. What?"

Now he was confused. "I thought you heard the recall

announcement I put out on the news and that's what upset you."

"What recall? What are you talking about?"

Tate stepped closer. "Sis, you've been asleep for like sixteen hours. I think your brain needs time to boot up. You seem confused and unable to think straight."

She pressed her lips tight and furrowed her brow. "What recall?"

Jon touched Tate's arm to get him to back off and let him handle this. "When I brought you home, I told you your phone had all those messages. You asked me to listen to them and call Adria with anything important. I did. Several of the messages were from Nathan at the Billings store and Theresa at the Bozeman store calling to ask what to do about customers calling saying they got sick eating their Caesar salad that they picked up at lunchtime."

Trinity covered her mouth with her hand, the metal brace on her broken fingers touching the tip of her nose. "Oh no."

"Exactly. So I called Adria and we've been working together with the hospital staff."

"Were people that sick?"

"A few. The lettuce was contaminated with E. coli. In one of my other businesses, we had to do a small recall of products that had a defective part. I kind of know the process, so Adria decided that I should take the lead and contact the Montana Food and Safety Bureau and the FDA and let them know we believed the lettuce was contaminated based on the sample that tested positive at the hospital. The FDA has since confirmed the E. coli contamination and is tracing the lettuce back to your romaine producer."

Trinity's eyes narrowed. "That's not right."

The doorbell rang. Tate turned and answered it, letting Adria and Drake inside.

Jon tried to finish his conversation with Trinity. "The tests are conclusive. The recall went out on the morning and afternoon news. They'll replay it tonight on the evening and nightly news. We phoned and emailed as many customers as we had contact information for, but we couldn't reach everyone."

"No. That's not right," she repeated, getting that confused look again.

He tried to be patient. "Take a second to organize your thoughts."

She gave him a dirty look. "I'm not stupid."

Adria put her hand on Trinity's shoulder. "He's not saying that."

He hadn't slept in two days, but still tried to hold back the hurt she'd think he'd be so callous. "You have a major head injury. Your brain is not working properly. You say it's not right. *Why* isn't it right?"

Her mouth tilted into a lopsided frown. She turned to Adria. "Hydro . . . hydro?"

Adria gasped, covered her wide-open mouth, then spit out, "Oh shit. Pregnancy brain. I forgot."

Jon waved his hand between them. "Care to fill me in?"

Trinity took a breath and went slow. "After there had been reports of several romaine recalls over the last few years, I knew we had to be careful about our supplier. Lettuce Harvest supplied all our greens until I read an article about a group of University of Montana students who were working with hydro . . . hydroponics," she said, finally finding the word. "They had a small setup and were supplying high-end restaurants with clean, organic greens. Because they are grown indoors and everything in the process is strictly controlled, the likelihood of contaminations like listeria and E. coli are nearly nonexistent."

Brilliant. Jon loved how she thought outside the box. "When did you change suppliers?"

"Last week at all the stores, but earlier than that at the Billings store, though I didn't tell them when I accepted . . ." She pressed her lips tight. "No, not the right word. Um . . ."

"Take your time," Jon coaxed.

"I received . . . No."

Adria's eyes went wide. "You went to the new hydroponic warehouse to look at the operation and sign off on verification that they met the quality standards we put into the contract."

Trinity sighed with relief. "Yes. And while I was there, I took *delivery*"—she beamed with a smile that she'd finally gotten her words right—"early and brought several boxes of greens to Billings because they ran out."

"Because of the Robertson wedding!" Adria grasped Trinity's arm. "So they'd switched over without even knowing. So what does that mean for the contamination and our customers getting sick?"

"You don't think it was the lettuce," Jon said for Trinity.

"Not if it was hydroponic lettuce. Can't be. The stores would have run out of the Lettuce Harvest greens early last week."

"You're sure?" He needed to be before he started digging further.

"As sure as I can be with you and the doctor warning me about not being able to think straight."

"But this makes sense to you?" Jon saw it in her eyes.

"Yes." She held his gaze, imploring him to believe

her. "Something else is wrong. I can't think of what it is, but it's something about Bountiful Foods."

"Okay." Jon remembered Nathan telling her she should take that deal. "They wanted to buy *Almost Homemade*, but you said no."

"Not about that. About lettuce."

"What about lettuce?" he asked, hoping to spark something more in her mind.

Tate held up his phone. "Tree Top Grocery recalled all their romaine lettuce about ten days ago because of E. coli contamination. They are owned by . . ."

"Bountiful Foods," they all said in unison.

Trinity sighed with relief again. "Yes. That."

Jon put his hand to her cheek. "You're really locked in with the produce news."

She nodded. "It hurts to think right now though."

"You're doing great." He brushed his thumb across her cheek and she leaned into his palm.

Drake chimed in. "So Bountiful had a recall of their romaine ten days ago. Did their grower also supply *Almost Homemade*?"

Trinity almost shook her head, but stopped herself before the pain really hit her.

"Try to keep your head still, sweetheart."

"I forget."

"It's automatic, I know, but seeing you in pain is killing me."

Trinity drew closer to him, and he loved that she was finally putting her earlier thoughts and feelings aside and remembering they loved each other. "Not the same supplier, but I remember Nathan saying they took a hard hit for that recall because customers feared all the fruits and vegetables were contaminated in the stores."

He thought about how aggressive Nathan became

when he thought Trinity was selling the store to Jon. "Is Nathan associated to Bountiful Foods in some way?" He sure did want Trinity to sell to them.

"His father owns it." An "ah-ha" lit Trinity's eyes before she closed them and connected all the dots in her head she couldn't earlier. "Nathan came to work for me because he wanted to be a chef and manager of the store to prove to his father he could run a successful business just like his dad. He wanted the inside track on the start-up. He is the point person for each new store we open because Adria and I can't be everywhere at once. But what if the job with us was just a ruse so he could scout the business for his father's company?" She opened her eyes and stared at him. "He cheated."

"I think you mean he used you." That's what she'd meant before about him trying to buy her company. Which was not what he'd been trying to do. At all.

He wished it would stop coming up though, because it kept coming between them. And that's the last thing he wanted.

"Yes," she agreed.

Drake hooked his arm over Adria's shoulders. "Well then, it's a good thing we have surveillance at all the shops."

Jon wished that were enough. "He manages the store. If he brought in contaminated lettuce and made up the salad kits with it, he'd have been smart enough to turn off the system."

"Which is why there is a secondary system that kicks in whenever someone other than Trinity or Adria shuts off the cameras."

Trinity grinned. "Paranoia pays off," she said to her big brother.

Jon got it. Drake had some issues a while back.

Adria's sister had been killed in one of their stores. He understood why Drake would take extra precautions with his wife and sister. "So you think we have a recording of him doing this?"

"I guarantee we do," Drake confirmed.

Jon thought of something else. "But there were cases of people getting sick from the Bozeman store as well."

Adria supplied that answer. "We had two early morning employees out sick, so the Billings store sent over some of their salad kits so the Bozeman team could focus on the hot food counter offerings for that day."

Jon thought that all made sense and everything tied back to Nathan. They still needed to prove it. But the state bureau and FDA would want to be sure. "We'll still need to test the hydroponic greens both in the store and at the source to be sure. We'll also want to test anything left over from Lettuce Harvest and at their farm to rule them out. Then the FDA and authorities can build their case against Nathan and Bountiful Foods if they can connect them to the sabotage."

"Let's go find out." Trinity turned to go back down the hall.

He took her arm and stopped her. "Where are you going?"

"With Adria and Drake to check the recordings and contact the police."

Jon, along with Tate, Drake, and Adria, said, "No."

Her brow furrowed again. "But I can help."

"The doctor said you need to rest. No bright lights. Only an hour of screen time and no stress."

"But . . ." Her lips scrunched into a disgruntled pout.

"You have a concussion, and your brain was bleeding inside your cracked skull not even a full day ago. No." He took her by the shoulders. "I couldn't stop what happened with Steph. Let me take care of this for you and make sure Nathan doesn't do anything else to ruin your business."

Drake stepped close. "I only brought Adria over to see that you're okay. I'm taking her home, then Jon and I will check the recordings and move forward with whatever needs to happen next with the FDA and authorities. We'll take care of it, Trinity. Right now, you and Adria need to take care of yourselves."

"But I can do this."

"Of course you can," Jon assured her. "You put all the pieces together. You figured out what is really going on here. I won't let Nathan tarnish the company reputation, tank your sales to devalue the company, buy it cheap, and slap an Under New Management sign on it to bring customers back."

As manager of the Billings store, Nathan knew a lot about their finances and that opening the two new stores had stretched them thin. A big recall and loss of customer confidence could sink them fast.

That's what initially made Jon come up with his ideas to help Trinity and Adria expand and not put everything at risk. But that didn't matter now. Stopping Nathan and restoring customers' faith in *Almost Homemade* took precedence.

Jon brushed his hand up her arm. "Let us clean up the mess and get *Almost Homemade* back up and running the way you want it. Right now, your health is more important than anything."

Adria moved closer. "I know it sucks. It's our baby. But Drake and Jon will bring Nathan down."

"Fine." Her stomach rumbled, reminding Jon she hadn't eaten in a good long time.

"You need some food and rest. I'll call and update

you as often as I can, but I'm betting we get the proof and Nathan is arrested in no time."

Tate walked out of the kitchen with a huge plate of lasagna and garlic bread.

Trinity held her hands out for it, eager to dig in, judging by the way her eyes devoured the food on the plate. "At least you brought one of my favorites."

"You probably made it. I took it out of my freezer." Tate handed over a fork.

Jon slipped his hand around the side of her neck and stared into her eyes. "Please rest."

She narrowed her gaze as she looked at him. "If I have to."

"You do." He nodded toward the sofa. "Maybe you can get Emmy to open up and talk. I'm worried about her. And you. But we'll talk when I get back."

She fisted her hand in his shirt. "I'm sorry I said you cheated. You wouldn't do that."

"Never. But I understand you were having trouble finding the right words."

"Still." Her frown deepened. "I don't like feeling confused about us."

"I love you. Try to hold on to and remember that."

She leaned in and pressed her forehead to his chin. He rubbed his hands up and down her back, trying to soothe her.

"I'll keep in touch, Trinity." Adria brushed her hand over Trinity's hair.

She looked up. "You're supposed to be on bed rest."

"I'm going." She took Drake's hand and let him lead her to the door.

Drake glanced back over his shoulder. "I'll meet you at the store in town. We can view the footage from all the stores on the computer system there."

"Okay." He turned back to Trinity after they left. "Thank God I don't have to drive all the way into Billings. I'm too tired for that."

Trinity brushed her fingers under one of his eyes. "How long has it been since you slept?"

"Two days," Tate said from his spot on the sofa next to Emmy, where they sat transfixed by the cartoon.

"Go eat your food, sweetheart. Drink some water, too. You've got to be dehydrated after sleeping so long."

"I'll take care of me if you promise to take care of you when you get home."

"All I want to do is spend time with you, so I can really take it in that you're okay and you're here with me."

"Then go do my thing, so we can do our thing when you get back."

He kissed her softly. "I love you." He wanted her to hear it, to believe it, so she wouldn't be confused anymore.

Chapter Twenty-Nine

TRINITY FINISHED her meal and downed two glasses of water. She felt better. But she didn't like the way Emmy stared at the TV, not speaking, not looking at her or Tate. The little one was never this quiet.

Trinity left the dining table and sat on the sofa at Emmy's feet. "Hey, sweetheart, do you want to play a game?"

Emmy stared at the TV, unresponsive.

"We could do one of the puzzles in your room or have a tea party." She wasn't up for much, but to engage the little girl, she'd do just about anything right now.

"No."

She'd take the one word and call it a victory for now, but she wanted more. Emmy needed to talk about whatever was going on in her head. "I'm feeling a little better today." She held up her hands and wiggled her sore fingers. She needed to trim and file the broken, jagged nails. Her broken fingers hurt, but not too bad. "Are you feeling better?"

"No."

Okay. Good. An honest answer. "I had a bad dream right before I woke up. It made me feel scared and a little confused. How are you feeling?"

"Sad." A tear rolled down her cheek and dripped onto Emmy's favorite stuffed bunny.

Trinity's heart ached. "Why are you sad?"

Emmy peeked up at her from behind Bunny's head. "What happened to the kitties?"

Trinity gasped. "Oh sweetheart, I'm so sorry we forgot about Puff, Dot, and Razzle."

"Puff and Dot are hers. Puff scratches me all the time. Dot won't let me pet her. But Razzle is mine. She sleeps with me." Emmy's lips trembled. "I hate her."

Trinity knew she meant her mother, not her beloved Razzle.

Well, she got Emmy talking. And she could do something about the cats. But she didn't know what to do about Emmy hating her mom. That feeling was real and justified after all Steph had done.

"Tate," she called, wondering where he went.

Surprisingly, he came from down the hallway. "Yeah. You okay? You need something?"

"It seems in all the drama that happened we forgot about Steph's cats."

"Razzle is mine." Emmy gave her a stern look.

"Um, yes. Razzle has two friends. Puff and Dot. Can you find out what happened to the cats? Are they still at Steph's place? Did a neighbor take them? Maybe Jon can pick them up on his way home?"

Tate pulled his phone from his back pocket. "On it."

Trinity stared at him. "What are you doing back there?"

"Looking into something. Let me find out about the cats, then you and I need to talk."

"Okay." She had no idea about what, but when something got Tate's attention, he held on to it like a dog with a bone.

"There we go, Emmy. Tate will make some calls and see if we can get the kitties." She had no idea if Jon even wanted them here, but if it made Emmy happy, he probably wouldn't care.

Emmy finally stopped hiding behind Bunny and sat up next to her. "What if no one fed them?"

"I'm sure someone thought about the cats before they locked up your mom's place. The police are very helpful. They wouldn't leave the cats alone in there with no one to care for them." She hoped that was true.

Steph hadn't been very cooperative. They'd had their hands full with her, their investigation, and making sure she and Emmy got the medical care they needed.

Trinity put her arm around Emmy's shoulders and drew her into her side even though it cost her. "Is there anything else you want to talk about now that we're looking into the cats?"

Emmy hesitated, hugged Bunny close, then looked up at her. "Will I get to live with Daddy all the time now?"

"Yes." No matter what happened with Steph, however the charges against her played out, Jon would never allow Emmy to go back and live with Steph. It would be a travesty if the court didn't side with Jon now.

"Are you going to stay here with us?"

"Trinity," Tate called, and waved for her to join him in the kitchen.

"I'll be right back." She hated not answering the little girl, but Tate stood just outside the kitchen staring her down, imploring her to hurry up with his intense gaze.

It took her a second to get up off the couch and be sure she had her balance, but once she made it to the kitchen, Tate took her arm and frowned.

"So the cat situation is tricky. I called Jon. He had no clue what happened with the cats and gave me the manager's number at the apartment complex."

Trinity rolled her eyes and wished she hadn't. It sent her brain and vision into a tailspin. She closed her eyes for a moment, then refocused on Tate.

"You good?"

"Yeah. Fine. My head," she said by way of explanation. "So the manager has the cats?"

"No. He knew that an older woman in the building had recently lost her dog, so he asked her if she'd like to take the homeless cats."

"Okay, can we talk to her and get them back?"

"Well, here's the thing. She took two. The gray-and-white and the black one."

"Puff and Dot."

"The orange one went to a single mom, who has a little boy."

"Crap. That's Razzle. Emmy's favorite."

"I have the number for both tenants, but it sounded like Emmy really only wanted her cat back. I mean, the older lady lives alone. She'll probably spoil those two cats rotten."

Trinity agreed, but if Emmy really wanted all of them back, she needed to try. "Call the single mom. Tell her that Emmy really loves her kitty and wants her back and because of the circumstances the other night, Razzle was rehomed without us knowing. See if the mom is willing to give the cat back. If we can make that happen, then maybe Puff and Dot can stay at their new home. But if Emmy wants them, too, we can always call the lady tomorrow and work that out."

"Okay, give me a few minutes. I'll see if I can get in touch with her."

"Thanks, Tate. My brain just isn't functioning on all cylinders today."

"I got this."

While Tate went back down the hall to make the phone call, she rummaged through Jon's kitchen, taking inventory of what he had on hand. Cooking always relaxed her, and she thought maybe she and Emmy could make something together. That would get both of them out of their heads and stop them from obsessing over what happened.

Unlike Steph's place, Jon kept the refrigerator stocked with Emmy's favorite fruits and veggies. She took out a package of chicken thighs from the freezer to cook for dinner later. In the pantry, she found a box of rotini. She could make some Parmesan butter noodles to go with the chicken. Emmy would love that. She smiled at the sweets Jon kept on hand to bribe Emmy and reward her for being good. Next to the jar of mini chocolate bars she left in his pantry sat a bag of miniature peanut butter cups and a bag of gummy worms. Behind them were two boxes of vanilla cake mix, three tubs of chocolate frosting, and three boxes of brownies.

She grabbed one of the brownie mixes.

Tate caught her before she called Emmy into the kitchen. "Okay. Single mom, Savannah, agreed to return Razzle, even though her son fell in love with her. She felt bad for Emmy. Liz is off work in thirty minutes at the spa. She'll swing by the apartment complex. I told the manager Liz is pregnant and can't be around the cat litter box. He said he'd go over to Steph's, clean it out, find the food, the cat cage, and have everything ready for Liz to pick up when she gets there."

"We owe him a nice thank-you and something for his trouble."

"I'm sure Jon can take care of it when he deals with Steph's place. Liz will get the cat from Savannah and bring it here."

"Thank you. I think this will make a huge difference to Emmy."

"I'm supposed to bring the horses over tomorrow. Maybe I should postpone with everything you two have going on."

"No. Bring them. It's another distraction for Emmy. She'll love it."

"Okay. Then that leaves you."

"Me?" She had no idea what he was talking about.

"You accused Jon of cheating on you."

She shook her head, setting off another round of dizziness, and silently scolded herself for not being more careful. "That's not what I meant. My brain . . . I have trouble finding the right word sometimes."

"You're doing well now."

"I slept a long time. My brain got the rest it needed, but I can tell the longer I'm up and doing things, the slower I start to feel."

"Then maybe I should hold off telling you what I found."

She gave him a dirty look. "Well, now you can't, can you?"

"Yeah, your mind is sharp enough to hear what I have to say. Come with me."

She followed Tate down the hall to the office Jon redecorated. "We shouldn't be in here. This is Jon's place. We should respect his privacy."

Tate ignored her. "Do you love him?"

"Yes."

"Do you want to make a life with him?"

"Yes."

"Did you believe him when he said he never wanted *Almost Homemade*, he just wanted you?"

"Yes."

Tate picked up a bound set of papers. "This is the proposal Jon was telling you about. I found it and this folder"—he tapped the file on the desk with his index finger—"in the trash, just like he said."

"Okay. He told the truth. I didn't think otherwise."

"But he never told you what he proposed." Tate waved the business proposal.

"No. We never got a chance to discuss it."

"I'm no businessman, but even I can see the genius in this plan. You know what else I see in these papers?"

"What?"

"That he really, truly means it when he says he wants you more than anything else."

Her eyes glassed over. "I know that, Tate." Her heart burst to overflowing with how much she loved Jon.

"Then you should accept both of these proposals."

She looked at them, but her vision still had floaters and stars and it was so hard to focus on the printed pages. "I can't read them right now. My eyes . . ."

"That's why I read them for you. I'll start with the business proposal. He didn't want to buy *Almost Homemade*. He wanted to expand it with you. He proposes giving *AH* an influx of cash to open new stores and sell your products at grocery stores. Some he owns. A couple he plans to buy, including the one right here in town. You will be partners. You and Adria own *Almost Homemade*. He owns the groceries and markets."

"Really?"

"You know your business. He knows his. The money he loans you will be repaid over time with a modest interest rate. If you pay it off early, your profits will soar way beyond what you're making now."

"We'd be working together." She liked that.

"He would oversee the business side of things, leaving you and Adria to focus on what you really love— cooking amazing meals for your customers. You'd of course have a say in all business decisions, but he'd take the lead on the expansion."

"That kind of sounds amazing. Adria and I have loved opening the new stores, but we spend more time focused on finding a building, renovations, hiring new people, and getting the operation up and running than we do being in the kitchens."

"You'd still be involved, but he'd take a lot of that off your shoulders because that's what he's good at. He also proposes having one of his business managers take point, and he'd direct that person and you'd all oversee him."

"Adria and I have talked about possibly hiring a business manager of some sort. Someone to help us with the logistics and things."

"I don't think you could do better than Jon and his people based on this very detailed and well-thought-out plan he has for working with you two."

"Wow. I had no idea. Why would he keep this from me?"

"It's like you said. You never got a chance to discuss it. I think while he was making his plans, he wanted to have it all perfect to present to you because if you said yes, that meant you'd be working together for a very long time to come."

"Is it strange that I can already see it? I know Adria dreamed of *Almost Homemade*, but it's become my life's work, too, and I love it and I want Jon to be a part of it."

"Then I think you should see this." Tate turned the folder on the desk and flipped open the top so she could see the papers inside.

"A prenuptial agreement?" They'd talked about sharing their life. He'd basically asked her to move in. "I guess that makes sense. He'd want to protect his wealth." He'd probably learned to protect himself dating Steph.

"This document isn't to protect him per se. It's to protect you."

"I don't understand. He's got way more assets and money than I do."

"But you were suspicious of his intentions. Nathan accused you of wanting to sell *AH* to him. Steph made you think he only started dating you because he wanted *AH*."

"All of that was wrong. Jon's not like that. I never thought he'd do something like that because of a business deal."

"He wanted you to be sure, so he put it in this document. He's not asking you to take one deal, he wanted to ask you to take *him* and the deal. If you agreed, and later down the road you two split for any reason, *AH* remains yours, any debt owed to him on the loan is forgiven, and you walk away clear. He keeps the grocery stores he owns." Tate tossed the last part out like that didn't really matter, because what mattered was that Jon wanted her to know the only thing he wanted was her.

It wasn't about the companies and money. It was about them working together and building on what they already had, but more than anything he wanted them to be husband and wife, equal partners in business and life.

"You should also know that I asked him about running cattle here."

It made sense. "He wants Emmy to grow up on the ranch."

"Declan and I want to expand the herd, but we'll need more land. Jon's got the land to run a herd as large as the one we've got at Cedar Top. You guys will expand the business, and you'll need more beef. Jon can supply it."

"He loves business, but his dream to run the ranch got trampled under all the Steph chaos." She thought more about it and realized why he'd put everything on hold. "He thought she might want to move back to California, which meant he'd have to go back, too, so he could be with Emmy. He'd have given all this up for Emmy."

"After what Steph did, Jon will more than likely get full custody. He can stay right here with you."

They could make a life together right here.

She touched her fingers to the papers. "I can't believe he threw this away."

"Your happiness is more important to him than money or any business deal. You had reservations about his offer, so he took it off the table and trashed it. He knows you love him, so he chose you over everything else just like he'd have chosen Emmy and gone back to California if that's what it took to keep his daughter."

"I can't believe it."

"You are his true love, Trinity. Is he yours?"

Her heart overflowed with love for him. "Yes."

"Then tell him you'll take the deal."

Everything became clear in her mind and heart. She knew exactly what she wanted and needed to do. But she needed a little time.

"How long until Declan and Skye's wedding?"

"It's next Saturday."

"And the rehearsal dinner is on Thursday?" She tried to remember the details stashed in her cloudy mind.

"Yeah. The whole family should be there, including Adria's sisters and Mom and Dad."

"Perfect."

"For what?"

"You'll see." She took the business proposal and the prenup and held them to her chest. "Whatever you do, don't tell Jon you told me about this."

Tate held out his hand, a black velvet box in his palm. "Then I guess I shouldn't tell him or you that I also found this in his desk drawer."

"Is that a . . ."

Tate grinned. "Want to see it?"

She shook her head. And regretted it again.

"How many times are you going to do that before you remember it hurts?" Tate scolded.

"I don't know, a dozen more maybe." She closed her eyes, waited a few seconds, then opened them again. "Are you sure that's for me?"

"I can't imagine he got it for Steph."

She cringed at the thought. "Okay. I'll need that for Thursday, but I'll leave it there for now."

"What exactly are you planning for Thursday?"

"If I can get Declan and Skye on board and Adria to agree, I'm going to accept Jon's proposals."

"Not sure what that all means, but if you need any help, count me in."

She'd need her whole family's help to pull this off, but they loved her, she loved Jon, and they'd help her make her dream a reality.

Chapter Thirty

J<small>ON THOUGHT</small> this day would never end. His head pounded. His eyes blurred. And he didn't even have a head injury to blame. Just overwhelming fatigue. All he could think about was Trinity and Emmy and all they'd been through the other night.

And that fuck Nathan piled on with his deceit and sabotage.

People were sick and in the hospital because Nathan wanted to force Trinity and Adria into a situation where they *had to* sell because they couldn't take the financial hit after spreading themselves thin with the new stores. Or maybe it was straight-up revenge for Trinity not taking the deal. Either way, Jon was taking him down.

Drake searched through the video footage.

Jon called the FDA and sent them to the hydroponics farm to test their greens. They'd confirm the contamination didn't come from there.

He sorted through Trinity's meticulous order forms and inventory lists and found all the evidence that showed when she'd used the last of their Lettuce Harvest greens and replaced them with the hydroponically grown greens. Then he contacted the farm that supplied Tree Top Grocery that was owned by Bountiful Foods and spoke to them about their recall, only to discover Bountiful Foods handled the collection and disposal of all the contaminated lettuce, which gave Nathan access through his father's company.

It might be circumstantial, but it was something to add to the case the police and FDA were building against Nathan.

Drake slammed his hand down on the desktop. "Got you, motherfucker."

Jon watched over Drake's shoulder as he rewound the video to show Nathan driving into the parking lot of the Billings *Almost Homemade*. He got out and went to the trunk where he pulled out four huge boxes of lettuce with the Tree Top Grocery logo right on them. "Son of a bitch."

Yes! They got him. Finally Jon could do something to help Trinity, instead of standing by helplessly. He'd take Nathan down and make sure he never hurt Trinity—or anyone else—again. She'd worked hard to build *Almost Homemade*, and he wouldn't let Nathan steal it from her.

Drake switched cameras to the one in the main kitchen inside the shop. Nathan immediately turned off the security system, then went to the office and turned off the camera system.

"None of the employees know that only Adria's and Trinity's passwords actually turn off the cameras."

"That way the employees can't steal from their employer." Jon thanked God they had the evidence they needed to prove Nathan sabotaged *Almost Homemade*.

Drake shrugged. "They can try, but we'll have them on video doing it."

Jon raised a brow. "Have you actually caught anyone?"

"A prep chef was stealing prime beef and reselling it to earn some extra cash. Trinity fired him."

The video continued with Nathan carrying out his potentially deadly plan. He pulled on a pair of latex gloves, unpacked all the lettuce, and set it on the huge prep table, broke down the boxes, pulled out the salad containers and a knife, and went to work making dozens upon dozens of salads until all the lettuce had been used. He stacked the prepared kits and filled the refrigerated cases in the front of the store, then put the remaining ones in the walk-in refrigerator in the kitchen. Presumably, someone on staff collected them along with the other salad kits that were taken over to the Bozeman store because they were short-staffed and couldn't make any themselves.

"He did it alone."

"Looks that way." Drake made a duplicate recording of the video.

Jon handed him the card from his FDA contact and the one for the local police detective working the case.

Drake sent the video to both officials' emails, then turned in his seat. "Nothing to do now but wait for them to arrest Nathan."

Jon sighed. "It seems rather anticlimactic."

"There can't always be a big takedown. But Nathan will serve time for purposely poisoning those people, *Almost Homemade* will be cleared, and Bountiful Foods will be implicated in this as well. Adria and Trinity can file a civil suit against Nathan and Bountiful Foods for their lost revenue and damage to their brand and name."

Jon agreed. "I wouldn't be surprised if everyone who got sick also filed suits."

"It's less than Nathan and Bountiful Foods deserve and all we're going to get." Drake looked as disappointed as him that Nathan wouldn't suffer more for going after Trinity and Adria.

Jon picked up his phone and accepted the call from the detective. "Did you get the video?"

"Watched it. We'll have him in custody soon. I'll let you know when that happens so you can put out a press release letting the community know who was really at fault."

"Thank you, Detective."

"You did most of the work uncovering his plan. The video is all the proof we need to back up your suspicions."

Drake tapped him on the arm and jerked his chin toward the door.

Jon turned and stared at the man who tried to harm Trinity's life. "Nathan. What are you doing here?"

"We're on our way. Stall him if you can," the detective said.

Jon kept the line open but held the phone in front of him.

"Is that Trinity on the phone? I need to talk to her, but she's not answering my calls. Neither is Adria." Nathan shifted from one foot to the other when Drake stood and eyed him.

"Adria is resting at home. She's not to be disturbed." The deadly warning in Drake's tone made Nathan take a step back.

The office didn't have much space, and Nathan kept the door at his back.

Jon wanted to know how far Nathan wanted to go with his scheme. "Why do you want to talk to Trinity?"

Nathan's eyes narrowed. "Those two own this place, yet they don't show up when there's a crisis. They leave *you* to handle it."

Jon didn't tell the staff what happened the other night. He'd let Trinity explain her absence and provide as much or as little detail about Steph's assault on her as she felt comfortable sharing.

"Trinity trusts me to take care of the situation and keep the shops operating smoothly." Although Trinity had suspicions because of the business proposal he never got a chance to articulate to her, Trinity still trusted him. She loved him.

"Yeah, well . . . She should be here herself. It just goes to show that running the business isn't her priority."

Drake crossed his arms. "I guess you think you could do a better job."

"The Billings store does far more business than this one," Nathan shot back.

"Given the larger population in Billings, it's not surprising the store's numbers are higher. It was a smart move for the women to set up shop there and in Bozeman once they had their flagship store running smoothly and worked out all the kinks inevitable in a new business venture." Jon used logic where Nathan, led by his ego, presented facts inaccurately.

"And now it's time to let someone run the business properly. I see the potential of what it could be, but they're too busy sourcing ingredients that increase prices and drop profits."

Jon didn't agree. "They've delivered on their promise to their customers. Locally sourced, organic, wholesome foods. Not only has *Almost Homemade* supported local farmers and ranchers—"

"You mean their family. Her brothers supply the beef. Her soon-to-be sister-in-law supplies the fruits and vegetables, the eggs, the chicken."

"Mostly, but they have other small farms right here

providing ingredients. Trinity partnered with a group of students growing hydroponic greens. She helped them expand their business. And as *Almost Homemade* grows, so will they along with us."

"Us? So you are buying the business." Nathan looked smug about catching him, but he only thought he knew the truth.

"No. But you're right. Trinity and Adria work with family. Trinity and I are building a life together, and when she needs my help with *Almost Homemade*, I will be there for her. Always." Jon didn't get Nathan's disdain for working with family. "If you're so against Trinity working with her brothers and sisters-in-law, why did you tell Trinity you wanted to work here?"

"I did it to prove to my father I can manage the business. He's seen the numbers for *Almost Homemade*. He agrees with me that I can build *Almost Homemade* into something as big, if not bigger, than Bountiful Foods."

Drake sneered. "So this was all about proving yourself to your father."

"He thought culinary school was a waste of time. But I showed him that I could be an asset even if I didn't work in some office all day."

"Good for you," Jon mocked. "But *Almost Homemade* is not for sale. Not now. Not ever."

"They can't recover from the bad publicity, the lost revenue because people are afraid they'll get sick, too, or the lawsuits that are sure to come from the people who got sick. Look at the store." Nathan held his hand out toward the shop beyond. "There are nearly no customers. It's going to take a lot to earn back their trust and bring them into the stores again."

Jon saw the detective walking in behind Nathan. "*Almost Homemade* is in the clear. I will make sure everyone knows it. And you and Bountiful Foods will be the only ones who pay for harming those innocent people."

Jon turned his phone and showed Nathan Trinity's face on the video call he'd initiated while talking to him.

She delivered the first blow. "You're fired."

The detective stepped up behind Nathan and pulled his arms behind his back and hit him with another verbal blow. "You're under arrest for tampering with a food product and attempted murder for deliberately poisoning people."

Nathan struggled as the detective clamped the handcuffs on his wrists. "You can't do this. I didn't do anything. It was just a bad batch of lettuce."

Drake tapped PLAY on the video on the computer on the desk.

Nathan's eyes went wide and round and filled with terror when he saw himself making the salads. "I turned off the cameras."

"You thought you did," Trinity said from Jon's phone. "But I have the best security guy in the business. And he's my big brother. He'd never let someone steal from me or tamper with the business that Adria and I built from the ground up."

Jon loved that she threw it in Nathan's face that the very family she worked with helped send him to prison. "You should have just taken no for an answer when she told you she didn't want to sell. Bountiful Foods has the resources to start a competitive business of their own. Why didn't you push your father to back *you*?"

Nathan's gaze hit the floor.

Jon understood. Nathan's father was willing to buy a successful business, but he didn't believe his son could build it on his own.

And now his son was going to prison for doing something desperate to please a father who would never give him the attention, praise, or approval he desperately wanted.

The detective gave him and Drake a nod. "Thank you for your assistance." He tugged Nathan out of the office with him, reciting his Miranda rights. "You have the right to remain silent . . ."

"You can't do this!" Nathan shouted back to Trinity.

The detective just kept pulling him along out of the shop.

Jon turned the phone back so he could look at his beautiful girlfriend. "How are you feeling?"

"Tired. But elated that he's been caught. Thanks for letting me be a part of it."

"I thought you'd like to see him take the fall and hear what he had to say."

"All of this because of his daddy issues."

It made him think of Emmy and how the problems with her mother would affect her as she grew up. "How's Emmy?"

"She opened up a little. She's really pissed at her mom. She said she hates her."

"I don't blame her. But I also know that's not good for her emotional well-being."

"No. But give her time."

"And she'll have you to show her what it's like to have a good, loving mom." He hoped he hadn't overstepped or pushed too hard, too fast for what he really wanted them to be to each other and for Emmy.

"She really needs to be reassured that we are all staying at the ranch together now and that she won't have to go back to her mom. While you're there, can you run up to my apartment and pack more of my clothes? There's a suitcase on the closet floor and an overnight bag. Just grab the stuff out of my dresser and in the bathroom, and that should be fine until I can pack up the rest."

He loved the matter-of-fact way she made it clear they were sticking together now. "Sure, sweetheart, no problem."

Drake grinned beside him. "So you guys are moving in together."

"I'm keeping him," Trinity said for Drake's benefit, and smiled at Jon from the phone.

"Cough if you're being held hostage," Drake teased.

"Hell no. My ribs hurt too much as it is. I sneezed earlier and thought my head might actually explode." Trinity closed her eyes, then opened them again. "Besides, I don't need to be rescued. I just need Jon to come home."

"On my way, sweetheart." And he couldn't wait to get there.

"By the way, Tate and Liz got Razzle back. She's here, in her cage, on the porch. I thought you could be Emmy's hero like you were mine today taking down Nathan, and return her to Emmy when you come in."

"What about the other two?"

"She seems to be the most attached to Razzle. The other two found a good home, but if Emmy wants them back, we can deal with that tomorrow."

"She'll probably be happy with Razzle. She complains about the other two. Steph didn't treat them well, but Razzle always seemed to be the sweetest."

"You look exhausted, Jon. Are you sure you're okay to drive?"

"I think I have just enough left in me to get home, kiss you, and fall asleep."

"Grab something to eat on your way. That will help keep you awake, and it's probably been forever since you had a decent meal."

He loved that she wanted to take care of him. "I will. Now say goodbye because you're supposed to limit your screen time."

"You called me." She glared at him, but it turned into another grin. "See you soon." And then she disconnected.

"You sure you want to keep her?" Drake teased, but there was a serious question in there about wanting to know Jon's intentions.

"Definitely. Forever if she'll let me."

Drake gave him an approving nod, and Jon stopped worrying that her family didn't accept him. Family meant everything to Trinity. And he liked the idea of having so many people to count on and trust to have your back. He didn't have any siblings. He hoped Emmy did one day. Until then, she'd have a lot of uncles and aunts and cousins from Trinity's side of the family.

Now that all the drama with Steph and *Almost Homemade* had been handled, he could focus on him and Trinity and building the life they wanted. He got her to move in. Now he needed to make it permanent and ask her to marry him.

Maybe it was too fast, too soon, but he didn't want to wait.

He wanted her to be his wife and partner. He wanted Emmy to have the mother she deserved. He wanted to have more kids and make a million happy memories that spanned the next however many decades they were given.

And he wanted it all to start now.

"Go pack her stuff upstairs. I'll get you something

to eat and a cup of coffee for the road." Drake smacked him on the back and walked out into the kitchen.

Jon trudged upstairs and into Trinity's apartment. He liked her place and imagined moving her things and incorporating them in their home.

It took him only ten minutes to fill the suitcase and bag with her clothes and bathroom stuff. He found Drake waiting for him at the bottom of the stairs with a bag of food and a takeout coffee cup.

"Adria has all the shifts covered at all three stores. Stay home with Trinity for a few days, make sure she's taking it easy. We'll see you at the rehearsal dinner Thursday night."

Right. He'd almost forgotten Declan and Skye were getting married.

That would give him time to come up with the perfect proposal and not steal any of the spotlight from them.

"Thanks for all your help, Drake. If I need any security work done at my businesses, I'm calling you."

Drake smacked him on the back again. "Be sure you do. We like to keep things in the family."

Jon stared after Drake as he walked out the back door to go home. It took Jon a second to follow him outside after that comment and absorb that Drake, and hopefully everyone else, considered him part of the family.

Trinity was a part of his.

He loved her. Emmy did, too, and she needed Trinity in her life.

Steph wasn't out of the picture, but she had been sidelined for a good long time.

But he still needed to deal with her.

That was a problem for tomorrow.

Tonight, he had a beautiful, kind woman waiting at home for him, and he couldn't wait to get to her.

Chapter Thirty-One

TRINITY SAT with her head resting on the back of the sofa, eyes closed, trying to think of nothing and just be calm and quiet. Emmy had her head on Trinity's thigh. Trinity brushed her fingers through Emmy's hair while she watched *Sesame Street*.

"Big Bird is too big," she announced out of the blue.

"I really like his flouncy feathers."

"When will Daddy be home?" She asked about every ten minutes.

"Soon." She hoped.

Tate left an hour ago with her assurance that she could handle Emmy for a little while alone. They'd already had dinner. Emmy had put on her pj's. It was still early, but Emmy seemed as tired as her.

Organ music played on the TV. Emmy counted with Count, the vampire, to find out the number of the day.

"One bat, two bats, three bats. Ah, ah-ah." She mimicked the Count's vampire laugh.

Trinity couldn't help but smile. "Very good, sweetheart."

"Three is the number of the day. I can draw a three."

"You are excellent at numbers."

The front door opened and Emmy scrambled to get up.

Trinity opened her eyes and watched Emmy launch herself into her dad's legs as he held up the cat carrier so she didn't bang her head on it.

Jon rubbed his hand over Emmy's head. "Hey, sweetheart, how are you?"

"You were gone so long." Emmy looked up at him with a scolding frown.

"I'm sorry. I had to take care of some business for Trinity, but look who I have . . ." He brought the carrier down to Emmy's level and Razzle head-bumped the cage door and meowed.

"Razzle!"

Jon unlatched the door and let Razzle jump into Emmy's arms. The cat accepted the fierce hug from Emmy and nuzzled her head into the little girl's cheek.

"You got her. Thank you, Daddy. Thank you." Emmy leaned into Jon, unable to hug him properly with her hands filled with cat.

"You're welcome, sweetheart."

Trinity stood back, watching the sweet scene. "Honey, Puff and Dot found a home with a nice woman who lived close to your mom's place. Is it okay with you if they stay with her?"

"Do they like it there?" she asked.

"Yes. And the woman lives alone and really wanted to take care of them."

"Okay." Emmy took Razzle and headed for the hallway. "Come see our new room, Razzle. We get to stay here now. No more Mommy's house."

Jon's eyes filled with anguish. "She's really upset about her mom."

"*At* her mom. Not you. She feels safe here. And you

brought back her kitty. I have a feeling that will make all the difference in the world to her. Plus Tate is bringing the horses tomorrow."

Jon's shoulders slumped. "I don't know if I'm up for that. I'm so damn tired."

"One of the guys from Cedar Top will come by in the morning and at night to care for them for as long as we need him. He's got a young family and could use the extra cash."

"Done."

"Also, Tate said you're going to run cattle for *Almost Homemade*."

"He mentioned it to me, and while I intended to make this a working ranch again, I—"

Trinity touched her fingers to his lips to stop him. "All Tate needed to hear was that you want to be a rancher again, so he's already got a plan in place. He'll fill you in. But since you've got your hands full with Steph, Tate thought the guy he's sending is a hard worker and has earned a better position and can be your ranch foreman."

"Done. He can have the job as long as he wants it."

Trinity smiled. "I knew you'd say that."

"Yeah?"

She slipped her hands up his chest and around his neck. "You're a good man. My man."

He leaned down and pressed his forehead to hers. "Yes, I am. For as long as you want me."

"I'll take forever if it's on the table."

"Done." Then he kissed her like he hadn't seen her in forever. He held her gently in his arms because he remembered her cracked ribs, and it was the sweetest thing to know he kissed her with a desperation she felt, too, but restrained the rest of himself to protect her from further pain. "I really wish I could have spent the day with you and Emmy."

"Thank you for working with Drake to take down Nathan. I really enjoyed watching Nathan get what was coming to him. Maybe a little too much."

"Revel in it. He'd have enjoyed taking your business and rubbing your nose in it." Jon sighed. "About my proposal . . ."

She touched her fingers to his lips. "I completely understand what you wanted now."

"You do?" His eyes narrowed.

"Yes. And I think it's worth revisiting soon, but right now you're exhausted."

"Give me a few minutes to bring everything in off the porch. We definitely need to set up the litter box and Razzle's food and water. You can unpack your stuff in a couple of days when you're feeling up to it."

"You do that, then get in the shower. I'll read to Emmy and we can call it a night."

"You're not supposed to overtax your eyes and brain."

"I think I can manage a couple of books."

Jon stepped back, but kept his hands at her waist. "You took a shower and changed. The doctor said I was supposed to watch you in case you got dizzy."

"Are you upset, or disappointed you missed it?" She gave him a teasing smile.

He sighed out his mock devastation. "Mostly disappointed." The sexy grin and light in his eyes did her heart good.

"Tate sat outside the cracked door and played a game on his phone with Emmy while I took a very short shower."

Jon brushed his hand over her hair. "I just can't bear for anything else to happen to you."

"Then help me stop worrying about you so my brain can shut down and we can both get the sleep we desperately need."

"All I want to do is hold you and crash."

"I'll meet you in bed."

"I'd like to hear that every day for the rest of my life, please."

"Done," she mimicked him, and gave him a sexy grin as she slipped out of his light embrace and went to Emmy's room.

Her heart fluttered with anticipation after hearing Jon so easily talk about them being together forever. She couldn't wait to see his face when she carried out her plan to make that happen.

Chapter Thirty-Two

Jon woke up with Trinity plastered to his side, one leg thrown over his, her long hair draped over his arm. Heaven. Pure and sweet and perfect.

He stretched to look at the clock and she snuggled in closer. He hadn't slept that well in a long time.

He'd like to make love to her. Slow and easy, taking his time. But she was in no condition for that with her ribs, head still in a fog, and the dizzy spells that came over her. So he settled for turning on his side and gently pulling her close.

She wrapped herself around him and kissed his neck. "Feeling better?"

Of course she'd ask him that, when she was the one seriously injured. "I woke up with you. I can't possibly be any better."

She leaned back and smiled at him. "You're sweet in the morning."

"I'm sweet to you all the time."

"True." She dipped her head back under his chin and hugged him closer.

He slipped his fingers into her silky hair, avoiding the long line of stitches. "How is your head this morning?"

"Slow. Like yesterday, but once I'm awake a little longer, it gets better. There are things floating in my eyes."

"Do you still have a headache?"

"It's not so bad this morning."

He gently rolled her to her back and slipped his hand up under the T-shirt he found her in last night. His shirt. And God, it looked good on her.

He checked out the bruising on her side. "Did you ice this yesterday?"

"On and off every couple of hours." She put her hand over his. "Jon. I'm okay."

"I know. It's just . . ." He lightly traced his fingers over the bruises. "I think of what could have happened."

"It didn't. I'm fine. And we are moving on with our life together with Emmy, and for now, Steph is out of the picture."

He wished for good. Except for Emmy's sake. He'd endure Steph's presence in their lives when necessary. "I think I'll go deal with her apartment today."

"You don't have to do that. I rented a storage locker and hired a cleaning crew and movers to go there and empty the apartment a week from Monday. All of Emmy's things will be delivered here that evening."

He stared down at her, even though she still had her eyes closed. "You were supposed to rest yesterday and not stress about anything."

"You took care of my business. I took care of yours. Well, your personal business."

"Sweetheart—"

"We both know you didn't want to deal with it. Unfortunately, you have the unpleasant task of going to see Steph. If I were you, I wouldn't put it off. Her lawyer left you three messages at the house. I can't imagine how many times he called your cell."

"I ignored all six calls. She wants me to pay her bail so she can be out while she fights the charges. For the first time, her family, especially her father, has refused to clean up her mess. So far anyway." He couldn't believe her dad refused to get her out of jail.

Trinity's eyes opened. "Are you going to pay her bail?"

"No fucking way." He reined in his temper, and Trinity relaxed beside him because he wasn't going to come to Steph's rescue again. "I've given her every chance to be a good mother. She can't even manage being a decent person."

"Then let the court handle it and let it go."

"If she's smart, she'll make a deal and serve her time."

Trinity gave him a look that clearly said she didn't think Steph was ever smart about anything.

Fair enough. He just wanted to drop the subject, but conceded, "I should go see her just so she knows where I stand on Emmy."

"You need the closure." Right again.

She read him so well.

"Tate is going to be here in an hour with the horses. I'm going to get some coffee and make Emmy breakfast so she's ready for her big surprise. Are you coming? Or do you need more time to relax and let your eyes adjust to the light?" He'd kept the drapes closed in here and where he could in the rest of the house so she wasn't bombarded by bright lights.

"I'm coming. I think I'll sit up for a few minutes and get my balance before I try standing."

"I'll come check on you in a few and help you up, so you don't fall."

"I think I'll be okay. I'm going to do what the doctor said and take it slow."

"No horseback riding for you today," he teased, knowing full well she wasn't allowed up on a horse in her condition.

"I can't wait to see Emmy's face."

He kissed her softly. "I love looking at yours and having you here with me."

"So sweet in the morning. Remind me to stay in bed with you as long as possible."

"My pleasure." He kissed her again, then made himself get out of bed before things got too hot between them and he possibly set back her recovery.

He pulled on a T-shirt and sweats to cover the boxer briefs he'd slept in and headed down the hall. He stopped in Emmy's doorway and found her in nearly the identical position he'd seen her in last night when he kissed her good-night, even though she'd already fallen asleep. Razzle lay by Emmy's side, her arm draped over the cat.

Razzle spotted him, slipped free, ran off the bed, past him, and into the bathroom across the hall and straight into the litter box. "Good girl."

He liked the cat. She looked like a masked superhero kitty with the orange fur around her eyes and spreading over her ears and the back of her head, like a cap. The rest of her was pure white.

He left Razzle to do her business, went to the kitchen, thanked God someone had made the coffee and set the timer, found two mugs in the cupboard, and poured for himself and Trinity.

Razzle raced in and immediately found the dry food feeding container and water bowl. She chowed down.

Emmy came in rubbing her eyes. "Hi, Daddy."

"Hi, sleepyhead."

Razzle ran over to Emmy, brushed her body against Emmy's legs, then ran back to her bowl.

Emmy giggled. "She's happy here."

And so was his little girl.

"Let's have some breakfast."

"Peanut butter toast." Emmy loved melted peanut butter.

"Take a seat." He got out two pieces of bread and popped them in the toaster.

Emmy climbed onto the stool at the breakfast bar.

Trinity walked in wearing his shirt and a pair of black leggings and squinted at the bright light coming in the front window.

"Sorry, sweetheart, no window covering in here."

"It's okay. You have coffee, which is better." She picked up her mug and took a sip, then went and sat next to Emmy. "What's for breakfast?"

"Peanut butter toast." Emmy leaned into Trinity.

"Excellent. I should add that to the menu at work. Maybe your dad will add some strawberries to both our plates, too."

"Ooh, that sounds good." Emmy smiled up at Trinity and petted Razzle, who had jumped up into her lap.

Jon took out two more slices of bread. "I'll do that." He appreciated that Trinity rounded out Emmy's meal with some fruit without forcing it on her. If Trinity wanted it, Emmy did, too. He liked that she wanted to emulate Trinity. She couldn't have picked a better woman to follow.

Better than her own mother.

Sad. It hurt Jon's heart to think about how Steph harmed their little girl.

"So Emmy, your dad has something he has to do today, so you'll be hanging with me. My sister Liz is coming over with the dress I need to try on for my brother's wedding."

"Do I get to go to the wedding?"

"Absolutely. We're going as a family." She met Jon's gaze with a reassuring smile that erased his earlier glum when he thought about Steph.

He needed to start looking forward and not back. He needed to focus on the two people who loved and needed him.

He needed to put Steph in the past, because for the next however many years she was in prison, she didn't need to be a part of their everyday lives.

"Do I get a pretty dress, too?"

"Of course." Trinity sipped her coffee.

He served Emmy her breakfast and went to finish Trinity's. "I can take her shopping for something tomorrow."

"If you don't mind, my sister said she'd pick something up in Emmy's size that matches what I'm wearing."

Emmy's eyes brightened with excitement.

"I can give her some money for the dress when she stops by later."

Trinity set her mug on the counter. "I've got this. I want to do it for Emmy."

"Sweet," he mimicked her.

"Are you guys going to get married?" Emmy asked, looking from him to Trinity and back.

"Yes." He waited to see if Trinity contradicted him.

"When?" Emmy bounced in her seat with excitement, nearly toppling Razzle off her lap.

"Soon," Trinity replied, though he hadn't even asked her yet.

He planned to, right after her brother's wedding. If she was ready, why wait any longer?

They ate breakfast together, Emmy chatting about everything and nothing to Razzle and them. It felt like this was how it had always been, yet it was new and . . . perfect.

Before he knew it, they were all dressed and ready to start the day when Tate drove in with the horse trailer.

"Who's that?"

"Uncle Tate," Trinity said, like it was a done deal, they were all family. She opened the front door and let Emmy loose to run right for Tate as he got out of the truck.

Tate scooped her up and held her to his chest. "I missed you, tiny tot."

"You saw me yet-erday."

"*Yesterday*," he corrected. "And that's right. I did." He touched his nose to Emmy's, then leaned back. "Today I brought you a surprise from your dad."

Jon stared at the two and his heart grew too big for his chest. Emmy beamed with delight. Tate treated her like she was his little one. Emmy had an uncle. In fact, she had three. And aunties. Liz walked around the front of the truck, holding a garment bag over her shoulder, and hugged Trinity one-handed.

"What did you bring me?" Emmy asked Tate.

"Well, I think I'll let your dad show you what he got you."

"I got Razzle back *yes*-terday."

"I heard. I can't wait to meet her." Tate handed Emmy over to Jon.

He walked to the back of the trailer and waited for Tate to open the gates.

Emmy squealed, "Horsies!"

Jon thought he might be deaf, but no.

Emmy hugged his neck. "Thank you, Daddy. I love them."

"You haven't even met them yet." Jon backed up a few steps as Tate led the first horse out.

Trinity walked over and took the big white-and-gray mare's lead rope. "This is my horse, Luna. She's a sweet girl."

Jon walked Emmy up to the horse.

Trinity took Emmy's hand and helped her pat the horse down her long neck.

Emmy's eyes went wide. "She's soft."

Jon backed up so Trinity could walk Luna down to the barn and Tate could bring out another of the horses.

"This one is yours, tiny tot. His name is—"

"Brownie," Emmy called out to the chestnut horse.

Jon laughed with Tate. "No, sweetheart. That's a great name, but he's called Baxter. He's very gentle. The little girl who used to ride him got too big for him, so she thought you'd like to have him."

"I do want him." Her sweet earnest little voice made Jon and Tate grin.

Tate handed the rope to her. "Then he's all yours."

Jon put his hand on the rope just to be on the safe side, though Baxter was more interested in watching his buddy Red come out of the trailer.

"He's a nice one, too?" Emmy watched the larger horse come closer.

"Yes, baby. He's real nice. His name is Red."

"Hi, Red." Emmy waved to him over Baxter.

Tate handed the rope to Jon. "Uh, you weren't expecting this, but apparently *she* comes with Red."

"Another horse?" He hadn't expected four, but he had the stall space in the barn, so why not.

"Not exactly." Tate disappeared into the trailer and came back out, but with the horses in the way, Jon couldn't see what he led out until he heard a loud bleating noise.

"Is that a goat?" He couldn't believe it.

Tate walked around the horses and, sure enough, at the end of another lead rope stood a very pregnant goat. "Her name is Pippa."

"She's not a pig." Emmy frowned at the goat.

"No, she's not, tiny tot, but she has a mad crush on Red despite her being in the family way from another goat."

Emmy gave Tate a confused look.

"Pippa is going to have a baby goat," Jon explained.

"Really? When?" Emmy wiggled to get down.

"In about a week," Tate stated. "It cost you an extra fifty, but my friend threw in a bunch of feed. He thought he could separate Red and Pippa, but she had a cow." Tate grinned at his joke.

Jon laughed. "So you thought why not bring her along to join the menagerie."

"Trinity will probably start her own goat milk cheese business now."

Jon laughed again, because Trinity was that enterprising.

She and Liz finally joined them.

Trinity took one look at the goat and crouched in front of her. "Look at you. I think you and Adria are both carrying twins."

And just like that Jon realized he had no chance. He was now the proud owner of a goat, plus one. Or two. They'd see in the next week or so.

Emmy cooed to the goat. Pippa loved all the pats and attention. She didn't try to bite Emmy or knock her down, so Jon relaxed.

Tate eyed him. "We good?"

"All good," he confirmed, smiling as Emmy brought her hands to her chin and squealed, "She licked me."

Trinity stood, but wobbled until she got her balance with Liz right beside her steadying her with a hand to her shoulder. "I think I'm going to go inside and get out of the sunlight." She hadn't worn her sunglasses.

"I'll go with her," Liz volunteered, leading Trinity back to the porch.

"Let's get these critters settled into their new home." Tate took the lead rope for Red and the goat and led them down the driveway to the barn.

Jon picked up Emmy and led Baxter, though he mostly followed Red.

Tate called back to them. "So there's a big cattle auction next week. I know you've got a lot on your plate, so if you want, I can go. We'll get this place up and running in no time."

"Sounds good," he heard himself say, even though he did have a lot going on right now. But he wanted the ranch, Emmy and Trinity, and the life they made here.

"Then it's settled. You're going into the family business."

As in Jon was now a part of the suppliers for *Almost Homemade*. He loved it.

It didn't take them long to put the horses in their stalls, feed and water them, then make Pippa comfortable in another stall with lots of hay in case she went into labor and delivered her kid.

Tate closed the stall door. "The renovations to the barn turned out great. The animals should be really comfortable here."

"Thanks for picking up and delivering them here. I appreciate it."

"That's what family is for. Please get medical clearance from Trinity's doctor before you put her on a horse."

"Trust me, that's not happening unless I have written consent."

Tate slapped him on the back. "She's a stubborn one, but I think she's taking this head injury seriously. How did she sleep last night?"

"Like the dead. Me too, actually." Jon tickled Emmy's belly. "And Emmy slept with Razzle last night."

"Everyone had a friend to sleep with then." Tate gave him a knowing look that Jon didn't touch with a ten-foot pole.

Jon looked at the house and out at the rolling green landscape. "What do you think, Emmy? Will it be fun living out here and riding the horses?"

"This is the best, Daddy." She hugged his neck again and he felt like Father of the Year.

This was the life he wanted for Emmy. Happy. Carefree. Filled with fun and sun and learning about taking care of the animals and land just like he did when he was a kid.

They walked into the house and he stopped short when he saw Trinity standing in the living room showing off the beautiful blue gown she wore to Liz and Tate.

"It's gorgeous. The cut is perfect." Liz looked at Trinity with sheer joy in her eyes.

Jon agreed. Everything about the dress showed off Trinity's curves and golden blond hair to perfection. "God, you're beautiful."

"So pretty." Emmy squirmed to get down.

He set her on her feet and she ran over to Trinity and touched her leg to feel the dress.

"Soft. Shiny." Emmy hugged Trinity's thighs.

Liz held up two tiny dresses. "What do you think of these?" One was blue, the same shade as Trinity's dress. The other a pretty vibrant purple.

"Why two?" he asked.

Liz held one, then the other up to Emmy. "We'll see which one fits her best."

The alarm on his phone went off. He'd completely lost track of time. But he needed to meet with Steph and her attorney.

"Time to go?" Trinity asked.

"Yeah. Are you okay? Outside, you seemed off."

"Just the sunlight messing with my eyes. I'm good now. Liz is going to stay awhile so we can catch up. Go. I'll be here when you get home."

"You're sure?"

"Yes. Put the past in the past and let's move on."

"Where are you going?" Emmy rubbed her hand over Razzle as she wound her way through Emmy's legs.

He went to her and crouched low. "I'm going to see your mom."

Emmy backed into Trinity's legs. "I don't want to go."

Trinity brushed her hand over Emmy's head. "Only Daddy is going."

"You're staying here with Trinity and Aunt Liz. I'm just going to talk to your mom about what happened and about her going away for a long time. That's all. You are staying here with us. Okay?"

She nodded, but stayed close to Trinity.

"Do you want me to tell your mom anything?"

"She's mean. I don't want her." Emmy turned and hid her face in Trinity's thighs.

"Okay. I'll tell her. I'll also tell her that this is your home. This is where you belong. This is where you will stay." He hoped that eased Emmy's mind.

Emmy peeked back at him. "Promise?"

"I promise." He held his arms out.

She hesitated for a second, then launched herself into

his chest. He wrapped her in a big hug, careful of the bruises on her backside. "I love you, baby. I won't let anything happen to you ever again."

"And Trinity will be the mommy now," Emmy demanded.

He took her face in his palms and held her away so she could see he meant what he said. "Yes. She is." He kissed her on the forehead, then let her go.

She immediately went back into Trinity's embrace.

"I'll take care of her," Trinity promised.

"I know you will. With your life." He kissed Trinity, then left her and Emmy to go do the one thing he didn't want to do but needed to do to end this chapter of his life so he could start a fresh new one with his girls.

Chapter Thirty-Three

JON WALKED into the visiting area at the jail where Steph was being held and took a seat in front of her just as the guard closed the door behind him. Steph's lawyer set up the visit, so she knew he was coming. Still, seeing her in the prison-gray pants and shirt, her skin pale and washed out, eyes bloodshot with dark circles under them, took him aback.

"How did we get here?" she asked him, and he gnashed his back teeth. "You said you'd take care of us."

"I gave you a roof over your head and support when you needed it. You beat Emmy. You left bruises on her. You attacked the woman I love in front of her."

Steph rose and slammed her hands on the table. "I wasn't going to let her take my daughter."

The guard observing them walked forward. "Remain in your seat and keep things civil or you will be taken back to your cell."

Steph huffed out an exasperated breath and fell back into her seat. She glanced at the door. "Where is she? Waiting outside?" She meant Emmy.

"She's at home. With Trinity."

"You didn't bring her!"

"Why would I bring her to jail to see you after the way you traumatized her?"

Steph waved that away. "I'm sure she's fine."

"She's not fine. She has nightmares. She goes quiet for long periods of time. She clings to me and Trinity. She thought you abandoned the cats. Luckily, Trinity arranged to get Razzle back."

"They're just cats. What about all my stuff?"

"The apartment will be packed up and your belongings moved to storage."

"But my trial won't be for months."

Jon had a talk with her lawyer before he came in for their meeting. "Why didn't you take the deal the DA offered you?"

"*She* had no right to come into *my* home. I was defending myself and Emmy."

He tried to hold on to his temper, but she didn't make it easy. "Trinity witnessed your boyfriend spank and shove Emmy to the floor. She had every right and responsibility to check on her and make sure she was okay because you'd left our four-year-old alone outside while you were getting drunk and high. I have the pictures of you passed out. I have pictures of the bruises you left on her the night you beat her and attacked Trinity without any provocation. You could have killed her."

"And now she's living in your house, sleeping with you, spending all your money, playing mommy to *my* little girl."

Trinity hadn't spent a dime of his money. In fact, she seemed to care less that he had it. She cared more about him and Emmy than anything else. "You want to know what I love about her?"

"I don't give a shit."

He knew that. He told her anyway. "Family matters. Trinity cares more about the people in her life than anything else. *You* only care about yourself and how much you can get from me, your dad, your friends. Everything is about you. When Emmy was born, you tried so hard to be a good mother to her. I appreciated that you took good care of her. But as she got older and required more of your time and effort, you simply couldn't be bothered and she suffered because of it. And that all ends now."

"You can't keep her from me."

"I have an emergency order giving me full temporary custody, so even if you get out on bail, she stays with me. I've filed for full custody, and I'll get it because you made sure a judge would give it to me after what you've done to her. You hurt her. You betrayed her trust in you. And because of that, you won't see Emmy again for a long time. I'm not sure that even when you get out she'll want to see you."

"You're going to poison her against me."

"I never badmouthed you to her and I never will. I told her I was coming today. I asked her if she wanted me to tell you anything."

"What did she say?" Steph made it sound like it mattered to her, but Jon had learned nothing really mattered to Steph unless she got something.

"She said, 'She's mean. I don't want her.' Then she asked if Trinity would be her mommy."

She spread her fingers wide on the table. "You can't do this to me."

"*You* did this. You made your own daughter afraid of you. You made her believe she doesn't matter to you every time you neglected her and didn't put her first. *You* made her think you don't love her. I don't think you love anyone but yourself, if you're even capable of love at all."

"That bitch is not going to be her mom. I'm her mother."

"Not anymore. You want to go to family court. Fine. I'll be there to testify about everything you've ever done to our daughter and to me. Trinity will get up on that stand and tell everyone how you attacked her. I hope it doesn't come to it, but if Emmy has to testify against you, she'll tell the court how she thought you killed Trinity right in front of her."

"You can't do this." Steph hadn't accepted the reality of the situation, or the severity of the charges.

"You're charged with assault, felony battery, and child abuse along with several other lesser charges. You'll be lucky if you're out by the time Emmy goes to high school. By then, she'll be old enough to make her own decisions about seeing you. Until then, Trinity and I will raise her. Trinity will be the only mother Emmy really remembers. And right now, that is the only thing that gives me comfort and hope that Emmy will find her way past this troubling time and be the happy, carefree little girl she used to be before you hurt her."

"I'm her mother!"

"I wish you'd taken that responsibility and privilege seriously. I wish you'd loved her enough to be the best version of yourself, because the woman I dated years ago was fun and happy and excited about becoming a mom. Maybe that was all a figment of my imagination. Maybe you changed. Whatever happened, you're not who I thought you were. You're not the mother Emmy deserves."

She crossed her arms and fell back in her seat. "So you're just going to replace me."

"I always intended for you to be a part of Emmy's life. You took yourself out of the picture. You showed

Emmy that you don't deserve her. Maybe one day you can fix that. I don't know. I'm not fixing things for you anymore. This is the last time I'll come to see you. I'm not paying for your lawyer or bailing you out."

"Jon, please, I need your help." Panic laced her words and filled her eyes with desperation. She leaned in, her eyes pleading. "My father refused to come. He said he didn't condone child abuse, especially when it came to his grandbaby." Her eyes glassed over at her father's unprecedented dismissal of her pleas for help. "He cut me off."

Jon would keep in mind that Steph's father had drawn a line for Emmy when they asked to see and talk to her.

"I helped and helped and helped and everything progressively got worse. I didn't hold you accountable. But the law will this time. So you're on your own." He stood and stared down at her. "I'm going to make a life with Trinity and Emmy. We're going to be a happy family together." He turned and started to walk away.

"She's mine. You can't take her from me forever. When I get out, I expect to see her."

Jon turned, knowing that day would come eventually. "When you finally do see her again, I hope you look at Emmy and see what an amazing young woman I know she'll turn out to be, because she's got a strong, smart, independent, loving, kind, sympathetic, generous woman who raised her as her own. I hope you thank Trinity for doing the job you should have done and realize that she was there every day for Emmy because *you* made it impossible for you to be there yourself."

Jon walked out, not caring one bit about all the things she ranted at the top of her lungs as a guard tried to subdue her and shut her up. He didn't have to listen to it anymore. He wasn't responsible for her anymore. She'd severed the ties that bound him to her because of the daughter they shared.

Emmy was with him and Trinity now, where she belonged, and with two parents who loved her unconditionally and would never harm her.

Yes, Steph was still Emmy's mother.

But Trinity would be the mom Emmy deserved and the woman she looked up to and aspired to be. When Emmy faced Steph again, she'd be a strong, confident young woman who could stand on her own because that's the kind of person Trinity would show her how to be.

Chapter Thirty-Four

"HE'S HERE, Trinity!" Adria called out from her position by the front door.

Trinity's stomach fluttered with anticipation. She'd planned everything down to the last detail and in a matter of days. With a head injury. Everything, except Jon's response. She had no idea what he'd think of this wild idea. Or if he'd even agree to go through with it.

He might think she needed her head examined again.

"Go get him," her dad encouraged. He and her mom had come home to see her in the hospital and to help Declan and Skye get ready for their wedding. Next week they planned to buy a place in town so they could be here to welcome Drake and Adria's twins. Drake stood by with Declan and Skye, Tate and Liz, and her mom, who gave her a quick hug before she passed.

"Smile, sweet girl." Jon's father helped her into the long coat she'd brought to hide her dress. "He needs a good surprise in his life."

She hoped Jon liked surprises because she had a doozy.

Noah and Austin, the husbands of Adria's sisters Roxy and Sonya, and the rest of the guests sat in the chairs that had been set up earlier in the restaurant's banquet room, which had been decorated to look like the inside of an elegant cabin. Barnwood paneling adorned the walls, string lights with Edison bulbs draped from one side of the room to the other overhead, and an explosion of flowers Trinity had ordered from the local florist completed the stunning room. Pink roses, white hydrangeas, fuchsia-colored snapdragons, and pink and white peonies filled vases on all the tables and lined the aisle.

Roxy, Sonya, and Adria waited for Trinity in the alcove between the banquet room and the front of the restaurant.

Trinity slipped through the doors and scooted behind the table they set up so that Jon wouldn't get a glimpse of the bottom of her dress as he walked in with Emmy. He glanced from her to Adria, Roxy, and Sonya.

"Hey, sweetheart. Are we late?" The closed doors to the banquet room threw him off.

"No. You're right on time." She looked down at Emmy dressed in her beautiful purple dress. "You look so pretty, sweetheart."

Jon noticed Adria wearing a dress nearly identical to Emmy's. "What's going on?"

The three ladies looked to her.

Jon's eyes filled with questions.

Trinity took a breath and dove in, knowing everything was going to be okay because Jon loved her. He wanted a life with her. And she couldn't wait to get started.

She flipped open the satchel on the table and pulled out the business proposal he never gave her.

His eyes narrowed. "Where did you get that?"

"Tate found it in your office trash the day after I came home from the hospital."

"Sweetheart, I told you not to worry about that. It's not important."

"I hope you don't mean that, because Adria and I discussed it and we'd like to sign with you with a minor change to the agreement. Adria's sister Sonya"—she held her hand out toward her—"is an accountant. Adria and I would like to hire her as the accountant for the new business. She's more than capable of overseeing both your grocery store expansion and the growth of *Almost Homemade*."

Jon eyed her, surprise mixed with a bit of confusion and hope. "You're serious. You want to partner with me."

"Adria's other sister, Roxy"—she held her hand out toward her—"backed us when we opened. She's a silent partner. We'd all like you to be our other partner." She smiled at Jon, excited and hopeful and wanting him to see it. "It's a great plan, made even better by the fact that Adria and I like to do business with family."

Jon's smile widened. "I'm all for that."

"Great. But there's only one thing that would make partnering with you in business better for me."

"Anything," he said without hesitation.

She pulled out the prenup. "We become life partners."

Jon grinned and tilted his head, his eyes alight with enthusiasm and surprise. "Are you asking me to marry you?"

"I love you. These last few days have been wonderful, living with you and Emmy on the ranch, having dinner together, watching you teach Emmy how to ride a horse, feeling so connected to you. I want more of that and so much more. I want you to be my husband and partner and the father of our children. So yes, will you marry me?"

"You name the day, and I will be the one waiting for you at the altar."

"Thursday. You still owe me that dinner we never had. I thought we could do it here, tonight."

Emmy clapped her hands. "I kept the secret."

Jon glanced down at Emmy, then at her, his focus on the unnecessary coat she was wearing, and his eyes went wide. "You mean we're getting married today." That sounded like a yes to her, but she wanted him to say it.

"Declan and Skye rented out the whole restaurant for their rehearsal dinner. All of our family and friends are waiting inside with the flowers and cake and everything we need for a wedding. But all I need is you."

"Trinity." Her name was an answer to everything. "Yes. I'll marry you." Jon couldn't believe she'd put all of this together in less than a week. He had no idea what to expect. He didn't care. So long as she said I do, he was good.

He tried to get past Adria so he could kiss Trinity to seal the deal, but she held him back with a hand to his chest. "Business first." She handed him a pen.

He signed the business contract he'd put together with his attorney and initialed the small changes they'd made to it. He signed the prenup knowing they'd never have to use it.

He held the pen out to Trinity. "Partners?"

She signed both documents with her usual determination and confidence, then looked him in the eye. "Partners."

Adria quickly signed the business deal, and it was done.

A gentleman appeared behind him. "If you'll sign the marriage license, please. Trinity has already completed the required blood test."

He wanted to ask when she'd done that, but didn't because the amazing woman had planned a whole wedding this week without him knowing about it. Granted, he took Emmy to school each morning and picked her up at the end of the day. Because Trinity couldn't go in to work because of her head injury, he stopped in at *Almost Homemade* and completed whatever list of things she gave him to do and check on.

And that's how she got me out of the house so she could plan our wedding.

He signed the license and smiled at her. "You know, next time you send me out on a bunch of errands and have me running your store for you, I'm going to know you're up to something."

"From now on, I want to be up to everything *with you.*"

He couldn't help the wide grin or the way his heart beat faster with the excitement humming through him. "Deal."

"If you'll follow me, Mr. Crawford, I believe the ladies will join us in a few minutes."

Jon reached out for Trinity's hand. She gave it to him and he kissed the back of it. "I'll see you at the altar."

"Deal," she mimicked. "Oh wait." She pulled out the black velvet box he'd stashed in his desk after he'd taken his grandmother's ring to the jeweler and had them replace the center stone with one much larger. He did it the day after they were called to Emmy's school and Trinity had been everything Emmy needed her to be that day. "Is this for me?"

"Remind me to scold Tate for snooping."

"Oh." Her face fell. "It's not mine."

"Yes. It's yours. I planned to propose to you next week after Declan and Skye were married. I didn't want to steal the spotlight from them, but I guess all they want is for you and me to be happy."

"True. And they know once I get an idea in my head there's really no stopping me."

"True," Adria, Roxy, and Sonya said in unison.

He lifted his chin toward the box in her hand. "Do you like the ring?"

"I haven't looked at it. I wanted it to be a surprise when you gave it to me." She handed over the box.

Emmy stared up at him. "I'm the flower girl."

"And a beautiful one. You stay with Trinity then, and I'll go take my position and we'll make Trinity officially your mommy."

Emmy bounced on her feet. "Yes."

The day he returned from seeing Steph and told her that Steph would be out of her life for years, Emmy asked if she could call Trinity Mom. It made his heart ache to know that his little girl wanted Trinity *instead of*, not in addition to, Steph. But he knew she would be loved and thrive with Trinity in her life, so he told her yes. And when Trinity woke up from her nap because she needed some quiet time to help heal her injuries, Emmy asked, "Can we make brownies, Mommy?" Trinity's eyes had filled with tears that silently rolled down her cheeks, but she said, "Of course," and held her hand out to Emmy.

And that was it. Emmy called her Mommy all the time now. When he stayed for sharing time at her preschool, she told the whole class she got a new mommy who made the best brownies and gave the best hugs.

Jon turned back to Trinity. "Hurry up." Now that he knew they were getting married, he wanted her to be his wife immediately.

He followed the justice of the peace into the banquet room and was immediately taken aback by the smiles and clapping.

His father came forward holding a pink rose boutonniere and pinned it to his lapel. "Now I know why Trinity asked me to wear my nice black suit." She'd laid it out on the bed for him with a basic white dress shirt and simple black tie to match.

A photographer took their picture, capturing the moment. Trinity had thought of everything.

"You ready for this?" his dad asked.

"More than I can say." He thought about how he and Trinity met. "You know, I met Trinity on a Thursday, that first day I came back to town and I found her dragging you out of the house. I thought it might be the worst day of my life if I lost you."

"Turned out to be a good day. I was fine and you met her."

"We had some difficult Thursdays in between, but I think getting married today, on Thursday, is the perfect day."

"Every day you get to spend with the love of your life is the perfect day. Today, let the past go. Be happy with your wife and Emmy. Enjoy the life you make together."

Jon hugged his dad like he hadn't done in a long time. "I will, Dad. Thanks for encouraging me to move back home and reminding me what's most important."

"Family, son. Nothing else matters more."

Jon pretended to straighten his father's tie. "Looking sharp. Will you stand up with me and be my best man?"

"I thought you might ask." And no doubt Trinity had asked his father to wear a similar black suit like his and gave him the matching boutonniere as well.

They walked down the aisle. He nodded to each of

Trinity's brothers and their respective wives and fiancée, waved to his aunt, uncle, and cousin, who he hadn't seen in years, and smiled at Roxy and Sonya sitting with their husbands, he guessed. He'd get to know them better later. Especially Sonya, since they'd be working closely together on the new expansion of *Almost Homemade* and his grocery business.

Tate had also bought and delivered nearly fifty head of cattle to his place. His new foreman had hired two ranch hands. They'd expand that fifty head soon, but right now, he had a working ranch set up and ready to thrive.

He had everything he wanted and needed. It made his head spin because it had all happened so fast, but he loved it. All of it.

When he reached the front, the couple sitting there stood to greet him. The man held out his hand to shake. Jon took it.

"I'm Trinity's dad. We don't have a lot of time to talk now, but we will once you all are married. She's told us a lot about you and your little girl, Emmy. Can't believe we get a son-in-law and a grandchild in one day, but we sure are happy for you all."

Jon couldn't believe the warm welcome. "Thank you, sir. I know this may seem fast. I mean the first time we're meeting is at the wedding."

Mr. McGrath shook his head. "Trinity's a smart girl with a big heart. When she loves, she loves deep. Ask her stubborn brothers. But she never loved a man the way she loves you. We see that in her. We hear it in the way she talks about you."

"I had no idea she'd spoken about me to you."

Mrs. McGrath touched his arm. "Every Sunday the kids know they're getting a call from their mama. Now we're back in town to stay awhile with the grandbabies coming. So we'll have time to get to know each other. I can't wait to spend time with Emmy. We've been waiting to spoil our grandchildren."

"I'm sure she'd love that."

Mr. McGrath smiled. "Who knew the youngest would give us our first granddaughter?" He slapped Jon on the back. "I better go walk your bride down the aisle. As fast as she put this wedding together, I bet she can't wait to get it done."

Jon liked Mr. McGrath.

He kissed Mrs. McGrath's cheek. "Thank you for coming and embracing me and Emmy."

"Welcome to the family."

He felt welcomed and included and amazed by how Trinity's family rallied around her when she needed them whether it was at the hospital when she was hurt or when she was putting together a wedding in a matter of days.

He took his place between the justice of the peace and his dad.

Soft music began to play as the back doors opened and Emmy stepped into the room wearing the pretty purple dress he'd brought her in, and a halo of tiny white roses on her head. She held a basket of red rose petals and tossed them on the floor in front of her. She smiled so bright his heart melted. She hadn't been this happy in a long time. When she got close to him, she ran the rest of the way and buried her face in his thigh. He scooped her up and held her close.

"You did so good, sweetheart."

"She's coming."

Actually, Adria walked down the aisle next, carrying

a bouquet of white roses. She looked beautiful in her purple gown, her baby bump very prominent. But she glowed when she winked at her husband, Drake, as she passed him and took her place on the other side of the justice of the peace.

The wedding march began and everyone stood for the bride.

His heart pounded as he waited to see her walking toward him. And then there she was on her father's arm, gorgeous in a classic white gown that had a scoop neckline and hugged her curves to her waist, where a crystal-encrusted belt wrapped around her. Layers upon layers of white billowed around her hips and legs to her feet.

"Princess." Emmy hugged his neck and stared at Trinity.

She looked like an angel with her golden hair falling in thick curls and a crystal headband sparkling in the overhead lights. The black-painted ceiling with the tiny white splotches that looked like a million stars made the room feel like they were outside.

And there was his heaven standing right in front of him.

Her father took her hand, kissed the back of it, whispered, "Be happy," and held her hand out to him.

Jon stepped forward and took it.

Trinity stood before him and Emmy, smiling with a lightness and love that lit up his heart.

"You are so beautiful."

The smile brightened to megawatt.

He set Emmy down between them and held her hand. Trinity took Emmy's other hand, and he and Trinity looked to the justice of the peace.

"We are gathered here today to witness the union of Jon and Trinity and Emmy."

Jon turned to Trinity and saw the confirmation that she'd been the one to include Emmy in their ceremony.

"Marriage is the promise between two people who love each other, and who trust in that love, who honor each other as individuals, and who choose to spend the rest of their lives as partners."

Jon shared another knowing look with Trinity.

"No matter what challenges you face, you now face them together. The successes you achieve, you now achieve them together. The love between you joins you as one."

The justice of the peace turned to him. "Do you, Jon, take Trinity to be yours? Do you promise to keep living, learning, loving, and growing together for the rest of your lives?"

"I do."

"Do you, Trinity, take Jon to be yours? Do you promise to keep living, learning, loving, and growing together for the rest of your lives?"

"I do."

"Do you have the rings?"

Jon pulled the box out of his pocket and plucked the ring from the velvet holder, then handed the box to his dad.

Trinity handed her lush bouquet of white flowers to Adria and accepted the ring she handed to her.

"Jon. Place the ring on Trinity's finger and repeat after me."

Jon slid the ring on her hand and watched her eyes light up.

The justice of the peace told him what to say and he

repeated, "With this ring, I give you my heart. All that I am, all that I have, I share with you. Wear this ring today and every day so that you will always have a part of me and my love with you."

Jon thought the vows, promises, and symbols were really heartfelt and touching, but he added, "This was my grandmother's ring. With an upgrade." He brushed his thumb over the large center round diamond. "She and my grandfather were married for sixty-two years. May we be even luckier than them."

Tears gathered in Trinity's eyes. "That's beautiful, Jon. Thank you."

He squeezed her hand, then held out his left one.

She slipped a thick gold band on his finger. "This was my granddaddy's ring. He loved me as fiercely as he loved my grandma, because I was his princess." Trinity glanced down at Emmy because that's what she'd called her, then met his gaze.

The justice of the peace recited the vows, and Trinity held his hand in hers and poured out her love to him. "With this ring, I give you my heart. All that I am, all that I have, I share with you. Wear this ring today and every day so that you will always have a part of me and my love with you."

"By the power vested in me, I now pronounce you husband and wife. You may seal your promises with a kiss."

Jon pulled Trinity in for a kiss that promised a lifetime of love and happiness.

The crowd cheered and Emmy pressed into both of their sides, her little arms wrapped around them.

Jon reluctantly broke the kiss and stared into Trinity's eyes. "This was perfect."

"I'm so glad you're happy."

He couldn't be happier. "I am because you're my beautiful wife."

She beamed with joy, then crouched next to Emmy. "I promise to be the best mom I can be to you." She sealed that promise with a kiss on Emmy's cheek.

He picked Emmy up and held her at his side, took Trinity's hand, and they turned and faced their family.

"I give you Mr., Mrs., and Emmy Crawford," the justice of the peace announced.

Everyone clapped and cheered again.

Jon set Emmy down again and she ran to Trinity's brother. "Uncle Tate!" She climbed into his lap and hugged him.

"What can I say, the ladies love me." Tate smiled. Liz smacked him on the shoulder and laughed with everyone else.

After everyone came up to congratulate them, and Jon thanked Declan and Skye for turning their rehearsal dinner into his and Trinity's wedding, they all sat down to dinner. The drinks flowed, toasts were made, everyone danced, and he reveled in the fact that Trinity wasn't just the love of his life, she was his wife, his partner, his true love.

Epilogue

TRINITY AND Jon rode the high of their wedding into Declan and Skye's wedding at Cedar Top Ranch two days later. It was a beautiful country affair. She'd never seen Declan so happy and carefree. Skye was beautiful and glowing in a gorgeous white gown. When they kissed at the end of the vows, everyone saw and felt the love between them. And when they were announced as Mr. and Mrs. McGrath, Trinity smiled at her mom and dad down in the front row, watching with pride and joy as their last child married the one he loved.

At the outdoor reception, Jon leaned in and kissed Trinity over Emmy, who sat in the middle of them and said, "I still think you were the most beautiful bride ever."

With all that love in the air, it wasn't surprising that babies followed, starting with, of course, Adria and Drake's twins . . .

PROUD PARENTS,
ADRIA AND DRAKE MCGRATH,
WELCOMED TWINS!
JULIANA—6 pounds, 4 ounces, 20 inches
AND
JAMES–7 pounds, 3 ounces, 21 inches

IT'S A BOY!
PROUD PARENTS,
LIZ AND TATE MCGRATH,
WELCOMED
WYATT—7 pounds, 5 ounces, 21 1/2 inches

IT'S A GIRL!
PROUD PARENTS,
SKYE AND DECLAN MCGRATH,
WELCOMED
BROOKE—6 pounds, 8 ounces, 19 inches

IT'S A BOY!
PROUD PARENTS,
TRINITY AND JON CRAWFORD,
AND BIG SISTER EMMY
WELCOMED
LUKE—7 pounds, 9 ounces, 20 3/4 inches

Keep reading for a sneak peek
at the first book in Jennifer Ryan's
new Wyoming Wilde series

Coming soon from Avon Books!

Chapter One

"**C**HASE! WAKE UP!"

Chase shot up in bed, the rat-a-tat-tat of automatic gunfire and the blast of explosions going off in his head overlaid with a newer nightmare, the ghostly image of a beautiful blonde staring up at him with dead eyes and blue lips. His unwelcome brother's scowling face only made things worse.

He sucked in a ragged breath and shook off Hunt's hand from his shoulder. "What the hell are you doing here?" It took Chase a minute to figure out where *here* was because everything inside him wanted the last twelve hours erased from reality. He didn't want it to be true. He didn't want to be held responsible for another death.

Hunt's narrowed eyes went wide. "You OD'd and nearly died. Where else would I be but here to force you back on the right path? Again." The last time Hunt tried to set him straight he'd arrested Chase and had gotten the DA to agree to a deal, rehab instead of jail.

"Why bother?" Hunt obviously thought Chase threw away sixty days of rehab the second he got out. "You don't care what happens to me." Sometimes it felt like no one cared about him anymore.

"Because Mom would have wanted us to look out for each other—even if I hate you." Hunt knew just how to slice open old wounds and make them bleed all over again.

Their mother died seven years ago and nothing had been the same since. His father and brothers blamed him, but he'd done what he thought was right for his mom. She begged him to help her die on her terms. He did it to spare her more pain, so she could die in peace even if she had to do it without her beloved boys.

Chase fell back in the hospital bed and turned away from his brother only to come face-to-face with his younger one. "You too."

"Yep." Max gave him a condescending frown. "I think you might have set the record for relapsing after getting out of rehab. Sixty days in and you OD in less than one day out."

Only he didn't. His Army buddy Drake did him a solid and asked his girlfriend, Adria, if Chase could crash in the apartment over her shop for a couple days. He needed a minute to figure out how to go home after rehab and rebuild his demolished life.

All he wanted to do was see his little girl and that meant facing her mom, Shelby, and convincing her he'd changed his ways and wanted to put Eliza first.

He prayed he could make Shelby believe him.

"Why are either of you here?" After his mom's death, his father banished him from their ranch. His mom made him promise to make his dad see reason and let Chase rebuild and repair the failing business. She wanted all of them to always have a home at Split Tree Ranch.

Their family tree had definitely split, leaving his branch broken on the ground while his father and brothers stood against him and kicked him off the ranch and out of their lives.

But he'd kept his promise to his mother and left them all with a business plan and the money to carry it out. The only way to get his hands on a chunk of money without putting them further in debt had been to join the Army and take the big bonus they offered him at enlistment. He needed to escape their hatred and anger and find a place to go and a purpose. He got both, and a new kind of family with his brothers in arms. Knowing he wasn't welcome at home but he was needed in the service, he reenlisted after his first term ended and sent the bonus he got for that to the ranch, too.

At the time, he thought his service and helping his family was his penance.

It turned out to be his undoing.

He'd served, and served well, but the battles left him scarred, battered, mentally unstable, and ultimately addicted to the very painkillers they gave him for the wounds that healed on his body but not in his mind. That kind of pain never ceased.

His brothers didn't come today because they cared. They came to pile on the punishment.

Juliana's haunting face filled his mind. Last night seemed like another nightmare, but it had been all too real. Watching Juliana die because he'd been unable to hold it together long enough to save her killed him. He'd seen her collapse. By the time he got to her, her heart had stopped. He tried to give her CPR, but his demons reared their ugly head. He had some sort of panic attack and couldn't breathe and passed out. She died because he'd buckled under the pressure.

It had never happened to him in the field under heavy

fire, but seeing a young woman, so bright and fresh with so much life left to live drop dead right in front of him broke the last shred of whatever he'd been hanging by these last many months.

"We're here to take you back to rehab."

Right. They wanted him out of sight, out of mind.

But he didn't have a dime to his name. He'd spent everything he had for the sixty days of treatment and therapy.

Right now, he couldn't even pay his child support.

Shelby told him he didn't need to until he was back on his feet. Shelby could support Eliza on her own. She told him Eliza needed her daddy and that meant he had to do whatever it took to bring *him* back, because the man he'd become was not the daddy Eliza deserved.

He stared up at the ceiling tiles and shook his head. "I finished rehab." He'd done the work. Now, he wanted to get his life back. He'd missed too damn much time with Eliza. She deserved better. He wanted to give it to her, even if he wasn't quite sure *how* to do that.

He picked up his phone, hoping it still had a charge.

What if Shelby left him a message? What if she needed him? What if something happened to Eliza?

His thoughts spun out and his breathing turned sharp and desperate when he stared at the black screen, his phone completely dead.

Hunt took his phone and set it on the table. "Look at you. You're so desperate to call your supplier—"

"I'm not doing drugs," he snapped, trying to keep from losing it. "Is Drake around? I need my stuff." His military buddy had helped save his life more than once. He got Chase into the same rehab where Juliana had stayed, though she'd arrived after him and left before him.

Hunt planted his fists on his hips. "Dude. Focus."

"I need to charge my phone. It's important."

Hunt stepped aside and revealed the military duffle bag sitting against the wall behind him. "We picked up your stuff this morning before we came here."

"Is my charging cord in there?"

Hunt rolled his eyes, annoyed as hell, but Chase didn't care. Hunt pulled the cord out of the top of the bag. Chase snatched it out of his hand and plugged in his phone and the cord to the wall behind his hospital bed.

The second the phone lit up with the battery-charging symbol, he pressed the side button to turn it on and stared at the spinning circle as his phone went through its start-up.

Hunt swore. "You need to face reality, Chase. You OD'd. You nearly died. Again."

"I'm not using!" He'd gotten clean and worked with a therapist to quiet his demons, even if he couldn't kill them.

"You can't lie to us, man." Max leaned forward. "We're not buying your bullshit anymore. The doctor said you're using."

Only he wasn't. He couldn't explain how he OD'd last night. He hoped Drake could fill in the blank in his mind. It had happened before, losing time. PTSD, anxiety, and depression had taken over his life along with the drugs. He just needed to talk to Drake to figure out what happened to Juliana and him last night. Because he felt like he was missing a huge piece of the puzzle that landed him in a hospital bed.

"I'm not taking any more of your accusations and blame and anger. Go home. I don't need you." He needed to see Eliza.

She needed him. She wanted him. She was the only

person in his life who loved him. Because she didn't know who her father really was, or what he'd done, she accepted him as is.

He had a chance to be the man she needed, because at two, she didn't know there were bad things in the world and he was one of them.

"You need to get your shit together." Hunt liked to throw out orders like that without any idea how hard that was for Chase after all he'd been through. He expected Chase to snap out of it. He wanted Chase to find a way to undo the past and make everything right.

If Chase could do that, he would.

All he could do now was accept that all the bad shit in his past happened because he'd done the best he could each and every time he'd been faced with impossible decisions. And when it all got to be too much, he'd hidden in a prescription drug haze meant to kill the pain, but all it did was make things worse.

And nearly cost him everything.

Get help, or you will never see Eliza again, Shelby had ordered him, her words and angry voice still ringing in his ears.

The thought of never seeing his little girl had him immediately calling Drake for help before he even left Shelby's driveway. He'd gone to rehab the next day.

He'd learned his lesson.

He wouldn't make the same mistake again.

And even though what happened last night left him reeling, he knew the only way to get through it was to feel it, no matter how bad it hurt.

His phone came alive with a series of dings and pings as emails and text messages blew up his phone.

He ignored the emails and tapped Shelby's text string. She never really said much, but what she sent him was better than anything in this world. Pictures of Eliza started downloading, one after another. Her smiling face stared at him and all the tension went out of his chest. He breathed for the first time in twelve long hours.

When he was serving overseas, he got a picture a day. She'd even hooked up a private web cam in Eliza's nursery. He could log in with his password anytime and see his little girl in her room. Some days, the pictures and seeing the livestream were all that kept him sane. And Shelby hadn't stopped now that he was stateside. At some point every day she sent him a picture.

He'd spent every night in rehab watching his baby sleep.

Three pictures popped up today. They went a long way to stitching up his bleeding heart. In the first picture, Eliza stood in front of the fireplace with a piece of paper with an *I* made out of multicolored buttons glued on it. Above her head on the mantel sat a picture of him. A selfie he'd taken and sent to Shelby to show Eliza while he was overseas. Behind him in the photo, nothing but desert sand spread out as far as the eye could see. The second picture showed Eliza on her swing in the backyard another piece of paper in her hands with the word *Love* spelled out in animal stickers. And the last, Eliza in the princess chair he sent her for Christmas with her finger pointed at him and another paper with *You* spelled out in glitter.

His sweet girl liked to stick things on everything. The walls, windows, and doors when her mom wasn't looking and forcing her to use paper.

Hunt closed in on him. "Chase, put the phone down and pay attention."

Chase didn't like being loomed over. At all. "To what? You telling me what you think I did. What you think I am. What you want me to do. Seriously, haven't

I done enough for everyone? Haven't I paid enough? Lost enough? You guys don't even want to be here. So why are you? Go home and leave me the hell alone."

"When you're left alone, you get high."

"Not anymore." It was never about some high. He needed an escape from his thoughts, to turn off his brain, so he didn't have to remember or feel or do something he couldn't take back and end it all.

Eliza needed him to *be* better. So he was going to *do* better.

"So if you won't go back to rehab, what are you going to do?" Max asked, sounding genuinely interested, even if Hunt still wanted to kill him for what happened with their mom.

"I'm going home."

"To the ranch?" Max's eyes went wide with shock. "Dad's not going to like that. He's—"

"As stubborn as you," Hunt interjected, cutting off whatever else Max intended to say.

Hunt and Max exchanged a look. Hunt pushed harder. "Where exactly do you plan to stay?"

He didn't know. Somewhere close to his girl since he no longer had his furnished apartment in town. Everything he owned was in the bag next to the hospital bed. "I'll figure it out." He hoped he had enough on his credit card to get him a motel room for a few nights so he could go and see Eliza and find a job before he ended up on the streets like so many other vets who struggled to assimilate into society again.

Hunt narrowed his eyes, one side of his mouth drawn back in a derisive frown. "Great plan."

Before Chase got a chance to tell his brother to fuck off, an officer walked through the door. "Chase Wilde?"

His heart raced. "Yeah." He had a flashback of Hunt slamming him into the ground, yanking his arms behind his back, and cuffing him. Hunt had taken great joy in arresting him.

"I came to get your statement about what happened last night." The officer checked out Hunt and Max, then focused on him again.

Of course Hunt couldn't keep his damn nose out of Chase's business. "I'm Hunt Wilde. Willow Fork, Wyoming PD. Is my brother under arrest?" Lucky for Chase, they were in Montana, so Hunt had no jurisdiction here, but he could still use his badge to steer the officer into doing what Hunt thought Chase deserved.

When Hunt arrested him back home, that had been rehab. Now, he wondered if Hunt wanted him locked up behind bars. For his own good, Hunt would say, but Chase knew it was revenge, pure and simple.

The officer raised a brow. "For attempting to save a woman's life?"

Hunt stared at him wide-eyed.

Chase crossed his arms and stared at his lap. "You said it. Attempted. But I didn't save her."

"Tell me what happened," the officer prompted, pulling out a pad and pen to take notes.

Chase glanced at Hunt, who crossed his arms over his chest and glared down at Chase as if to say, "You better not lie."

Chase told the truth, despite how horrible it was. "My buddy's girl let me stay in her place above the shop where it happened. She said I could eat whatever I wanted from the kitchen. I headed down to find something when I heard Juliana yelling. She sounded angry and desperate, so I rushed in to see if I could help her.

The second I saw her, she collapsed to the floor." Chase could see it all too clearly in his mind. "She just crumbled. I couldn't get to her fast enough to stop her fall." He could still hear the crack of her head hitting the polished cement floor. "When I reached her . . . I knew it was too late. Her eyes . . . She didn't have a heartbeat. Training kicked in. I started CPR."

"You gave her mouth-to-mouth," the officer added.

Chase nodded. "I did, then yelled at the guy—I think he worked there—to call for help, but he was out of his mind, ranting. I tried to help her, but then . . ." It all went black.

"You passed out. You were dosed, just like Juliana," the officer supplied.

Chase's heart and breath stopped. That never crossed his mind. Of course, he hadn't been able to think past losing Juliana so quickly. One moment she was vibrant and alive, and the next she simply dropped dead.

"I was dosed?" He really couldn't believe it.

"Yes," the officer confirmed. "Luckily Juliana's sister Adria arrived on the scene and injected you with naloxone. It took two doses. But she saved your life."

Hunt put up his hand. "Wait. Are you saying someone else dosed Juliana, and then Chase ingested the drug while giving Juliana mouth-to-mouth?"

"Exactly. We have it all on video."

Chase ran his hands over his face. "I thought I had some kind of blackout."

"No sir," the officer assured him. "You did everything you could for Juliana, but nothing would have saved her with that much fentanyl in her system."

"Fentanyl." No wonder it took him down so fast. Fentanyl was a hundred times more potent than morphine. He'd been addicted to oxycodone. Same opioid family, but nowhere near as deadly. Even a small dose of fentanyl could kill.

"We're looking for the suspect who fled the scene. Seems he dosed her with what he thought was heroin. Turns out he bought a bad batch. The fentanyl-laced heroin had already killed six people. We were in the process of tracking down the suppliers and letting the public know . . ." The officer shook his head. "It's a tragedy she died the way she did when she'd worked so hard to get clean." The officer stepped closer. "I hope this doesn't set you back in your recovery."

"I'm good." In fact, he felt a hell of a lot better knowing he hadn't caused Juliana's death. But the weight of her loss and how Adria must have felt trying to save him when she knew her sister was gone just killed him.

He needed to contact Drake and check on Adria. He needed her to know how sorry he was for her loss and that he really had tried to save Juliana.

The officer turned the page in his notebook. "I just need your contact information for the file. I'm sure the DA will want to talk to you if this goes to trial."

Chase rattled off his cell number.

"And your address?"

Chase shook his head. "Don't have one right now, but I'm headed back to Wyoming and you can reach me on my cell."

"Good luck to you. And I'm glad you survived."

That's what I do.

Though sometimes he'd wished he hadn't.

But that was behind him—he hoped—even if the nightmares were still fresh in his mind.

The officer left him alone with his brothers again.

He glanced up at Hunt. "You were saying something about me using again?"

Hunt looked away.

Max sighed. "It sucks that girl died. It could have been you."

Hunt unlaced his arms. "Remember that, Chase, the next time you want to use."

Chase rolled his eyes and wanted to offer up another *fuck you*, but the nurse came in with some papers.

"Mr. Wilde, you've been cleared by the doctor and can go home."

Yeah, he didn't have one of those, but seeing his little girl sounded great. If Shelby allowed it.

He'd jump through any hoop she put in place. He'd do whatever it took. He'd show her he wasn't a deadbeat dad. He cared. More than she knew. Because even if she didn't know it, she'd saved him.